The following review from James O'Brien
– now of LBC Radio –
appeared in August 1996.

This book, published by a small independent company but written by a mammoth talent, is almost impossible to summarize. Benatar's lyrical skill is such that he can sustain plots bordering on the incredible, populate them with characters simultaneously sympathetic and chilling, and weave the whole into an effortless and beguiling masterpiece in modern fiction. He is a writer who can thread reincarnation and a time-travelling Lucifer through a fantastical 90s morality tale without once stretching the bounds of credulity. There are two tales in this volume. *The Return of Ethan Hart* is the sort of book you start reading especially slowly as the final pages arrive – wishing you could prolong your visit to the world conjured up by Benatar's engagingly twisted imagination. A damaged and disappointed middle-aged man is afforded the opportunity to live his life differently but personal revelations soon call into question the real price of the bargain he has struck. Benatar manages to observe the mind-numbing minutiae of end-of-millennium life and paint our tiny triumphs and failures on to the canvas of two thousand years of flawed humanity. *Recovery*, the other story, is also about second chances and being given the freedom to change one's life. Here, a young American with no memory and a mysterious photograph is led on a trail back through fifty years of unremembered history and experience. His mission emerges as slowly as the identity of the woman in the picture and, as tension inexorably builds, both conspire towards a gripping conclusion. Book of the month. Discovery of the year.

Stephen Benatar

Recovery

6.6.09

For Vasanthi

Stephen Benatar;

Welbeck Modern Classics

First published by Welbeck Press 1996

This edition published by Welbeck Press 2008

Welbeck Press
Flat I, 4 Parsifal Road, London NW6 1UH
Telephone: 020 7433 8084

ISBN: 978-0-9554757-2-6

Cover design: John Murphy

Printed by:
Broadfield Press Limited
75 Broadfield Lane, London NW1 9YS
Telephone: 020 7482 5282

For
Henry Fitzherbert
and
– naturally –
John Murphy

INTRODUCTION

The following book is made up of two wonderfully readable novellas, *Recovery* and *The Return of Ethan Hart*. When it first appeared in 1996, *Recovery* was placed second but Stephen Benatar has now, sensibly I think, changed the order so that the title story leads. This is important, because although the two tales are to all intents and purposes quite separate, both are concerned with recovered memory. And in each, the recovery of lost or hidden memory is inseparable from discovery or uncovering of the past. And this in turn leads to a kind of self-discovery for each protagonist. So *that*'s who I really am…

It is often said that modern writing is haunted by the question "Who am I?" And it is as frequently suggested that the answer post-modern writing returns to this question is, "no one person at all." "Je est un autre." Rimbaud's famous phrase finds an echo in the formulation of the great Portuguese poet, Fernando Pessoa, "to be one self is not to be." That this has led to the making of much heavily self-conscious prose and poetry, all of it poring over the question of personal identity, seems to me beyond doubt. The shelves of university and college libraries groan with the weight of books created, so the least sceptical of readers is sometimes bound to feel, in order to have theses written about them, all bearing titles such as *The Ordeal of Consciousness in X*, *Unstable Identities in Y* or *Ontological Insecurity in Z*. (And no, I'm not making these up, and they are by no means the worst examples.) The good thing about *Recovery* is that it is the work of a born writer, and comes without any of the baggage toted by more self-conscious – and less gifted – authors. It does what all the best writing does. It makes you suspend disbelief. So that although the stories are in a strict sense incredible, they invite

I

you to go along with the question "What if...?" What if a man waking from an amnesiac blanking out of his memory ends up by seeing his own long-dead fiancée as she repeats the moments that led to her death? What if a man finds that he is repeating his life and realizes that he may be condemned to do so again and again until the last syllable of recorded time?

I don't want to give too much away of either story, because to do so would snap the thread of suspense which in each so teasingly leads us to a brilliantly-imagined conclusion, the routes by which we get from beginning to end. But it seems worth noting that what makes them so compelling, so *readable*, is Benatar's great skill in making us believe in tales which, in bald summary, are pure hokum. How does he do it?

In several ways, I think. First, he tells the stories so naturally that you almost forget to tell yourself that what you are reading isn't strictly believable. Well, why should it be? If art is art because it is not life, then fiction is fiction because it is not fact. But of course we are used to fiction inhabiting a world of realism, one that deals not in *what if?* but with *as if. Recovery* is in many ways intensely realistic. But it is also fantastic, an exercise in storytelling, and Benatar is the best kind of raconteur. He holds you not so much with a glittering eye as with the dramatic opening of his tales, those hooks that reel you in.

Okay. Don't panic. You'll soon make sense of this.
And there, in that window, your reflection.
Young. Clean shaven. Hair dark blond.
T-shirt, jeans.
Pockets!

These are the opening sentences, placed as separate little paragraphs, to the title story. We know before the end of the third line that the protagonist is male – and we infer he's seeking enlightenment as to whom he is, rather than merely admiring his looks. Hence the exclamation mark after *Pockets* – for pockets may at once give hope and supply information. For what has happened to him? Has he been mugged? Is he drunk? Who

II

exactly is he, *where* is he, and – if perhaps he *has* succumbed to an attack of amnesia – why? What is he running from?

The Return of Ethan Hart is quite different but equally effective.

Have you ever dreamt that you lived in another time? I did, just a night or two before my life changed.

Here, the buttonholing is unashamedly direct. "My life changed." No need to ask the man to tell us about it. He's going to, anyway. And once the tales get into their stride, which they quickly do, you are gripped not merely by their strangeness but by the matter-of-factness with which they are told, as if, incredible though they are, they are, when all is said and done, pretty ordinary slices of life.

This attention to the dailiness of things is deftly managed. Much of *Recovery* is set in middle England at the end of the Second World War, and Benatar is very good at providing vivid glimpses of that time without indulging in any historical overload. The story is blessedly free of those self-advertising pieces of careful research which inadvertently but paradoxically remind you that what you are reading is only fiction. Instead, when a young woman agrees to pose for her photograph, "I smile like the Bile Beans girl and although I don't exactly flash those pearly whites I snatch up one side of my frock, strike what I hope is an alluring pose and for a moment imagine an interesting new me on the cover of Picture Post." This is entirely believable. The young woman's wish to look attractive is balanced by a dash of self-deprecating wit, a kind of springiness of mind which will make her more attractive still to the American airman she is about to meet and fall in love with. Their love story and its outcome is the stuff of many novels. What gives *Recovery* its especial distinction is the real regard Benatar shows for both of them and the brief, uncertain time they have together, one that incorporates their vividly described escape to London for V-E day and night…

And like all true novelists, Benatar has the trick of bringing to life even the most marginal of his characters. The London

III

landlady, who later takes the young woman in, drinks gin, smokes Passing Cloud cigarettes, prefers cats to men, and her talk is spiced with the idiom of the day, as when she tells her new lodger that she looks 'peaky' or 'not half as bonny as you did'. But her warm-heartedness comes across not as cliché but as proceeding from genuine, womanly concern. What could be a walk-on caricature becomes three-dimensional.

The same holds true in *The Return of Ethan Hart*. To take one instance. Chapter 12 is occupied with an episode where on a hot Sunday lunchtime the teenage Ethan is required to dash some miles to see a family he doesn't even know, and at one point finds himself held in conversation by a woman who tells him that the weather is "Real close and muggy. Full of all these horrid gnats and midges." A lesser writer would have used the woman as a means to get to what he 'really' wants to concentrate on. What that may be you will have to read the story to discover. I wish merely to note that Benatar's ear for the terms and rhythms of ordinary speech is so accurate that the woman herself is made as real as anything else in the chapter. And I should add that his handling of dialogue is never less than convincingly assured.

But one tiny moment in this story is enough to tell you that you are reading the work of a true writer. It comes in Chapter 15 where Ethan, brooding over what will happen to him in extreme old age, worries about how and indeed whether, once he enters on his second century, *he will manage to get his toenails cut*. Beckett said that the test for any writer of any worth was whether he was able to imagine the details of his characters' lives, 'the reek of onion on the breath'. In this as other matters, Benatar easily passes the test.

But above all, the Benatar of *Recovery* reveals himself to have a masterly skill at manufacturing ways and means to entice you into reading on. He's the consummate trickster, the writer-as-conjurer whose most commanding trick is always to make you turn the page. To take an example almost at random. When young Ethan sits down to write a school essay and, without explanation either from him or his creator, finds his pen and thoughts seized by a figure from mythic history, you wonder how the devil this has happened. (As it turns out, the cliché

IV

makes good sense.) But you are also bound to reflect that Ethan is a kind of surrogate novelist, the conduit for vividly realized characters and voices, as Benatar himself is. Of course, the story eventually offers an explanation of sorts for this act of possession, this tale within a tale, and we read on to find out what it is. But explanations can go only so far. They certainly can't uncover the root cause of writerly talent. That is and always will be mysterious.

John Lucas
Poet, writer and critic
Professor Emeritus –
Universities of Loughborough and Nottingham Trent
Summer 2008

Recovery

The Return of Ethan Hart

Recovery

Recovery

1

Okay. Don't panic. You'll soon make sense of this.

And there, in that window, your reflection.

Young. Clean shaven. Hair dark blond.

T-shirt, jeans.

Pockets!

Oh, but for heaven's sake, containing what? Just a tissue and a silver hip flask (empty, yet so well-handled that the chasing's pretty worn) plus the snapshot of a woman who's at present unfamiliar. Nothing else. No billfold. No credit cards. No change. You guess you must have lost your jacket.

Left it behind you someplace.

But…only try to think now. Where exactly are you?

Exactly you're outside a narrow building in Foley Street W1 (since you've now moved along from that barbershop window, taken a step or two to the right, and there's a street sign overhead: *City of Westminster*).

London, then.

The front door of the building is open – ajar – could you be the one who's neglected to close it? Maybe you rent one of the offices? Maybe you were visiting? Maybe you'd just stepped back into the sunlight and then…wham! This! Where am I? Or more to the point – *who* am I?

The door is green and dingy. Beyond it you see pale blue walls; navy blue lino. The offices listed comprise that of a textiles company on the first floor, a school of fashion on the second – and, yes, you gaze at the plate with a mixture of nervousness and validation – a private detective on the third.

You ascend the steep and narrow staircase. Bare wood. Loafers would resonate; your sneakers make no sound. On each of the three landings the walls remain pale blue. Grubbily pale blue.

The detective's name is Newman. "Good evening," you say, when he opens his office door – your watch has told you that it's nearly six. "I know this is going to sound a little odd…" And then you stop.

You're American!

American!

_ You concentrate on the man before you. The guy could still be in his thirties; but later on you learn he's forty-four, a youthful forty-four; tall, lean, roughly your own colouring. Grey-suited; smart. You're patently a stranger to him.

His office breaks with the general theme of blue. Cream walls, grey carpet, green drapes. Plants on the windowsill. A David Hockney print.

Filing cabinets, reference books, a computer, cafetière –

My God, though. I'm American!

I sit across the desk from him. On my way up, of course, I'd been hoping he would say I'd only just left – and that he'd been on the point of chasing after me with my jacket.

"Have you tried the floors below?" he asks.

I shake my head. "Textiles? A fashion school? I don't think they sound very much like me."

"How do you know what sounds very much like you? Perhaps you've been doing a spot of modelling. You're working your way through Europe?"

"Oh, yes. Sure." I watch him fiddle with a paperclip. We've dismissed the possibility of my having been mugged. A mugging might account for the amnesia but I don't have any bruises; nor did I need to pick myself up off the sidewalk; nor would any mugger have left me with my watch. "Anyhow," I say, "at least it was providential that if this *had* to happen it should have been outside the office of a private dick."

Newman concentrates for a moment on the pulling open of his paperclip. "Mightn't it have been more providential," he asks, "outside the entrance to a hospital? You see, I can't help thinking it's a doctor you require…or even a good night's rest. Not a detective."

2

He has a kind face; attractive manner. Yet rejection is still rejection, however pleasantly it's couched.

"Okay. Supposing you're right? Where'd you suggest I get that good night's rest?"

"That's why I said a hospital. I could have said the embassy. But there's also the question of whether or not you'd be better off sedated."

After three seconds or so, I get to my feet. "Apparently," I say, "there's something one never forgets – even with amnesia. Everybody likes to be paid. But I thought that once I'd found my jacket... Or have you forgotten? This watch is a Rolex!" My voice betrays an odd blend of sarcasm and swank. "Yellow gold; eighteen-carat. Costs upwards of nine thousand dollars." I sound like a salesman.

He looks a bit nonplussed. Suddenly he grins.

"How do you know all that?"

This reaction is disarming. I remove my hand from the doorknob. "You're right. It is sort of weird, isn't it?"

"You don't remember buying it?"

"No, nothing like that. Clearly I'm a guy who's very well-informed."

He laughs. There follows a slight pause.

"I'm sorry," he says then. "You know, it wasn't the money I was thinking of."

I don't respond.

"No, that isn't wholly true. But what *is* true is that I was also worried about my not being the person best qualified to help."

"And I had this hunch you might be. The person best qualified to help."

"Well, as a detective I, too, am a great respecter of hunches." He holds out his hand and with a rueful smile indicates the empty chair. He says, "I have a flat in Golders Green and you'd be welcome to its spare room."

So naturally I sit down again and he makes us both a cup of coffee. Strangely, even before I've tasted it, I realize that I don't take sugar; in the same way, for instance, I haven't forgotten that the year we're in is 1990. (Though plainly there can't be any hard-and-fast rule: until I'd heard my own voice I'd taken it for

3

granted I was English.) "So what are we going to call you?" he asks. "My own first name is Tom."

"How about X?"

"No way. How about Tex?"

I pull a face. "Do you really see me as some aw-shucks, bowlegged cowboy?"

He only smiles. "Now, where's that snapshot you mentioned?"

I produce it from my back pocket. He studies it a moment. "Have you any idea how *old* this is?"

It's certainly black-and-white. It's certainly creased and shabby. I suppose that, earlier on, my aim had been only to recognize the face. Apart from that, I hadn't noticed much.

He hands it back. "Look at the hairstyle," he says. "Look at the line of the dress."

He's right. I guess it can only have been pure shock which – on the sidewalk – had prevented me from seeing. "Second World War," I murmur.

"Or possibly straight after."

"But that's crazy. Why would I be toting around the picture of some girl who by now must be an old woman?"

"Your mother, perhaps?"

"Oh, come on. What normal guy carries a pinup of his mother? Well, practically a pinup?"

He regards me in a thoughtful way.

"I reckon you're probably in your mid-twenties, yes?" I've already told him I've caught up on my reflection. "So, if you were born some twenty years after the war, why do you have a wartime snapshot in your pocket? And the likelihood is, too – because of the church behind her – that she's British. How does that tie in with the fact of your not being?"

How indeed? I gaze again at the woman's picture as though the answer to his questions can be determined in her face. But then I get distracted by something which is surely more deep-seated than her prettiness; and suddenly I find myself wondering, with strange irrelevance in view of all my problems, what might have been her circumstances around that instant when the shutter closed.

4

2

"Trixie, why not save your film for something special? This is sheer waste."

"Oh, bollocks, Roz. Don't hold yourself so cheap. Come on, just flash those pearly whites."

That's rich. Me hold myself cheap. I know damned well how she got hold of that film. I've seen the chap who gave it to her. Preferable, if you ask me, to pay the price on the black market. Or better – far better – to use that ex-RAF stuff, even if they do say that half the time it doesn't work.

Anyhow, being the soul of obedience, I smile like the Bile Beans girl and although I don't exactly flash those pearly whites I snatch up one side of my frock, strike what I hope is an alluring pose and for a moment imagine an interesting new me on the cover of Picture Post.

"Oh, that's nice, hold it," she cries; and then, picture taken, with quick change of emphasis: "Yes, that's nice! Right in front of the church, too! Supposing the vicar saw? He'd think that Betty Grable had come to Suffolk."

"Well, if he'd really think that, let's go in and offer him a second chance."

To go in is the whole purpose of the exercise. I've wanted to do this ever since the first weekend she and I came here, which was nearly two years ago, in the summer of '43 – but both on that occasion and the ones which followed (Trix being a Philistine) we never got round to it. I hadn't learned to be assertive.

So now it could be something of an anticlimax.

But it isn't.

I think the first thing that strikes me is the radiance. Except for the west window the stained glass has all been blown out by enemy action and – as though deliberately to compensate – the light can now flood in through wholly clear replacements, emphasizing the loftiness of the nave, the slenderness of the pillars, the fine proportions of the roof. I wish I knew all the names, because for someone who enjoys looking round old churches I'm pretty unversed in the terminology. I suppose I'm a dabbler who likes the inscriptions and the pews and the paving stones: the connection with past lives. Along with the stillness and the sense of awe. The splendour.

There's a magnificent and brightly coloured pulpit. There's also a wonderfully elaborate organ case and a tall painted screen celebrating some of the saints and angels. It's sixteenth-century but touched up in Victorian times. A typed card charmingly informs us that St Jude – as restored – became very like the rector.

I'm admiring this delightful screen when I hear Trixie talking to someone. This turns out to be a gum-chewing American airman, boyish-faced though burly and bull-necked.

"Excuse me for butting in," she's saying, "but I couldn't help overhearing. Sounds like you and me are in the same boat. Being dragged around to get a bit of culture by our educated friends!" I feel I'd like to slosh her.

"Our boring, educated friends!" returns the airman. "That is – no, lady, I'm sorry – I certainly didn't mean yours; I meant that highbrow over there."

The fellow whom he indicates smiles vaguely at Trixie but continues to give his main attention to a small wooden man in armour who apparently strikes a bell on every hour. "Say, Walt, come here a minute. This little guy is getting all set to do his stuff. Any second now."

"Hey, Roz," shouts Trixie, "you don't want to miss this."

I cross over to where the three of them are grouped; there's no one else in sight but even so I tell myself crabbily that the church is much too full.

"Come on – hurry! This is Roz," says Trixie, while I'm still ten feet away. "And I'm Trix."

"Glad to know you," says her big, good-humoured new acquaintance. "I'm Walt. And my friend here is Matt."

He's hardly spoken when the little man in armour strikes the bell.

And the highbrow laughs.

As he does so my churlishness begins to fade. His pleasure is infectious. Besides – it occurs to me I would have missed out but for him.

"Cute," says Walt. "And you'd always know this guy was English."

"Why?" asks Trixie, so willing to enjoy the joke she's already started giggling.

"Reminding us it's teatime. And there's a nice place for tea we noticed on our way to be religious. You ladies care to join us?"

I'm about to decline but Trixie says, "We'd love to!" and glares at me no less tellingly than if my careless talk were costing lives.

She and I know the Sugar Loaf Tearooms. Their bread and carrot cake and soda scones are all delicious and the bread doesn't even have that greyish tinge. We're obliged to queue for a table. The teashop has a holiday atmosphere – not unexpected in a seaside resort on the first warm Saturday of spring. It's the twenty-first of April. The noise level is high and becomes even higher, breaks into cheering and applause, when a waitress – poor woman – drops a loaded tray. (Tearooms for the moment have lost all their gentility. Thank God.) The building is one of the few in Southwold that survived the fire of 1659 and the timber beams speak of precisely that: survival. Indomitable spirit. It's a good place and even without the Americans is probably where we'd have ended up.

When at last we get our table, conversation becomes less superficial. We already know they're stationed at Halesworth, some eight miles away, but now we hear more of the details. They're members of the 5th Emergency Rescue Squadron. They specialize in air-sea rescue work. Walt talks with enthusiasm about their lifeboat-carrying B-17s, their CA-10 Catalina amphibians and in particular their P-47 Thunderbolts. For a minute I wonder if he should be telling us all this but then I realize that at this stage it can hardly matter. He also tells us – probably sensing the need to recapture Trixie's interest – about the time last August when Glen Miller came to Boxted. (They had moved the short distance to Halesworth only this January.)

Trixie wants a rundown on every piece of music that was played, and descriptions not simply of the late major – no one still believes, unhappily, that after all these months he can be referred to any longer as just missing – not simply of him, but of almost every member of the band. While Walt does his best to satisfy her I take the opportunity, surreptitiously, to have a good look at his friend.

Matt's full name is Matthew Cassidy. Before, in the church, it hadn't occurred to me he was especially handsome; only that I liked something about his face. But now I must have got my eye in, for handsome he undoubtedly is. Coarse fair hair – though not as short as you'd expect an English officer's to be; blue eyes, straight nose, firm jawline. For what I think must be the first time, I really know what 'clean-cut' means; even his wrists and hands seem to exemplify it. I am twenty-four and probably have never felt so stirred by the way a man is put together.

Or am I allowed to dignify this and say that of course his whole personality must have contributed? That I'm speaking of the full package?

Walt exhausts the charms of August 6th and of the sweet strains flooding through the main hangar on that golden Sunday afternoon. "We were sitting on the wing of a B-24 that was being serviced – you remember, Matt? And, ladies, I don't mind telling you, it was swell but it sure made us feel a little homesick."

"Yes, I'll bet," I say. "But at least you'll soon be getting back there, won't you? Though do you realize: you haven't told us yet where home is?"

"For him, Connecticut," says Walt. "San Francisco, for me."

"Oh, then you must know that song!" cries Trixie. She starts to sing it. "'San Francisco…open your golden gate…'" Heads turn towards our table and she giggles and feigns bashfulness. "I remember Jeanette MacDonald singing it in that film with Clark Gable and Spencer Tracy and the earthquake. I suppose the song's called 'San Francisco'. I can't remember what the film is."

"'San Francisco'," Walt supplies and we all laugh. I get the passing thought that it was calculated (Trixie is by no means the

8

dumb blonde she pretends, any more than I'm the brainy brunette she also claims) but it's still quite funny.

"And I once read 'A Connecticut Yankee in King Arthur's Court'," I say to Matt. "So I'm well up on where you come from, too."

This time it's only him and me who laugh. Trixie is too busy saying to Walt, "I liked that film; I found it ever so inspiring. Spencer Tracy's in the one we're going to see tonight. It's called 'Without Love'."

"Well, is that right? We've been wanting to catch up on that movie for months. Didn't you say so just the other day, Matt?"

"What?"

Walt has to remind him meaningfully of what he had said so emphatically just the other day.

"Oh, sure," Matt confirms. "I've been boring everybody senseless!"

We arrive at the Electric Picture Palace in time for the full programme – and bypass the longest queues by going in the dearest seats and needing to stand on the staircase for only a few minutes. The full programme comprises a second-feature, the news, Food Flashes, trailers, a Pete Smith Speciality, a medley of tunes on the theatre organ... I'm always pleased to get my money's worth and so, I find out now, is Matt, "even down to your God Save the King," he shamelessly confesses. But Trixie and Walt decide not to see the end of the big picture (so that we'll have longer in the pub) and Matt and I fall in obligingly.

"You didn't mind?" he asks, as we walk together a short way behind the other two – who proceed first arm-in-arm and then, soon after, arm-round-waist.

I shake my head. "But I'm not the one who's been so frantic to catch up with it."

"In fact, I have an admission." I'm sure he already surmises, from the little he's drawn out of me, that he isn't really spoiling my enjoyment. "I found it talkative and dull."

"Oh, what a letdown! I'm truly sorry."

"And irritating! All those 'by gums' which were clearly meant to be so full of charm!"

9

"I know! You sat there almost waiting for the next! And what about her proud and tearful memory of her dying husband – who 'grinned that grin of his'? I think I'd even have accepted a couple of extra 'by gums' in exchange."

"Careful! Two more might have brought us to screaming point!"

So in a way, although the film undoubtedly had entertaining moments (which we conscientiously acknowledge), we have more fun pulling it to pieces than we got out of watching it.

"Anyhow, despite all that, it was a good night out at the pictures. A very good night," I add on impulse.

"For me, too. Though I'd have to say not entirely on account of the movie. I don't know if you gathered that."

"Thank you for treating me."

Then we talk about how wonderful it is that the last blackout restrictions have finally been lifted and that the streetlights are on again; no more being obliged to carry torches which could only be directed at one's feet. No more need, even, for headlamps to wear a covering – nor traffic lights – although admittedly there isn't much traffic now except for bikes. It's like a glimpse of El Dorado to see the light from the pub spilling out across the pavement.

Through the open door there comes the welcome of a singsong,

> "Yes, we have no bananas,
> We have no bananas today,"

which suggests that dealings in contraband must be at a remarkably low ebb, since a bent old seaman with a beard and runny nose tells me while we wait for Matt and Walt to do battle at the bar – well, he tells Trixie too but she plainly isn't listening – that the Lord Nelson has a dormer window on its seaward side, from which signals could be flashed to smugglers coming in below the cliff, and that there's many a whispered tale of blocked-up passages which once led from the cliff into the cellars. Matt gives the man one of the two glass tankards he's brought, and heroically returns to fetch himself another. By the time he comes back, Walt and Trixie have been able to muscle their way onto a crowded bench – she's sitting on his lap – and the seaman has swallowed his drink and has moved off in search of some other sucker (Matt's phrase). "The artful old lush – well, good luck to him," he says.

We then decide to join the group around the piano; yet just as we get there it disbands. So we eventually manage to edge into a corner, holding our glasses up high, apologizing as we go and meeting with cheerful reassurance. We could of course have taken our drinks outside and sat on a parapet overlooking the sea but, despite the cardigan I'm now wearing, the night feels chilly. Besides – it's exciting to be part of a good-natured crowd that's soaked up the warmth of the day, even if at times it's a little difficult to hear what each of us is saying. He asks where Trixie and I are putting up in Southwold and I tell him about Mrs Herbert's guesthouse.

"It's simple but seems luxurious compared to our farm-worker's cottage – where the plumbing is so primitive it's sometimes hard to get rid of the day's caking of mud."

"No wonder you need to escape."

"But it's a good life, being a land girl."

"Will you be in Southwold next Saturday?"

His question takes me by surprise. "Well, usually we only get away once every – "

"I wish you would," he says. "We could meet earlier in the day and go for a picnic – fit in a swim. I think I could probably wangle us a jeep."

"It sounds fun. I – "

"And I'll take care of the picnic. I mean it. No arguments." He looks round briefly. "I guess Walt's probably making similar plans with Trixie…aiming to get off on their own." I glance round too; we both smile. "But Rosalind?" Suddenly he seems embarrassed.

"Mm?"

"I don't quite know how to put this, without sounding bigheaded. But, you see, back home... Well, back home I'm engaged to be married."

11

A slight dip of disappointment – silly, I suppose, on the strength of merely a six-hour acquaintance. Come to that...not such a slight dip, either.

"Congratulations, Matt."

"You'll still come out next Saturday? Maybe even Sunday as well?"

"I'd like to."

"I damn well wish that I was free tomorrow. You're just about the nicest person I've met in England. And that's not to say England isn't very full of nice people."

"Thanks. And you must tell me about your family and your fiancée and we'll keep our fingers crossed that the weather next weekend is at least half as good as today's."

I laugh.

"Especially if you're serious about that swim."

3

The detective takes the snapshot from my hand. "I think it's time we shut up shop," he says.

"I can't help wondering who she is."

"Naturally you can't."

His apartment is on Finchley Road, over a bakery called Grodzinski's. "I like this area," he tells me. "Bus conductors cry, 'Get out your passports, we're coming to Golders Green!' But that's what's good about it. Jewish. Cosmopolitan. Lively."

"Maybe. But my trouble is – can I really believe in any private eye who doesn't come from Southern California?"

"I know. I sometimes have the same problem."

I ask about his average day.

"It may not inspire you with confidence."

"But I can't take my business anyplace else, can I? Especially when you've just bought me a toothbrush and washcloth. Did Sam Spade or Philip Marlowe ever do as much for any of *their* clients?"

So he mentions process-serving. Debt-collecting. Surveillance work. Investigating cases of pilfering for a company which doesn't want to call in the police. Carrying out a lot of grindingly tedious research. "I'm not sure what's average. Certainly not becoming involved with missing heiresses and stumbling upon fraud and ancient unsuspected murder. Probably just sitting in the office and hoping for business."

"Like this afternoon?"

"Like this afternoon. Your timing was impeccable."

I ask him other things, more personal things. "No," he says, "no wife nor family. Obviously I've never met the right girl. Not yet."

However, although his tone is light, I get the feeling he'd rather not talk about his private life. Well, fair enough.

We listen to Elgar and drink Scotch while waiting for the supper to be done; he's boiling some potatoes and has put the contents of two packets of Lean Cuisine into the oven: fillets of cod with broccoli in a white sauce. He's also put some Riesling in the fridge.

After supper we channel-hop: half-watch, amongst other things, ten minutes of a programme on Pirandello. I scarcely take in any of it, but Tom says, "Sometimes I feel *I* might be a character in search of an author. Or may have existence only in the minds of others." He smiles at me. "God knows how the world works!" he says.

One thing is fairly certain. He's drunk far more of the wine than I have. I go to bed quite early.

This could be a mistake. For the first time in several hours I'm alone with all the haunting speculation. Just what is it, exactly, I'm so anxious to forget?

Maybe it's this, maybe it's that. Maybe I'm a guy with a broken marriage, a failed career, a smashed ambition; with a terminal illness, a kidnapped child, a dead wife. Maybe I'm wanted by the police. Wanted on a charge of tax evasion, drunken driving, manslaughter, murder…

Surprisingly, I eventually manage to sleep.

Tom wakes me with a cup of tea.

"And…?" He sounds too eager. "Has anything come back?"

"You mean, anything apart from 'I tort I taw a puddy tat' or 'I know a bank whereon the wild thyme blows'?" This morning I'm finding it hard to hide a growing note of bitterness.

But he ignores it. "Do you want to shower before or after breakfast? And how do you like your eggs?"

While we're eating he says:

"About that snapshot. During the night I had an idea. Suppose your father was over here in the war? Long before he thought of marrying your mother he met this English girl. The war ended and they lost touch. But now, when he heard that you were coming to London, he asked you to try to trace her."

"Why?"

"Nostalgia, perhaps?"

"Yes, but I mean if he cared that much why didn't he come himself? The guy's had forty-five years in which to look for his little buttercup."

"What I'm saying is – suddenly he has this strong desire to take stock; to come to terms with his past."

"And this is the sort of thing you'd get your son to do for you?"

"Depends," says Tom. "Whenever he's here himself he's probably with your mother. And maybe it's something you could speak of more easily to your son."

"Well, I don't know… I don't know if I buy that."

"It's just a theory."

After a moment, though, I give a shrug and do my damnedest not to sound perverse. "And I suppose it's the only one we have. Okay, then. Why not?"

Tom stirs his coffee. "Actually I'm hoping there could be another woman somewhere. A bit more contemporary."

"Meaning a wife?"

"A wife or partner. Anyone who – by this time – might have raised the alarm."

I pause in the act of buttering toast. My God, I'm a bastard! (And perhaps that's why I've got amnesia: simple self-disgust.) Oh, yes, I've certainly wondered what sort of wife I may have left behind. But up to now I haven't thought there could be someone not so very far away who's maybe feeling desperate;

who, apart from having a missing husband, could be seriously unsure of how everything operates in a strange country – could be worried about funds – could be encumbered by a worried child, or even worried children. Oh, Christ! I've been thinking only of myself.

My possible wife, child, children, parents...presumably I have parents, who at some point will need to be notified? All these begin to acquire, not faces, not personalities, but at least some sort of real and suffering existence. No longer simply adjuncts.

I also start to wonder about my father and that girl.

4

At last it's Sunday morning!

And at any minute now I shall be seeing him!

But, heck, I was being *far* too optimistic, hoping to do so yesterday, hoping to contrive *two* Saturdays off in a row.

Quite late into the evening, in fact, I was still busy with my milking after what would have been, in the normal way, a dreary day of weeding and hoeing and muck-raking – dreary, I mean, if I hadn't had this morning to anticipate, plus the bliss of a soak in the Crawfords' own bathtub to wash away not only the grime but the smell: muck-raking is a chore which permeates! (And, shamelessly, I had every intention of ignoring – for once – those regulatory five inches.)

At any rate he'd been easy to contact at Halesworth and very understanding about the necessary change in plan; we must have spoken for over half an hour, which in itself made up a little for the lost day. (He'd rung me back, after the first set of pips.) Though even after half an hour I'd found it difficult to say goodbye. On the other hand, this hadn't prevented my cycling away from the box in the village singing at the top of my voice and speeding down hills – well, slopes! – with my feet off the pedals and my hands off the handlebars.

15

His voice had sounded just so nice; and his conversation had been so easy and so civilized. We'd even mentioned Shakespeare's birthday, which had fallen on the previous Monday. And there, as Trixie would have said, *there* was culture for you!

Because although I like the people I mix with – they're kind and helpful and I learn from them some fascinating lore – their talk is never what you'd call relaxing, mainly on account of the dialect; and with our German prisoner-of-war it's not merely the dialect, it's the whole wretched language barrier; we smile and nod and mime (and the mime often makes us giggle) but it's not a conversation. Trixie of course is usually full of chat, yet recently she's been thoroughly moody, since she too had planned on having yesterday off and not all her wheedling could accomplish it. ("I'll do a bunk!" she'd said "To hell with them!" But her 'bunk' didn't take place till nearly nine o'clock last night, when anyway she was perfectly free to go. However, she ran out waving her crimson-painted fingernails – not so much in farewell as to get them dry – and it was the bounciest I'd seen her since the previous Sunday. "Now don't do anything I wouldn't do, Roz!" Followed, naturally, by its inseparable and very boring rider.)

And now I'm feeling pretty bouncy myself, waiting in the lane and savouring the smell arising from the earth, the gossamer on grass and hedges, the stillness which surrounds me: a stillness only deepened by the gentle cry of a ringed plover – or is it perhaps a stone curlew? Savouring, too, the sheer pleasure of my yellow coat.

This, a Christmas present from my mother (the kindest mother imaginable: she must have used up every coupon she could save, swap, steal or scavenge), is fastened with a tie belt and a single button at the neck and has a nice jaunty swing to it. Because I haven't worn it very often it still feels special. With that and my best frock – actually the one I was wearing last weekend, which is a bit of a shame but can't be helped, a print of green leaves on a white background, eye-catching without being gaudy – with those and my leather gloves, classic black shoes, Jacqmar headscarf and carefully painted legs (it was Amy

Crawford who drew the line down the back for me, taking a lot more trouble than Trixie ever does), I feel today that Vogue is more my spiritual home than Picture Post. I wonder if this will instantly occur to Matt. Will he draw up, jump down, give a deeply felt whistle and sigh for his disloyal abandonment of Rita Hayworth? Poor Rita Hayworth.

Amazingly, he doesn't. He jumps down from the jeep all right but forgets to give that whistle. And although he tells me I look nice, he adds far too soon for someone genuinely dumbfounded that he hopes he hasn't kept me waiting.

"No, you're extremely punctual. You had no trouble finding us?" It's been a journey of some twenty miles.

He shakes his head…a bit absently? (Certainly he doesn't appear to be dumbfounded; but is it merely wishful thinking that makes me see a look that might be construed – very loosely – as appreciative?) "All I had to do was follow your excellent instructions."

"And your still more excellent Ordnance Survey?"

He grins. "Well, that helped a bit."

"I hear they're talking about starting to replace the signposts."

"Oh, where's their spirit of adventure?"

I observe drily that I'd better call him Marco Polo; or Dr Livingstone if he'd prefer. He glances at the sky. Pulls up the collar of his raincoat.

"Better call me Scott of the Antarctic! What happened to all that warmth we had a week ago?"

"And just now you sounded so courageous. Don't let me think that, after all, they breed them lily-livered in Connecticut! Oh, but talking of which…"

We are going to spend the day in Cambridge – yet I'm wondering if, before that, he'd be interested to see Groton. John Winthrop, the man who became an early governor of Connecticut, was born in Groton.

"I've been doing my homework for you." And, yes, it's almost as if I'm getting ready for some test. "John Winthrop sailed for North America in 1630, on board the Arabella, along with seven hundred Puritans, two hundred cows and sixty horses. However, by the time the ship reached Massachusetts Bay, two

17

hundred of the immigrants had died at sea – well, either at sea or shortly after landing. Then another hundred decided to return to England."

We are still standing in the lane – a lane that's twisting and leafy, full of cowpats and tractor ruts.

"Those, I'd say, were definitely the lily-livered ones!" He nods, decisively.

"You think so? After the voyage out I'm not so sure they mightn't have been called the braver element...no matter how base. And, by the way, seventy of the animals had died as well."

"Thank you for doing your homework. And you're right, I'd sure be glad to see where it began. In New London County there's a town called Groton that was named for Winthrop's birthplace. But I didn't realize he came from round here." He adds after a moment: "Come to think of it, how did you?"

I tell him that when he'd spoken of Connecticut last Saturday, something had stirred at the back of my mind. But I hadn't been able to pinpoint it.

"Gee, I'm impressed."

"Gee, I'm pleased that you're impressed. Actually I'm quite impressed too. Well, let's face it: it is impressive."

Yet first, even before Groton, I want to show him Polstead.

So we get in the jeep, which is fun, I've never ridden in a jeep before (although later it will prove a little cold) and off we drive to Polstead. There I show him the pond where witches used to undergo their trial by ordeal and into which somebody, allegedly spellbound, once drove a coach and four horses. The site must have been a bit jinxed: by the early nineteenth century there were so many ghosts roaming about it that an exorcism came to be thought desirable. But poor Reverend Whitmore could have been a forbear of Will Hay: after death he was himself seen driving a horse and trap along the lane to the rectory – and presumably not a man to be outdone by anyone, it was claimed that he was headless.

"Headless?" cries Matt. "My God! But why?"

"Obviously an arch-bungler."

"Then how was he identified? Was his head sitting there on the seat beside him? Wasn't there a danger it might roll off?"

18

"I think you have a gruesome streak."

"What tosh!" (More British than the British but I don't at this point comment.)

"And if you have" – I give a kindly smile – "in Polstead we can pander to it."

"That's nice." He asks if I believe in ghosts.

We have left the jeep at the bottom of the hill and are now walking up a pleasant footpath to the top of it, from where I want him to see what must be one of the prettiest village greens in England.

"I don't know. I certainly believe in an afterlife – in the survival of the spirit – if that's of any help."

He says it isn't much, but as I feel that way and as it's Sunday, oughtn't I to be in church?

"Well, it doesn't follow; though I'd be happy to go, if you would."

"Yes," he replies, slowly and rather unexpectedly. "Actually, I think I'd like it."

But since the morning service isn't due to start for half an hour we wander around the green.

Facing the green is the Cock, with its attractive inn sign.

"Will it be open when the service ends?"

"Straight out of church and into the pub – tch, tch, Lieutenant Cassidy! Do I approve?"

"I think you've got the emphasis wrong, Miss Farr. What you mean is: oh, boy, do I approve! I saw you knocking back your Adnam's the other night. And the word, my dear, is Lootenant."

I tell him he's in England now: land of village greens and fine old pubs and men who answer to Leftenant. Land of Maria Marten and the Red Barn.

He stares at me in some perplexity. Just as he was meant to.

"Come. I shall lead you now down Marten Lane for the terrifying climax to this fleeting interlude of Grand Guignol. Not for the faint-hearted."

I take him by the hand. It seems so natural that I'm almost unaware of having done so. His own hand closes around mine; and from then on continues to hold it. Firmly.

It needs only a few minutes to reach the thatched cottage where Maria Marten used to live. The red barn is there no longer, having been destroyed by fire.

"Maria was a mole-catcher's daughter," I tell him, "William Corder a rich farmer's son. One night he lured her to the barn with promises; and indeed wrote to her father announcing they were married – married and very happy. But Maria's mother kept having dreams about the barn... Finally she persuaded her husband to go out and excavate. And then, of course, Maria's body came to light. Are you bearing up manfully?"

"Gee, I don't know, it's tough."

"Well, anyway, Corder was discovered near London, in a place called Brentford, where – thanks to an advertisement – he had found himself a rich wife. And guess what: they were running a seminary for young ladies! But in August 1828 he was hanged at Bury St Edmunds, in front of a crowd of ten thousand. The hangman sold the gallows rope at a guinea an inch and a book about the trial was bound in Corder's skin, which the prison doctor had farsightedly removed for that very purpose. What do you have to say to that, Lootenant?"

"Enterprising. Though I guess it was a fairly limited edition."

"Just one copy; still on display in Bury Museum. Like to go and see it?"

"Any chance we'd be allowed to fondle it?"

"Oh, don't!"

We begin to retrace our steps. But something impels me to stop again and look back at the cottage. "Actually we make light of it, we turn it into melodrama, we pull out all the stops. But this is a real person we're talking about: silly perhaps but probably kindhearted and hopeful and trusting. Poor soul. At the end she must have felt terrified. We ought to say a prayer for her when we're in church."

"Wouldn't some interpret that as being a little late?" He smiles at me, then adds: "The idiots!"

"That's right. What idiots."

"After all," he says, "how much do any of us really know about the complexities of time?"

I regard him suspiciously. But his expression appears guileless.

"And in any case," he continues, "supposing that time *is* just linear. God himself is outside time – presumably, then, he'd have had knowledge, even on the night she died, of the prayer you'll say this morning for Maria Marten. And so, if you believe in prayer, you must also believe it may have eased the pain for her, it may have helped her die less fearfully."

He pauses.

"I'm saying all this as though you weren't already perfectly aware of it. Forgive me."

"No, it's good to hear it put in words."

So we make our intercessions for the murdered girl; and I throw in one for William Corder also, on the principle of judge not, lest ye be judged...

The service, which began at eleven, is only sparsely attended. The church is Norman, primitive and simple. In the nave arcades, the arches are of brick; the clerestory also. Since the Normans are not supposed to have used brick, as we are later informed by the vicar, these are thought to be the earliest bricks made in England since Roman times; earlier than Coggeshall. The vicar is clearly proud of his church; he's a gaunt old man with snowy white hair, a shuffling gait, a soft voice, and some difficulty in hearing. His sermon is gentle, not very inspiring. But at least the hymns are mostly ones I like and played in a comfortable key.

At the end of the service he's of course standing by the door and as there are so few for him to say goodbye to, Matt and I talk to him about the church and the weather and the redecoration of the church hall (we have been invited to it for a cup of coffee and a biscuit but have made excuses; I already know that neither Camp Coffee nor Bev is what Matt most appreciates about England – and, anyhow, by now the Cock will probably be open). But the vicar has just asked where Matt's home is. And when at last the old man hears the answer he suddenly exclaims that some twenty-five years ago he himself spent time in New Haven, with a family called the Taylors, who lived in...he struggles to remember the name of the district, or the road, and Matt, equally pleased and almost equally frustrated, struggles to assist his recollection. Professor Taylor taught History at Dartmouth College…

And then, by one of those wonderful coincidences, Matt knows exactly whom he means, because the college mentioned is his own Alma Mater. And although he didn't study under Professor Taylor, he's not only spoken to him on several occasions but once came close to dating his youngest daughter, Jo – Meg – Beth? He's sure it's something out of 'Little Women'…

"Meg! Yes! Yes, you're right! Oh, just a baby at the time! Of all the most extraordinary things! Now, who would ever have believed…?"

The two of them stand beaming at one another and I reflect that Matt may shortly change his mind about the coffee but he doesn't and he's right: after that initial explosion of excitement there's disappointingly little to sustain it. The talk deteriorates into stilted references to the rivalries between Yale and its nearby competitors; to the fact that the Winchester repeating rifle ('the gun that tamed the West!') and Samuel Colt's improved repeating revolver were both developed in New Haven. Could that say anything significant one wonders – ahem – about the law-abiding nature of the city's inhabitants, or possible lack thereof? And remind me now: what is the name of the river on which the town is built? (The Quinnipiac, sir, which is what the city itself was once called.) Ah, yes, and it's even more industrialized these days, I'm sure. And are your people – er – in industry? (Yes, sir. My family's in the meatpacking trade.)

I sympathize with Mr Farlingham. What kind of comment runs trippingly off the tongue regarding a family that works in the meatpacking trade?

"Ah, yes. How interesting! Meatpacking, you say…?"

There's a pause.

"Well, it's been great meeting you, sir, and we certainly enjoyed the service. Daresay we'll be here again before too long."

Pure courtesy, of course. Nothing but the most fundamental form of politeness; the Americans are famed for it.

But, even so, my heart leaps up – rejoicing.

5

"Come on, Tex, watch the birdie. Say cheese."

"I might say any number of things but cheese wouldn't be among them."

"All right, say up yours; yet at least try not to grimace while you're doing it."

Tom pulls the film out and waits for the picture to materialize.

"Okay, that's fine," he says. "Now let's go in."

The police station is on Savile Row, near Piccadilly. Tom has a friend there, someone whom he got to know during his own time on the force. Sergeant Payne is powerfully built, gap-toothed, beady-eyed. He's certainly no beauty.

"Jim, this is Tex."

"Ritter?" the sergeant asks, shaking my hand.

"Who knows?" My own dryness matches his. "That's why we're here."

"Still looks pretty good, though, doesn't he," says Tom, "for someone who's been dead for roughly fifteen years?"

Then he explains.

"Too bad," observes his buddy. "I was hoping for a chorus of that thing from *High Noon*. 'Do not forsake me oh my darling.' Might have enlivened a bleak Tuesday."

I can understand why the two of them are trying to keep the tone cheerful but I have a fleeting image of a female face, strained, heavy-eyed with fatigue, and again I'm shocked at the ease with which I'm able to forget the pain of others. (I now feel sure there must be others.) It makes no difference if the face belongs simply to the woman in the snapshot. For the time being, because that photo's the only thing I have to go upon, at least she can stand proxy. A slightly misplaced symbol, maybe – the gaiety, the liveliness – but never mind.

Do not forsake me oh my darling.

The sergeant checks the computer for anybody of my description recently fed into it. We watch without speaking. I realize I'm drumming my fingers on the table by my chair.

23

The computer gives us nothing.

"Okay, then," says the sergeant. "The card index at the Yard. I'll phone and have them do a run-through." He hesitates; it's as though he's apologizing in advance. "You see, Tex, missing persons only get priority if it's known they may be ill or vulnerable in some way…people can go walkabout for weeks. Or months." He shrugs and looks to Tom, wryly, for confirmation. "Years."

But I'm the one who answers.

"Vulnerable? I suppose mere amnesia doesn't count, then?"

The sergeant says, "Yet who would know you've got it? Apart from us?"

"I can't remember." This is intended to sound as bitter as some of my remarks earlier on, but they think I'm being funny – and reluctantly I also end up smiling. "Naturally you mean apart from us, a textiles company, a fashion school, a barbershop, a sandwich bar and the receptionist working late at the dental practice opposite."

"Opposite?"

"Opposite Tom's office."

Tom, once more, explains all this. "We were trying to discover what Tex was doing in Foley Street."

"A dentist, for God's sake?" says the sergeant, as if a fashion school were quite to be expected.

"We guessed he hadn't just received treatment; but it could have been a checkup."

"Americans on holiday have checkups?"

"How can we even feel certain Tex is on holiday? He might be working over here. And yes, before you say it, the embassy is most definitely one of our next ports of call."

"Oh, he's incredibly thorough, your friend Tom." For the second time I think I intend only irony, but there's a trace of pride there too. "We even went into a pub, several shops, whatever offices were still open, a café, a Spanish restaurant…"

"Okay! Okay! Stop!" The sergeant holds up his palms as if to ward off blows. "I'm convinced of it. Half of London knows you've got amnesia. But that still hasn't got you onto the computer. Not yet, at any rate."

"And I don't understand it. If I've left my jacket behind, along with my passport and all my money and traveller's cheques, wouldn't my wife, or my parents, or others on the same tour – I mean, if I *am* on vacation – wouldn't someone have realized by now that something's wrong?"

But nothing can alter the fact I don't appear on that damned computer.

Nor in that damned card index at the Yard. (The sergeant's call had been speedily returned.)

He tips back in his seat. "Don't worry, though. I'll keep my eyes peeled for anything that comes in."

Tom produces the picture he took earlier…"in case you can't get hold of us and – with any luck – are called on to put someone out of their suspense. We shan't be at the office; a message at home will probably reach us faster." He jots down details to do with nationality and appearance. "How are Bridget and the girls?"

"Bridget will want to know when you're next coming to supper."

The sergeant shakes my hand again.

"Relax, Tex. Think how in time you'll laugh at all of this and even see it had a purpose – that's what my granny used to say."

It's rather a sweet thought: great big Sergeant Payne learning at his wise old granny's knee.

On the sidewalk Tom takes more photos.

"But why? You say that, anyway, all the hotels and boarding houses would get in touch with the police."

"True. Yet if you're over here on your own it could take them time to realize you were missing. The chambermaid would see your bed hadn't been slept in but might assume you'd spent the night in someone else's or that you'd gone out of London for a while. Or the people she'd report it to would definitely assume that. And reception staff, of course, only work in shifts. So therefore…"

"So therefore I can stop bellyaching about expenses? Is that what you're trying to say?"

"Yep. You read me like a book. And each hotel will have to have a picture, so that the staff who come on later in the day…"

I frown slightly but not at the price of photographs. "How many hotels?"

"Oh, hundreds. Especially if your Rolex is misleading us and we need to lower our sights to the bed-and-breakfasts."

Despite his smile, 'hundreds' doesn't prove that much of an exaggeration. During the next eight or nine hours, while concentrating solely on the larger and grander establishments, we hand out thirty photographs – together with thirty of Tom's printed cards – and realize there are still innumerable places we haven't been able to cover. (And the prospect of the bed-and-breakfasts is truly terrifying – even if, mostly, we may get away with just making phone calls.)

"Tom, I don't know how you can stand this sort of grind, day after day. The monotony, the disappointment."

"I don't do it day after day. In any case it's simple. That old thing about hoping for the best while only expecting the worst."

"Newman the philosopher," I say. "Newman the philanthropist."

"You also learn to ignore the jibes."

"But clearly not how to recognize a compliment. A sincere compliment."

"Sincere, then, but half-witted. After we've eaten I'll take you to the hospital."

"Right. Only thank God we *are* going to eat."

He nods. "I feel we've earned ourselves a good dinner. My treat, not yours. Are you exhausted?"

We go to Rules in Maiden Lane. Steak and kidney pudding, homemade raspberry ice, Stilton cheese, undoing all the benefits of last night's Lean Cuisine, if either of us was actually needing to lose weight.

We drive back to Golders Green along Tottenham Court Road. Suddenly Tom makes a right turn and pulls up outside a hospital. University College. Accidents and Outpatients.

"My God, he means it!"

He smiles at my expression. "No, I know somebody who works here. Let's see if he's around."

He knows damned well that he's around. Dr Ramtullah, who isn't much older than me and who may be one of the gangliest

26

creatures I've ever encountered, gives Tom a hug as though he would wrap his arms about him twice, and fills his small office like a loose-limbed spider with an Oxford accent.

After he's questioned me quite lengthily, he spends several minutes parting my hair with his fingers, running his hands across my neck, feeling my temples, forehead, nose, jaw. He looks inside my mouth; shines a torch into my eyes. He seems very conscientious but apparently discovers nothing. He returns to his chair.

"So what's the treatment?" inquires Tom.

"Wonder-drugs, you mean? I'm afraid there's no drug yet invented which can restore a lost memory."

"All right, no drug," says Tom, "but what about hypnosis?"

The doctor gives a shrug. "Personally I would recommend you to wait until the amnesiac state has resolved itself naturally."

"Why?"

"Because, although a hypnotist may tell you that hypnosis can take care of anything, I and a lot of others are sceptical: we believe there are still areas that remain outside its province. Even if we're wrong, it would undoubtedly take time, several sessions at the very least. My own feeling is that left to itself," he inclines his head in my direction, "your memory will return within a week."

"And if it doesn't?"

"And if it doesn't…well, then by all means think about hypnosis; I should be happy to refer you. Yet be prepared for disappointment."

He adds: "In any case, I would still favour the more natural method. If you are subconsciously blocking out some memory which is painful, I should prefer that it come back at a speed you can cope with."

Dr Ramtullah unwinds himself. He stands up. We all do.

"Well, Tom, why don't you bring him back next Tuesday. In the meantime, Mr Tex, rest as much as you can. Try not to worry. And be patient."

"Ranjit's a good chap," says Tom, while we descend in the elevator. "Did you find him reassuring?"

"Not especially. I found him patronizing."

27

"I'm sorry. That's only his manner. He doesn't at all mean – "

"And what about you? Do you at all mean…?" I draw breath. "It's nearly ten o'clock. We weren't seen by accident. You must have telephoned at some point, yes? Since we all know how incredibly thorough you are."

He admits that he did.

"Then why couldn't you have told me?"

He sighs. "I suppose I thought you'd make a fuss."

"Well, I'm damned well making one now. I resent being treated like a ten-year-old."

"So would I – who wouldn't?"

"Yes. Well. Please remember that." And all through the silent ride back to Golders Green I refuse to let my knowledge of his good intentions mitigate the offence.

When we get home he offers me a whisky. I decline. I leave him in the sitting room with the curtest of goodnights and a closing of the door which is practically a slam.

But following a good ten minutes in the shower I return in penitence. He is sitting with his feet up – listening to a tape with a tumbler in his hand.

"Sorry about that."

"Tex, I apologize as well."

"Won't let it happen again." I smile.

"And even if it does I reckon we might just about survive. Who could deny you must be under the most enormous stress? Come and have that drink."

The tape he's listening to is 'Chanson de Matin'. Is it the music itself or only its title that seems to convey to me a message of hope?

Or is it simply that I've made my peace with Tom?

28

6

Because of the weather, Matt had thought it wiser not to bring a picnic: "I guessed we might feel snugger in a pub." ("Wot, no swimming!" I inquire.) Sitting in the Cock I tell him of the Fox and Hounds – equally attractive – so, sight unseen, he decides we'll lunch at Groton as soon as we arrive.

A good decision. We feel well-fed and much warmer by the time we're looking at the Winthrop birthplace, which is really quite ordinary: a white two-storey building with a tiled roof, small-paned sash windows, gable at either end. But we stand there loyally for several minutes and try to think of things to comment on.

Then we go back to the jeep.

"Full steam ahead for Cambridge!" he decrees, slapping his hands together. "And wouldn't it be swell if we could also take in Grantchester?"

"In Connecticut they breed them ambitious," I declare.

"Not so much ambitious. Merely anxious to make up for lost time."

"But why haven't you seen all these places before?"

"Who knows? Laziness? Lack of opportunity? Lack of the proper person to see them with?"

"Oh, well," I agree, airily. "Probably reason enough."

Groton lies amid some of the most beautiful scenery in the county; this is the edge of Constable country. From time to time we even see a windmill. Matt compares the twisting Suffolk lanes to that strip of Roman road which runs out of Halesworth – and of course to the detriment of the latter – but we hadn't yet met a large car coming in the opposite direction (a car, incidentally, whose occupants he'd needed to salute) when he happened to voice that particular opinion.

"Oh, yes, naturally it still holds. Do you see me, then, as someone who lacks constancy?"

It's about half-past-three when we arrive in Cambridge. We park the jeep and wander through the town and look inside the courts of several of the colleges. ("Matt, just listen to those blackbirds!") I feel the rightness of the day compounded when we enter Trinity through the Great Gate and a nice old boy with red complexion, thin silvery hair and a grubby pullover engages us in conversation, discovers Matt comes from New England, and reveals that John Winthrop was a student here. But in the end he has less to say about Winthrop, who apparently wasn't an object of scandal, than about Lord Byron, who undoubtedly was. Our guide turns out to be one of the masters of the college. He leads us across to the magnificent Franciscan fountain in which it is said that Byron used to disport himself naked.

The old man chuckles.

"He's also alleged to have climbed onto the roof of the library and added certain…embellishments…to the statues up there."

As we walk out of Trinity, Matt echoes my own feeling.

"I had a hunch today was going to be special."

"That kind of hunch is very often fatal."

"Agreed. However, today I had a kind of hunch it wouldn't be."

We're now strolling along the Backs, hand-in-hand. We sit down on the riverbank and watch a soldier skilfully propel a punt. His companion is leaning back on a bed of cushions and although the weather is still a long way from being warm the fitful late-afternoon sunshine – impressively forecast by one of the farmhands – makes it look inviting.

"Maybe we could do that?" suggests Matt.

"I'm told it's not as easy as it looks."

"Surely you can't have forgotten that you're talking to a man whose forefathers survived the Arabella?"

The passenger in the punt has red hair that falls about her shoulders. I admire it – then append rather casually: "Your fiancée? What colour's *her* hair?"

He answers less casually. "Not a lot different to yours."

"Mousy? Poor girl. Do you have a snapshot?"

He takes out his wallet and passes me a photograph. "Meet Marjorie."

"My goodness! The face and figure of a film star!"

"In fact that's what she wants to be. She's done a bit of summer stock." Is there an element of dryness there? He adds neutrally: "And her father hobnobs with some of the best-known names in Hollywood."

"Where did you meet her?"

"She was engaged to my brother,"

I hadn't even known he had a brother.

Now I discover that he hasn't. "Tom died of bone cancer. Three years back."

"Oh, my God. How awful. I'm sorry."

"Yes." He remains silent for a while but then continues. "Marjorie was left desolate. She may look… But the truth is she's intensely vulnerable and if you'd seen the way she pined for Tom… It fell to me to try to get her over it, help her to recover her courage. And gradually, before either of us had realized…"

"She was enormously lucky, then, that Tom had a brother like you." I recognize a certain amount of dryness in my own tone; a dryness which I honestly do my utmost to eradicate.

Matt returns the snapshot to his wallet.

"No, I was the lucky one, to have a brother like Tom. Marjorie would have been okay, eventually. She's the kind of girl who brings out the protective instinct in practically any man she meets. Even a guy like me."

"Why do you add that?"

"Oh, I don't know. Wasn't thinking, I guess." He picks a blade of grass and starts to chew on it, lying back and leaning on one elbow. "I guess I used to see myself as being pretty weak."

"Weak!" The surprise is genuine.

"Thank you for that – but, yes, I often used to think so. Before my brother died, before I realized that Marjorie could ever view me as any kind of…well, as any kind of a replacement. And in a way that's why this stint in England has been so good for me. I know that sounds selfish but it's shown me I can cope. That I can cope the same as anyone."

"But what on earth made you think that you were weak?"

He rolls onto his back, throws away the blade of grass. "Well, for one thing, I suppose, I find my father a bit formidable. My mother's also got a very forceful personality. I'm fond of them both and missed them like hell when I first got to England but –"

He laughs. "That's another thing, of course. Homesickness is hardly a great sign of strength."

"What an idiotic remark…for a highbrow."

"I've no idea," he says, "why I'm telling you all this. Well, actually, yes I have. From the start I've found you remarkably easy to talk to."

"I'm glad." I wish I could have met him earlier, during that period when he missed his home.

But suddenly I get a consolation prize (and almost wonder if he might be telepathic).

"You know, Rosalind," he says, "I really found you at the right moment. I'd been feeling fairly low, what with Roosevelt's death; the discoveries at Buchenwald… Well, of course, everybody had. I'm not claiming any special sort of sensibility; don't get me wrong. But that Jack o' the Clock was the first thing to make me smile in days. I had nearly told Walt to find someone else to go with him to Southwold. In fact I did but he was surprisingly insistent."

"Good old Walt. And you did more than smile. You really laughed."

"I know. It was a true liberation."

I lie back, feeling happy.

"And then, too, see how you've taken me out of myself today! John Winthrop, Maria Marten, Meg Taylor, Lord Byron. Though I give you my solemn word," he says hastily – albeit with a touch of mischief, "I am *not* making light of Maria Marten!"

We decide to take a punt to Grantchester. Yes, at first he gets the pole caught but then he quickly grows proficient and his movements become a joy to watch.

> "Oh! there the chestnuts, summer through,
> Beside the river make for you
> A tunnel of green gloom…"

Also he recites the whole of 'The Soldier' – at Dartmouth he majored in English – and gets it word-perfect. It's a memorable experience: drifting along a lovely river on a fine spring evening (the sky has at last got rid of the remnants of its cloud) and listening to a moving poem well spoken against the very setting which inspired it.

We tie up the punt and for a wonderfully enchanted hour we ourselves roam England's ways and love her flowers and feel we have hearts very much at peace under an English heaven. Is war still raging in the Pacific? Bloodshed, pain, bereavement? Even boredom, muddle, apathy? We poke our heads round the gateway of the Old Vicarage and try to put the clock back forty years to when the poet would have been eighteen, try to picture him running across the lawn, sitting on that wrought-iron seat, standing on the very spot where we ourselves now stand. 1905. It's easy to imagine – in such a place, on such an afternoon – that we have turned into time travellers who have stumbled upon a secret door into that sunlit, safe, Edwardian world; at least, Matt cautiously amends, sunlit and safe for those who had a good income. We admire the exterior of the church; we look for his name on the village war memorial (there it is – Brooke – after Baker, Blogg and Bolton) and think a little, too, about those other names imprinted on the stone. Then we eat a proper English tea, high tea, in a proper English cottage, with a proper homemade sign outside its door. And afterwards, while still not quite of this world, while wandering through some twilit balm-filled extension touched with just sufficient melancholy to sharpen our appreciation of it, we wend our way back to the punt and give a florin to the boy who's been left most proudly and willingly in charge.

However, once we're in the jeep returning to the farm, tranquillity soon disappears. And how! Pity all the life of field and hedgerow. 'You're in the army, Mr Brown'…'The Lambeth walk'…'She'll be coming round the mountain when she comes'…'It's a grand night for singing'…

But then he must have seen me shiver (it *is* cold riding in a jeep after the sun's gone down) for with his free hand he pulls me towards him and I lay my head on his shoulder and we drive along less boisterously for the remainder of the way.

As we get closer to home I tell him he must come in and meet Fred and Amy and have a mug of tea and a sandwich. The

Crawfords stand to some extent *in loco parentis* and I would vaguely feel I had to do this anyway, even without the urge to show him off and give him something hot and let him see the farm by moonlight, for the house is moated and therefore picturesque as well as merely old. I could have shown it to him in the morning but had felt then that this was the better way to do it. Another time – and I was now fairly certain there was going to be another time – he could look at it by day.

I can see he's making an impression on the Crawfords: I've never heard them talk so animatedly to somebody they didn't know. They even turn down the wireless: Albert Sandler and his Palm Court Orchestra playing 'Bells Across the Meadow'! As usual, the lamp has the faint aroma of paraffin about it but its light spreads a soft glow over the kitchen and the range gives out the same style of homeliness, with the kettle now boiling once more and whistling gently on the hob. Fred, stringy, weather-beaten, with slightly protuberant eyes, talks about the execution of Mussolini, the supposed cerebral haemorrhage of Hitler and the dropping of food bombs on Holland. Amy, mending towels, the typical farmer's wife, rosy-cheeked, round, comfortable, talks about the children and the difficulties of making do. ("I have eighteen people to feed; two gallons of broth to prepare each evening!") Then Matt asks about the moat and Fred's well away: protection against peasant uprisings, wolves and winter floods and cattle thieves – well, that's only the start of it. Fred's an authority.

Therefore it's nearly a quarter past ten when Matt again stands up to take his leave – and this time is allowed to – fairly late when you consider we all have to be up so early (although as yet there's not been any sign of Trixie). He hesitates about whether to give me a goodnight kiss, then does so, on the cheek, which is exactly right.

In bed, in our small room with its sloping floor and equally sloping ceiling, I drunkenly review the day and suddenly I'm aware of a tremendous sense of loss, an awful ache of longing in the abdomen. Already.

I don't want to lose him!

Can't bear the thought I'll have to lose him!

34

7

We get to the embassy at half-past-nine and discover it's been open for an hour. We're directed to the Upper Brook Street entrance. A man in front of us has his attaché case looked into but we're okay, neither of us is carrying anything. Oh, yes, Tom has a bunch of keys in his pants pocket. So he has to hand it over for a minute and once again pass through the metal-detector. Parking the car has taken all the coins he had – and the money he's lent me wasn't in change.

American Citizen Services is to the right and up some stairs. A Marine security guard watches as we go inside. The young woman who greets us from behind her counter sounds Irish rather than American. I explain that I've lost my passport. ("Start easy," Tom had advised. "Don't throw it at them all at once.") Totally unfazed, she hands me a form and asks us if we'd like to sit while I complete it. We go a little further in and the place opens up to resemble a vast modern bank: airy and pleasant with all the walls, desktops and partitions either cream-coloured or grey, and the carpet adding a bluish tinge. Typewriters, computers and printers introduce a lighter shade of grey. There are anomalies, of course: a vase of flowers, a large and leafy plant, the U.S. flag drooping from a staff topped by a golden eagle.

We sit on plastic chairs and glance through the form: Application for Passport Registration. Initially there doesn't seem a lot I can fill in. It starts with name, date and place of birth. Social security number. But then I find the next six questions to be simple. For my mailing address I give Tom's. I tell them my gender; that my height is six foot; the colour of my hair, light brown; my eyes, blue. For my home telephone number they get Tom's. (They get his business phone as well – that makes a seventh field not left entirely blank.) After that, it's permanent address and occupation. Father's name, father's birthplace, father's date of birth. Is or was father a U.S. citizen? Then comes my mother's maiden name and a request for *her* details. Then it's back to me. Have I ever been issued with a U.S.

passport? (If yes, passport number, issue date and disposition. In this context, what does *that* mean, exactly? Neither of us knows.) Have I ever been married? (If yes, date of most recent marriage.) And so on. In other words, not without problems for someone like myself. Tom points out a note on the reverse side: if no birth record exists, a circumcision certificate might help to prove identity. "Oh, yes, extremely funny," I reply.

"Or family Bible records," he smiles. "I find that equally endearing."

I put the form into a tray on another counter, more in an attempt to appear willing than because I think it's of the slightest use to anyone. In the space for the first answer I have finally written – God help me – Tex Newman. (It could have been John Doe but that's even worse.) As Tom indicates, they must have something to address me by, when they summon me to interview.

Which happens surprisingly soon. An athletic black youth at the counter tells me my form appears to be lacking many essential details. I reply that I'm faced with certain difficulties that I should like to explain to someone. He glances at the five or six people waiting and – conceding that the matter may be complicated – decides to pass me on to a superior. This lady, he informs us, is the supervisor in charge of Passport Citizen Operations. What is equally impressive is that she, like the clerk, doesn't keep us hanging around: no more than three minutes before we're on our feet again.

She's an angular woman with greying hair piled high and spectacles dangling from a golden chain. She's British. She means to interview me over the counter but Tom asks if it couldn't be done in an office.

And it could. We pass through a door whose lock is opened by pressing the right combination of studs and she leads us to a room with grey Venetian blinds, the same grey-blue carpeting, and a striking vase of gladioli next to her typewriter.

We all sit. She gazes at us from across her desk with an air of solicitous refinement.

"Well, Mr Newman, as I was saying, I'm afraid that this form requires – "

36

"I'm not Mr Newman. I'm sorry but it's a good deal more complicated than that. You see…"

And I put her in the picture.

"Oh, you poor young man!" Mrs Bradley puts on her glasses and picks up my form again – finds nothing there she hadn't found before – replaces it upon her blotter. She takes off her glasses, sucks one of the hooked ends for a thoughtful moment, then leans forward eagerly. "I don't believe we've ever experienced quite this problem before…although strangely we did recently have occasion to assist an amnesia victim once he had recovered most of his memory." She holds this out to me, almost literally, as a solid inducement to hope. "But tell me, have you seen a doctor?"

I assure her that I have.

Tom makes a suggestion.

"Oh, I'm afraid not," she answers, most regretfully. "You need to understand, there must be millions of passports issued yearly in the U.S. and even if we *could* transmit a picture to every passport office in all the fifty states, it would be almost impossible to match it up."

She smiles at me and pulls a face of deep apology.

"And supposing that your passport were issued in 1983, when the renewal period was made longer? Your photo would now be seven years old and, who knows, seven years ago you might have been just eighteen or nineteen…with spots and a crew-cut…?" She shrugs, eloquently.

This is dispiriting. "You mention all fifty states," I say, "but doesn't my accent pin me down to someplace on the East Coast?"

A short pause. "Oh dear," she says. "I must confess to being a little out of my depth here. You've set me a conundrum. So perhaps if you wouldn't mind waiting for just a minute…?"

It turns out to be more like fifteen. She sends us one Mr Herb Kramer, who's about forty, big, sandy-haired, blue-suited. He comes in alone and shakes our hands with warmth. Mr Kramer is the vice-consul.

"I believe I've been made conversant with your plight. I have to say a case like this puts us in a difficult position."

"Not half as difficult as the one it puts me in."

"No, I'm sure." He laughs, genially. "You see, our problem is we can only provide assistance to someone we know to be an American citizen. You'll realize that given your memory loss this becomes a little awkward?"

"But my accent?"

"Yes, your accent. People do sometimes come to us with the most authentic-sounding…" He looks at me intently; looks at Tom; looks back at me. "Oh, hell. At a guess I'd say you come from New England. I'm a New Englander myself."

"That's what I'd have said, too." (On both counts.)

"However, I doubt there'd be much value in communicating with the New England passport offices; there's no way to systematically search their records. But I'll tell you what we can do. We can send a cable to the State Department on the chance that someone might have started an inquiry."

He's perched on the edge of Mrs Bradley's desk, pensively stroking his moustache.

"What's tantalizing is to think we could already have received a cable from them. Or from some other post. A caller might actually have been right here asking about you. Every last detail could be sitting there awaiting us. But without a name to enter into the lookout check…" He spreads his hands. "So we have nothing to fall back on but the memories of our staff. Just now Mrs Bradley and I were questioning everyone on duty today. Unfortunately without the least bit of success."

"Thank you, anyhow."

"Well, it's our job, of course. Your accent leads us to believe you're American and therefore we'll assume you are." He says this in a fairly businesslike way but then he smiles. "Unless we happen to unearth some discouraging thing to the contrary."

"Like what, for instance? That I'm a natural born mimic who's spent time in New England?"

"Oh, believe me, it happens! I notice, by the way, you're not totally uninfluenced by British speech patterns."

This doesn't strike me as being loaded but I do reply that, seeing it from his point of view, my claim could unquestionably be a hoax. "Nice work if you can get it."

38

"Exactly. Oh, you'd be surprised at some of the tricks people try to pull. Also, you'd be surprised at some of the ingenuity they put into them."

"Do they, so far as you know, ever manage to get away with it?"

"I doubt it. Our tests are extremely stringent. We look for very special responses."

"Such as?"

They both laugh.

"And even apart from those tests," says Herb Kramer, "one very swiftly develops a sixth sense."

Although I acknowledge that his answer will be meaningless: "And your sixth sense regarding me?"

"That you're genuine. Can I ask you a somewhat personal question? You have no credit cards nor traveller's cheques. What's your financial situation?"

"A real pain."

Again he laughs. "Sure thing; must be! But the reason I ask is that it's possible for us to give you assistance in getting back to the States. We'd make contact with the Department of Health and Human Services and they, if necessary, would help you find a place to stay."

I like this man. He seems to come from almost the same class of human being as Tom. I like his attitude of innocent till proven guilty. I like his tact, as well: the way he doesn't actually ask what I'm managing to live on. To say that Tom is keeping me would most likely convey a seriously misleading impression, especially to a man who, however well-disposed, is trained to be cynical. Even considering it in passing is something that makes me realize, all over again, how exceptional Tom is, and how incredibly lucky I was to have come across him. Unthinkingly, I flash him an affectionate smile, which could possibly confirm any suspicions my compatriot may have.

Herb Kramer takes my form and scribbles down some notes. Tom gives him a couple of photographs. The vice-consul promises he will do all in his power to speed up the inquiries.

He escorts us to the entrance (Mrs Bradley waves cheerily from a far corner and mouths the words "Good luck!") and we leave the building in a fairly optimistic frame of mind.

We need all the optimism we can get. There's another day of visiting hotels ahead of us.

8

We'd had a date for the following Sunday.

This time it's Matt who has to change the plan. He phones on Saturday. I run into the kitchen without taking off my wellies. They're caked in mud. Already I can see wet lumps strewn across the tiles.

"Rosalind, I really am sorry. What about next Tuesday?"

"Next Tuesday?"

"V-E Day."

"Are you sure, Matt? I listened to the lunchtime news. They claimed it was still only rumour."

"Oh, Miss Farr," he says.

"I see. Privileged information, Lootenant? A tip-off from Uncle Sam?"

"A tip-off from Donald Duck. And Donald Duck tells me you'll get Wednesday off as well." Yes, the wireless had certainly spoken about two days' national holiday, just hadn't been able to say when. "He also wants you to know Walt and I will be driving down to London to be right in the thick of it – and looking for two brave girls who might be interested in joining us."

"Well, I admit, I've always had a very soft spot for Donald Duck."

"Must be reciprocal," he says. "He's got you some nylons – no more cold legs in jeeps!" (And no more aggravation, either, with the tan cream and the eyebrow pencil!) Matt adds that if he puts them in the mail tomorrow they ought to get to me on Monday. His thoughtfulness has to be exceptional.

Therefore it's hardly fair to take advantage. "I know this is going to sound stuffy. But you wouldn't consider, I suppose…? I mean, before we leave for London…?"

The wireless had also spoken about arrangements being made by the government for a morning thanksgiving service to be held in towns and villages across the country.

"I guess I know what's in your mind."

"You do?"

"But I was thinking of after we'd gotten there, not before we left."

And it's absurd: why should my eyes begin to water?

"Yet you're right," he continues. "St Paul's will be too crowded – and maybe even a bit too grand? Besides, God knows what time we'd have to set out. So how about our old friend Mr Farlingham? After all, it's nearly a week since we said we'd look him up and I reckon by now he must be missing us."

"Oh, bless you, Matt. I imagine you're aware you must be psychic?" The church at Polstead is nicer than the one nearer home, where the party from the farm is going. Trixie and I find St Leonard's a little too austere – even at Christmas or on Easter Sunday. "Just so long as you can square it with Walt," I mention, smiling.

They get to us at half-past-eight. (And Donald Duck was right: V-E Day! – and the war in Europe most wonderfully and most beautifully brought to a glorious end!) They were supposed to be having a guided tour of the farm by daylight but after the violent storm of a few hours back the ground is far too muddy. Never mind, at least they can see the moat and the farmyard – which are the pretty-pretty bits – and say "Wow!" and "Gosh!" and "Gee!" in most satisfactory style.

Then we take them into the kitchen. Today there are about a dozen gathered there – still, at *this* hour! – mostly with braces dangling and collars attached only by a back stud; they're drinking strong tea, half-listening to the radio, not openly excited but companionable, content, smoking their Woodbines or the cigarettes they roll themselves. Werner sits there with the rest, in no way ostracized but understandably subdued. I make the introductions. Nods, handshakes, pleasantries (for the most part

41

unintelligible – several times I have to translate). Matt goes to chat with Fred, while Walt helps Amy carry off her three hitherto protesting sons to get them smartened up. Then Trixie and I start packing into baskets the picnic things we'd been preparing when Matt and Walt arrived. We haven't told them yet and no doubt they both confidently expect (being men and being American) to march at any time into any restaurant and have their pick of whatever's printed on the menu; but with all the millions prophesied to be in London today, the reality will quite assuredly be different. We weren't Girl Guides for nothing.

We leave the farm at roughly nine-thirty. The children, with their scrubbed knees, grey flannel suits and shirts, school ties and caps – and patently smitten with hero worship – have begged to be allowed to come to Polstead. They climb onto our laps, mine and Matt's and Trixie's ("Though if you kick me and snag my nylons," she says, "I'll bloody well use one of 'em to strangle you!") and spend their journey first enjoying the novelty of the transport and after that the novelty of the decorations in the village. (The novelty of air-sea rescue work has finally – and mercifully – been permitted to subside.) Masses of bunting. Prams, cycles, cars all bear their flags…so why not ours, Matt and Walt get asked reproachfully. The three young Crawfords point pathetically to other children carrying flags. So what, says Trixie – other women wear rosettes. I try to cause a diversion by pointing to a Scottie trotting along beside its owner with a rosette at its neck and, strapped around its perky little body, a coat which also exactly matches hers.

The church is really crowded – how different to nine days ago! Yet Mr Farlingham is just as shuffling and unflustered. Before long he'll surely have to stand down for one of the younger men returning to civvy street, but today he has a helper, someone not much less decrepit than himself.

We learn from the printed sheet which we've all been given (or been asked to share) that the service is to follow a set line: Thanksgiving for Victory. Maybe most of us could have predicted the choice of psalm, 'O give thanks unto the Lord, for He is gracious', but possibly it has seldom been said *en masse* with so much sincerity. Mr Farlingham chooses a passage from another psalm for his text, 'When the Lord turned again the captivity of Zion', and after a shaky start his sermon, this time, by the grace of God, manages to rise to the occasion. The whole service is as uplifting as the church bells which are now being heard again throughout the land; I imagine we shall really appreciate the peal of bells from now on, and still feel grateful that never once in all the long years of silence (silence, except for that one November Sunday when we celebrated Monty's victory at El Alamein) did they need to warn us of invasion!

On our leaving the church Mr Farlingham doesn't at first appear to recognize us. "Professor Taylor," Matt reminds him, with a grin. "New Haven, Connecticut."

"Why, yes, of course," says the old man. "My nice young couple from some weeks ago!" And to me: "I think you said that you were Meg. God bless you, my children. God bless you. And a very happy peace!"

"The same to you, Mr Farlingham."

There are tears in his eyes. He calls after us: "And to your father and the family! Oh, if only your fine president had been alive to see this day!"

We don't immediately return to the jeep. Matt wants to find a shop where he can still buy flags. I tell him he doesn't stand a chance. But marvellously, ten minutes later, he's earned the right to shake his head at me indulgently: "O ye of little faith!" The children are ecstatic; our stockings run an even greater risk. The jeep itself now sports a flag as well.

And Trix and I now wear rosettes.

We drive the young Crawfords back to the farm. One of them (Matt's, thank heaven!) is complaining, sulking. In a way I feel tempted to plead his cause – *their* cause – but I can see that it's impractical and know it's not for me to be magnanimous. "We'll bring you back a souvenir! Something nice for each of you." Yet, even there, the instant I've said it, I'm aware that I've been rash.

But then, after we've waved goodbye (poor Dick refuses to respond), phase two of this auspicious day begins.

It's inaugurated by Walt, who's still the driver. "Right! London! Here we come!"

And he makes excellent time, despite a last-minute mistake which puts us on the wrong side of Oxford Circus and loses us some quarter of an hour. By ten-past-two, however, we're back precisely where we wanted to be and driving around Trafalgar Square ("But are you sure this can be London, folks? There isn't any fog!"). I haven't seen so much traffic in years, certainly not since the coronation. Where on earth have people found the petrol? But, anyway, we're lucky with the parking: Northumberland Avenue, near the river. We walk along the Embankment to Westminster and mingle with the crowds streaming in across the bridge, all making for the Ministry of Works. Whitehall's packed but not impenetrable and thanks to the size of Matt and Walt – their shamelessness as well (but they defend themselves by saying that they were only doing it for our sakes!) – we end up in a very good position.

Hardly have we reached it, moreover, before Big Ben strikes. Three o'clock. All eyes are looking at the balcony. Mr Churchill must now be on his way.

And then he's there, that rotund, well-loved figure in the dark suit and bow tie, watch-chain stretched across the waistcoat, white handkerchief showing at his breast pocket. A tumultuous cheer bursts out.

Yet this is soon replaced by a silence almost more amazing.

It now becomes official: the Channel Islands have been liberated – Norway, too – and hostilities will end at one minute past midnight.

Tears mix with laughter. The name of Eisenhower and mention of 'our Russian comrades' provoke a further storm of clapping.

"Advance, Britannia! Long live the cause of freedom! God save the King!"

The buglers of the Scots Guards sound the ceremonial cease-fire. The band strikes up the National Anthem.

Eventually, Mr Churchill is permitted to depart.

And next stop the palace. Again the four of us do well. The central balcony is hung with gold and scarlet. At about a quarter-past-four there's a frenzy of cheering as the King himself walks onto it.

He's in naval dress but bareheaded. He stands alone for a few seconds, waving to us with his nice yet serious smile, and then the Queen comes out. She's wearing powder blue. She raises her hand and joins him in acknowledging the roar of cheers. "Jesus but she's swell," exclaims Walt.

The two princesses make their appearance. Princess Elizabeth in her A.T.S. uniform – also bareheaded – stands at the side of the Queen, while Princess Margaret, in blue, stands next to her father.

People wave their flags and hats and scarves like crazy. When the royal party returns inside, the crowd sings, "For they are jolly good fellows," and although many hundreds leave the forefront of the palace, most of us remain; scarcely another five minutes have gone before voices are shouting "We want the King!" and this refrain is taken up in every quarter. It's interspersed with another chant. "We want Winston! W-I-N-S-T-O-N!" While we wait an Australian soldier climbs the gates of the palace, waves his flag like a baton and leads us in community singing.

Roughly an hour later Mr Churchill does indeed join the royal family on the balcony – following his arrival in an open car, when, to a rapturous reception, he stood and waved his hat, and mounted policemen had the heck of a job clearing him a pathway. Now he stands between the King and Queen and flourishes his cigar in greeting to us all. Being last to leave the balcony he gets a special round of cheering and applause.

When we do at length tear ourselves away we go back to the jeep and eat our picnic. Afterwards, in Piccadilly Circus, we see a British sailor, a GI and a Pole perform a striptease; they get plenty of encouragement. (Trixie exhorts Walt and Matt to join in and is almost set to have a go herself.) An American paratrooper whose face is covered in lipstick is asking all the women in his path to add to his collection. From Trixie he gets perhaps more than he had bargained for, a real smacker on the lips, and from me a laughing peck upon the cheek.

"Here!" says Matt. "These damn Yanks! What nerve! It's time I got in on this!"

I brush my lips against his cheek in similar friendly fashion. He looks at me…and then returns this gesture with a close embrace and proper kiss.

I'm aware of his erection.

Aware, as well, of my own arousal.

Disorientating.

The next few hours pass in a blur. I know that Walt and Trixie decide to leave us. I know that at some point we find ourselves in the blessed serenity of Westminster Abbey, where people's heads are bowed in thanksgiving and where the pilgrimage to the tomb of the Unknown Warrior appears unending. I know that at some point we're standing beside the lake in St James's Park. I feel quite sorry when it's time to hear the King's speech.

We infiltrate a small hotel near Piccadilly, with probably a hundred others, to listen on the radio.

We've arranged to meet Walt and Trixie outside Rainbow Corner, in Coventry Street, where, two or three years back, the American Red Cross set up a club for GIs. Pushing our way through, we find all faces turned towards a lamppost outside the London Pavilion as an RAF officer and a red-bereted airborne officer compete to climb to the top with a Union Jack.

Ten minutes later the Stars and Stripes is fastened next to it – and then the Russian flag as well: the three Great Powers fluttering side by side.

Even women are trying to climb the lampposts. A bit further on, a girl in a red coat earns the crowd's approval. I can imagine the swirl of colour from up there: the carnival caps, the uniforms, the women in their prettiest frocks. The sashes of bunting. The flowers and ribbons of red and white and blue, pinned either in the hair or on the clothing. Viewed from the lamppost it must be wonderfully impressive.

Tonight nothing is unsuitable. Evening garments saved from prewar days, full skirts, hobble skirts, backless dresses, long-sleeved day dresses; strangely you don't see many pairs of slacks.

We get to Rainbow Corner.

"Isn't this great!" Walt greets us. "Who said the British never let their hair down!"

"I don't know," I reply, a little drily. "Tell us. Who did?"

"But listen, kids, we've managed to get two hotel rooms in some little place called Bayswater."

People are trying to get enough stuff together to start a bonfire in the middle of the street; there's even a hawker's barrow to which a strip of card is still attached ('Flags of all the Allies'). "Some bloody profiteer trying to charge five quid for a single Union Jack!" self-justifies the swaggerer who's commandeered and overturned it. There's much aggressive laughter. I say to Matt: "I thought that we were driving back tonight."

"Me, too. Walt? What is all this?"

"Don't be a schmuck. Me and Trix managed to pull a few strings." They look at each other proudly. "In fact, we just about had to move heaven and earth – didn't we, babe? 'Cause who in their right mind wants to be driving back to camp through half the friggin' night? Matt, you sap! This is Victory-in-Europe Day! Hasn't anybody told you?"

Trixie grips my arm, imploringly. "Come on, Roz. Don't be a spoilsport. You know how much you like the lad."

She adds in a whisper, "And you needn't worry. We've even been and got some of those…well, thingamabobs. So everything's been taken care of."

Oh, Trix. You'll maybe never guess how much I do like the lad. Nor how sorely tempted I could feel.

But it wouldn't be right; I know it wouldn't be right. And I don't mean just because of Marjorie or because of morals. It's all much vaguer than that. More the thought of some seedy jumped-up boarding house in Bayswater, its every nook and cranny let out to servicemen and their girls at hugely inflated prices, and of some oily little clerk peering with a knowing smirk at what we've written in the register.

I look at the pavement, see that somebody's been sick. Transfer my gaze to the upturned barrow in the middle of the road, where things seem to be growing increasingly unpleasant.

"No," Matt says quickly. "You two take the jeep. I guess it won't be any problem getting rid of that second room." He suggests we all meet up again at noon the following day.

I slip my hand into his – and squeeze – and hope this pressure will tell him my reaction was in no way a rejection of Matt Cassidy, only of Bayswater. But, after all, I remind myself: isn't he the Great Clairvoyant? The Amazing Mr Mind-Reader? Surely he already knows.

"Then what are you gonna do?" asks Walt. "Wander round the streets all night?"

"Why not? There'll be more than enough going on. It's all part of history and we don't mean to let a single moment of it pass us by."

"That's right," I say. "And even if we do change our minds I know my mother would be glad to put us up." I plan to ring her, anyway, as soon as I get the chance – simply to say, Hello, isn't this great, just listen to London. "Chesham's only some twenty-five miles away."

Matthew grins. "In other words we could take the jeep and these two can walk or thumb a lift."

I agree, cheerfully. "Plenty of trams around! Pity about the taxis."

Trixie looks at Walt and gives a tolerant shrug. "The pair of them are loony but so far as I'm concerned they're more than welcome to the jeep – eh, sweetheart? In any case, *we* won't be walking. We'll be flying, more like!"

9

Thursday. I spend an aimless day on my own. Am unable to concentrate on books or newspapers or television. Go for a walk on Hampstead Heath and do a small amount of marketing, even a bit of vacuuming. Can't stop worrying about my future. Or my past.

I now look back almost with fondness on our hours of trekking round hotels.

Cooking the evening meal is the only thing that affords me any true escape. All that cutting meat and bacon into cubes, peeling shallots, slicing mushrooms and onions, foraging for garlic and bay leaves and thyme, searing and browning and sprinkling and stirring. Pouring in cider. The sauce is rich, the chuck steak tender. By halving the quantities, I've cooked enough – allegedly – for three. Tom and I dispose of it with ease. He even wipes some bread around his plate, then round the cooking pot. "Perhaps," he says, "we shouldn't have gone to reception to ask about missing guests. We should have marched right into the kitchens to ask about missing chefs."

"It would certainly have gotten us as far."

He tells me he's employed a firm to phone the bed-and-breakfasts.

"I've also been faxing off copies of that snapshot to various contacts round the country."

"Why?"

"To try to identify the church. With a magnifying glass one can make out a fair amount of detail. I spent an hour at the Royal Institute of British Architecture. Hoped that Pevsner or some other authority might come up with the answer."

"I don't see that it's important. She was only a day-tripper."

"Any pudding?" he asks.

"Cheesecake." I start to clear the dishes and Tom gets up to help. "No," I say, "*I'll* do it!" My tone sounds testy.

"Why just you?"

"Earn my keep."

"Balls." He continues to help. He says after a minute, "No, I agree with you. About the photo. It does have an air of holiday. But at the moment it's the only thing we've got."

He hesitates.

"And if we locate that church it will at least give us an area to home in on. Maybe we could even publish the picture in the local press."

"In the hope that our doing so will produce my father's name?"

"It could do."

"I'd have thought he'd have produced it himself – if he was missing me."

Tom bites his lip. Doesn't answer.

"Oh, sure. Not that anyone does appear to be missing me." There hasn't been any word from Herb Kramer. Nor from Sergeant Payne.

"No… Well, I'd say it now looks increasingly as though you came to London on your own."

"No loving wife? No family?"

"Not here at all events."

"Or anywhere, I guess. A married man doesn't vacation without his wife. And I was hardly dressed for business."

"Perhaps you were taking the day off."

"On a Monday?"

"Why not?"

"I can't continue to impose on you like this."

"That's a dazzlingly logical progression!" He grins that grin of his – the one that had stopped me leaving his office within the first fifteen minutes.

This time it doesn't work so well.

"Having everything bought for me: T-shirts, socks, shorts. Even having to take pocket money, for God's sake! Couldn't I find a job someplace; someplace I wouldn't need a permit? Get myself a room?"

"If that's what you want. It's not what I want."

"I don't know." I'm spooning coffee into the filter.

"What don't you know?"

"Your friend said amnesia could sometimes last for years."

"He thought it more likely to last a week."

"But *you* don't, do you? Otherwise you wouldn't be working so hard to try to trace this woman? And supposing you're right and he's wrong? If I had a job I could at least be starting to pay you back."

"Ranjit said you needed rest. Not that I think your shopping – cleaning – cooking – are really what he had in mind. Frankly, I'm not all that worried about your paying me back. The thing that does worry me…"

"What?"

"You sound so negative."

"Negative? Because I feel you're wasting your time looking for some woman who…well, even if she turns out still to be alive…?"

"Yes?"

"I don't see the point, that's all. Because, in this instance, I'm inclined to side with the experts. If medical opinion truly leans towards a week…"

He looks at the two pieces of cheesecake he's now transferring from their box. I expect some comment on my change of tune. I reckon I should have known better.

"When you put it that way I'm not honestly sure I see the point myself."

Possibly I now wear a slightly sheepish look. I shrug. "I guess you want to make me feel we're making progress."

"No. I think you'll have to put it down to more than that. Let's call it instinct."

"Instinct?"

"Gut feeling. Something that's hounding me on. I just believe we've got to find this woman."

10

And then the lights come on!

The lights come on! And some of London's most historic buildings are seen floodlit for the first time since the coronation.

St Paul's…

Two sections of the A.T.S have brought their mobile searchlights, have turned their beams on the cathedral. A third picks out the dome and its surmounting cross from a bombsite lower down the hill.

In the precincts, people either sit on the protective coverings to the cellars or – like us – they stand in groups around the searchlights, watching the girls in charge.

One of the girls talks to Matt and me. She's blonde and pretty and wears a lot of shiny scarlet lipstick. "They never could get it, could they? Don't you think that's sort of symbolic?"

Sort of miraculous, too. This splendid old structure stands triumphant in the midst of devastation, having watched over London through all the fires and explosions of many hundreds of air raids. Inspirational in its isolation. Surely as imposing now as it must have been at the time of its completed resurrection.

Plenty of other buildings are adding to the glow that hangs above the city. From the top of the hill we can see the brightly lit newspaper offices in Fleet Street, also the lofty tower of the Shell-Mex edifice, illuminated by flares which are constantly changing colour. All this is the more impressive since we've again been without any form of street lighting for a week (it wasn't restored to us for very long!) and shall have to be without it for a further ten; it's only for tonight and tomorrow – such beneficence.

Walking back along the Strand we pass dozens of men and women sitting on the kerb, raising tankards and toasting the victory. (All the pubs tonight are open until twelve.) We have to stand aside for sailors marching six abreast with linked arms and singing 'Tipperary' – a song more of the last war than of this. However, it makes a change from the equally dated 'Over There', which even Matt, good American though he is, feels we've had quite enough of for the time being. Anyway, me, I much prefer 'Yankee Doodle Dandy' to either of them. That's another song we're hearing pretty frequently.

We get back to Buckingham Palace just before ten-thirty, and at precisely the appointed minute all the floodlights and lamps above the gates are switched on to bathe the great grey building in pools of soft white light. As this happens, cheer upon cheer bursts from the delighted crowd. Word goes round that the two princesses, escorted by Guards' officers, are now walking amongst us. We hope to catch a glimpse of them close to, until a quarter of an hour later they once again appear with their parents on the balcony; after that we reckon it's time to see Big Ben and the Houses of Parliament, while we still have the chance. People say the lighting will go off at twelve.

But we get detained in Whitehall. The Grenadier Guards are playing 'Land of Hope and Glory' to a crowd which is uncannily hushed until, little by little, the people themselves start to sing the words. Tears mist my eyes. Then we have a further view of Mr Churchill – this time in his siren suit and black homburg – taking over as conductor.

We'd like to stay in Whitehall but there's still something we've been told we shouldn't miss. The view from Waterloo Bridge is panoramic. St Paul's in one direction; Parliament in the other. Ever-shifting searchlights making tracks into the sky. Many of the wharves lit up. Lamps shining on the bridges and Embankment. The magnificence of County Hall. Trains moving slowly in or out of Charing Cross. All mirrored in the water. Magical. Even when we pull ourselves away we have to keep stopping to look back. Matt bemoans the fact we haven't got a camera. I ask him why. You can't encapsulate enchantment.

Afterwards, we make again for Piccadilly Circus, the true vulgar heart of the West End, the place which always calls you back. (Whereas we find we couldn't now return to Waterloo Bridge, for fear of disappointment.) A floodlight plays across the site of Eros, although Eros himself is hidden behind tiers of seating. But when the floodlight gets turned off a universal groan bursts out. It isn't even midnight.

However, searchlight beams soon swing across the sky. A column of men and women forms at once – each person with both hands upon the shoulders of the reveller in front – and goes marching off down Coventry Street with a drummer beating a tin box.

Then the floodlight is switched on again. The crowd had earlier shown signs of dispersing but now it begins to be drawn back.

The underground's still open. Police are marshalling people in and out. Near one exit a woman faints. The night's grown sultry; we've seen ambulance after ambulance. Despite their clanging bells these appear to make progress only with bobbies walking in front or riding on their running-boards. A U.S. military police van, slowly forcing its way across the Circus, is brought to a prolonged standstill. Before it finally disappears, along Piccadilly, about six men are sitting on its roof. I agree with a fellow in a dinner jacket, and an older woman in a veiled and wispy hat, this certainly shows a fair degree of insouciance.

53

So, perhaps, does a small family party inching its way from the opposite direction in a flag-bedecked governess cart. But what about the pony? A bonfire is already blazing – complete with effigy of Hitler – airmen are letting off fireworks. (Not that the pony seems in any way disturbed.) Little groups gyrate around the flames or else form into crazy, jigging circles. Crocodiles of dancing civilians – many with masks and streamers and wearing grotesque fancy dress – keep pushing their way through. Flashes of news photographers. Shouting, singing, laughter. Din of rattles, bells, whistles, bangers, rockets. Trumpets, too. Champagne corks. (Champagne flows; we see dozens drinking straight from the bottle – nearest us, a little party of Norwegian airmen and sailors flourishing a huge Norwegian flag.) It's a night of noise and brilliance. Suddenly we turn to one another…and know we've had enough.

"Maybe we're hungry," says Matt.

It isn't something I've thought about, yet now I realize it's true. The restaurants and hotels fronting on the Circus have closed their doors (and Swan & Edgar's and other shops have barred all their windows) but anyway I suddenly remember the nearby Trocadero, which years ago I used to think so smart. In fact it goes with its location – it's a bit vulgar: lots of elaborate decoration and variegated marble in the neo-classical style. But it's large and there's only a short queue waiting for tables and people do seem to be leaving.

Here, too, the champagne flows. There appears to be no rationing of it whatsoever, unless the fact they're charging six pounds a bottle can be seen as rationing. (And obviously it can't. "Rosalind, it's only money and that looks like nectar they're giving in exchange. So please. Quit worrying." I do…to the extent we eventually work our way through two bottles. It's been a thirst-making kind of night – as we now, rather belatedly, realize.)

Matt also orders scrambled egg, which goes surprisingly well with the champagne, considering it's made with powder and sits so solidly upon the toast. It resembles a moist yellow cake – fun to cut slices from.

We then have castle puddings with jam sauce: a far cry from the *crêpes suzettes* I'd eaten here before the war, with a young man I had thought the very acme of sophistication. But I feel tonight I wouldn't change dried egg and castle puddings for any amount of roast duck or sophistication or balanced menu planning.

At the Troc, moreover, I find a nice lavatory – not such an easy undertaking in London at the moment – and a nice telephone, not only working but actually unqueued-for, on which I ring my mother. Matt then pays our bill, leaves an extraordinary tip for the waiter (it must be a good night for waiters, porters and the like) and we return, feeling fortified, to face the hubbub.

Before two-thirty, however, we are back in Northumberland Avenue and by this time the crowds have definitely diminished. Matt has little trouble in getting to Baker Street, and from then on our way is clear. We should arrive in Chesham by four.

"We might just beat the milkman! Are you sure your mother's going to greet us with such squeals of joy?"

"Of course I am. She said she'd put the key under the mat and make up our beds and leave us out a snack. If she's awake she may get up and say hello; if not she'll meet you in the morning."

"To which she's looking forward."

"To which she's looking forward."

"I think you must be drunk. You've already told me all of this."

"Well, if I must be drunk you must be drunk. Which is by far the more dangerous. In my opinion." And I put my hand on his, to offer him assistance with the steering.

"No. Women have a lower tolerance to alcohol." He smiles at me, smugly.

"Are you sure?"

"Completely."

"Life isn't fair. Why do men have all the fun? What nice hands you have."

"Thank you. You have nice hands as well."

55

"One of the first things I noticed. So strong. And nice. And…nice." I caress the hand with my forefinger, stroking the hairs on his wrist and causing them to stand up.

"That's nice too," he says.

"Everything's nice. It's a nice night. It's a nice drive. It'll be nice to introduce you to my mother."

But in fact I don't introduce them. They meet the following morning (no, the same morning, of course, just further along in it) when she knocks on his bedroom door and takes him in a pot of tea. Amazingly hangover-free, I am by then wallowing in my (once again!) unashamedly deep bath and have told her he'll enjoy being pampered. Apparently she means only to extend a simple word of welcome but finishes by staying while he drinks three cups of tea, for he, too, is remarkably clearheaded. She hears a lot about his life at home.

And yet she doesn't hear about Marjorie. I discover this while the pair of us are preparing a very late breakfast, and the omission strikes me as significant. I know I mustn't get my hopes up. But I can't help wondering why he hasn't made even one passing reference.

I surmise he learned comparatively little about my mother, not because he isn't a sympathetic listener – which, heaven knows, he is – but rather because her life now is basically so awful she doesn't like to talk about it, not even to me. She was a widow for four years; remarried when I was sixteen. And how my stepfather changed! Though I'd always thought the generous and attentive suitor very suspect, even I was unprepared for the mean, lazy, tyrannical brute he turned into. And the sheer rapidity of the transformation made one question one's own sanity almost as much as his. I wanted her to divorce. She spoke about the need to honour your commitments, whatever the enormity of your mistake. Later on I could have added to her knowledge of that enormity. On a night three years ago, while she was at a meeting of the Women's Institute, he tried to rape me. Stupidly I wasn't able to tell her and he made out that my avoidance of him, yet more assiduous after this, was solely due to jealousy.

If I hadn't known that he was currently in hospital I could never have contemplated even this short visit. I see my mother very rarely – mainly on snatched meetings in London. It's a wretched situation.

Though Matt has heard all this from me (except, that is, for the final cause of my departure, which I'd attributed entirely to the fact I wanted to feel more involved in the war effort – up till then I had been working in a canteen) the man hasn't been mentioned by the time we start on breakfast. We're given eggs and bacon. Shell-eggs and two rashers of bacon! I have no scruples about knowing we are doing the husband out of his but I wish my mother wasn't making such a sacrifice, especially since Matt and I – he at his air base, I on my farm – in general do quite well. She says she finds fatty things slightly rich at the moment. Fresh eggs make her liverish; people just aren't used to them.

The time goes by too quickly.

"I suppose, though, you two have to get to your appointment and I must go and see your father in the hospital." She had spent most of the preceding day there, which seems to Matt and me – although of course we don't tell her this – a wholly criminal waste of what Mr Churchill has called 'the greatest day in all our long history'. But she assures us the nurses did everything they could to bring an air of celebration into the wards and that she listened to the wireless a good deal, which was all extremely moving. I gaze at her and think, Oh God, just forty-seven and your life is over.

"I wish we could have stayed longer." The front door comes between a branch of the Home & Colonial and the small Astoria cinema.

"Well…it's been real nice, ma'am. You're everything your daughter claimed."

"And more," I add, "much more. But please go to the doctor, get that checkup. I'll ring you in a few days to find out what he said."

"Oh, what a nag! Goodbye, my darling. God bless you. Remember me to Trixie." She gives me a hug. "Goodbye, Matthew. This has been such a pleasure. God bless you. Good luck." She gives him first a handshake; that too becomes a hug.

"You're going to be so late." Another hug for me – this time an especially long one, as though she really can't bear to let us go. "But no, it doesn't matter if you're late, just so long as you get there in the end. Take care."

Then Matt hands me into the jeep. She remains on the pavement, waving, until we've turned the corner by the Food Office.

11

For this evening's supper I've prepared only a salad but Tom comes into the apartment – or, rather, into the kitchen – brandishing a bottle.

"Southwold!" he says.

"Well, fine. Is that better than Bordeaux?"

"Oh, most amusing. How would you fancy a day out in Suffolk?"

At the table he elaborates. "And here's something else. I went to school with a bloke who hosts a TV show on Anglia every Saturday; and although of course it's pre-recorded, what's a mere thirty-second insert, in the name of helping out a friend?"

It turns out that he means tomorrow.

He actually means tomorrow…

We get to Southwold just before noon. From the moment we cross the causeway over Buss Creek and Tom tells me 'buss' means a square-rigged herring smack – he's clearly done his homework – the last of my reservations has gone. I love the Georgian houses and the fishermen's colour-washed dwellings; the long sandy beach and little harbour. The town is built on a cliff-top and its views take in bracken, heath and marshes, as well as the sea. Side streets widen into large green spaces, one of which contains six cannon; another a white lighthouse. Outside an inn, barrels of ale are being lifted from a dray. The drayhorse responds with endearing nuzzles to my overtures of friendship.

I tell him I'll bring him sugar from the bar. Before we get there, Tom asks about overnight accommodation and we're lucky, they do have one remaining room. Anywhere else would have been a letdown. The Red Lion dates from 1623 and began life as a hostel for mariners.

Following lunch we visit the fifteenth-century church, which must be one of the great ones, Tom says, even for Suffolk. We look at the spot where long ago she posed for a photograph, this woman who's the reason for our being here now. I experience a pang of regret. Almost of shame. Why so much resistance – yes, all along the line – to our trying to find her?

What in God's name was I afraid of? What devil has been aiming to prevent me?

There's a little wooden man in armour: an unusual, fascinating timekeeper. While I'm admiring him and just about to call across to Tom something rather strange happens.

"Tom! Hey! Tom!"

He's been gazing at the brightly painted pulpit and looks around inquiringly.

But now I feel a bit foolish.

"Oh, nothing. It's just that I suddenly thought I must have been here before. Sorry."

Afterwards we go to a men's outfitter's, where I choose a pair of trunks; Tom has brought his. We walk down to the beach, which at a closer view turns out to be composed less of sand than of shingle. The water's cold but lovely. I feel free, cleansed, weightless. Relieved of worry. Drying off, Tom stretches out to sunbathe. I prefer to sit and let my gaze wander. My eyes come to rest for a minute on the frankly unattractive pier.

And abruptly I get a second sample of that feeling I'd experienced earlier. "That feeling of…well, of having been here before," I say.

Tom sits up, clasps his hands beneath his thighs.

"Well, now, I wonder. Could you have been here before?"

I look at him and wait.

"I mean, just supposing," he goes on, slowly, "just supposing you've been on the trail of our mystery woman in the past? Why should we necessarily assume that this is the first time? Suppose in the past you even found her?"

There's a pause.

"Well, it's an intriguing possibility," he announces finally. "But unfortunately I don't see where it gets us."

I feel disproportionately let down. I feel a stubborn need to pursue this line of speculation.

"And, come to that, I imagine there's no reason why at one time or another I couldn't have been here on vacation?"

"Oh hell," he says. "Let's take another dip. Then we can visit the local fortune-teller and have her clear up all such piffling question marks."

I laugh. "I haven't been to a fortune-teller since – "

Tom jerks his head round. Stares at me.

"No, it's gone. Damn it."

His tone is thoughtful. "But perhaps now we really are getting somewhere. Tell you what: let's do it, let's actually do it – go to a fortune-teller."

So we make inquiries. And come up with Madam Sonia.

Madam Sonia has her consulting room above a baker's in the High Street. Her appearance, like her setting, has little of the exotic, little of the fairground booth. Despite soft golden hair and unlined skin she must be in her seventies, even late seventies. Good carriage, careful enunciation, a pleasant face. She wears a simple summer dress of white daisies against a mauve background – with mid-length sleeves and a knitted mauve scarf whose ends hang to her waist. Matching mauve pendant – bracelet – earrings.

Tom sees her first. I sit waiting beside a table with a yucca on it and some magazines. On the wall there's a print of a girl with flowing hair and a gauzy dress; a girl who's gazing at her image in a lake. At a guess, I'd say the picture dates back to the twenties. It's entitled 'Fair Reflections'. My own fair reflections need to occupy me nearly half an hour.

"Sorry to be so long, dear." As I go in she gives me a warm smile. Directs me to sit on the other side of a small, square, baize-covered table.

"Have we ever met?" God knows why I should ask her that. She doesn't look familiar. No further flash of déjà vu. At least, not of the same order as before.

"I don't believe so, dear. Though I could be wrong."

60

"I could be crazy."

"Oh, don't say that!" She smiles again; grows serious. "I wonder what was on your mind to make you think we had."

I answer slowly:

"Mence Smith. Gypsy costume. Golden earrings." I listen to what seems like the echo of someone else's words.

My own take repossession.

"Your surname," I say, "isn't by any chance Mence-Smith?"

"No, dear, it's Wheeler."

"I told you I was going crazy. Let's make a start, though, shall we?" She'd informed us that she mainly reads palms; uses tarot cards.

She's giving me an odd look. Not greatly to be wondered at.

"You know, when I began in this line, I used to wear Gypsy costume. Golden earrings, too. I felt it was expected of me. A splash of flamboyance to brighten up the drabness of the war years."

"You and Paulette Goddard, both. Not to mention Marlene Dietrich."

"I suppose it's still the same. At the pictures. Audiences don't want to see their fortune-tellers dressed by C & A. What colour was this costume, dear?"

"Red. Studded with stars and moons." Well, it would almost have to be, wouldn't it? Choice between red and mauve and orange – one chance in three. I open my eyes again. "Shawl was black and gold."

She nods. "If it was here I'd show it to you. But I don't live on these premises any longer – although I've always worked from them. There used to be an ironmonger's below. The name of it was Mence Smith."

Curiously, I'm not all that surprised.

"There's a woman," I say. "I don't recall having met her and yet some sort of link exists between us." I take out the snapshot. With one end of her scarf she gives her spectacles a polish. They've been sitting on the table.

"Who is she, dear?"

"I don't know. But I think she must have come to see you. I feel her presence here."

61

She gives me back the photo. "I wish I could say that I remembered."

I lay first one hand and then the other, palms upward, on the green baize. Her bent head is sometimes less than a foot away; her finger tickles as it runs along the lines.

After that she unwraps a deck of cards from a piece of pink silk and asks me if I'd like to shuffle it.

Then, "at no extra charge, dear," she brings out her crystal ball.

Finally she opens her purse and takes from it two folded ten-pound notes, handing me one of them. "Please return this to your friend. I'm sorry. Your past seems wrapped up in a shroud. I can't understand it."

I'd like to tell her to keep the money; she's certainly worked for it. She may be a phony but at least she's an honest phony. And I divine more than mere bewilderment: I hear silent calls of deep distress. When I tell her about my amnesia I sense an instant rush of warm relief.

"Ah, well, yes. That would account for it."

Our positions then become reversed: she ends up trying to give *me* comfort. "...so very frightening. But regard it as a test, dear. Try to hold onto your faith." (Do I have any? I'm not so sure.) "Hold onto it fast." She tells me she will pray for me; then after a decent interval asks if Tom and I can find our own way out. She suddenly sounds tired.

On the faded wallpaper inside the entrance there's a framed photograph of this corner of the High Street, taken, it says, in 1942. I hadn't been consciously aware of it but the name of the hardware store is clearly legible. Mence Smith & Son. I undeniably have a gift for picking up on things, albeit unintentionally. And fast. I think I'd better not mention this to Herb Kramer.

Or even to Tom. I give him back his ten pounds but don't speak of the Gypsy costume or the hardware store. It doesn't seem worth it. Besides... I don't want him to feel I'm only making cheap claims.

The woman wasn't such a phony after all. She'd asked Tom if he worked to uphold the law in some way; thought at first he was a customs officer – amended it to policeman, then to private investigator. "To begin with, she merely said I had an office in London (not too much of a gamble there) but then told me it was very close to Great Portland Street – how could she have known that? She asked if we were visiting Southwold on business. 'I'm aware that's rather vague, dear, but I conjecture it might have had something to do with church architecture during the war. I can sense you being drawn towards St Edmund's.' Well, Tex, even if by chance she had actually seen us there, I'm sure neither of us said anything about the war. So in the end I was reasonably impressed. She told me nothing much about my future but I began to think she might tell us quite a lot about your past."

Yet I'm assailed again by bitterness. "Some hope! She didn't even comment on my being American." But that's an ungracious remark. I immediately feel remorse.

And say so.

"Well, anyhow." Tom glances at his watch. "All part of our jolly jinks at the seaside. Right? And if we hurry back to The Red Lion we may just have time for a drink before the programme. What's more, I think we're probably going to need one."

The TV lounge is empty and the show we've come all this way to see is abysmal. Even hefty double Scotches can't improve it.

Tom runs a hand through his hair. "But who am I to criticize? If Simon and I should ever compare bank statements…"

"And now for something a little different," this banker's pet announces. "Before in these programmes, sometimes with very great success, we've often set out to trace a long-lost brother or sister or cousin or friend. Well, this evening we're looking for a mystery woman, a beautiful and charming and vivacious young mystery woman, nameless and quite unknown to most of us (yet perhaps not to all; that's what we're hoping for, of course), who once upon a time posed for her picture outside St Edmund's Church in our very own Southwold. And here she is, ladies and gentlemen! This photo was obviously taken many years ago, maybe as far back as the Second World War. But look at it long and hard and it's just possible that one of you may be saying to yourself at this very minute, 'Why, isn't that old Edna or Rita or May...?' Well, if you are, there's a Mr Tom Newman staying tonight at The Red Lion in Southwold who would dearly love to hear from you. As I say, he's only there for tonight, so if you have even a hint of a whisper nagging away inside you, please, please, do a nice man a good turn and make another of Simon's friends wonderfully happy. The number you have to ring is..."

Then, after he's given it twice, Simon, in a very smooth transition, asks the studio audience to put its hands together for a Mrs Jan Millington, who has been waiting half a lifetime to see her wildest and most cherished dream come true... Tom switches off the set, with an apology both to Simon and to Mrs Millington, and we tell the desk clerk that in case anyone should need us we'll now be reachable upstairs. I take off my sneakers and throw myself down on one of the beds. Tom paces restlessly between the window and the telephone.

Time goes by. We don't say much. Eventually he asks: "Why doesn't the damned thing ring?" It's a question he's proposing to the world.

And then the damned thing does ring.

"Newman here..." (Now I'm sitting up but after a moment Tom wrinkles his nose at me, wryly.) "Oh, Simon...yes. It was great. I really owe you one... No, there hasn't been, not yet. It's early days, of course." They don't speak very long.

"It really doesn't matter," I say, when Tom replaces the receiver.

"No, you're right, it doesn't. We're going to get the answer anyway. And if we don't have it by Tuesday we'll think about hypnosis." But he sounds dispirited and I actually pray for the telephone to ring.

It doesn't.

Instead, there comes a knock at the door.

Again the atmosphere grows tense.

Again there follows anticlimax.

On the threshold stands a chambermaid.

Tom bids her good evening but has a job concealing his impatience. "If you're here to turn the beds down – thank you but please don't bother. We can see to it ourselves."

64

"No, I'm here because I saw that programme on the telly."

A moment of stillness. Of suspension.

"I couldn't get away quicker because I wanted to wash my hands and tidy up a bit. Try and make myself beautiful." She gives a nervous snicker. "I hope I didn't keep you."

She's an elderly rawboned woman with bleached hair and too much lipstick, too much eye shadow, too much mascara. They don't go with her uniform. They don't go with her demeanour. Even now, when she's surely on her best behaviour, her expression indicates that life has been a disappointment.

Tom's voice already holds excitement. "Then did that snapshot seem familiar?"

She gives him a coquettish glance. Maybe she thinks she looks about forty years younger than she does.

"I'd be surprised if it didn't," she answers. "Seeing as I'm the one that took it."

12

During our return to East Anglia we decide to make a short detour; the weather has stayed warm and it's only mid-afternoon. Back to Southwold, then. "Shall we inquire," suggests Matt, "into their plans to change the name of the church? In memory of our meeting?"

"My, they *do* breed them ambitious in Connecticut! What's wrong with just a wall plaque?"

From the back of the jeep Trixie answers us lugubriously. "And that won't take them long! Four measly little words! *They met. They parted.*" It's been growing more and more obvious that following all our recent excitement a reaction has set in.

"Oh, come on, babe, that's the Monday morning blues catching up with you on Wednesday." Walt, who's sitting beside her, sounds uncomfortable and Trixie's reply isn't going to reassure him.

"Monday morning blues?" she exclaims, bitterly. "Rest-of-my-life blues, more like."

"Nah, don't say that. And, anyhow, it's still possible Matt and I have something up our sleeve. Eh, buddy?"

"What sort of something?" Already a faint display of interest.

"Oh, nothing much. Just a dance at the camp next Saturday. Even if people do say it's going to be a dilly."

"Dance! Next Saturday?" Trixie has the maybe enviable ability to coast along breezily from one highlight to another and not look much beyond the next in line, so long as there actually is a next in line. "But why didn't you tell us sooner, screwball? The idea of it! Keeping a surprise like that all to yourselves!"

"We only heard about it Monday."

"So? And today's – "

"And we decided," puts in Matt, overriding her, "that we wouldn't mention it until tonight. In case things felt a bit flat by the time we got back from London." There's no trace of irony, but there is a note of worry, and he looks at me without a smile. "Rosalind? You'll come to it, won't you?"

"Of course she'll come!" cries Trixie. "Think she's barmy or something? You try to stop her, that's all! Eh, Roz?"

"We really weren't taking the pair of you for granted."

But he's misread my hesitation. *It's a farewell dance, isn't it?* That's really what I want to say.

Yet instead: "You bet I'll come. It will be wonderful."

Walt is wholly at his ease again. "You and the rest-of-your-life blues!" he teases. "We ought to go and see that woman we noticed the other day – her signboard, you remember – Madam Something-or-Other."

"Oh, yes, let's! That would be a giggle. I'd forgotten about her."

I feel perverse. "But what makes you think she'll be open?" The shops around Leicester Square most certainly were – Matt and I went looking for those souvenirs I'd promised the young Crawfords – but suddenly it seems to me Walt's being insensitive. It's just too easy to fob Trixie off with a dance and with having her palm read.

Yet on the other hand, if he can't respond to her cri-de-coeur in the only way she'd wish, I suppose there's not much else that he can do.

"Oh, pooh!" says Trixie. "At the seaside! It'll be like August Bank Holiday! Like how it used to be. Course she'll be open. Everywhere will."

"Madam Trix…!" says Walt, proudly, even proprietorially. And indeed she turns out to be right – if 'everywhere' doesn't include places like the ironmongery in the High Street, over which Madam Sonia has her premises.

"And what about us?" asks Matt. "Rosalind, would you like to have your fortune told?"

"I don't know. Do you think she might come up with a tall dark stranger and travels to a distant shore?"

"Bound to."

"Well, I don't mind lashing out five bob for that. What I couldn't stand is spending hard-earned cash and having to listen to the truth."

It's providential that when we get there Madam Sonia doesn't have a client. She suggests she see Trixie first, that Walt sit in the waiting room, and that Matt and I come back in an hour.

So we again go searching for presents for the children and this time we're lucky: we find wonderfully right Dinky Toy models of a red double-decker bus, a tram and a taxi. "And God forbid anyone should mention," smiles Matt, "that on V-E Day there wasn't so much as a single cab allowed out on the streets of London!" He attempts to pay for these three purchases himself – I don't see why he should pay for even one – but eventually settles for our going halves. Then we saunter back through the town, which probably has never known a Wednesday quite like this. But from a distance we see that the pier is even more crowded. (Red, white and blue are still the colours of the day.) It's not an especially appealing pier; in fact we both think that Southwold deserves better. Leaning against some railings for a while, we study the coastline, which is a lot more rewarding, despite the quantities of barbed wire.

We arrive at the fortune-teller's only a minute after Trixie and Walt have left. There's a message to meet them at the tearooms.

Madam Sonia looks about thirty. Apart from her shawl and earrings and allegedly Gypsy dress, the two most striking things are her voice and the flawlessness of her complexion. Her voice is loud yet melodious, each word so carefully enunciated you might think her a pupil of Professor Higgins.

I go in first and – when she's finished with me – sit waiting for Matt while abstractedly gazing at the sentimental picture of a pre-Raphaelite beauty bending over her image in a lake. It's called 'Fair Reflections'. I rather wish someone would come along and give her a hearty shove.

But perhaps this has less to do with *her* reflections – no matter how complacent – than with the practically unbearable nature of my own.

Later, *en route* to the tearooms, we compare notes.

I remark as cheerfully as I can: "She isn't bad, is she?"

"Why? What did she tell you?" Am I imagining it or is he as well – now that our two days of diversion are nearly at an end – experiencing a growing weight of depression?

"Well, I have to admit, not enough about tall dark strangers or trips to foreign shores. The future got short shrift. But she was fairly good about the present and the past."

"Same here…but we already know about the present and the past."

"For instance, she told me I was working on the land, which, if it was a guess, was reasonably inspired. There isn't any straw behind my ears, is there? You can break it to me gently."

"Not behind yours," he answers. "I don't know about Trixie's."

"Well, that's a point, of course. But then she spoke about my home situation. Was there a stranger in the house? Was one of my parents dead? It struck me that she truly has a gift."

He nods – though only after hesitation. "What else? What about…well, what about next week? Next month? Next year?"

I laugh and shrug and hold on tightly to his arm. "Oh, all the usual."

"What's that?"

"Plans in a state of flux… Uncertainty about the course one's life is going to take… At this point, however, wouldn't that apply to most of us?"

Besides, she'd already seen Matt and knew he was American; had probably sensed how much I cared for him.

"She also prophesied a change of job – well, naturally. A change of scenery – well, again, I'd never have guessed that, would you? As I say, she was far less good about the future." (And I certainly don't want to burden him with her predictions of approaching hardship.) "Oh, look, we're nearly there and you haven't given me one hint of what she said to you!"

"Nothing of any interest!"

He kicks a pebble into the gutter.

"Oh," he says, "she was okay about a lot of it. Strained relations with my dad. Death of someone very close." The need to be fair gradually wins out over his humour to be grudging. "Better than okay, in fact. She even told me that I come from a town where she could see a large university, lots of water and, listen to this, a theatre I often attend that she thought was named after a well-known composer."

"And?"

"I guess she meant the Shubert."

However, with a slightly lopsided smile, he then adds: "But it wasn't named after the composer. It was named after the Shubert Brothers. S-H, not S-*C*-H. It's a chain of theatres all across the States."

"Well, that's quite good." And it is, too, despite the woman's error, surely understandable in someone not conversant with life in America. I try to remember if in London (or anywhere else I know) there's a theatre which sounds as if it might have been commemorating a composer.

"So why," he asks, "if she's so blasted hot on some things, can't she be a bit more informative about others?"

"Oh, they never are. Never are. Damn 'em!"

I'm not actually sure if that's true, but anyway I've said the right thing. Suddenly he grins and gives my arm a squeeze. "Yes, that's right. Damn 'em all to hell!"

But already I've had second thoughts. I rapidly recant. "No. It's as I mentioned before. What sane person would seriously want to know the truth about their future? I mean, if they were powerless to change it."

Why not admit it? I don't even want to know the truth about next Saturday. Not any longer. Is the dance really a prelude to

69

departure? Is the date all settled for the pulling out of the entire squadron? Earlier – if only in my thoughts – I may have been patronizing about Trixie: about her not looking much beyond the next highlight. If so, I apologize. Now I decide I'll follow her example.

13

As Tom stares at the chambermaid she takes a picture from her pocket.

"Look. I been carrying this around now for more than forty-five blinking years."

Tom misunderstands her.

"No, I don't mean always in my overall. I live here, you see. Got a tiny bedroom on the top floor."

"Well – good God – this is great! I don't know where to start."

He smiles.

"Oh, first by asking you to sit down, obviously. My name is Newman, Tom Newman. And this is…well, this young man is a good friend of mine who may have some connection to the lady in the photograph…" I nod at the chambermaid, who by now is seated, a little stiffly, in a small armchair with a striped cover. "It's all a bit complicated, but… Well, now then, you are Ms – ?"

"Morris. You can call me Trixie if you like." She folds her arms, unfolds them. She lets her hands rest limply in her lap. They look stringy and uncared for.

"Right. Trixie. And the name of your friend there?" The photograph is safely back in Trixie's pocket. "At least I take it she's your friend?"

"Oh, yes, we used to be – quite close we were – you see, we both worked on the land. Land girls. That's where we met."

"And her name."

"Rosalind. Sounds fancy, doesn't it? Rosalind Farr. We called her Roz, though, and she didn't mind – she was never stuck-up or anything." But then a touch of asperity enters a tone that in any case is slightly shrill. "Though probably the Farr bit got changed to Cassidy – and that's what I hope it still is, of course." She adds: "Well, naturally."

"Then you've lost touch with her?" I can hear Tom's disappointment.

"And that's putting it mildly! Haven't seen her since 1945. There were a couple of letters after that but she'd even stopped writing by early '46. I suppose she went off to America; forgot about her old friends."

"America?" Tom gives me a meaningful glance.

"There was this Yank she was in love with."

Trixie pauses and seems to be struck by the undercurrent of disapproval she catches in her own voice.

"Well, I don't know if I ought to say this, not to strangers, though I suppose it can't do no harm. Water under the bridge and all that. She got herself knocked up. And so I thought…well, maybe you're too young to know about it but there was this American war brides scheme…"

Tom nods. He bites his lip. "And the American's name, you say, was Cassidy?"

"That's right. Lieutenant, he was. Lieutenant Matt Cassidy."

"Matt? Matthew…" Tom repeats the name in full, slowly. He looks at me with hopeful eyebrow raised.

I only shrug and shake my head.

Trixie also looks at me. It's the first time she's given me her close attention. "You're a Yank too," she says, rather matter-of-factly. "That right?"

I haven't spoken up till now and I suddenly become aware of it. "How'd you guess?"

"Because you all seem to have that special sort of look. I can always tell. You and him, now. If it wasn't for the differences in clothes and hairstyles and the like…yes, I'm not being daft…the pair of you could almost be related." (Tom, behind her, raises his arms in a boxer's gesture of victory.) "I'm right, you know. And I can prove it to you. Upstairs I got another photo."

After a minute she gets up to fetch it. Tom says: "And by some miracle you haven't saved those letters which you mentioned? But no. No one could be that far-sighted!"

On her return she carries a battered-looking album. The three of us stand in the centre of the room, under the main light, Tom and I on either side of her, while she, with a forgivable air of self-importance, turns its pages.

"There," she says. "That one at the bottom."

And we all look at the likeness.

*

It's after midnight and we're in our beds.

"Well," Tom says, "back to the embassy on Monday. There may be hundreds of Matthew Cassidys living in the States but there can't be too many who hail from New Haven in Connecticut and whose families worked in the meatpacking industry."

He laughs.

"And, into the bargain, a handful of bonuses – i.e., the dates your father was over here, the bases where he served, even the name of his American fiancée and the fact he'd had an older brother, who died in '42. Good old Trix! What a memory! And good old Herb Kramer, also – none of this should take too long to sort out – you'll soon be shinning up your noble family tree and waving to all those cheering relatives on board the Mayflower!"

Then why don't I feel more optimistic?

Why, in fact, do I have the jitters?

I try, as best I can, to fight them back.

"Tom, tell me something. Do you think I ought to go to that address? The one she wrote her letter from?"

"Yes, why not? If you want to. Though after all this time I don't suppose there'll be anyone there to remember her. To remember your mother," he amends, as though it's impolite to use the pronoun.

Want to? No, 'want to' isn't quite the phrase that *I*'d have picked. "You don't think you're jumping to conclusions?" I ask.

"Why?"

"I just don't get the feeling she's my mother. No flash of recognition like the one I got when I saw that picture of my dad."

"But that was different. You were recognizing yourself, not him."

"Even so." I'm lying on my back, hands clasped behind my head, staring at the branches of a horse chestnut that are still visible in the moonlight – it would be good if they could tap me out a message. "You know what I believe? I believe my father's just died and my mother, knowing about this woman in England, knowing about…Rosalind…sent me here to trace her. It might have been a promise she made him. Or one that I did. Or it might have been the carrying out of something in his will."

In the semi-darkness I turn my head in Tom's direction with a slow smile.

"In other words, you crazy dick, it's pretty much what you said last Tuesday. But I still don't feel I'd have been carrying around a pinup picture of my own mother…which was definitely *not* one of your better notions, I submit. With respect."

"Okay. What you say does sound…well, I suppose it does sound feasible. Apart from anything else, I'd think your mother might be a good deal younger than Rosalind. Actually, Rosalind could quite easily be *her* mother. Perhaps it's your granddad whom you look like?"

"But then, can't you see, my objection still applies. Pinup of my grandmother? I don't think it changes things."

Tom sighs and I interpret this as being a reluctant form of assent.

"In which case," I say (implying a logic which I'm not certain actually exists), "maybe we *had* better go to Hampstead. Or I had. You're probably right about there not being much point but…"

"Why just you?"

"Because we've found out who I am. More or less. Like you said, it's only a matter of time now. Soon we'll have the name of the hotel where I stayed in London – my identity, my money, my documents. I can't go on forever keeping you from getting on with your work."

By 'identity' I suppose I mean merely my given name, or names. Cassidy! That, too, may take a bit of getting used to!

"Yet there's still something that worries me," says Tom. "How you came to be wandering about a capital city without even a penny piece in your pocket, let alone a credit card."

"Perhaps I'm naturally extravagant and this time I'd simply gone out for a stroll, determined not to part with so much as a nickel. Not so much as one red cent."

"Perhaps." But, again, he doesn't seem convinced. Any more than I do. I'm sure that to both of us my theory comes across as being enormously far-fetched. Not to mention (unless I make a habit of behaving so bizarrely) enormously coincidental.

In the morning we find a message from Trixie that's been pushed beneath our door. It's folded around an enclosure.

"I told some fibs last night. I loved Roz but I was jealous. It just didn't seem fair. I told you how she got pregnant. I didn't say how she'd already had the baby by the time I stopped hearing and how full of it she was. That's why I pretended I couldn't find this second letter – not even sure now why I kept it. It was me who didn't stay in touch. You see, I never answered her, not either of her letters, just couldn't face the thought of it. And also, what was really mean, I never told her that I had that picture of her boyfriend, perhaps she never knew I'd taken it. But I didn't for one second think he'd gone and ditched her – not like she did – knowing old Roz it was probably just some silly hiccup, not that blinking Marjorie she always talked about, and nothing like my own case where I knew I didn't stand a chance. Anyhow I thought I'd got over all this long before last night. But I can't pretend as how I got much sleep..."

Her message finishes by saying she won't be at work today, or tomorrow, because she's off to Yorkshire for a short break. She asks us to give Roz all her love when we finally find her.

"*When*?" I say. "I guess she means *if*."

I'm pretty certain Tom will contradict me. But he doesn't. He remains silent.

"Should we leave Trixie some flowers?" I ask. "Or wine? Or chocolates? I mean, as well as a bit of cash, naturally." I feel happier now about suggesting further outlay.

Anyway, Tom would soon have come up with the same suggestion. "Yes, we'll definitely find her something." He means alongside the originals of my father's snapshot and the letters, all of which he wants to get photocopied.

I'm surprised.

"Photocopying on a Sunday?"

"No, but I was wondering. If the room isn't taken, why don't we stay over until Monday? That would mean we could enjoy a nice relaxed Sunday by the sea, yet still get back to London in plenty of time to see Herb Kramer..." But here his voice tails off; his attention elsewhere. He has now opened Rosalind Farr's second letter – which, to some extent, I seem to have been fighting shy of.

"This one," he says, "is dated March 5th, 1946."

As Trixie had implied (but I'd forgotten) it's a happy letter. Yet the penultimate sentence possesses a poignancy that leaves us silent for a moment.

"'It will be wonderful to see you and we'll have tremendous fun, just make it soon.'"

I've been standing at the window, staring again into the branches of the horse chestnut. "Oh, hell," I say.

"Well, it wasn't your doing."

"No. Then why do I feel as though it were?"

"Because you've got a name like Cassidy. Which probably means you're a Catholic. Which probably means you have a Catholic conscience."

He puts his hand round my shoulder.

"Which probably means, in short, that all of it – absolutely all of it – is your doing!"

14

I wish I could have stunned him with a new dress, preferably something long. (But at least he's never seen my cobalt blue, which I wore to the Troc in 1939.)

I wish I could have had my hair done.

I wish I could have stupefied him with my jitterbug. (Or anyway, I mean, have had the fun of being able to fantasize a little.)

No, forget all the rest of it. I wish that as soon as we'd got there we could simply have enjoyed ourselves.

Because everything's laid on for our enjoyment.

The dancing takes place in the main hangar, which is festooned with crepe paper. Balloons are hung at the entrance to the base and Chinese lanterns brighten several pathways. The refreshments are extraordinary, not just the profusion but the variety. Naturally I exclaim as much as anyone and hope that once I've tasted them I may even start to feel hungry.

Fat chance.

I'm not the only one without an appetite. You see them everywhere: the couples who are either clinging in barely concealed unhappiness or else putting on an act. I, too, am putting on an act.

I hate it.

And I resent Matt for appearing so very much as normal.

We walk out of the hangar into fresh air. From somewhere comes the unmistakable scent of wallflowers. Can someone on the base have made a little garden?

He's not aware of it, he says, but that isn't to say it hasn't happened. "You're not cold, are you?"

I shake my head.

"Yet after that great heat in there…" He offers me his jacket. "Wiser not to risk a chill."

Who cares about a chill, I want to ask. Who cares about being wise? He puts the jacket round my shoulders. I don't trust myself to thank him. The last thing I want right now is kindness.

We stroll a short way in silence. Not holding hands. Not linking arms. Nothing.

"Rosalind?" he says. "I am going to see you again, aren't I?"

"On Monday, you mean, when your train leaves? Oh, yes, I'm pretty sure they'll let me get away. And if not...I'll come anyhow." But the smile I give doesn't in the least negate my briskness.

"You know that isn't what I meant."

"What, then?"

"I don't know." He shrugs, and suddenly I see that, after all, he too has been pretending. "I've got to try to work things out."

"Why? What is there to work out? You don't owe me anything. You're engaged to a nice girl back in Connecticut and I knew that all along. It's been fun, I'm glad to have known you, Matt. We'll have to write to one another and, who knows, someday you and your family may come to London or I and mine may come to New York and – "

"Sweetie. Please don't."

"Don't what?"

"Listen. Just answer me one thing. Will you miss me when I'm gone?"

"Oh, Matt." My voice quavers, treacherously.

"No, but what I mean is – how much will you miss me?"

"Darling, this is pointless. Let's go back and dance."

"No, it isn't pointless... Because... Well, you see..."

I give up every effort to be bright and brittle and to hold him at a distance.

"You know how much I'm going to miss you. But do you really want to make me spell it out and have myself in tears? That would be a fine way to finish, on a night so obviously intended to produce only pleasure and high spirits. You almost have to laugh: the band playing 'The sun has got his hat on' while nearly everywhere you look..."

"I love you, Rosalind."

"There! Now see what you've done." I fumble for my hanky.

He doesn't let me – pushes my evening purse aside. I mumble that his shoulder will get wet; he doesn't seem to care.

Eventually I have to pull away. It would hardly be romantic to wipe my nose against his shirt.

"But, Matt, do be sure that what you decide is what you really want. We've known each other for three short weeks. Heightened atmosphere of wartime, of wartime coming to an end. It's two years since you've seen Marjorie. Maybe one can forget a bit in two years but the minute you set eyes on her again – "

"Now you make it sound – what we feel for one another – " (because I had finally let on, a second or two before my nose began to run), "now you make it sound like some starlight-on-the-ocean holiday romance."

"I only want to be sensible. I only want to be fair." But how fair is it to come out with what I now come out with? "I shall love you, Matt Cassidy, until the day I die – and beyond that, too, if I have any say in the matter, but – "

I don't get any further. Suddenly he lifts me off my feet and whirls me round. "No! No buts! That's all I wanted to hear. Don't say another word." He kisses me, ecstatically. "And *now* let's go in and dance!"

What's more, I perform one or two pretty nifty pieces of jitterbug in the shortish time remaining. I'm only surprised the other dancers don't give up and stand in an admiring circle – allow us room to show off our agility. They always do in films.

"Oh, you'll love America!"

We're on our own again and once more riding in a jeep. I can't think how he's pulled it off, considering the number of men there are at Halesworth.

"You might also get to care for Britain," I remind him.

"I already do. Though I still can't say a whole lot for your coffee." There's hardly any alteration in his tone. "You spoke earlier about a fine way to finish off things – wasn't that the way you put it? – on a night so obviously intended to produce only pleasure and high spirits."

I look at him and start to smile.

At that, he takes my hand and lifts it to his lips. He has avoided touching me till now; is evidently much fairer than I am. "Have you ever been to The Red Lion? In Southwold?"

I tell him that Trix and I have had drinks there a couple of times.

In fact I might have been scared to go back with her. I remember her, on that last occasion, queening it at the bar and adopting an ultra-refined accent in which to order pink champagne. She hadn't made herself very popular. "Someday," she'd said, "I'm going to run a little place like this. Waitresses and porters and chambermaids all at my beck and call. Yes, someday! You'll see."

But I don't mention this and he completes what he was saying. "Well, the desk clerk may be getting his forty winks but I guess if I make it worth his while he won't mind losing two or three."

"Oh, you Yanks. You think mere money can accomplish anything."

"No. If I thought that, I'd book for tomorrow night, as well."

But suddenly he has to brake, to avoid something which dashes out in front of us. We think it was a fox.

"No," I say, "I'm *sure* it was a fox. It had to be."

"Why?"

"Like calling out to like. It heard the voice of its brother."

15

"Where did Trixie say he came from?"

"New Haven."

"No, over here," I say. "Which U.S. base?"

"Oh. Halesworth."

"Yes, Halesworth. Would it be much off our route?"

He looks it up in the guidebook. "Airfield built in 1942 – 43, intended as a bomber station," he reads. "Only eight miles from Suffolk coast. Ideally placed for escort fighter operations."

"Why?"

"Range, I suppose."

As we approach Holton, the village near which the base was built (two miles out of Halesworth), I find it a moving

79

experience to be driving through this flat East-Anglian countryside where so many of my compatriots served during the war. I think of all those young men who flew up into the skies nearly half a century ago, so many of them never to return.

"But please don't imagine you're going to absorb the flavour of an airfield," warns Tom. "I gather that most of the land has gone back to agriculture, that a good portion's now given over to turkey farming."

We discover there's one small omission in the guidebook. Part of the perimeter has provided the council with a special course for novice lorry drivers.

And, yes, of course it's sentimental, but there's somehow a sadness in seeing the destruction of any place where life's been lived intensely. It's possibly worse when you can still distinguish outlines. An employee of the turkey farm, a stocky and grizzled man with bow legs, leads us to those spots where the main runway would have been and the control tower and the hangars.

"Two thousand yards long," he says, pointing to the runway – you can just make out the traces. "And then, of course, the Nissen huts…funny to remember there was accommodation here for some three thousand."

He's made quite a study of it, points out where the T2 hangars would have been. "Did you know Glen Miller came to Halesworth? 6th August 1944. A Sunday. But a busy day for Major Miller: Boxted before he came on here."

We're standing maybe at the very point where he'd played. It isn't hard, for a moment, to hear 'Moonlight Serenade' or 'String of Pearls' flooding that main hangar, drifting out across the airfield.

But then you remember that you're now on a turkey farm and that facing you is a pool of evil-smelling effluent.

We leave the hangar site and start walking towards what was once the Admin block – though, frankly, I've lost interest. The sooner we return to London the better. I make a last attempt to feel my way into my father's shoes…this stranger's shoes; to experience one fleeting second of what he himself may have experienced. I close my eyes and try to will something to come to me out of the past. But no. Nothing. I open them and find I've walked on some wallflowers. Wild – incongruous – defiant: even in competition with the effluent they give off a warm and spicy smell. I meet Tom's amused, inquiring glance and shrug self-mockingly. "Okay, you're right. I should have had more sense. But I bet you anything he brought her here at some point. And probably to hear Glen Miller." Unexpectedly, the notion gives me pleasure.

*

At some point as we're driving back to London I think about the half-brother I have never met. I wonder which side of the Atlantic he may now be roaming.

<u>16</u>

In the garden and just outside our window there's a pink-blossomed horse chestnut. I lie in bed on Monday morning and gaze into its branches and at the sky beyond…and think why can't the sky be gloomy. The time's just after six and Matt is still asleep and looking peaceful. It's a pity to wake him but selfishly I want to. I trace his brow with my forefinger. Yet he only stirs and smiles and turns over and I haven't the heart to persevere. I'm not sure what I do have the heart for: certainly not the drive back to Halesworth, the chaos at the railway station, the journey home with Trixie, the greetings, questions, commiserations. I don't know how I'm going to get through any of that. Not the next few hours, nor even the next few days. (Or weeks. But returning to the farm will undoubtedly be the worst: the place where Matt brought me back after Cambridge, just a fortnight ago, and where I felt so close to him and proud. The place where he and Walt collected us last Tuesday and where both Trixie and I sang as we got ready. The place where only the day before yesterday they'd come to pick us up for the dance and where I'd

81

last seen all those familiar surroundings – seen them in *his* presence. Yes. Returning to the farm will be the hardest.)

But I had been wretched, of course, when they had picked us up for the dance – would it help to remember that?

And at least – from the time I had wept onto his shirt and my whole situation had so miraculously altered – I think I had made the most of every moment. Every precious moment.

That is, until the previous evening. At dinner. When the truth had suddenly hit me.

In fourteen hours he will be gone.

True, we still had the night ahead. But I wanted a whole lifetime of nights ahead, of days and nights ahead, and I wanted it now. Suppose that anything should happen to him? After six years of war one was attuned to the possibility of accidents, of people never coming back. Suppose *Matt* should become one of those buried statistics in some government file, or a name in the local press, or an inscription on a war memorial – how deeply, when it really came down to it, how deeply had I truly cared about Baker, Blogg and Bolton? Or even about their loved ones? Their families?

I knew last night that Matt felt just as miserable as me but at least for him there are all the distractions of homecoming to lessen the misery. I almost wish there weren't. In my heart I want him to feel every bit as lost as I do.

Scarcely a noble sentiment…and in fact I only admit to it as I gaze blindly into the branches of the horse chestnut and look mournfully at the squat brown radiator below the window. Yesterday Matt had spread out our washing along this as though he were mounting an exhibition at the Victoria and Albert. He several times sought my views – *and* my compliments – on the matchless skill of his presentation.

Then I really do wake him. We ought to be out of bed in half an hour.

Breakfast isn't a lot of fun. Indeed it's pretty awful. Will I ever again, I wonder, be able to come back here when I'm on my own or with anyone but him?

(Perhaps it's just as well, I tell myself severely, I am *obliged* – and by the law of the land! – to return to the farm.)

Anyway, this could be the last time I shall ever see The Red Lion. My days in Suffolk must surely be coming to an end.

But we've hardly driven twenty yards when vague splutters occur and I think I shall be seeing it again quite shortly: apparently Matt's forgotten to give the engine any water. We don't go back to the hotel, however; there's a charlady who's been polishing a shop window and it's easier to ask her for some. Afterwards Matt returns the empty jug, punctiliously deciding against leaving it on the doorstep when the door itself is open – although it certainly isn't yet opening time. But on his way out he pauses. And then, presumably at some inquiry he's just made, the woman must have gone to fetch her boss, because an elderly man now emerges from the back and smilingly unlocks the glass top of a table. Evidently a showcase. In spite of my depression I wonder what I may be missing and hastily get down from the jeep.

"Go away," says Matt. "You're spoiling the surprise."

"Ah, then? Is this the young lady in question?"

Cadaverous, stooped and sparsely ginger-haired, the owner doesn't seem to know me, despite my having been here with Trix on maybe five or six occasions. It's a fascinating place, full of secondhand trinkets and pictures and family photographs; books, cutlery, gramophone records, ewers, basins, wireless sets; all sorts of things from threepence to ten pounds. It's this incredible price range which makes you feel that potentially you could unearth huge bargains.

All you have to do is scavenge.

For Matt, though, there hasn't been time. And since he's shooing me away so peremptorily I still can't see what's drawn his attention.

But then he says, "Oh well, since you *are* here, you may as well help. This gentleman has been kind enough to interrupt his breakfast…" And he reveals to me the object he's been looking at.

Companionably, by my side, the charlady sounds wistful. "Never saw another which was half so nice!"

It's a ring I'm being shown, one that's studded with pearls and turquoise, and is certainly attractive. "I think it dates from about 1875," the man tells us.

But then Matt says: "Rosalind, here's what actually caught my eye." And now he picks up another ring, again Victorian, also gold but this time far from delicate: black-enamelled, with a heart-shape at the front that has a flower and leaves etched on it, the leaf motif extending round the band. Well-defined gold tracery lightens the effect of the black.

"Oh, sweetheart, this one!" Brazen hussy; no question of Matt-oh-but-you-shouldn't-you-can't-possibly-afford-it. "This one – please!"

"You're sure? Try them both on. Don't be swayed by the prices."

The enamelled ring is cheaper – although, naturally, far closer to ten pounds than to threepence.

It has engraving on the inside. If there had been any doubt before, this would instantly have dispelled it. 'Always. Emily and Robert. May 1, 1840.' I swiftly form a picture of Emily and Robert – and who cares a jot if it's impossibly idealized? What matters is the sense of strong connection with the past. The date, the passion, the commitment. *Always*.

The owner of the shop stays neutral. His charlady can't manage it.

"Oh, it's dismal – would fast bring on the willies! You take the other one, my pet." She tucks a wisp of greying hair back under her beige rayon scarf, as if scared too much exposure to Emily and Robert may start to turn it white.

"Is it dismal?" asks Matt, gently – not specifically of her. "Why should a mourning ring be more dismal or more spooky than any other that's antique? Obviously, when any ring is that old, whoever wore it first must now be dead."

Stupidly, it hadn't even occurred to me that it's a mourning ring.

"And, pet, it's much too big for you. It's really supposed to be worn by a gent."

But Robert must have been slim-fingered. It *is* too big, admittedly, but it doesn't look ridiculous. A clip will hold it firm.

84

I try on the turquoise ring as well. "Ah…," says the charlady, on a sustained and dreamy note.

I smile at her.

"It's no good. I'm sorry. You're right, this is exquisite. But it's the other one I want."

"I hoped it would be," says Matt.

I reach up and kiss him on the cheek.

"Well anyhow, my pet, we really wish you joy of it. And it's nice to know it's being rescued by a couple like you. I sometimes feel it's awful how these ever so personal bits and pieces…what you'd think by rights ought to be seen as proper heirlooms…"

We all agree with her. "I promise you," I say. "One day *this* will become a proper heirloom!"

There's a fairly sober pause in which it seems likely we're all thinking back a hundred and five years; or else thinking forward another fifty or sixty. "And now," says the owner, "I wonder if there's anywhere I can lay my hands on some little box…?"

Matt says: "I don't suppose you'd have one of those clip things my…my fiancée mentioned just a while ago?" It's the first time he's ever used that word, in connection with myself.

I wish there was something I could get *him*. A candlestick? Warming pan? If he and I weren't about the only two adults in this world who don't smoke I could have bought him a cigarette case – I can see an attractive one. But unfortunately the rings they have here for men (other than mine, other than mine!) are disappointingly ordinary. Even the signet rings.

Actually I'd thought about buying him something before, a thank-you gift for all his generosity, but I'd been too worried about putting him under any kind of obligation – what I mean is, making him *feel* he was under one.

It's not an omission, though, that spoils my enjoyment of the moment. (Incredible that enjoyment could inform *any* moment so close to his departure!) And I shall mail him something, do so at my leisure and choose the really perfect gift. In the meantime he can have my exquisitely coloured and patterned pebble, truly gemlike, joyfully salvaged from the stream in which we paddled yesterday whilst eating our sardine sandwiches.

Mr Wilton doesn't have a clip. But in any case he recommends me not to bother. He says that a clip could easily cost three bob – and fairly soon wear out – when at a proper jeweller's, and for roughly the same price, I could get the ring cut down and expertly soldered. I say I'll act on his advice.

Neither can he find us a suitable box. He simply wraps the ring in tissue paper…but he knocks ten shillings off the cost of it, "as a small engagement gift, and with all our good wishes and warmest congratulations."

"I hoped that bit would come in handy," Matt tells me later, with a smile.

"I don't blame you. It could also serve as a useful sort of prelude to proposal."

"But I thought we'd covered all that. How else…the sort of plans which we've been making…?" He pulls into the side of the road.

"Even so, it would be nice to have it actually put into words. Call me an old-fashioned girl."

"I'll put it into writing if you like."

The echo of this undertaking clearly lingers on ("Rosalind, will you marry me?" "Oh, darling, this is such a surprise!"), because afterwards I say: "You really will write as often as you can?"

"At least six times a day."

"No, I'm being serious."

"I'll be back to get you very soon. The first minute I'm out of this crazy uniform – "

"Oh, Matt, how long…how long do you think…? There's really no chance of your being sent to the Pacific?" Oh, God, I couldn't stand it if he were.

"No, none at all."

He swears he isn't humouring me. "By gum! Can't you see I'm not grinning that grin of mine!" He grins that grin of his.

Back on the road, a little reassured, I say, "But there's no need for you to come over to collect me. More romantic, yes, but not so practical. On my own I could probably get on a liberty ship more easily. Even onto a Constellation. Besides, it would be cheaper."

"The money isn't really so important," he says. "You're marrying into… But, anyway, I'll fill you in on all those rather boring details when I write." Then he laughs, self-consciously. "No, what an affectation! Money isn't in the least bit boring."

He has to drop me at the railway station because this morning no girlfriends would be welcome on the base. The train is due to leave in just over an hour, at ten. The Americans will start to embark some twenty minutes earlier.

Since my instincts are all to be alone, I'd vaguely thought of wandering round the town – or, more probably, taking a brief stroll outside it. But I should have realized! The station is already filling up. There are people approaching from every direction…most of them young women. Some are carrying babies, some accompanied by mums. What even looks like whole families have come to make farewells: the Yanks have found a lot of friends in the neighbourhood and life is going to be extremely dull without them.

The station is a small one, not built for such a multitude of well-wishers. It's no kind of junction where expresses roar through to more important destinations, leaving a legacy of soot and smoke and grime. It's a place with flowerbeds and a rockery, hanging baskets, wooden benches. Fields and hedges stretching out beyond. You could refer to it as sleepy.

But not today. Today it sounds more like a football stadium before the match or even (oh, God!) more like the Mall on V-E Day – except that there aren't any fireworks and there's absolutely no cheering and absolutely no singing.

There's a great resounding cry, however, when the Americans begin to arrive; and that's when the real pushing starts. If you don't catch sight of your man before he boards the train he may be lost to you forever. Women are jumping up, straining on tiptoe, standing on benches, crying out for Jack or Joe or Bill, even climbing onto one another's shoulders. Their babies, many of them bawling and red-faced, are raised above their heads. One woman holds up a placard – "I love you, Rob, please marry me" – while two others, less pathetic, share a banner which reads, "Don't forget us, lads, you're welcome back at any time."

Then I spot him and frantically wave my arm while calling out his name.

"I was so afraid I wouldn't find you."

"Me, too," he says. "Thank goodness for your yellow coat!"

I cling to him. "Matt, will you slip my ring onto your finger? For just an instant? So that I'll always know I'm wearing something which…"

It fits him well. I see an expression cross his face which looks like a mirrored image of everything I feel myself.

"Don't, my darling," he says. "Remember, if *you* cry, *I* cry. Please don't do that to me."

He hands me back the ring. An instruction comes over the loudspeaker: all airmen to get on board. The instruction has to be repeated. Several times.

"Oh, Christ, I haven't got a photo!"

"Photographs!" I exclaim. It seems so ludicrous; such an improbable oversight. "I haven't got a photograph of you!"

"I'll send you one," he promises. "You send me one, as well."

I nod. I can't get out the words. But then I remember something…dip my hand into my pocket; not so easy in this fearful crush. All the Yanks have now embarked, although Matt is one of the lucky ones who's ended up with space beside a window. "I've got a snap that Trixie took! Three weeks ago! I meant to let you see!"

The whistle blows. My fingers find the photo. One edge is caught up in the lining; it's difficult to free – like in some panic dream. The train's already moving as I thrust the snapshot in his hand. There's hardly time for one last kiss before the engine picks up speed.

"There'll never be anybody else! Never! *Never*!" I don't know if he hears.

I stand there blowing kisses – everybody does – until none of the heads or arms or waving hands is any longer distinguishable. The final carriage rounds a bend. Only a plume of smoke remains.

Gradually the people on both platforms turn away. Drift aimlessly towards the exits.

At least half of us are crying. Some of us, howling.

I lean against a piece of metal on the wall – advertisement for Mazawattee – and feel first faint, then sick.

It's there that Trixie finds me.

"I never said goodbye to Walt," I tell her, tonelessly.

We walk a short way from the station. By now the crowds are thinning out. "Oh, Trixie, isn't this awful!" We hold each other's hand. The tears are pouring down our faces.

We go and have a cup of tea...no, several cups of tea. But every time we think we've got ourselves under control a fresh attack of sobbing starts. The waitress stares at us indifferently.

Trixie gets the giggles; they're close to being hysteria. "Look at the two of us sitting here in our posh dresses and laddered nylons. And both with these soppy little evening bags. No wonder that the fat cow stares!"

Our own train leaves in roughly an hour. While we're waiting for it, not wanting to return to the station one minute earlier than we have to, we listlessly look about us for a jeweller's.

But I've decided to ignore Mr Wilton's advice. I don't trust the soldering. However expert. I don't trust it not to damage the inscription.

Besides, it wouldn't any longer be quite the same ring which Matt has handled. Briefly worn.

And I might even need to leave it and have it posted back to me. I couldn't do that. What if it got lost?

Anyway, I want to wear it.

Wear it immediately.

Wear it forever.

No. A clip will do just fine.

17

Herb Kramer is impressed – as he damn well ought to be. With so much information on my father, and even a photograph, he's confident he'll soon have news – "maybe only a matter of hours! And didn't we just prophesy you came from that part of the world?" Again he escorts us to the main door.

Tom and I pause on the sidewalk. "One-twenty-five," he says. "Time to feed the inner man."

But no, I tell him. I'd rather be getting on with things. Getting them over with.

"Then why, if you feel like that, don't I come with you?"

"No point."

He hesitates. "All right. So don't forget: Central Line to Tottenham Court Road, Northern Line from there to Hampstead."

He directs me to the Bond Street tube. The car is parked the other way, maybe a mile from where we stand.

"Good luck, Tex. I reckon I'll probably stay at the office till half-past-five."

When I've crossed the road I glance back. Tom raises his hand. "And don't forget," he calls, "you haven't eaten!"

Old fuss-budget – I don't know, I guess I feel this huge affection for the guy – in Oxford Street I buy a large banana.

(Yet…no particular fault of the banana…after just one bite I have to stop myself from throwing it in a bin.)

I get to Hampstead half an hour later; ask at least six times for Worsley Road. One old man with an oversized Adam's apple scratches his head and keeps on telling me, "That sounds familiar, son…now if only I could lay my finger on it…where was it you said?" There's a post office nearby but I'd maybe have to stand in line for ten or fifteen minutes. In a bookstore I ask to look at street guides. There's a Worsley Road listed in E11 and a Worsley Bridge Road in SE26. Worsley Road in NW3 apparently doesn't exist.

Not in the early nineties, that is; but sure as hell it existed in the middle forties. I need to check at the town hall.

On my way I pass a police station. The desk sergeant is about fifty. He remembers that Worsley Road is now called Pilgrim's Lane, although it used to be simply the continuation of it. It's very near.

I walk the length of Pilgrim's Lane, feel a spurt of satisfaction on seeing faint remnants of the *ley*: a superimposed street sign at the further end. House numbers have been changed. But in her first letter to Trixie, Rosalind had spoken of a bombsite being

90

next door. There's only one three-storey house adjacent to something that's comparatively new. I walk slowly up the front steps; scan the names beside a row of bells; choose for starters the apartment on the lowest floor.

I realize, of course, that at two-thirty on a Monday afternoon the whole house is likely to be empty. But I wait for maybe half a minute – am about to put my finger to the next bell up – when I hear the opening of an inside door and shortly afterwards find an old lady eyeing me with interest through a chain-restricted aperture.

"If you're a Jehovah's Witness or a Mormon…if you're selling double glazing or encyclopedias…then I'm sorry but the answer's no."

"Nothing like that, ma'am. I'm trying to trace somebody who lived in this house immediately after the war."

"I lived in this house immediately after the war."

"You did?"

"Immediately before it too. Which war are we speaking of?"

"Second World War, ma'am."

She's quick, though. She sees my disappointment. "No, I haven't gone senile, young man. I'm almost ninety years of age but I'm sure I have a memory practically as sharp as yours. I was born in this house – I was married from this house – and God willing I shall die in it, too. I think you'd better come in."

She conducts me to her sitting room, the first door on the left off the hallway. She looks trim in a black pants-suit, green roll-neck and red sneakers. She moves with agility.

"Put Henry on the floor," she says. It's a choice between that or disposing of two leaning piles of books which occupy another chair. "I trust you aren't allergic to these things?"

"No, ma'am. On the whole I'd say I like them."

"I approve of your reservation. To say you like cats would be as foolish as to say you like people. Or children. Some cats have characters that just aren't likable. And I apologize for the smell. Who is it that you're trying to trace?"

"A young woman called Rosalind Farr. Well, at the time we're talking of she was certainly a young woman."

"And a very lovely one."

"What?"

She smiles at me, enjoying my surprise. "I told you. I've lived here, on and off, for nearly ninety years."

"But I can't believe that it should be so easy." It doesn't seem quite real.

And yet there's nothing unreal about *her*, this amazing old lady whose pants-suit is covered in cat hair and whose anklets and underclothing, along with a blouse and a night robe and some dish towels, are airing in front of an unlit and antiquated gas fire. "Yes, I remember her vividly. And it wasn't just the niceness of the creature, it was the circumstances which attended her stay here. May I ask the reason for your interest?"

"She was a friend of my father's."

"Your father?" She stares at me intently, stops stroking the large gingery creature in her lap. "And by any chance, then…can your name be Cassidy?"

For a moment I stare back at her. "But how…? How on earth…?"

"Mine, by the way, is Farnsworth. Jane Farnsworth." She resumes her rhythmic strokes. "You know, it's not such a mystery. It's just that you're American and your father was a figure of some importance in Rosalind's life. So for as long as I retain my faculties it's not a name I'm likely to forget. Matthew Cassidy."

"That's it, ma'am. Matthew – or Matt – Cassidy."

"Alias, the sod."

I can't believe I've heard her right.

"Excuse me, ma'am?"

"Young man. Don't say that I've managed to shock you! How much has your father ever told you about Rosalind?"

"Not a great deal," I reply, carefully. "But at the same time…" The thing is, I don't want to put him in a worse light than I have to, and speaking about the baby and possible desertion may not even prove necessary. I suppose I could tell her the truth regarding the condition I'm in, yet I feel reluctant to sidetrack her.

In any case, my answer seems to do. She gets to her feet, puts the cat back in the chair, offers me a drink.

92

"A cup of tea if you want it, but we could always pretend the sun has sunk below the yardarm. At this stage in my career I'm seldom without a drop of gin."

"That would be great," I say.

"Well, at least I see he taught you manners." (I guess she's referring to the fact I too have risen.) "Or perhaps it was your mother. Would you like to be the barman? You'll find all you need in that cupboard over there – except the ice. Oh, and you Americans are always so mad-keen about the ice!"

"Not me, ma'am. Bad for the digestion. Never touch the stuff."

"May God forgive you. And I don't mean for the lie; I mean for being such a nauseating charmer like your father... And don't be stingy with that gin or *I* won't forgive you – far more to the point. You can be as stingy as you like with the tonic."

While I fix the drinks (trying to ignore the smeary appearance of both tumblers) Mrs Farnsworth moves across to a glass-fronted cabinet in one corner, full of porcelain and knickknacks and flanked by two tall plants in saucers on the floor. "Here's something which I think might interest you."

I can't see what it is but when I've put the glass into one hand she stretches out the other and uncurls her swollen and arthritic fingers.

I let out a startled exclamation.

In her palm lies a black-enamelled ring.

"Then evidently *this* is something which he told you about?" Yes. Evidently. My memory may be starting to come back to me. "But why so shaken?" Her eyes are the eyes of a china doll, wide and blue and scarcely even faded.

"I'm not quite sure, ma'am. Disappointment?"

"Disappointment? And at what, may one inquire?"

"That finally it must have meant so little to her."

"Oh, stuff! Your father jilted her, of course."

Her hand is still held out to me; she now extends it even further. She repeats: "I thought you might be interested." I have to steel myself to take the object from her.

I say, "It's a mourning ring, isn't it?" *Always. Emily and Robert. May 1, 1840.* Somehow I'd foreseen I would discover an inscription.

She sips her drink and goes back to her chair. Even with just the one free hand she picks up the cat so deftly I barely have time to think about assisting her.

"Do you know something?" Reflectively, she holds her tumbler to the light. "On the very first occasion I saw Rosalind it could have been out of this selfsame glass – out of these two selfsame glasses – that we drank our gin-and-tonics then."

She laughs and adds some comment about how rarely she ever breaks things, despite the clutter she unfailingly creates around her. But although I hear her voice I gradually lose track of what she's saying. She's left me in possession of the ring.

I return to my chair, nearly falling over Henry, the disposed and wheezing, still contented tabby. I sit and set my glass down on the floor. Then I place the ring upon my finger. I do this impulsively. The fit seems well-nigh perfect.

"It must have been too loose for her?"

Though did I actually say that or just think I did? Suddenly I feel confused. I don't know where I am.

Not only where I am but who I am.

Okay. Don't panic. You'll soon make sense of this.

You're in a room. There's a voice. A woman's voice.

Talking about ice.

Ice?

I make a real effort. I concentrate. I whisper.

"Rosalind…?"

Then I try it again but this time with considerably more authority.

This time it's practically a shout.

"*Rosalind…!*"

94

18

"I'm sorry? What was that?" My mind had wandered for a moment. Suddenly I'd thought I heard my name being called, though from a distance. Maybe it was a father or a brother summoning home one of those girls who'd been bouncing a rubber ball against the side wall of the house (there's a gap caused by bomb damage). As I came along they'd been chanting tirelessly, in time to every bounce, "Deanna – Durbin – wore a – turban – of red – and white – and blue." But it would be quite some coincidence if one of the girls happened to be called Rosalind. I must've imagined it.

"Only that if I had a fridge," she repeats, "I could offer you some ice. But I haven't, so I can't. And who needs ice, anyway?"

She passes me my gin.

"Thank you. What a treat!"

"Question of priorities," she says. "And contacts."

From her appearance you'd never suppose she had that kind of contact. Nor indeed that kind of priority. Although she must be in her middle forties she looks too delicate, too childlike. It's only her voice – a bit gravelly – which somehow prepares you for this far more vigorous note.

Certainly the kitten doesn't. Under one arm she carries a Siamese. Sometimes – when, for instance, she's dispensing gin or lighting cigarettes – he climbs up on her shoulder. "Can you believe it? I thought I didn't like cats! But then along came Rex." Often she raises one of his front paws to place a quick kiss upon its pad. "Cheers!" she says. "And to the length and happiness of your stay here!"

"Cheers! Thank you." Rex watches with interest the death throes of a bluebottle trapped on the flypaper overhead; his hind legs are planted in her lap. "But, Mrs Farnsworth, I don't want to mislead you. I'm not really sure for how long – "

"Not Mrs Farnsworth. Jane."

"Rosalind."

"Ah. 'From the east to western Ind there is no jewel like Rosalind.'" A misquote but she recites it with a flourish;

although, when she waves her tumbler, she has the sense to do so carefully. "Well, anyway, at least we can drink to the *happiness* of your stay here."

"There is one other thing," I remark, slowly. I'd been hoping for a few more sips of the gin before I had to bring it up, but I suppose that, if I'd been strictly honourable, I'd have broached it before accepting the gin in the first place. This is the one point on which I don't intend ever to be underhand. "You see…well, the fact is…"

I laugh. This is ridiculous.

"The fact is: well, I'm pregnant."

It suddenly occurs to me that perhaps I oughtn't even to be drinking gin. I tell myself I'd better not finish it.

Jane Farnsworth claps her hands. "My congratulations!" Although I've taken off my gloves and she's admired my black engagement ring it's possibly escaped her notice that I'm not wearing any other. "When's the baby due?"

"Mid-February."

"About six months." She extracts a further cigarette from the open packet of Passing Cloud on the arm of her chair. "But these days, what with the housing shortage, it takes a long time to get settled. You mustn't worry that anybody here will object to having a baby on the premises."

"You're very kind," I say, "but I hope that before he's born I shall have joined his father in the States. Matt's an American, you see."

Soon afterwards my landlady conducts me upstairs. The journey may inspire some reservations – a passing glance at the lavatory and bathroom proves a bit dispiriting and the stair-carpet could definitely do with a brush – but the room itself isn't bad. I've been lucky. I came to Hampstead on the merest whim. But when I'd started walking down the hill I saw a board on which this room was advertised, the only room on it, and at just thirty-five shillings a week. The newsagent told me he had put the card there scarcely ten minutes before.

So after Jane leaves I stretch out on the divan and do little else but count my blessings. Eventually, though, I get up to inspect drawer linings, wardrobe space, the number of hangers provided, exciting things like that – and then to unpack my suitcases. This done, I carry the rickety table from the centre of the room, set it under the window and bring across a chair. Later I shall go out to explore a bit, start to stock up, maybe buy myself some flowers. But for the moment I want to finish the letter I began this morning on the train.

To Matt, of course.

I haven't told him yet about the baby. For one thing, I have only just found out myself – well, had my suspicions verified. (Suspicions? *Certainties*!) Partly, maybe, I do feel a little nervous about telling him. My own initial reaction, already a good two months ago, wasn't by any means unmixed. And obviously I want to do it in the right way, not just hurl it at him in a postscript. But today the first priority is to send him my new address. Perhaps I'll give the matter a bit more thought after I've got this current letter posted. I feel it's never too soon to start on another one.

I wish he felt the same. But with the best will in the world some people – when it actually comes down to it – are simply lousy correspondents. Hmm. At least six times a day! Lootenant, are you *sure* I can have caught that quite correctly?

I must write to Amy, too, to let her know I'm settled and to apologize for being peevish – I'd been so hoping to have another letter before I left. Also, of course, I want to tell her where I am, in case there's anything to be sent on (pray God!). My peevishness found outlet in something of a diatribe over the raw deal we land girls have received from the government. It's particularly unfair when compared to the way the women in the armed forces are being treated. People like Trixie and me have been demobbed with practically nothing. In fact, you should have heard how Trixie was going on about it only a few days back, while cheerful philosophical old me was then shrugging it off in a manner that must have been infuriating! Poor Trixie. I ought to write to her, as well. She's now working in a restaurant run by an aunt of hers in Norwich.

But what letters I do receive from Matt – well, this goes entirely without saying – are delightful. For quantity, his performance can only aspire to five percent. Quite pitiful! For *quality*, it has to score a hundred! Yet how I wish he'd get a move on. I'd like to know what arrangements regarding my transport he considers best. The other day there was a demonstration outside the London hotel where Mrs Roosevelt is staying. U.S. war brides who'd marched there to petition her had paraded up and down carrying their babies, a mute proclamation (or not so mute) more eloquent than the traditional type of placard: "We want our daddies!" I envied them the opportunity of being able to do even that much.

I suck the top of my mottled pen cap. Next door the girls are still playing on the bombsite but have now combined with a gang of boys to play tag. Having told him a little about the house and about Jane, I start another paragraph.

"I'm sitting by the window, which overlooks a strip of horribly neglected garden. Tomorrow I'd probably be out there digging this up for vegetables if I didn't have to be out instead finding myself a job. Something totally frivolous and undemanding! I shall ask to spend my days spinning endless daydreams ('All I do, the whole day through, is dream of you!') and thinking up excuses to work you into every conversation, whilst patiently awaiting the photograph which I'm beginning to think you never mean to send (!!)…"

But suddenly I realize it's five o'clock and that in half an hour the shops will all be closed. I acquaint him with this daunting fact, scribble a typically loving farewell, then rush to the postbox on the corner of Pilgrim's Lane – where, having first prayerfully kissed the envelope, I follow it into the opening with my dopily protective fingers…trying to reassure myself it hasn't crumpled already (it's only a very *thin* little envelope) or somehow taken a wrong turning, or got itself stuck in a crevice, right at the start of its journey.

*

"In the whole course of my life I've never kept anyone in reading matter as prodigious as this – and since I don't guarantee to keep it up, my darling (particularly with so signal a lack of response!), I suggest you make the very most of it while you may. On a bus this morning I actually heard some fellow saying to his mate there's no such thing as love – only lust – and you can imagine how superior and pitying I felt as I sat there straining to hear more… I was on the bus en route to find that job I spoke about yesterday – and find it I most incredibly did! You remember Oxford Street, the bit of it between Oxford Circus and Tottenham Court Road, which we mistakenly drove along with Walt and Trix when we first arrived in London? Well, in that part of it there stands a large and dignified department store called Bourne & Hollingsworth. And in this large and dignified department store there happens to be a large and dignified perfumery department. And in this large and dignified perfumery department there yesterday existed a splendid opportunity for a…*no*, quite wrong!…for a slim, smart, invariably soignée – and, indeed, wholly wonderful – young woman like me. I wrote, of course, that I would go for something frivolous, yet little did I know how cleverly I prophesied! From muck-raking to attar of roses in one fell swoop! Can anybody stop this girl? I start on Monday. The money isn't much but neither thankfully is the rent I pay Jane, and the members of staff I met today all seemed pleasant and helpful. What's more, there are the perks of the trade – perhaps from now on these little billets doux will be discreetly scented? What about your own little billets doux, my darling – although the scenting of them, whether discreet or otherwise, may remain optional? Already, even if I know it doesn't make sense, I look wistfully at the table in the hall every time I pass, and half-expect a miracle. I know what will happen the moment I see an airmail envelope addressed to me – my throat will go all dry and my pulse will start to race as though you'd just walked through the door. I think I'll even begin to get these symptoms as I leave my room each morning…as I start running down the stairs…"

*

I still haven't told him about the baby. What is it I think? That for some reason he'll be so upset he won't want anything more to do with me?

Oh, yes. Sure thing. That's my Matt.

That's the boy I fell in love with.

19

The next morning there could be something for me. If a letter had arrived at the farm yesterday, Amy would have readdressed it immediately.

Nothing in the first post.

There's always the second, though.

And the final one, mid-afternoon.

But if it doesn't come by then it may not come for ages. Matt knew the date on which I'd be leaving Suffolk; he also knows how long a letter takes to get to England. Well, roughly. So if I don't hear today, it must mean he's waiting for my new address – which he won't receive till Monday at the earliest. Oh God, dear God.

So my first full day of exploration is marred by constant fretting, although it's a good day by and large and I keep having bursts of sanity when I realize how I'm getting all worked up over nothing – one tardy letter in the context of a whole life? And possibly, too, he'll turn out to be blameless: mail can get held up even in peacetime. I suppose it can get lost as well. Which would be upsetting, naturally, but hardly a tragedy. And Hampstead with its intimate, artistic atmosphere, its network of irregular back streets, its charm and history and interesting shop windows (yes, even now), not to mention those acres and acres of rolling, wooded countryside…Hampstead is enough to offer consolation.

Or, anyway, distraction.

Nevertheless, when I return to Worsley Road and find that the hall table holds nothing for me, I put in a trunk call to the farm.

And after Amy's surprised, enthusiastic greeting, I explain I thought she'd like to know I'd found a job. "And how are Fred and the children? And is everybody missing me, most dreadfully?" But what I really want to hear, of course, is something very different. *Oh, and by the bye, Matt's letter came today. I've sent it on.*

When it seems there's nothing left to say, I ask if there's been any mail.

Before I phoned I told myself I'd rather have certainty than suspense. Now I wish I'd stuck with the suspense.

After a supper of Welsh rabbit, a meal I generally enjoy but this evening find difficult to finish (and even getting down my sweet and sticky orange juice seems hard), I decide to make another call.

"Oh, hello, my darling." Thank God it's usually my mother who answers. If it isn't, I instantly hang up. "I'd been hoping you might ring."

"You'll get a letter in the morning. But having told you all my news in that" (*Dearest Mummy, your loving daughter's pregnant*…) "I suddenly thought wouldn't it be nice if we could spend the day together. I mean tomorrow, because I've found a job that starts on Monday. I've got a room near Hampstead Heath, so I can easily meet the train at Finchley Road…"

"Oh, my sweetheart, I'd love to. But this weekend…it's really such short notice…"

I suggest that, even if he can't manage for himself, she could surely leave him a sandwich, or something cold, or something he could warm up.

"No, darling, it isn't that. Truth be told, I'm feeling a little tired and you mustn't be offended, but…"

I'm not offended. Just disappointed. And sulky. (Even though it's probably better she should have time enough to assimilate my bombshell.) She asks about my job – and the room – but doesn't want me, she says, just to repeat what I've written and make the call needlessly expensive. "Anyway, the main thing is you're well. And Matthew? How are things with him?"

"God knows. I haven't heard a word. I feel cross."

"Oh, please don't, my darling. I remember when your father and I were engaged and then he suddenly had to go away. Only for a month but I wrote him fifteen letters, would you believe! I got just four in return. There was nearly a divorce before there was a marriage."

I laugh and find it helpful being reminded. But even so my moodiness persists. I mention very pettishly that he hasn't even thanked me for a silver hip flask which I sent. I recognize that I, too, am tired. (Besides, I'm pregnant; pregnant women are allowed to be moody.) Earlier in the day I'd been planning to spend my evening telling him about the baby. But now I think – well, no, I don't feel like it. Four letters in exchange for fifteen still seems about the going rate. So maybe two can play at that game. Yes, Mr Cassidy. Two can start to agitate and wonder.

It's a decision which I rapidly regret. Of course, it's not in any way binding and yet I discover that I'm obstinate. I make a compromise. I'll go on writing but won't actually post anything until I've received his next letter.

I write about five sides a day and my letter reaches thirty sides. Forty. Fifty. But then my average starts to fall. Dramatically. By then it's hard to retain even a semblance of good cheer.

And every morning, yes, the closing of my door, the running downstairs, the sifting through the pile on the hall table, the philosophic shrug. Continual disappointment; continual slowing of that optimistic heartbeat. The same thing every evening, basically in reverse. Over the weeks, disappointment turning to deep anger. To disbelief . To desperation.

My attitude at work begins to change. At first my job enabled me to think of other things, to chat with colleagues, learn about the stock, try to be of service to my customers. But the women who are buying perfume – and, even more, the men who are buying it for them – are usually in a carefree mood. They haven't heard about austerity. You see a lot of adoration.

One morning I set out as normal, having largely given up on hope, when suddenly I spot an envelope exactly like those which Matt used to send. I give an excited exclamation, rush forward – and find it's from Australia. A convulsive sob bursts out of me just as Jane, in dressing gown and carrying Rex, emerges from her bedroom.

"Oh, Rosalind, my dear, whatever's the matter?"

"Nothing. Late. Must dash. Goodbye."

"Look in again one evening and have a little drink. I'd enjoy that."

"Yes, all right." I only want escape.

What follows is a time of nightmare. It's the day I finally face up to things. It's the day I finally say to myself: He isn't going to write again. He's going to marry Marjorie.

He isn't going to write again, he's going to marry Marjorie. (I'm on the tube.) He isn't going to write again, he's going to marry Marjorie.

But hasn't got the guts to tell me.

Or maybe not the callousness. The cruelty. He's aware I'll get the message. It could be less upsetting for me, if this process can be gradual. Perhaps that's the way he figures it.

In any case it's over. I shall never see him again.

The whole day has a weird feeling of unbalance. Nothing seems quite real. I observe things at a distance, hear even my own voice as though it comes from someone else's mouth. (You'd think that this might dull the pain.) Reality is only restored, briefly, when the afternoon culminates in a dropped bottle of scent, glass shattering as it hits the floor. After that I faint.

Well, anyway – thank God! – at least I don't throw up.

*

"Four ounces of My Sin. I felt it slip, it happened in slow motion. We'll reek of it for weeks."

"But did they make you pay?"

"No, they're good about those things."

"Well, you've been there two months. More. They must know by now you're not cack-handed." The inevitable fumbling for a fresh cigarette. "Why were you crying that morning when you left?"

"I wasn't crying. I was only – "

"And you don't look half so bonny. I know I'm being inquisitive but has something happened? Between you and Matt?"

I hesitate – and shrug – and force a smile.

"I suppose you could say so. Something? Nothing? Either would be accurate."

"And?"

"And it's over."

She pauses. "Are you sure?"

"Yes, I'm sure."

"Then he's a fool. Here – let me fill your glass. And you'll be better off without him." I've never asked about her ex-; wonder suddenly if she's going to speak about him now. "But does the bastard know you're pregnant?"

However, she soon realizes she's on the wrong tack. I refuse to become one of those women a man feels it's his duty to reclaim. Make an honest woman of.

So she contents herself with remarking on the fact I now wear a wedding ring.

"Oh, well," I say. "Needs must, I suppose. Life is full of compromise."

My tone encourages her. "Anyhow, who wants a man, when they can have a dear sweet precious pussycat? Isn't that right, my pretty darling?" She sees me smile at both her own soppiness and that of her purring Siamese. "So what went wrong?" she asks quietly, after a pause.

I sigh. "Jane, it's the usual story. Some very clichéd holiday romance. I'd fooled myself that it was more."

"*More*? My perfect dream: one holiday romance per year. From which you'd run like mad the moment it threatened to get serious."

"Well, anyway – as I think I told you last time – I realized from the start he was engaged. So by disappointing me, at least he hasn't disappointed the girl who had the prior claim. You have to give him that."

"No, not at all! I have to give him nothing. You mustn't be a nauseating saint."

104

"Oh, I didn't say I don't resent her. And I resent the fact it was Matt's brother whom she loved; I mean if she loved anyone. Her transfer to Matt seemed wholly a matter of convenience. That's what really gets me. I promise you I'm not a saint."

"Still, love, it isn't only her, is it? It's – "

"Anyway, we'll leave it there, shall we? I swear to you I'm over him."

Her look is plainly sceptical but at any rate she doesn't challenge me. "You may not believe this," she says, "yet in the end you'll find it's better to be self-reliant."

A little to her surprise I acquiesce. "Yes. Looking back I hate the way that everything depended so entirely on the smile or frown of just one person." (And I even tell myself that I *shall* come to believe it, in time – for I can certainly sympathize with such a point of view.)

"Let's drink a toast, then." She considers. "Confusion to the fellow! He had no right to make you look so peaky."

I also raise my glass. "And may he think about me now and then and know an instant of regret! The occasional, unexpected pang!"

But Jane gives a gasp of annoyance.

"Sweet Lord. Let me interpret. What was his second name?"

"Cassidy."

She lifts her glass again; pauses, to indicate that here is the really serious toast, the truly definitive version.

"Sod Matthew Cassidy!" she says.

20

That's all very well, but as I stand looking from the window of my room, I think: Sod you? No, not quite. And is it really true I'm over you?

But all the same. I'm certainly not going to mourn you, not any longer. We'll make out, Thomas and I. And in a way it'll be a comfort just to know that somewhere over there you're still around, it isn't quite as though you're dead. (One day, even, when he's old enough, Thomas may begin to feel curious, curious enough to want to come in search, and then the two of you could possibly become close...well, anyway, let's hope!) But I only wish I had a photograph. I'm so afraid I'll start to forget what you look like. And a faceless blur, I feel, wouldn't be of great comfort.

Oh, what the hell...who needs comfort? We'll be okay. We'll be okay, won't we, Tom? The human race hasn't survived this long by whining and feeling sorry for itself. Agreed, my love?

I often talk to him like this. I don't mean to Matt, I mean to the baby inside me: the baby who sometimes kicks quite hard now and who is very much a presence; at five months I have grown large – gratifyingly so. I'm aware that perhaps it's not too different to Jane and her Siamese but already I see him as a confidant, a boon companion.

The following Sunday, for instance, I'm on Hampstead Heath, sitting on a bench watching a young woman go by with a pram. An older woman who is almost certainly her mum is walking alongside. I fold my hands complacently across my stomach.

"This time next year, my darling, that could be us: you and me and your gran. Your gran is going to be so proud. She's already knitted you some blankets. So from the start, my lad, only the very best. And definitely no stigma. People will say, 'There goes that smashing boy Tom Cassidy, pity he never knew his dad – who died in the Pacific.'" (At work I've now told my colleagues it was because I couldn't bear to talk about Matt's death that I'd gone back to using my maiden name. Luckily, even during my earliest days at the store – and despite the poetic licence of my letters – I had continuously hugged him to myself and done whatever I could to hide my exuberance. These days, I wear my wedding ring and let them call me Cassidy. But obviously – as soon as I judge our son sufficiently grownup to know about such things – I'll search for the gentlest and wisest possible means of telling him.) "It's a shame, Tom, but it isn't the end of the world. Especially not when you remember this. A boy's best friend is always his mother."

The two women with the pram pass my bench on their way back. The older woman smiles at me.

"Just like a girl's is."

*

A girl's best friend is her mother.

When I was a child, the churchyard in Chesham was always one of my favourite haunts. Not only was it pretty – and peaceful – and private; I liked the old man who tended the graves, and the flowers that people left on them, and above all the names and the dates and the inscriptions. It was a place where I used to read my Violet Needhams and my Daphne du Mauriers, find sunshine and security, set off on wild adventures – from the age of eight, say, until the time my father died (when, following his funeral, I never wanted to return, not even, as so often happens on the screen, to linger at his graveside and talk to him of day-to-day events or matters of the heart). But now, on this cold and grey November afternoon, scarcely thirteen years later, it isn't my father who is chiefly in my thoughts – although he is certainly there and at one point I remember him, on the evenings when I met him from the train, hurrying forward with his warm and eager smile, dropping his briefcase on the platform and lifting me high and then tossing me yet higher. When we got home, his greeting to his wife was invariably more sedate but just as loving. "Hello, my Sylvia..." I can still catch that precise inflection. "Hello, my Duncan," she would say.

"Rosalind, your mother was one of the kindest people I ever met." Mrs Morley walks beside me as we leave the churchyard.

"Yes. Thank you."

"And how pleased she must have been to hear she was going to have a grandchild."

"Yes."

"If it's a little girl will you be naming it after her?"

"Yes." I can only bring myself to speak in monosyllables. My handkerchief is crumpled in my hand.

107

Her husband – I mean my mother's – moves up purposefully to join us. To my dismay Mrs Morley, believing she's being tactful, soon wanders off to leave the two of us together.

He's tall and rangy, with a severe, not unattractive, face. "Well, then, I've been hoping to get you on your own. Perhaps now your mother's gone we could try to be friends again, Roz. Like we were in the beginning."

No, we were never friends.

"I can appreciate you should have been upset about it at the time – about that little incident when I'd been drinking more than was good for me and I didn't know what I was doing. But it was all such a terrible misunderstanding. Why not come back where you belong and make a home here for your nipper?"

I simply turn and walk away. I don't go back to the tea which a couple of neighbours have very kindly organized. I plead misery as my excuse and the two elderly ladies accept it with compassion. I couldn't endure having to listen to more sympathetic platitudes or further fond remembrances. The dusty carriages and the anonymity of the Metropolitan Line are the only familiar things I feel that I can cope with.

The last time I saw my mother it had been with Matt.

"Goodbye, Matthew. This has been such a pleasure. God bless you. Good luck."

I picture her standing on the pavement outside the Astoria. I can see Margaret Lockwood looking out over her shoulder. The film being shown is one I'd hoped that I might see with Matt: 'I'll Be Your Sweetheart'. But perhaps 'Without Love' was more appropriate.

"Goodbye, Rosalind. Goodbye, my darlings. You're going to be so late. But, no, it doesn't matter if you're late, just so long as you get there in the end. Take care," she says.

*

Four weeks later Christmas comes. I'm glad that none of my memories of spending Christmas with my mum is of very recent date.

On Boxing Day, Jane and I redecorate my room.

"This was the nicest present you could possibly have given me," I say.

"No," she replies, "it needed doing, anyway. It was a cheating sort of present." Even while she's on her knees to paint the skirting board, eyes half closed against the constant spiralling of smoke, Rex is draped like a fox fur round her shoulders.

"I wish everyone could cheat on me so gracefully. You've made my Christmas happier than I could ever have imagined."

For it had hardly augured well, a few days back, when Congress had finally passed an act on behalf of the alien spouses of U.S. servicemen, expediting their admission into America.

"Thomas is going to love all this," I say, as I look at the wallpaper rolls which we'd dashed out to buy, almost on impulse, late on Christmas Eve.

"I sincerely hope so. But, my dear, I'm sure it isn't wise to keep on calling him Thomas. What problems if Thomas should turn out to be Thomasina!"

"Oh, Jane – he *wouldn't*!"

"That's precisely what I mean."

I laugh at the way she's risen to my bait. "No, please don't worry. I would love Thomasina just as much. It's only that somehow I know..."

"I wish you'd write and tell the father."

"The sod? Can we be talking of the sod?"

"The sod has money and he ought to pay."

"But I don't want any part of his money. I don't want any part of his money or his pity. If I can't have his love – and obviously I can't – the only part of him I want is Tom."

"Pooh! You sound like the heroine of 'Back Street' or some Bette Davis weepy. Oh, bugger!" she says. "I can see there's nothing for it but to place my trust in karma."

It takes me a moment to work this out. "You're talking of reincarnation?"

"And retribution. In his next life he'll experience all the wretchedness he's brought to you in this."

I smile. "Oh, but have you thought? What if the buck stops here?"

109

"Meaning?"

"Meaning that in my last existence *I* might have been the man. That this is the justice I deserve, not Matt."

"Huh!" She gives a sniff.

The room is finished by New Year – except for the curtains I am having made and the carpet I'm still looking for. Also I intend to buy one or two pieces of good furniture to replace some of the more shoddy items. Nothing to do with Jane, all these expensive acquisitions, but since I've heard from the solicitors that my mother's left me over a thousand pounds I feel I can afford to be extravagant. Eventually I shall move out of Worsley Road and rent a self-contained flat and then the antique rocking chair and the Queen Anne chest of drawers, the carpet and the standard lamp, possibly the curtains too, will naturally come with me. This knowledge of the amount of my legacy relieves me of a lot of worry. Apart from anything else, it will see me comfortably through the period surrounding Tom's birth, as well as give me two or three months at home before I need to find a woman to look after him. (And talking of the will, I don't know how usual this is but I've instructed the solicitors to go to the flat themselves to obtain the pieces of jewellery and other keepsakes so carefully enumerated. Also the knitting.) Bless my mother, whom I was too self-absorbed to realize was even ill, let alone dying.

My baby is born at noon on the 12th February 1946. My waters had burst at night after a day of fairly frenzied activity: of giving not simply my own room but the bathroom and the lavatory and the stairs – the landing, the hallway and even the front steps – a really thorough clean. People had said that because he was my first baby he would most probably come late. But in fact he arrives bang on time.

Yes.

He.

Thomas.

Blond hair and blue eyes just like his daddy. Seven pounds three ounces. I only wish my mother could have seen him.

No, *that* isn't the only thing I wish, of course not, not at all. I have to keep suppressing thoughts of…well, of where he might

110

have been born and of the different set of circumstances under which he'd then have made his entry into this world, and of the different set of visitors who would then have been coming to see us in the hospital. (But here in Hampstead I have Jane, and the young Australian couple from the floor above me, and some of the girls from Bourne & Hollingsworth, and the curate from Downshire Hill, and they're all of them so kind.) And it's funny to think how, even in those far-off and unfamiliar surroundings, with a different home and nationality and future, Tom would have been exactly this same baby, this identical selfsame baby.

And his mother couldn't have been any prouder of him in America than she already is right here in England.

On March 5th I write to Trixie.

"...so, Trixie, believe me, he really is beautiful – and not just in his looks either. But I won't go on. Let me simply state that Thomas Duncan Cassidy is probably the best baby on earth, just about the most wonderful thing that ever happened to me, and then I'll take pity on you and shut up for the time being. I return to work in May. When that happens Jane will look after him during the day. There's nobody I'd trust him to more willingly and she's promised to cut down on both the Gordon's and the Passing Cloud whenever she has the care of him, and also on her – occasionally – unguarded language! But what if I miss the moment when he starts to crawl or says his first word or pulls off some other equally momentous coup? He looked so pleased with himself this morning when he merely sneezed – a bit surprised for a second but then quite shamelessly proud, inviting me to join in with his full ten seconds of self-congratulation. I hate to think of everything like this I'm going to lose. But I suppose one has to work – although bother – what a nuisance – why? Before I do go back, however, what about that visit I suggested? At the moment there's an empty room in the house – this would be a good time. Surely your aunt would let you get away? We could moan to our heart's content about men in general and American men in particular and of course I'm dying for you to see Tom – though naturally he won't be at his best and I shall never stop telling you how if you'd only come just one week earlier... So you can see I have lots of jolly treats in store for you. No, seriously. Jane says she can babysit whenever we want to get away – films, shows, shopping – anything – which is the one big advantage of bottle-fed babies! It will be wonderful to see you and we'll have tremendous fun, just make it soon. In the meantime much love and look after yourself – God bless, Roz."

*

Five weeks later and still no word from Trixie. I wonder if I was clumsy, appearing to gloat a bit over Tommy. Walt's gone and poor Trix may feel she hasn't got a thing.

In any case, it doesn't seem she's going to come.

Today Tom and I, we'll take our walk up Rosslyn Hill, stroll as far as the Everyman, look at the stills of whatever pictures they've got showing. I don't need any groceries. It's a nice morning: the children playing hopscotch on the pavement, an errand boy whistling as he cycles into Pilgrim's Lane, the delivery man from Pitt's Stores – the shop at which I'm registered – waving to me cheerfully as he passes in his van...they all add somehow to an atmosphere of holiday. I could almost believe there might be sea just over the rise at the end of one of these peaceful sunlit streets and tell myself that if I meet an ice-cream vendor I might indeed stop him and buy one. I really shan't want to go back to work in four weeks' time, just as the summer is properly getting under way and we could be spending long lazy days on the Heath, with lots of reading for me and lots of kicking and crawling for Tom.

But Trixie? Is there nothing I can do to make things right?

After we've passed a stationer's on Rosslyn Hill it occurs to me that at least I could send her a postcard. There's a revolving stand outside the shop and so we turn back and I know that it's ridiculous but as I take each card from the rack I hold it out above the pram. "Now which do you think she'd prefer: a picture of Keats' house, or Kenwood, or the Old Bull and Bush, or Jack Straw's Castle...?" (I've already told him that when Trixie

112

comes she and I are bound to spend some evenings in the pub. "It's great fun, sweetheart, with everyone standing round the piano and belting out the old songs, some of the new ones too, 'Let him go, let him tarry, let him sink or let him swim, he doesn't care for me, nor I don't care for him…'" Well, Tom's certainly heard that particular song before!) There are some maybe who'd think me crazy carrying on to a mere eight-week-old like this and obviously I must soon rid myself of the habit because later on I shan't want to embarrass him, nor treat him as a little adult, nor appear in the role of the possessive mum seeking to live at secondhand through her overburdened child. But just for the moment, I tell myself…

Anyway, there's a fellow who comes up to me who clearly doesn't regard me as at all crazy: a sergeant major who's carrying a cheap brown suitcase so carelessly packed that ends of clothing are escaping from under its lid. But it's really the size of his Adam's apple that almost mesmerizes me and I pray he hasn't seen my fascination. The road he wants is somewhere near; it sounds familiar and if only I could lay my finger on it, I tell him, smiling. I point in the direction where I have a feeling it may be. As I do so I notice that I've still got a postcard in the other hand. But if both my hands are in front of me then neither of them is holding onto the pram. Nor, it further strikes me in a moment of heartstopping clarity, have I yet put on the brake. I whirl around. I see the pram careening down the hill. I see it careening down the hill and off the pavement and into the road.

My own scream mingles with the scream of tyres.

21

Over forty-four years ago…and yet the echo of that scream reverberates. The old lady stares at me. She looks appalled. Have I gone as pale as she has?

It feels like months since I first came here.

To Pilgrim's Lane.

"Forgive me, ma'am," I try to say. "I'm sorry."

It seems that the cry just now had come from me.

22

"I shouldn't have told you," she says.

But she hasn't told me.

Not more than just an outline.

The rest I knew.

"Even for myself," she says, "it seemed the end of everything." She pauses for a moment, glancing across at some enticing parallel time curve. "Tom would have been well into his forties by now… And he was going to be my godson."

"What?"

She recollects herself. "I think perhaps you ought to leave." She pushes the startled feline off her lap and rises unsteadily. "I'm sorry. We've both been very much upset. Just give me back the ring and…"

Ah, yes, the ring. I hold up my hand and stare blankly at the ring. She draws it off my unresisting finger.

"I should never have told you," she repeats.

Her voice, which earlier had struck me as quite deep, almost gravelly, now seems thinner. My God, but how she's aged! I remember how she painted and wallpapered and stood on stepladders and shifted furniture and helped me unroll my carpet…

But no. I am still… Well, evidently I am still very much confused.

114

I remember seeing a movie with my brother. I remember not only the movie; I remember where we saw it. At a movie house in Hartford... I remember how the woman had changed in that – grown old and wizened, from having been so young and beautiful – changed, frighteningly, in only a matter of seconds.

It really feels as if my past is growing closer. It seems I simply have to summon up the energy, cast off this terrible weight of deadness. That's all it will require, I guess, to make the final breakthrough.

Energy.

"Perhaps," she says, "you might return some other day?"

I still gaze at her in only partial understanding.

"I was saying, I think it's time for you to leave." She tries to urge me to my feet by pulling at my shoulder.

In doing so, she drops the ring.

I pick it up, rise slowly from my chair. My limbs feel leaden. "Why did she give it you?"

"She didn't."

"But...?"

She says impatiently: "They brought her back here in a state of shock."

"Who did?"

"And then the doctor sedated her." Her responses seem a bit awry. Is it her or is it me? "For several hours I sat by the bedside, held her hand. He came back, gave her a second shot, said she wouldn't wake until the following day. He was a fool. I shouldn't have trusted him. Ought never to have left her. They shouldn't have brought her here in the first place. She woke up in the night..."

"Yes?"

She looks at me almost as if I'm not there any longer. Her look seems to pass right through me.

"And that's something else that's going to haunt me forever. The way she must have felt when she woke up and found herself to be alone."

After a pause, her eyes refocus, perceptibly. "Somebody found the ring on the staircase. One of the lodgers."

"But for God's sake!" I say. "What happened to her?"

"She disappeared."

"Disappeared?"

"Walked out of the house that same night. Never came back."

"But people don't just disappear."

"The police said otherwise. If that's what they want to do. And if they want it desperately enough."

"But she was drugged – a zombie. Wandering aimlessly. How could they not have found her?"

She makes no answer.

"Did she have a suitcase?"

"No."

"Nothing?"

"Just her handbag. That and one of the cuddly toys that Thomas had been given. She thought it might have grown to be his favourite."

"But no clothes?"

"The frock which she'd been put to bed in; the coat I'd taken from her cupboard and spread on top of her for extra warmth. I don't know if there was anything else – underwear and stuff like that – squashed inside her handbag."

"And money? What about money?"

"She had a post office account."

"Then couldn't the police have traced her through that?"

"No."

"But why not?"

"Nor could they trace her through her ration book."

"Excuse me, ma'am – but why in the hell not?"

"Simple. They finally assumed that Cassidy wasn't her real name."

For several seconds I merely stare at the old lady. "My God!"

Then: "Oh, my God!"

"She'd always wanted her son to be called Cassidy." She says it quite calmly.

"But surely you told them?"

"No."

"No?"

"It was the name she'd been going by for months. There was no reason to suppose she'd now revert. Besides, after a few days

116

I decided to respect her privacy, her right to choose. If she didn't want to come back I didn't mean to force her."

"But she wasn't in a fit state to know *what* she wanted."

"She didn't want continual reminders of Tom – that much I could be sure of! I telephoned the farm in Suffolk; in case she might have returned there. But I didn't tell them anything, pretended only that I'd lost her new address. Also, I was going to try to get in touch with a friend of hers, Trixie, in Norwich. But as I say. By then I'd decided that Rosalind had the right to self-determination." The old lady's tone had recovered much of its authority. "And, anyhow, if she were dead what difference would it make?"

"Excuse me?"

"Oh, yes. I already thought she might be dead."

"No." I shake my head. "No, ma'am. No."

"I suggested they should drag the Leg-of-Mutton Pond. That's where she often used to go and sit with Tom. But they said it was a costly operation and there wasn't enough evidence to warrant it." She pauses. "And it wouldn't have brought her back, either. Would it? So what the hell?"

At last I manage to reply. "No, ma'am. She isn't dead. Rosalind is not dead."

She actually smiles at me – a small smile – touches my wrist for a moment with one arthritic hand. "My dear young man. How can you sound so positive? You don't know anything about it."

"All I do know is, she can't be dead. She can't be. I assure you."

"What nonsense."

"It's instinct, ma'am. Conviction. Not nonsense."

"I can't make you out, Mr Cassidy."

"And besides. If she had intended only to jump in some pond, why would she have taken her purse?"

"Forgive me, that's naïve."

But then she offers me another gin.

"And if you like," she adds, "I could go and rustle up a sandwich."

In view of recent events both offers are surprising.

I accept the first, decline the second. After I've fixed the drinks we spend ten minutes looking at some snapshots. (The pictures of the baby show how beautiful he was. Rosalind wasn't simply being partial in what she had written to Trixie.) There are several of her mother. "Yes, her mother. I feel that I'd have known her anywhere."

"Well, of course. There's a very clear resemblance. Change the hairstyle, slim down the face…"

"Mrs Farnsworth? May I see her room?"

Her indecision – whatever she may say – has little to do with any possible objection from the present tenant, who won't be back, I finally hear, until after six. It has more to do with her unvoiced fear I could be schizoid. You don't have to be a clairvoyant to perceive that.

"But why would you want to see it? I needn't tell you it's completely changed."

Yet we do go up. And there are certain things that won't have changed: the doorknob, the window, the shape of the room, maybe even that maze of hairline cracks across the ceiling. The wallpaper was hers. So were the curtains – dirty, discoloured, faded – but still hers. "What about the bed…?" At the moment it's unmade but Mrs Farnsworth doesn't seem to notice. And Mr Turnbull need never realize he's had visitors. "Would it have been in that same spot when Rosalind was here?" It fits neatly into an alcove.

She nods. I sit on the edge of it, tentatively. She points out – a bit drily – that it wouldn't have been the same bed.

"Is there any piece of furniture that would have been the same?"

"Oh, my dear young man." She partly contradicts what she had told me at the start. "Wait until you're ninety and someone asks you to describe a room when you were half that age. Possibly the chair was here. Possibly the table."

Now I go and sit on the chair, put my hands on the table. A table small and square – rickety and badly scarred.

In the middle of the room, beneath a forty-watt bulb.

It's twenty to ten. The couple next door has just returned from what I'd be willing to swear was a day of begging, combined with several hours spent in the pub. In a while they'll probably start to bawl at one another. For the moment, though – and running true to form – they've already switched on their wireless; and equally true to form have switched it on at full volume.

> "It's a grand night for singing,
>   The moon is flying high
>   And somewhere a bird
>   Who is bound he'll be heard
>   Is throwing his heart at the sky…"

I want to beat against the wall, I want to scream at them to stop. Almost any song but that, almost any song but that! I press my hands against my ears. I can't shut out one decibel.

I'm sitting at the table, hunched into my yellow coat, watching the shadow of the light bulb swing in the draught that blows from door to window. And my hair is stringy, my dress is creased and stained, my whole appearance…slatternly.

But the room I'm sitting in, it's not the room in Worsley Road.

The light bulb is flyspecked and unshaded, the partly-drawn curtains thin and skimpy. The filthy nets aren't even hanging right. The bed looks as though bedbugs might infest it.

Tom's Dalmatian puppy sits on the pillow. There are times when I can scarcely bear to look at him. And yet always when I go to bed I take him with me. I cry into his fur.

Not just during the night, either. I spend three-quarters of my day attempting to sleep. But whether I'm in bed or elsewhere – for instance, sitting at this table – my thoughts fly back repeatedly to that one unchanging topic.

If only I'd stopped to ask Jane if she wanted any shopping. Other mornings I had done so.

If only I hadn't made that extra piece of toast.

Which was pure greed…especially with Tom getting so impatient to be taken out.

Selfish and greedy. No wonder his father had finally seen through me; decided on escape.

119

But all my life I've been selfish. Who would deny it? A selfishness pointed up, only last year, by the death of my mother.

I should have realized she was ill, should have realized it for months. Ever since the early summer she had been mentioning a number of minor things. *Apparently* minor things. If only I had paused to listen; to think about someone other than myself. *Truly* think. *Truly* listen.

That beggar now...he'd only asked me for a cup of tea. Oh God, the price of just one cup of tea...

And I'd wanted to give it to him, too. That was the dreadful part. The sun was shining. I'd been feeling happy. I'd even thought about ice cream; just a few minutes earlier I had actually thought about buying an ice cream! And then, while even in the act of pulling open my handbag, with the old man's eyes already watching and grown hopeful, I'd suddenly remembered. I had only a ten-shilling note and a couple of farthings. And I was too mean to part with the one and too embarrassed to offer him the other.

But why hadn't I asked him to wait? I could have changed the money in a shop.

Oh God, a ten-shilling note – and with that I might have bought the life of my child!

And the life of my child's children.

A ten-shilling note – and with that how many hundreds and thousands of lives might have been purchased?

But the sins of the mother.

Shall flatten.

And splatter.

And destroy.

On each of these words I bang my fist down on the table. (Oh, if only I could have been the one to be flattened and splattered and destroyed!) Bang my fist down hard, with intent to make it hurt and bleed; then stare at it, amazed, as though awoken from a trance... In fact, I've done more damage to the table than I have to my hand. I lay my forearms on the splintered wood – place my head on top of them – and howl.

"Oh, I don't know what to do! I don't know what to do!"

I slide down from my chair; slide down deliberately. I crumple on the floor. I crawl across the carpet.

"My dear, you're ill."

There's an old lady leaning over me.

"I'm going to call the doctor." She lays a trembling hand upon my shoulder.

"Who are you?" I ask.

"My name is Farnsworth. Jane Farnsworth. You've just been…"

Jane? Jane Farnsworth? But the woman standing before me has wrinkled skin, white hair. How can this possibly be Jane?

The carpet is worn. In places, threadbare. Even where there's any pile left, some of it is matted with the spillages of countless years of slovenly behaviour. Is this my carpet? My own beautiful, expensive carpet which I saw in a shop window and hoped at once I might possess? (She's right, I'm obviously not well… Am I wandering? Have I gone out of my mind? But I don't want any doctor.) My fingers dig into my prized, once-lovely carpet. My fingers are tanned and strong and have a scattering of hair. These fingers can't be mine.

Yet in that case what's become of me?

What am I doing here?

Five minutes later, I am standing at the front door.

"That carpet? That was hers, wasn't it?"

"The one upstairs?" She doesn't even question how I knew. "Yes, I forgot about the carpet."

But then I just don't get it, ma'am: how could you ever have allowed…?

She replies as if I'd spoken.

"I sold most of her belongings, gave the money to some charity. But I felt there should be one or two things left to commemorate her presence…or her passing. But, it's true, I oughtn't to have left the carpet: an act of vandalism against the very person I loved best in all the world. Are you certain you'll be well enough to travel?"

"I'm truly sorry to have put you through all this."

"We could always ring to get a taxi."

"No, ma'am, you've been very kind. I'm fine. I appreciate your hospitality."

I'm fine. Yes, ma'am, only one thing wrong with me now – even if that one thing does, as it happens, threaten to be terminal.

You see, ma'am…I'm remembering.

23

I don't know how I get back to Tom's office. *Was* it by taxi? Or was it by tube? Or bus?

Or even on foot?

And I don't know what time I arrive. It could have been a year since our parting in Grosvenor Square – whereas it's not yet a full week since I first walked up this steep and narrow staircase.

"You're earlier than I expected," says Tom. He sounds preoccupied.

"Why? You told me you'd leave at half-past. Or *probably* leave at half-past."

"Yes. Half-past-*five*. Not four."

"And now it's – ?" I look at my watch. "Oh, you've got to be kidding!"

Yet this is addressed only partly to Tom. Partly it's addressed to the watch itself – which has obviously gone haywire. Says nine-forty-five. Clearly, I can't have looked at it in some while…although I definitely recall having done so in Pilgrim's Lane, when it had given me two-thirty. I slip it off, in disgust.

But it's a service it requires, not a shake. I leave it on a corner of Tom's desk.

"I'm sorry," he tells me. "I'm not sure about your watch, but I think my brain could benefit from a shake. Otherwise, instead of saying you were early I might have asked what's taken you so long."

He pauses.

"Because going by your expression, I'd guess you didn't have much joy."

122

"*Joy*?"

"But then we never thought you would. Not really."

"No, Tom, you're right. I didn't have much *joy*."

"I'm sorry. It's a pity." It suddenly strikes me he isn't looking all that great himself. "Although as it turns out…"

"What?"

"Although as it turns out," he says, "it doesn't matter."

It doesn't matter! I'm tired. Surely I can only have imagined he said that?

But he sees my astonishment. He rapidly explains. "I mean – because we now know what happened to her." He gives a sigh.

"Oh, yes? And how? How do we now know what happened to her?"

He starts to fiddle with a paperclip. He's always fiddling with some goddamned paperclip.

"I went to St Catherine's. Looked for a death certificate. Found one."

"You can't have."

"I'm sorry, Tex. 1946."

"No."

"Yes. I'm afraid so."

"Then you've made a mistake, that's all. If she'd really killed herself the police would have gotten in touch with Mrs Farnsworth. She'd been reported missing." I remember the mix-up over names. "But, anyhow, she's not dead."

Tom doesn't answer immediately. "Tex, I didn't mention that she'd killed herself. Who's Mrs Farnsworth? Tell me what you found out."

"Why? You said it doesn't matter."

He waits for me, in silence.

"Landlady," I mumble. "Still living at the same address. What I found out…"

"Yes?"

"…was how her child got killed." I find it difficult to think about, let alone to say it.

"Whose child? Rosalind's?"

"And how she blamed herself for this and ran away from where she'd been secure. How she went to live in squalor

123

because she thought she needed to be punished." It occurs to me I'm babbling.

"Where, in squalor?"

"Oh, for Christ's sake. Why's that important?"

"What I mean is, if it were known where she had gone to, why was she reported missing?"

"Obviously, it wasn't. Can't you understand? It *wasn't* known where she had gone to."

Tom lays aside his paperclip. Lets out another sigh.

"Tex, why have you let it get to you like this? Last week, you didn't even want to go to Southwold; it was I who had to push. But since then… Well, since then it's become…"

"What?"

"An obsession."

This time the silence lasts longer.

"There are things that I've remembered. Things I wish I hadn't." I shrug.

"I see," he says. "I'm sorry." He picks up the paperclip again. "Do you want to talk about them?"

"No."

"You don't think it might help?"

A further pause.

"Things like…oh, for instance…like I'm married. We don't much care for one another. Not sure we ever did. I remember she wouldn't have children. Partly it was fear; partly it was the sheer inconvenience of it. Worry that she'd lose her figure."

But it isn't necessary to elaborate – to burden him with more. I recall a time when she'd believed she was pregnant: the hysteria, the recriminations, the demands for an abortion. As it happened, her period had been about a week late, but she'd miscalculated and thought that it was two. Afterwards, no apology. No hint of shame.

I can't go back to this.

"All the same," I say, "the rotten state of our marriage… I suspect that in some ways it may have been *my* fault more than hers."

"In any case, it's not so tragic. People do claim there's life after divorce."

124

"Yes – and another thing they claim: that if you're born to wealth, then money's not important. Untrue. It seems I've always let the dollar sign dictate."

Yet though I can remember this, although I can remember many things, there are still a number of gaps in my knowledge. Serious gaps. For example, I don't yet know my full name. I don't yet know the name of my hotel.

"Well, damn it, Tex, you're young. You talk as though it were too late for children or for working out priorities. You talk as though you were an old man."

"And that's the way I feel right now." I give a wan smile. "Perhaps I'm older than I look."

"'The Picture of Dorian Gray'? Now there was a fellow who had trouble with priorities."

"And you know something? I guess I could be nearly as despicable."

*

One thing I do remember is a dream. Or, more accurately, a nightmare. I must have had it often; it's vivid and insistent.

And amazingly prophetic – concerning as it does a hired detective. Yet he's not at all like Tom. Nor does his office compare with this one. It's far shabbier; less welcoming.

But the snapshot I show him is the same, even if my motive for tracing the woman in it has also changed. (It appears I've turned into my father. However, I don't plan to see Rosalind – I only want to find out if she's happy. Because, if she isn't, I must do whatever I can to set things right, while remaining completely anonymous.) Nor does the search proceed along the same lines. It's confined to London. A London of some forty years ago.

Yet, although the motive and the search are different, the outcome's similar. I discover that she's dead.

Flattened beneath a tube.

Suicide, but not premeditated. She was standing on the edge of a platform. She had no thought of death – well, certainly no more than usual – only of the awfulness of life.

125

Then suddenly she saw the train.

She didn't even think. There wasn't any time to think.

But how do I know what she was thinking? Or wasn't? Somehow, there had taken place a terrifying fusion. Terrifying…yet utterly desired. In my dream, although I hear about her death only in the office of a private detective, suddenly I am transported back – transported back screaming – to watch it happen.

And not simply to watch it happen. Even to feel as though it's happening to myself.

And to wish I could have saved her.

*

"But how did she do it, Tom?"

"I don't know."

"Tell me!"

"Tex, it was forty-four years ago."

"Maybe. But I still need to hear."

So finally he gives in.

"When I left St Catherine's I went to the records office of the borough in which it occurred."

"And?"

"Strangely enough, it was this one."

"Well, how very convenient! But – believe it or not – that wasn't what I was asking."

He tells me then without preamble.

The telling doesn't take long, however. As soon as it's over – and perhaps only to end the silence which follows – he asks me wearily if I'd like him to make coffee. "Sorry. I wish there was something stronger I could offer."

"No – not for me." I stand up. "Anyway, I've got to go."

"*Got* to? Why *got* to?"

I can't give any answer. Almost from the start, haven't we been aware of intangible compulsions?

"What will you do?" he asks. "First you'll go and have something to eat, obviously. But after that…why not see a film?"

126

I nod – knowing that I'll do nothing of the kind. "But, Tom? Why d'you think she was here? In this neighbourhood? She wasn't working at that store any longer."

"What store?"

"Department store. Bourne and Something."

"Hollingsworth. Closed down years ago. Why was she here – well, who can say? She may have found herself some other job in the area."

"No," I reply. "Too close to the one where she'd been happy." But oddly I'm not suggesting this; I'm asserting it. "Well, yes, that's it, of course! That's why she came back. To have a look at the place where she'd been happy. To have a look at it for the last time. To stand somewhere in a doorway and watch them coming out, the people she'd been working with. That's it – isn't it?"

"What film do you think you might see?"

"No, I'm not in the mood for any movie. I may just wander round a bit. Window-shop. Or simply head for home." Again, though, I'm secretly aware it won't be that.

He jumps up. "Come on, then! Why do I suppose *I* have to stay? What's so beguiling about the booming stroke of half-past-five?" Then he sees my expression; misinterprets it. "Oh, it may have been getting on for six when you found me here last Monday! Okay, I admit it. But in any person's life there's got to be *one* moment of supreme foolishness."

"No, you don't follow me. I wasn't surprised you might be wanting to leave early, I was only – "

"Yes?"

"I was only thinking I'd like to get away on my own."

I'm unhappy about having to say this. I'm scared it will come out sounding all wrong. Hurtful. Insensitive.

And – for a moment – it seems as if it has. "Hey, listen. That's the second brush-off in a single day! I may start to feel rejected."

"You've been good to me, Tom. I'm sorry I've been difficult."

Now he really has been fazed.

"Tex, I was *teasing*. Why shouldn't you want to get away on your own? That was a *joke*! I'm aware it was a pretty feeble one."

"Sure. But I still mean it."

"Well, I'm glad you still mean it." He pauses. "And, by the way, 'difficult' I could almost be persuaded to accept. 'Despicable' – never in a month of Sundays."

"Thanks." I give him a hug. Although it's short, it aims to express more than just my gratitude.

Then I make for the door.

"*Au revoir*, Tom. Take care."

"And you, Tex. See you later."

After a moment he calls out.

"No – wait – you've forgotten your watch!"

I gesture that I can't be bothered to return. By then I'm nearly at the next landing. He says that – all right – *he* won't forget it when he comes.

"That's barbed," I say. "You're talking to someone who's recovering from amnesia."

"Poor fellow," he laughs. "You call that an excuse?"

It seems we're struggling for normality.

24

Out in the street I feel so utterly alone.

I turn back abruptly, thinking to rejoin him.

However, a woman comes out of the main door, blocking my retreat. A minute earlier I'd been vaguely aware of her standing at the entrance to the textiles company, trying earnestly to gain admittance. She's thin and sandy-haired, wearing a sleeveless dress and sandals. She asks me something which I don't quite catch.

"Excuse me?" It's stupid, but it's automatic.

She's been holding out a leaflet. Now she thrusts it in my hand. She repeats the last part of her question. She has, maybe, a Scottish accent.

"…born again?"

"Oh, Christ." Normally I'd have caught on sooner. "Yes!" I say. "Yes! Yes! *Yes*!"

I crumple up her leaflet – toss it down – turn back to the sidewalk. Not, in all likelihood, *her* idea of born-again. But who cares?

Oxford Street one way, Regent's Park the other. Heat and fumes and traffic; or water and greenery and the chance to think? I head for Oxford Street.

Yet, once arrived, I stand irresolute. Left or right? Tottenham Court Road or Oxford Circus? As little point to either.

Bourne & Hollingsworth.

"Bourne and What?" asks the guy.

"Large department store. Closed down now. Used to be someplace round here."

"Sorry, mate. Could tell you where John Lewis is."

So next I try a woman twice his age. "Yes, dear, you're right – along here somewhere. Terrible how quick one forgets. This side of the road, though. Perhaps that gentleman selling papers might know. I once got such a lovely pair of shoes at Bourne & Hollingsworth."

The news vendor also points me towards Tottenham Court Road. But he's busy and less patient.

A short way further on, I'm standing at the kerb, outside a shopping complex called the Plaza. I'm craning back my head when a policeman stops in front of me. He's fat and bluff and red-faced from the sun. His sleeves are rolled up.

"Can you help me, please? I'm looking for Bourne & Hollingsworth."

"Are you indeed, sir? Sorry to have to break it to you. You're about six years too late."

"I know. I'm looking for where it used to be."

"Then you're standing in the right place. Took up the whole of this block it did."

"Somehow I had a feeling it was here. Thank you."

He moves on. I stare up again at the complex. After that I turn and look across the road. I experience a brief moment of sickness

– even of faintness, almost of dislocation. I'm convinced of it: she'd have been standing in one of those doorways opposite.

Except that the doorways then would all have been so different. Or in fact would they; how can you tell? To my untutored, obviously un-British eye, the one I'm gazing at right now could easily – in the aftermath of war – have looked pretty much the same.

A bit rundown. Flaking paint. Rubbish blown in and left to settle.

And jeepers! This suddenly strikes me with the utmost force. If there *is* a God (and I seem to remember that, once, I may have thought there was) he must surely possess a sense of humour that's – to say the least – ironic.

Why? Because at present there's a woman standing over there in that particular doorway. And she's not simply standing there, goddamn it; she doesn't simply bear a passing resemblance to Rosalind, goddamn it; she's even – would you believe this? – she's even wearing an eye-catching yellow coat. (I can't remember if I saw in my dream that it was yellow or if this was something Mrs Farnsworth may have mentioned? In any case, it's exactly the kind of coat Rosalind was given by her mother – even down to the tie belt and single button at the neck. That one, too, had been dirty and in want of a good press.)

So, yes, God. You've an ironic sense of humour, all right!

But tricks aren't what I need at present.

Neither tricks nor mockery.

Though there is *one* merciful thing. At least this stranger doesn't mean to stay. I've hardly set eyes on her before she starts moving off in the direction of Oxford Circus – moving off with the walk of a person totally defeated. Well, lady, I can identify with that. I know exactly how you feel.

And my heart goes out to her. Amazing! At this moment, I wouldn't have thought that I could empathize with anyone.

I leave the shopping complex and head towards Tottenham Court Road, heaven knows why. And as I proceed, something bizarre crosses my mind, something just as bizarre as anything that happened earlier in Pilgrim's Lane. (Earlier? Wasn't it ten-forty when that song was playing on the radio?) "No, don't be so stupid," I tell myself. "Don't be such an asshole!"

But I can't help looking back from time to time towards the opposite sidewalk. Now there's only the odd flash of yellow as she swiftly gets absorbed into those rush-hour crowds: strangely colourless crowds in comparison to her. I give myself a mental shake and force myself forward, doggedly attempting to think of something else, anything, it doesn't matter.

So why then, again and again, do I find my footsteps faltering? Why am I still engaging – even as much as a minute, two minutes, conceivably *three* minutes later – why am I still engaging in that same mindless conversation?

"Have you gone mad? She's dead – you know she's dead. And even if she weren't, she'd now be old. That woman you've just seen…all right, dishevelled, ground down, helpless. But still young. *Still young*! So you can't give in to this! You – cannot – give – in – to – this! For the sake of your self-respect, for the sake of your health and future well-being… For the sake of restoring the proper balance of your mind – "

Abruptly I come to a standstill. Someone – I think it is a major or a captain – treads on my heels and apologizes. I glance about me at a London that suddenly seems as grey and washed-out as though it were coloured by my own despair. Or desperation.

I say the words out loud.

"Oh, fuck my health and future well-being! Fuck the proper balance of my mind!"

And then, almost before I'm aware of it, I have turned and I am running. Bumping into people, almost bumping into *things*. Sidewalk signs, bus stops, lampposts.

Also, I'm weaving through the traffic: traffic thankfully less dense than usual. *Far* less dense. Even so I'm provoking not just anger but actual oaths – mainly from two harassed cabbies and a bus driver who leans a long way out in order to harangue me. None of it's important. I'm breathless and sweaty. Again I catch a glimpse of yellow coat. I see it disappear into the subway. It's all that concerns me right now: the progress of a yellow coat.

131

I too, in time, hurl myself into the stormy sea converging on the subway. I do my best to penetrate.

But in the end I can't get down those narrow steps any faster than anyone else. Why couldn't she have stayed out in the open?

And then I realize. Oh God. I realize. How long since Tom had finished telling me?

That body on the line.

Here.

At Oxford Circus.

Realize? No – not realize. What's the matter with me?

A measure of lucidity returns.

"You're under stress and you're confused and you're in shock. You're only doing all this to have something to aim towards, aren't you – to find yourself a purpose? You're only doing all this to channel your aggression and your fury and your impotence."

All the same, I wish I'd got a closer look. I wish she hadn't moved away the second I'd laid eyes on her.

"Please let me through! I must get through!"

"Yes, you and a million others," says the man in front, turning his head ill-humouredly. He's a labourer with old khaki shirt and unevenly cut grey hair. "So take your turn and stop shoving and *everyone* will get through a lot happier."

Someone else, right next to me, is even more aggressive. He's wearing a dark city suit, red carnation pinned to the lapel, and there's an aura that's practically satanic about *him*. "Just wait your turn!" he snaps.

Then adds in quite a different tone:

"Besides… There's nothing you can do!"

He gives a queer laugh.

When I eventually make it down the steps, his words seem horribly prophetic. My sweat goes cold on me. I can't see her.

But there's a beggar woman on the concourse, holding out her palm to anyone who'll listen. "Few pennies for a cuppa tea, sir? Few pennies for a cuppa tea, lady?" My eye's caught by a fold of yellow that surmounts the ring of carrier bags behind her. I know immediately what's happened.

Yet, dear God. How on earth – how in the name of heaven – how am I ever going to find her now?

The dress! Oh, let her be wearing the dress in the snapshot! Black-and-white there, of course, but I'm well aware the leaves are green. Not brown or russet or any other shade. Bright green, on a white background. Oh, let her be wearing that!

And she is!

She is!

I spot her.

In all that milling crowd I actually do spot her.

But she's still a long way off: on the other side of a barrier and close to one of the escalators.

I vault the barrier.

"Hey, you, sir! *You*! Come back!"

The shout hardly registers. Yet when I briefly turn my head I see some outraged official now pointing me out to a colleague; get the impression that they mean to follow. Well, let them, who cares, haven't they anything more meaningful to occupy their time?

But the coat – the dress – it is you, isn't it? Yes, it's got to be! *Got to be*! If only you'd turn round and let me see your face!

The escalator is jam-packed.

Although it's a strikingly long one, by the time I get there she's nearly at the bottom.

I say it only softly to begin with.

"Rosalind…?"

But then I give it every ounce of energy I can.

"*Rosalind*!"

Yet with all the usual noises of a busy subway (there's even the distant moan of a saxophone) how far can one voice ever hope to carry? Those who do hear turn and stare at me dispassionately. The men look stupid in their stupid trilbies, the women in their stupid headscarves; all their senses addled by their stupid cigarette smoke.

"That woman down there! Please stop her! *Stop her*!" But she has now stepped off the escalator. "Please let me through! I *must* get through!"

People do their best to move over – more embarrassed than anything – but it scarcely helps. Is there another escalator after this? An old guy says there is.

But when I get to it the woman is a long way down.

"*Rosalind*!"

No response.

"That woman's going to kill herself!"

A man calls back to me, an able seaman.

"Where? Which one?"

"That woman in the white dress. White dress with leaves on! She's… Oh, Christ."

Again she's just stepped off. Is wholly out of sight.

But suddenly I know what I must do. The down-staircase and its counterpart run parallel. They share a broad dividing band. I scramble onto it. People gaze at me in fascination. Their smiles, their gasps, their staring eyes don't bother me. I think it's true that since I glimpsed her on the street I've hardly thought about myself.

It's weird, however…the thoughts that *do* occur. Up here the lighting seems dimmer and for the first time I notice that the steps have wooden slats. I'm struck by the heavy gloss on Rita Hayworth's lips – 'Gilda' is back at the New Gallery. Joan Crawford's, too: 'Mildred Pierce' at the Warner. And some newsreel theatre is showing the Wembley Cup Final, plus Shakespeare's birthday celebrations. Yes, definitely it's weird.

But wholly irrelevant. Like the cries of those two station officials now in hot pursuit. They're not getting through any quicker than me, though – their shouts no more effective than my own.

I jump down.

The crowds appear to have thinned a little. But on the platform – a platform which I've got onto roughly halfway along – people are standing a good half-dozen deep. I see no sign of her.

"Oh, God. Please help!"

I know the train will come in from the left. Panic-stricken I hear subterranean rumblings; but those are tubes for other platforms. I thread my way towards the edge of this one – reach

134

it – nervously lean forward and look in both directions. She's over to my right.

Yes, she's altered, certainly – damaged, bedraggled, bowed down – but just possibly, and for the merest instant, I may smile. "Rosalind, it *is* you!"

But then I yell:

"No, don't! Don't do it!"

Yet she still doesn't hear and anyway there's now a roar in the tunnel that's got to be the prelude to arrival.

"Rosalind! Don't! I promise you it's going to be all right!"

She doesn't hear.

I wave, frantically.

She doesn't see.

"That woman over there! She's going to kill herself!"

But no one, absolutely no one, appears to be taking notice; and the roar in the tunnel is growing tumultuous.

"Rosalind, I'm here! I'm *here*!"

Nothing.

Oh, dear God. What can I do?

The answer comes with quick, storm-centre clarity. Of course! I can create a diversion.

"Me," I say. "Not you."

For surely no two individuals ever jumped independently – and during that same small fraction of a minute – in front of the same tube.

The train is now out of the tunnel. Three seconds or less from where I stand.

Those ticket inspectors are pushing their way through the ranks immediately behind me. I feel the hands of one of them reach out to grab my arm.

But he's too late.

I close my eyes and throw myself forward.

25

Darkness.

There are screams and the grinding of brakes. There is pandemonium.

Which fades to silence.

The darkness starts to swirl, to clear. It turns from black to grey. Becomes a mass of billowing smoke.

Dense, soot-laden, proceeding from the funnel of an engine.

Still pandemonium, yes.

But of a very different order.

26

We are about to leave. At any second the stationmaster's going to lower his flag, blow on his whistle. He makes me think of that little guy in the church: Jack o' the Clock, preparing to strike the bell at the start of the new hour. But possibly I'd have thought of this, anyway: Rosalind's just given me her snapshot, the one taken outside St Edmund's only minutes before we met.

I've reminded her, too (no, not reminded; she didn't even know) about the photo Trixie took of *me* last Wednesday afternoon, also in Southwold, when we'd all stepped out of the Sugar Loaf Tearooms and taken hardly a couple of paces before my future wife decided to nip back in, to use their comfort station.

Oh, Lord. The shape of things to come!

"And believe this, darling. Believe this if you never believe anything again. This time I'll send for you."

"This time?"

Yes, why did I say that? Unaccountably, I shudder. Someone must have walked across my grave.

"I guess I was woolgathering – thinking how crazy I'd go if anything bad ever happened to you. Oh, sweetie, please don't cry! I absolutely promise: nothing bad ever *will* happen to you. I just won't let it. I think I'd die for you first."

"Well, if that's supposed to stop me crying, it isn't wonderful psychology."

"All right, I *know* I'd die for you first."

"Idiot. Say something heartening, like…'See you in three months.'"

"No, that's too long. See you in one-and-a-half. Two at the most. I'll either send for you, come for you, or arrange with Harry S. Truman…" But then we kiss; we cling. The train is beginning to pull out.

"Please look after yourself," she calls. "I love you so much! Without you in this world, I couldn't survive!"

"Same for me," I say. "I love you, too. Enormously."

"What?"

"Always," I shout back. I tap my ring finger. "Always! Always!" And I can see she understands.

Again she calls out after me.

"*Always!*"

27

We can no longer see the station, it's hidden round a bend. For the moment I don't want to talk to anyone – I want only to be left in peace. (And I've not the least idea where Walt is.) Squashed into my corner of the carriage I want to concentrate on Rosalind.

But I must be tired; even more so than I'd realized. I suppose I quickly fall asleep.

And have a dream.

Or a vision, or a revelation, or whatever you might wish to call it. For, actually, it's not like any dream I've ever experienced.

Because in it I see some guy who's a complete stranger. And yet I feel as much concern for him as though he were a member of my own family.

It turns out, after a while, his name is Tom.

137

Tom? To me, this has always meant my brother – and I've already mentioned to Rosalind my hope that if we have a son he will be called Thomas. "Darling, you have my word on it!" she'd said at once.

Yet, anyway, *this* Tom (who incidentally was wearing a dark blue suit, but one that in some way looked unfashionable) had just returned to his apartment – well, I guess that it was his. And when I say 'just', I mean maybe half an hour ago. The first thing he did was call out someone's name.

"Tex?"

There wasn't any answer.

Tom merely shrugged. He must have assumed that Tex – do people *really* call their children that? – might either have taken himself off for a walk or gone to see a movie.

But he seemed disappointed. You could tell this by the way he walked into the sitting room – even by the way he poured himself a Jameson's, sat down and took a wristwatch from his pocket. It was a Rolex. I have one like it – although when in this dream (for want of a better word) I shot back my cuff with a view to checking the resemblance, mine wasn't there.

I couldn't help wondering why he'd keep a Rolex in his pocket.

Then I decided he must have collected it from the repair shop. Probably within the last hour or so. Because when his sleeve rode up I saw something a good deal cheaper – presumably a stopgap.

And he had evidently missed it, the Rolex! He seemed to be admiring it now as he must have done when it was brand-new. Even when he reached out and activated some machine which apparently recorded phone calls in your absence – even then, he was still looking at the watch.

On the machine, there was a message he had clearly been waiting for. He looked expectant as he settled back.

"Hi! Herb Kramer here, from the embassy." (Which I guess means the *American* embassy, since the caller sounds like a native of New England.) "Have the information you wanted, Tom, as regards your friend, Mr Matthew Cassidy, of New Haven, Connecticut."

138

Oh, for Pete's sake! Dear Lord! Is my subconscious *really* that egotistic?

(Well, yes, actually – I suppose it is!)

"And most of it checked out, exactly as you gave it: meatpacking business, older brother who died in '42, Cassidy himself over here from '43 to '45, lieutenant in the United States Air Force, stationed at Boxted, then at Halesworth – both in Suffolk. And he married a Marjorie, too: a Miss Marjorie Carpenter, daughter of a very rich and eminent Connecticut family. All spot on. Except for one thing. No children. Also…and here's the heck of a coincidence. Admitted into hospital, in deep coma, last Monday. Condition critical. In fact, I put through another call some five minutes ago, 4.55pm British time. Old guy appears to be sinking fast; only an hour or so left, the doctors think. So I don't know where in hell that leaves our young amnesiac, do you? Why is life *never* simple? Call me as soon as you can, we'll try to figure something out."

Well, now!

Oh, my God!

Beat that!

So much *detail*. And so concise – so coherent! So memorable! How can it possibly be a dream?

And above all…so accurate!

(Except that, obviously, I am not going to marry Marjorie, and therefore whether or not the pair of us would have had children is irrelevant. But apart from this and the startling fact that I appear to be dying…plus the similarly wacky reference to some young amnesiac…apart from these three perplexing yet – one hopes! – fairly tangential things, the accuracy is phenomenal.)

But why, I wonder, why on earth should Tom have been asking about *me*?

At all events. He didn't listen to anything else. For several minutes he simply stayed put, still gazing at the wristwatch. Now not so much in admiration. More in sheer bewilderment.

Then he got up and went into the hall. Quietly opened the door to what was clearly a small bedroom. I guessed he must be looking for this mysterious Tex character; guessed it had occurred to him that Tex might have been there all along, sleeping.

Is Tex 'our young amnesiac'?

Though, whether he is or not, he wasn't on the bed. Tom stood in the doorway for a minute. He seemed to be reviewing the few personal possessions he saw lying on the carpet and the chest of drawers.

"But no children! Tex, that's absurd. We only had to glance at that photograph of Trixie's…"

He leans against the doorjamb.

"Oh, for heaven's sake! You looked so much like him you could practically have *been* him! And Kramer's seen the photograph! How can he say you aren't the man's son?"

Slowly, he goes back to his armchair in the sitting room, retrieves his drink. Listens to see if there's any further message – at least, one of the kind he wants. There isn't. He stares at the telephone as though suddenly willing it to ring.

"But Tex? Why *au revoir*? And what made you leave your watch?" He bites his lip.

I know what's in his mind. *Were these things significant? And – if they were – why didn't I realize it?*

"Some sort of payment?" he says, aloud. "No, that's nonsense! And you know I wouldn't have wanted payment. Not one penny." He smiles, a little wryly. "Not one red cent."

A moment later, he repeats that earlier phrase. "*Au revoir*…?"

Until the next time, he must be thinking. Yes… *Until we meet again*.

He takes a further slow sip of the whisky. He swallows it, notices his glass is almost empty, is about to drain it – probably contemplates refilling it – but then…

He disappears.

*

Tom simply disappears.

One second he's there.

The next…he isn't.

*

140

Well, I suppose in a dream a character can do anything he likes.

In a dream, yes.

But I still can't believe it was entirely that – even though, bit by bit, I'm being forced to accept it might have been.

Yet if I *have* dozed off for a while, here in this crowded carriage, I don't want any of my comrades to realize I'm awake. All those astonishing details, so clear to me a minute ago, they're already beginning to slip away. And it strikes me as important: I've got to do what I can to hold onto them.

For instance, I know Tom lived in a flat that unexpectedly transformed itself the instant he had vanished: suddenly possessed murals and stained glass and parquet flooring. What would any dream-expert make of that, I wonder – assuming, of course, I was still able to describe it? Stupidly, the only thing I can now recall with *total* clarity is the presence of a wristwatch. And I guess that's only because it was a Rolex – the sort I'm wearing now. (Yes, and I *am* wearing it. Why on earth should I ever have dreamt otherwise?)

Which reminds me. I'll be needing to adjust it soon – put it back a few hours. After two long years in a place you'd think that such a notion might bring either regret or excitement. But in fact it brings neither; predominantly I feel happy, relaxed, peaceful. I'm aware this may sound odd – when at one and the same time I ache for Rosalind. Yet somehow it doesn't seem a paradox. And despite the buzz of conversation all around me I keep my eyes tight closed, wishing to remain in my own private world for as long as I can – a world in which I now stand, quite suddenly, in someone else's back yard. Looking about me.

Did I say putting my watch *back* a few hours? Maybe I meant putting it *forward* – and not just by a few hours, either, but actually a few years. Because, incredibly, I guess it's our own back yard: mine and Rosalind's and Tom's! It's the sort of garden I used to read about in children's books. I'd tell myself that someday – when I was all grown up – someday *I* would have a garden exactly like it. But did I imagine it then with a picnic rug spread on the grass and a scattering of picture books and toys? There's even a rocking horse and a tricycle and several piles of building blocks.

And not only am I able to *see* myself. I can actually hear my voice – mine, despite its present gruffness.

"Fee, fie, fo, fum! I smell the blood of an Englishmun!"

I sniff the air, seeming to luxuriate in the appetizing aromas wafting towards me.

"Oh, goody! Bacon? Sausage? Steak-and-kidney pudding? No! Better than any of those! The unmistakable scent of little boy! There might be a little boy round here I could *gobble all up* for my supper!"

No answer, other than a giggle. Or, rather, a series of giggles.

"And, yes – *half* English, too! Mm! Where are you, my little one? Oh, where are you, my tasty precious?"

Slowly, I'm moving now towards a bush. I've got my arms raised above my head and am clearly all set to pounce. The giggles grow more nervous.

So I show clemency and swoop down fast. I release my two-year-old from both the pleasure and the pain of such anticipation.

I gather him into my arms.

"Again!" he says. "Now do it again, Daddy!"

"Again?" repeats the ogre. "Oh, no! Little pipsqueaks can't give orders to great big terrifying giants!"

He looks at me inquiringly – waiting to be told, in that case, what little pipsqueaks *can* do.

"First of all, they have to help me find their momma! They have to act like a really smart detective. They have to think *hard* and tell me where she might be hiding!"

My son hesitates for a second, then with a broad and cheeky smile points towards a tree. I approach it stealthily, finger to my lips, holding him closely in my other arm.

The instant before we get there, however, Rosalind steps out in mock dismay.

Though it isn't completely mock. "Oh, I can't stand it any longer! I don't know how you can love it so, my little angel. *I* find the suspense unbearable."

But our son disregards this.

"We've got you back, Mommy!"

He manages to sound both very serious *and* quietly gleeful.

142

My voice changes from a growling giant's – a ravening beast's – to that of your more average, mid-twentieth-century, American dad.

"Yes, we've got you back, me and this clever little boy of ours!"

And Thomas chuckles, apparently not in the least bit fazed by the rapidity of my transition. He puts his thumb in his mouth, lays his head against my chest.

"That's right, I've got you both back. Isn't that so, Tom? I've got you both back."

The Return of Ethan Hart

1

Have you ever dreamt that you lived in another time? I did, just a night or two before my life changed. I dreamt I rescued a woman from the Fire of London. She looked a little like Ginette, I mean Ginette when I first knew her, but she definitely wasn't French nor did she have brown hair. She was called Eliza Frink and was a favourite of the King. Although it's true I shared a bath with her, a very sexy bath because she said she wanted to reward her saviour, in every other way the dream appeared authentic.

It's not important, though, and I mention it only because a couple of days later, on March 28th 1992, I was taking a Saturday morning stroll through a nearby cemetery, not in London but in Nottingham, and happened to pass a grave which bore Eliza Frink's name. I must have done so before, of course, without my knowing. She hadn't been a Restoration beauty. She may have been an early Victorian one but by the time she'd lost four infants in as many years I doubt she had retained much sign of it. As always at such moments I wondered how I could ever dare to feel self-pity.

"Excuse me, sir, you've dropped your watch!"

The shout had come from a young man not far behind. He was tall and well-built, unusually handsome, and made me think of a current Levi's commercial. He also made me think of my son. By now Philip, too, would have been in his mid-twenties.

"Obviously my lucky day," I said. "Thanks." The watch had fallen onto grass. It was a good one but for some time I'd been aware its strap needed replacing. Since there was no one else in sight I wondered what the odds were against my being spared my proper punishment. Wasn't sloth a member of the seven deadly sins, which all led to damnation?

I expected him to continue on his way. But he saw the gravestone I'd been looking at.

"Some people's lives!" he exclaimed. "How did they ever stand it?"

"I'd say they had no choice."

"Yes, sir, that's true. Whatever may be wrong with the present, at least we do have choices."

I wasn't sure I appreciated the sir. And I thought fleetingly of Somalia and Bosnia, even of our own inner cities. I thought about the situation I myself was in. Ginette, as well. I'd have said that, in some way or another, most of us were still trapped.

"I'm sorry," he amended, "I talk as if we're all much freer than we really are." I found I was impressed.

But I answered only lightly. (Is it always the case that someone who's outstandingly attractive, whether they're male or female, can so quickly stir you from your apathy?) "Certainly the resourceful young have choices. Now more than ever."

"You mean, more so than when you yourself...?"

"Yes, definitely. For one thing, it wasn't the norm in the fifties to go travelling round the world with a back pack."

"But that's something you'd like to have done?"

I hesitated.

"I know that the person I am now would like to have done it, yes."

"What else would he like to have done, the person you are now? Differently?"

"Oh, what, in a nutshell? Just about everything."

He grinned. "No, that was a serious question."

"And I gave it a serious answer."

"So are you honestly saying that, if you could live your life again, knowing everything you now know, you would seek to alter...so much?"

"Undoubtedly I would."

He considered this a moment. Then suddenly he held out his hand. "Zack Cornelius," he said.

"Ethan Hart."

He was one of the few who didn't comment on the rareness of my name. I suppose his own was pretty seldom encountered. I remembered Zachary Scott, an American film star from my boyhood.

"*Ethan*?" he said. "Doesn't that mean 'perennial'?"

"But I believe you're the first person I've ever met who's known that."

And I felt touched by his courtesy. By his willingness to linger. We left Eliza Frink's grave (it was also her children's but there wasn't evidence of any husband) and followed a path meandering up the hill. On either side of it the grass was full of dandelions, which in the distance made big blurry clumps, decorative among the tombstones. We rounded a bend and saw a row of almshouses, surmounted in the middle by a clock tower. At this point there was an exit from the cemetery. "Canning Circus," said the young man, "the crossroads where the suicides were buried. Could you fancy a beer?"

We went to the Sir John Borlase Warren ("An admiral at the time of Nelson," replied my knowledgeable informant) and carried our pints through to its back yard, where I took off my sports jacket and we sat at a picnic table under a cherry tree. I offered him a cigarette.

But he didn't smoke.

"I wish *I* didn't. Yet my work is so dull I probably couldn't survive without."

He asked the anticipated question.

"Advertising. Nowadays I'm astonished I ever thought it interesting. Though I suppose we all change. What about you?"

"Psychology."

"Ah, then. That explains it. Why I've been unburdening myself so shamelessly to a stranger."

"I think it's more a case of our operating on the same wavelength. Very rarely do you meet someone with whom you click immediately."

If I'd been a girl, I could easily imagine falling in love with him. It wasn't just his blue eyes and his blond hair, his infectious grin. He had strength – charisma. You wanted to confide in him.

"But, Ethan, do you really feel so trapped?"

I gave a slow nod.

"By what, then?"

"Well..." I blew out smoke, deliberately. "A job I don't enjoy. A heavy mortgage. A stupid sense of resentment." I didn't add a sterile marriage – at least I was capable of holding *something* back. "Will any of that do? Just for starters?"

But I hadn't reckoned on the note of hysteria. I'd kidded myself I could keep it casual. I reached for my glass and discovered my hand wasn't any steadier than my voice. "I think we'd better talk about something else."

"Of course." He momentarily touched my shirtsleeve, gave a reassuring smile. "So how about the weather? Or…well, let me see, now…what about euthanasia? Or time travel?"

"A broad choice," I said. "But on a day like this I feel we ought to pick the weather."

"It's glorious, isn't it?"

"Do you suppose it's going to last?"

I'd been waiting for him to finish his drink. It was he who'd bought the first round.

"Perhaps we can deal with euthanasia," I suggested, "on my return?"

But he must have felt impatient. "Do you approve of it?" he asked. I was slightly bewildered.

"Well, yes, I suppose so. If the person's desperate and there's honestly no other way."

I spoke for a moment about safeguards. As a form of small talk it seemed a little inappropriate.

"Forgive me," he smiled. "Yes, you're right. It isn't something one should joke about."

Not that we'd actually been joking.

I came back from the bar. "We appear to be running out of options," I said. "I think we're only left with time travel." I loosened my tie and undid the button at my throat. "So what period would *you* choose to return to?" I'd forgotten that time travel, for some, meant the future even more than the past.

"Oh, it's not so easy for me. I'd have to think about it."

"Why wouldn't I?"

"But I assumed you'd already decided. To live your life again with memory intact."

A ladybird landed on my grey trousers.

"Just put the clock back? Okay. I feel I could settle for that. If youth only knew; if age only could!"

"Yes – right," he agreed.

I drew on my cigarette. "Next time round I shan't smoke!"

And next time round I'd be more sportive. Swimming, skiing, tennis. I'd have liked to be a great dancer. Also, of course, I'd be a traveller. A bon viveur. (Why not a Don Juan? That's something I'd definitely missed out on.) The possibilities were endless. I'd only been considering them a moment.

I stopped myself. Felt foolish. I wasn't the sort who got carried away. Not any more.

He raised his glass. "Cheers!"

"Cheers! I find this subject fascinating. There are more things in heaven and earth, Horatio, than are dreamt of in your philosophy."

"Indeed there are. Consult Dr Einstein."

"Or consult Dr Faustus." I watched the ladybird walk across a corner of the table. "But no, on second thoughts, not *him*. Don't really want to jeopardize my soul."

Zachary laughed.

"Ethan, it wouldn't be required of you. I give you my solemn word on that."

2

"Come in. And please forgive the mess." It was Ginette who normally said that but as she wasn't here (she managed a dress shop in the town) I found myself coming out with it instead. This was stupid, because there really wasn't any mess. What there was was shabbiness. The carpets for instance had come with the house and had looked worn even when we'd moved in, four years earlier. Likewise, the curtains. In that time, too, although we'd often spoken of the need to do things up, we'd never found the energy. Slothfulness again.

Now it didn't help that the sunshine was so bright.

But I needn't have worried. Zack was scarcely in at the front door before he was admiring a framed and blown-up photograph we had on the wall. This showed my grandmother when she was twenty – taken in the open air with her mother and her siblings. "You've plainly got a strong sense of family. You care about your origins."

I pointed out, a fraction dryly, that they could have been my wife's origins.

"But they're not, are they? I'm right in thinking this one here is your grandmother?"

"Yes. I'm flattered. She was very beautiful, wasn't she?"

"And the older woman next to her…her mother?"

"Not so difficult," I said.

"Oh, I'm only showing off! Could we have the light on? Now the sister sitting on her other side…Mabel?"

I stared at him.

"And this…Lilian? Julia? Ruth? Madge." He left a pause of some five seconds between each name and kept on looking at my face.

"That's uncanny," I exclaimed. "What kind of trick is that?"

"A small talent for telepathy?"

"Zack, I'm struck. But come on. What were the brothers called?"

This   time   he   scarcely   looked   at   me. "Frank…Howard…Stuart."

That was even more striking since I'd then done my best to block him, by trying not to think of my great-uncles' real names and by searching frenziedly for false ones.

"My goodness, hardly a *small* talent! God, I shall start thinking things like, 'I can't stand this man, I wish he'd go away,' not because they're true but because I know I mustn't."

He laughed. "Oh no. It's not so bad as that, I promise. And even if it were I'd be extremely understanding."

"Yes, I believe you would." I led him into the kitchen and got out two tumblers; I'd bought more bitter on the way home. I began to prepare some salad and some snacks. Zack leant against the worktop with his beer beside him. For the first time, indoors

152

and in the narrow confines of the sunny kitchen, I caught the subtle fragrance on his skin.

"Eternity," he said.

"Smells good."

"I ought to get you a bottle. Happy birthday, by the way. Many happy returns!"

"Is there a single thing that I actually needed to tell you this morning? I mean, that you couldn't have told me?"

"I saw those cards on the hall table." He smiled at me, innocently. "Do you mind if I wander a little?"

The dining room adjoined the kitchen; the sitting room was on the other side of that. He was gone for several minutes.

"The things I enjoy looking at are people's books and records and photographs."

"Sorry there aren't more photographs."

"Yes, highly inconsiderate! So where do you keep them? In a box beneath the bed?"

"Zack, you're losing your touch. There's an album in the linen chest."

I told him I'd fetch it later if he still wanted it, though privately I didn't think he would.

Apparently I had underrated his interest. After we'd eaten he asked again. We sat side by side in deckchairs.

"Ginette is very pretty. You make a handsome couple."

Made.

"Was Philip your only child?" He must have known he was; and this time he got the tense right.

Zack had opened the album at random. Now he went back to the beginning: babies and toddlers on both sides of the Channel.

But he didn't seem so interested in Ginette.

"How old were you here?"

I hadn't looked at these photographs in years. I found it, at best, a bittersweet experience.

"Eleven." Sloppily, we hadn't always bothered to write captions.

"Primary school?"

"Prep school."

"Here in Nottingham?"

153

"No. Amersham on the Hill. In Bucks."

The snap showed three of us, Johnny Aarons, Gordon Leonard and myself. My mother had taken it outside the school. All at once I made an oddly disconcerting connection: forty-four years ago, to the very day! Almost to the very hour!

Oh God, I thought.

"How well do you remember that afternoon?"

"I don't. Not at all."

Yet hardly had I said it before I realized I was wrong. I could almost *hear* my mother laughing. "Now, all of you please, no fidgeting this time, just watch the birdie!"

There was a pause as she again stared into the viewfinder.

"Come on, Ethan – and you, Johnny – let's have some really big smiles… Darling, I wish your socks weren't always round your ankles. Or that you'd sometimes have your cap on straight."

"Oh, Mum, do hurry up. We feel silly standing here, with everybody watching."

That was a slight exaggeration. The few stragglers who, from time to time, had still been coming out of the side entrance had merely called a quick goodbye.

My mother had suggested it: that instead of my having a birthday party she would collect me and my two best friends and take us to tea at Peg's Pantry: as many buns and pastries as we wanted – today no one would be counting – just so long as none of us was sick! Then we'd all go to the pictures; my father ran the only cinema in town. Happily, today's film was something we'd have chosen anyway. *The Three Musketeers.*

But I hadn't known she meant to bring her camera. And it seemed such ages until the shutter finally clicked and she professed herself satisfied. She was busy winding on the spool.

"Mum, can't you do that after? Gordon says he's starving."

"Oh, you liar! When did I say that?"

But anyhow it was too late. We had known at any moment Teddy might see us. And now indeed the front door opened and he came limping down the steps, leaning on his walking stick. "Ah, Mrs Hart. Good afternoon."

"Good afternoon, Mr Dallas."

154

"If I may be permitted to say so, how very well you're looking! What an extremely pretty hat!"

And I didn't simply recall all of this. I actually – literally – heard it.

Saw it, too.

For Zack and I weren't sitting in the garden any more. We were standing on the pavement opposite the school.

"Oh, my God! My God!" And then – how *woefully* inadequate: "My God, Zack! Can they see us?"

It had taken me fully a minute even to articulate that much.

"Yes. Or, rather, in a moment they'll be able to see *you* – they won't see me." He laid a hand on my shoulder. "But don't panic! Who's going to recognize you? Twenty years older than your mother, only five years younger than Edward Dallas…" He then asked if I'd like to speak to them.

"*No!*" I shook my head wildly. He seemed disappointed.

"Your mum's been dead for five years. I'd have thought at least you'd want to say hello. You were always fond of her."

"I was fond of both my parents."

Perhaps he couldn't gauge how absolutely *mind-blowing* this was? If I took the brief walk to the Regent I should now be seventeen years older than my dad. I could no longer blithely taunt him on his first grey hairs.

Zack laughed. "Even if you didn't go round to the Regent," he corrected me.

Another few seconds went by. "I think I've changed my mind." Could it be I was already starting to take it a little more for granted, this whole phenomenal situation?

"Fine. I guessed you would. But whatever happens don't let anyone sense you're more than just a passerby."

I crossed the road before I had a moment's chance to reconsider – or be put off by the racing in my chest. I heard my mother say, "Yes, I like it too when Easter comes a little late. It gives the weather time to pull its socks up." Then she added gaily, "Oh, do you think Ethan could be made to follow its example?"

She and Mr Dallas chuckled for rather longer than the joke deserved. I remembered my mother had always thought of

155

herself as somewhat scatterbrained. She must have found it reassuring to see her son's headmaster so manifestly smitten. How in the past could I have failed to notice?

The boys, standing silent and impatient, were the first to realize I was hovering.

"Excuse me," I said – a little shakily. "I'm looking for the train station."

I addressed myself to the three of them and left my mother and Mr Dallas to the enjoyment of their mild flirtation. I tried to drink in every detail. As much as the hat which Mr Dallas had admired, the red felt with the dark feathers, I'd completely forgotten her wine-coloured suit and those court shoes made of yellow suede.

Believe it or not, I'd even forgotten she had dimples.

And the boys. When asking for directions I'd looked chiefly at myself but Gordon Leonard very soon took over. I recalled that within a dozen years he would become a pop star and, ten years later on, something big in the City. But while we stood there that afternoon in Chesham Road directing a stranger to the railway station...at this period I considered he was wonderful, felt proud to have him as a friend. Never dreamt that when success came he would drop me.

The man kept staring at me, kept staring at my mother too, kept staring at everything, as though he were playing that game where you have to memorize the objects on a tray. There was something fishy about him, not just the fact he wore no jacket, tie or hat, and that his trousers looked strange. I got the feeling he wasn't even listening properly to what Gordon was telling him; I began to wonder if he was the kind who'd offer you sweets and want to take you on a long walk. But then I realized this was stupid. That sort didn't approach you while you were standing with two friends and your mum and your headmaster. So perhaps he was more interested in the open front door of the school, in casing the joint, as Buck Ryan might have put it. Anyhow. His behaviour was suspicious. He was smarmy, too. He said to my mother:

"May I congratulate you on three such helpful sons? You must feel very proud of them."

156

She smiled at me and although her smile was a bit constrained (was it my manner, my appearance, or something oddly familiar in my face; was it the vague suppressing of a mother's instinct?) it made me feel so close to her, so much a part of her young womanhood again.

"Thank you, but only one of them is mine. Perhaps it's Mr Dallas you ought to be congratulating. All three are *his* pupils."

Mr Dallas himself chimed in. "They told you the way to the station? Ask them to do it in Latin and see how helpful they are then."

This time we all laughed. So did Zack. "Disgraceful lot of sycophants," he said.

We were back in the garden. The album lay on the grass, between our deckchairs. I felt reproachful. "Why couldn't we have stayed there longer?"

"Ethan, you can go back any time you wish."

My readjustment proved rapid. "Though you do realize, don't you? I not only saw me, I *was* me; just for a second or so! It was weird!" I gave a sudden whoop. "But wonderful!"

"I wanted to convince you it was possible."

"Zack, who are you?"

He smiled. "Not Mephistopheles."

"No, I wouldn't seriously think that. But… Oh, God, I can't believe this. I can't believe any of it. And yet at the same time I believe it all. I reckon you're an alchemist."

"Sort of."

"What would I have to do in return?"

"Why do you assume you'd have to do anything?"

"Well…" I shrugged. "Nothing's for nothing in this life, is it?"

"But what I'm going to ask you isn't really in the nature of a price tag. I need to see how fully you're prepared to trust me."

I waited for a moment. Obviously he was in no great hurry to continue. "What, then?"

"The thing we were talking about this morning. A case of euthanasia."

157

3

I didn't know if he were serious. "Euthanasia?" I repeated, feebly.

"Ethan, it's no big deal. You told me you approved. So long as no one was abused."

"But the taking of somebody's life!"

"Mercifully. He's ill. He wants to die. You'd be doing him a service."

"No, I'm not sure."

"What about?"

"Any of it. It's too…"

"Way-out?"

"More than way-out. Unknown."

"Yes, of course. I can understand that. Anybody could."

Half-mesmerized, I watched a black cat creep along the garden wall towards an unsuspecting sparrow. Zack cried out a warning the second before I did. The bird flew off, the cat glared. It served to break the tension.

"Ethan, think it over. I shan't exert the slightest pressure."

He stretched and yawned; reluctantly stood up.

"All this sunshine. It must be tiring. I know it couldn't be the beer."

"Do you have to go?"

"Or the good lunch," he added. "Yes, I think I'd better. Give you a little breathing space."

"When shall I see you?"

"Whenever you like. A week from now? Two weeks? Longer?"

I, too, had risen. I squatted to pick up the album, heard the click in my left knee joint. "I was thinking more of – say – tonight."

"Tonight?"

"Or isn't that possible?"

"But what about Ginette? Won't she be expecting that you spend the evening together?"

"No. We often go our own ways." Why hadn't he realized?

"What, even on your birthday?"

"Oh," I said, "we don't celebrate birthdays. Not any longer."

"Well, if you're sure. I think that's sad."

"Back at the pub?" I asked.

"No – you'd better come to my place."

We went indoors. He wrote down his address.

"Zack? If I really did decide…"

"Yes?"

"To go back…"

He waited; carefully returned the Biro to its place on the worktop.

"Would I have to look the same?"

"Why? What's the matter with the way you look?"

I hesitated.

"I'm not talking of radical changes. Just a bit more handsome, that's all. A bit better built." I watched him playing with an orange, lobbing it from hand to hand. "A lot better built, actually."

"Isn't that something you can always work at on your own account?"

"But I couldn't make myself taller," I said. I smiled. "I couldn't increase the size of my penis."

"You seem to be under the impression you're placing an order at Harrods. What about the size of your brain?"

But then he held his hand up, fast.

"No, that isn't on offer. I suppose at a pinch I can agree to those other things. Provided you don't attempt to add to them."

In any case a higher IQ might change one's personality and I wanted – maybe this was arrogant – to remain essentially myself. It was also a paradox. I felt little love for the man I had become. I knew I was often small-minded and stingy and old-maidish.

But these, too, were things which I could work at. And *would* work at. Oh, my God, given a clean slate, how I would work at them!

"Hair dark instead of indeterminate?" was the one other thing I tried to slip in, hoping it might go unnoticed, yet at the same time subconsciously be taken note of. Verbally, he offered no comment, but in fact it made him laugh.

159

Before he left I asked what would happen when I had once more reached my present age. I was told I'd go on living until the day appointed for my death. "Which, I can assure you, is a very long way off." It had been unnecessary for him to add that; and I found it comforting.

But after death?

"I repeat, Ethan. Your soul is not at risk as a result of today's meeting."

"And what will happen to Ginette?"

"Ginette? Well, if she never married you, she'll clearly have travelled a very different path. She could be anywhere. Let's hope at least she's happier."

"Could scarcely fail to be," I said.

I went with him to the corner, stood in the sunshine watching him walk down the hill. He turned and waved just once before he disappeared. I felt a huge sense of happiness and energy and quiet excitement. All the more potent for its being so unaccustomed.

Ironically, it was only as I re-entered the comparative chill of the house, that I remembered something.

I had agreed to kill a man.

4

One wall and ceiling in his flat depicted a fiery sunset: crimson, orange, yellow – with whorls of gathering black. Another ceiling conjured up the night sky: velvet soaring dome, deep blue, pricked out with stars. In his bedroom, lucent waves lapped round the skirting boards, and stretches of silvery sand were fringed with palm trees. He had done it all himself. I hadn't been prepared for it. I'd walked past the pair of wheely-bins flanking an unimposing entrance, climbed the dreary staircase which served both upper flats, wondered why landlords so *routinely* perpetrated neglect, and then – suddenly –

Exotica!

It wasn't all so colourful. Zack himself was dressed in black. Shirt, trousers, socks, loafers…tonight he could have been in mourning. And yet once, when he turned away from me to draw some ink-coloured floor-length curtains and his blond hair was the only thing which for that instant remained visible, it made me think of the Olympic torch, burning brightly in a place of darkness.

Showing the way forward.

5

On the Monday morning I ran up to her bedroom. She was brushing her hair. She looked round in surprise. Normally I merely shouted from the hall.

"Have a good day, Ginette."

"You too, Ethan. Not that I imagine either of us will, especially." She turned back to the mirror and continued with her slow and rhythmic strokes.

Perhaps I would never see her again. I tried to feel something. I tried to remember her as she had been during the early years of our marriage, when she had still loved me and been passionate: forever thinking up small treats, gastronomic or otherwise: forever thinking up new ways to make me happy. I tried to picture her lying on the floor and helping Philip build Meccano. Running back down the shingle, bikini-clad and squeaking, ice cream dripping from the three cones.

But it didn't help. These were all memories from too long ago, incidents that seemed to have happened in another world and to different people. I couldn't remember them as real.

I said: "I'm sorry you have to work at such a boring job."

"Ah, well. That's life. I daresay most people's jobs are boring."

"I'm sorry that things haven't worked out better."

She appeared to have no answer to that; of course, there wasn't any. "Don't stop me or you'll make me late. Besides being late yourself."

"I'll wait if you like and give you a lift. It won't be any fun your having to walk through this." It was raining. Our freak springtime summer had come and gone in just one day.

"Good heavens, I won't melt! And I'd only feel hustled and imagine you were growing impatient." Her shop – which regarded itself as being exclusive – didn't open until ten. "There. Now you've made me smudge mascara."

My farewell to our home was equally bathetic. All I could manage was to speculate a moment on what other family might be living in it shortly – maybe in a sense already was – and how different it could all look by tonight, without anyone having rearranged a single ornament, far less picked up a paintbrush or had to mix adhesive.

Arriving at work I asked for Brian Douglas.

"Not here yet, Mr Hart." Iris, who operated the switchboard, seemed mildly surprised by my inquiry.

Zack had told me that in all probability Brian Douglas wouldn't be there today.

I asked again some half-hour later.

"No, he hasn't rung in."

Alone in my office I meant to tie up loose ends, clarify things for my successor…until I realized how idiotic I was being.

I had no affairs to put in order.

I didn't have to send off any cheques; make any apologies; ask for anyone's forgiveness.

It would have been nice to draw out all our money and rush with it to Oxfam. (The whole hundred and forty-seven pounds and thirty pence of it!) It would have been nice but it would have been dishonest. Almost flippant. That money would surely disappear at the very instant I did.

Incidentally I hoped that, at that same second, Ginette wouldn't be in the middle of serving a customer. The thought actually made me smile.

Because I was now totally committed – even if, admittedly, for the moment all the excitement had drained away; been replaced by trepidation. This wasn't on account of my life to come. Not at all. Whenever I thought of *that* I was fleetingly sustained. I'd have been distraught had the chance been

162

unexpectedly withdrawn. No, it wasn't my new life. It was what still needed to be done in my present one. The very last thing which needed to be done in my present one.

I trusted Zack – trusted him implicitly – but I only wished he hadn't asked me to give him proof. *Why* had he? Why on earth?

Yet when he said it was a fine thing I'd be doing for Brian Douglas I unreservedly believed him…despite that one insistent and perverse association: that contentious line between mercy killing and murder.

But, all the same, it wasn't *this* which worried me the most. It was more the notion of my assisting at a death, of possibly being called upon to be the prime mover. By nature I was squeamish. If injected in the arm I looked the other way. If exposed to violence on TV – or to scalpel or to forceps – I stared into my lap.

Whether it made things better or worse that I should know the person was debatable. It wasn't as if Brian Douglas was a friend or as if I'd ever had much to do with him. Apart from the odd good morning on the stairs, our paths had never crossed – and as far as I knew we had little in common. He worked in another department, was thirty years younger than me and in his natty suits and shirts and ties, his expensive, possibly handmade shoes, I'd always thought of him as something of a yuppie. I suppose that I'd been jealous; had hoped to fool myself by simulating mild contempt.

Though little had I realized! Imagine being bent on killing yourself at the age of twenty-five.

He had AIDS.

I knew this through Zack, not the office grapevine. Douglas had had the virus for years; a week ago he'd been told he had the full-blown disease. All the time I'd been faintly resenting him the poor man had been dying. Now I admired his coordinated clothing, nice haircuts, attention to discreet sartorial detail. I felt sorry it could only be in retrospect.

But apparently it wasn't the physical decline he couldn't face. It was the prospect of the suffering of his parents. The other things of course were factors – the pain, the pity, the indignity. The fear. But all these, Zack had said, were secondary.

163

"In any case," I had wanted to know. "Why doesn't he overdose on sleeping pills or something?"

Zack had told me it would be better to ask Brian. He was adamant about that. So I'd decided the question should be put almost the minute Douglas let me in.

One is so used to following certain lines of thought. Because of this I'd at first planned to drive to his home after work. *Work*? But then it occurred to me: why not go during the lunch hour? And then it further occurred to me, oh stuff the lunch hour, what's wrong with the present? Get the thing over with, you're never coming back, there could be someone else sitting in your place by this afternoon. *His* name on your door, *his* accumulation of junk filling all your drawers. So look sharp. Be decisive. Start as you mean to go on.

There was nothing I had to take with me. Not my briefcase, my raincoat, nor even my umbrella. (Yes, it was still raining but what the hell? Let me get wet, soaked to the skin, let me catch pneumonia. All equally irrelevant.) I felt free, despite my apprehension. I raised my hand in farewell both to Iris and the trio of typists working in the same area. "See you," I said.

Yet of course I never would – or if I did, it could only be because something had gone wrong. And with that jaunty little wave I headed on towards the main door. I offered no excuse. No further lies.

"But Mr Hart. The chairman has been asking for you. I was going to ring your number."

I said: "Tough!"

Then softened it a little.

"Iris, that's tough!"

I'd never been appreciated by the chairman. He had hinted frequently over the past four years that the reference I'd received from my former boss had bordered on deception. My former boss had been the head of a small London agency, which had folded during the '81 recession.

"So you can tell Mr Walters, please, he's a talentless and exploitative bastard who's only where he is because of a rich and well-connected wife. Talk to him about the milk of human

164

kindness and about trying to get his priorities in order." Coming from me, of course, that last bit was especially fine.

But I'd determined I ought to quit this place in style. *Start as you mean to go on.* My new slogan.

Her reply astonished me.

"But where's your umbrella, Mr Hart? Look out of the window! You want to take care of yourself."

"Iris, the umbrella's in my room. I'd like to make you a present of it." It was a good one; I hoped it would give her pleasure during the few hours she retained it. "So long, girls. I wish you every happiness – together with long and fruitful lives!"

It was pleasant to leave them all so open-mouthed. It was childish but at least it would provide them with interest on a particularly drear morning.

Finish as you mean to go on.

Brian Douglas lived some way out of the centre of town but Zack had mentioned the name of the area – Sneinton – and a telephone directory supplied the rest. It took me a quarter of an hour to drive there. I found a terraced house much like twenty others in the same street but this one looked better cared for – or was this just its window boxes and attractive curtains? I paced up and down for several minutes before I rang. Then I noticed I was arousing the interest of two women who, in spite of the drizzle, stood chatting on a nearby corner; and the notice of a teenager who was pumping up his tyres. The door was swiftly opened.

It was some time since I'd seen him; and the weeks had altered his appearance. Always lean, he was now thin, his shoulders bony beneath the open-necked shirt. But he was still nice-looking – in some ascetic way, even more so – and along with the weight had gone that air of complacency…which I might only have imagined in the first place. "You got here very quickly," he said.

"You were expecting me?"

But I suddenly realized he didn't know who I was. "I'm Ethan Hart, Mr Douglas." Although he nodded, his handshake remained formal. But it seemed insulting to elaborate further: I'm from the office, we sometimes pass each other on the stairs.

165

It would have been like saying *Do you always walk around with your eyes closed*?

He ushered me into his living room.

"What will you have? Tea? Coffee? Something alcoholic?"

I could have been the first to arrive at some weekly get-together – this morning, Brian's turn to play host.

Which struck me as commendable. But grotesque.

"That's very kind but – no, nothing, thank you." It amazed me that either of us could even be coherent, let alone mindful of the niceties.

"Of course. No drinking on duty." I could hardly miss the mockery. "I'll be having a whisky, though, if you don't mind."

"Then, on second thoughts, may I join you?"

It was Chivas Regal and we took it neat. I didn't think I had ever in my life drunk whisky before noon. He had poured doubles. We sat on either side of a fire with cosy artificial coals.

"Brian?" I said.

But I looked at the fire and not at him.

"Are you sure you really want to go through with this?"

"I've never been surer of anything."

"Yet suppose they found a cure tomorrow? Some kind of breakthrough?"

"Oh, don't! You'll tell me next that there are flowers and books and music. Sunshine and friendship. No, for God's sake! Spare me! Have you always worked in advertising?"

"More or less."

"Where were you last, before you joined Peach & Walters?"

"I set up my own small agency in London. Kept it going for around six years but finally had to bow out. Lost a lot of money."

He got up and poured himself another drink, as liberal as before. Anger and resolution and whisky. At least, I thought, unangry and irresolute, if the thing really had to be gone through, there could scarcely be a better recipe. He held the bottle out. I followed his example.

"I don't need advice," he said. "What I need is practical assistance. You know this incident has got to look like murder?"

"Murder!"

He seemed to think I had been better briefed than I had.

"Murder? But why? Is it a question of insurance?"

I had a hazy idea there were companies which would still pay up even after suicide. If the policy had been in force for long enough.

"No," he said.

"So why would you want a murder hunt?" I had to clear my throat. "And one that could possibly cost tens of thousands of pounds?"

"Yes, I feel sorry about that. But in the last resort I care more for my parents than I do for the taxpayer."

I intimated that I didn't follow.

He said, "It's simple. It would almost finish them to realize I was homosexual. Yet that's not the worst. They believe suicide to be the greatest sin on earth, a sin that would annihilate my chances of salvation. And they would blame themselves for it entirely; never feel that they could find forgiveness. Now do you understand?"

"Though if their beliefs are wrong...?"

"Of course their beliefs are wrong. What difference does that make?"

"You're obviously a good son."

It may have struck him as banal but at least it was sincere.

There was a pause. "Do *you* have children?"

"I had a boy who... He died when he was twelve."

I hoped he wouldn't pursue it. I shuddered. If I couldn't bear to think about a loss due to accident, how could any parent bear to think about a loss due to murder?

"What did he die of?"

"Run over," I said.

And yet, if I knew that I was going to get him back, why then, yes, naturally I could bear to think about it. It was just a matter of determination. Guts. I had the pattern right before my eyes. Brian Douglas wanted to die. I wanted to live. I wanted Philip to live. Surely I, too, should be capable of summoning up the strength.

"A good son...," he repeated.

"Yes."

"Ironic."

"Why? Just because you happened to be gay?" *Are you sure they're worth it, those bloody parents of yours*?

"No, I don't mean that. I think I have been a fairly good son. Give or take."

"What, then?"

"Oh, nothing. I was remembering a dream, that's all."

I'd have asked him to expand on this but suddenly he stood up. "So let's get on with it," he said.

For a moment I was paralysed. He started to push over chairs and tables, to hurl things to the floor. "Pull open those drawers," he commanded. "Tip out the contents." I stumbled when I rose to help.

But it wasn't drunkenness. Or, rather, if it was, I knew my head would all too swiftly clear. "And then? What happens then?" The words were barely croaked into existence.

"And then? My God! Haven't you been told *anything*?"

I shook my head.

"And then," he said, "you're going to drown me."

I forgot that he was meant to be the pattern right before my eyes.

"I can't!"

"Oh, yes, you can! You've got to. Bloody well got to."

"Drown you?" I had a vivid picture of trying to hold his head down.

I had imagined (although even then I had done my best not to) a polythene bag. I would first bind his hands, tie in place a polythene bag, then rush headlong from the room. I wouldn't need to watch him die. In fact I wouldn't ever need to return. With his final exhalation, I hoped, would come my own renewed *in*halation. That was vaguely the way I'd understood it.

I said, "I want to use a plastic bag."

"Christ, no!"

"But drowning…?"

"They tell you it's a peaceful way to go. There even comes a point when you'd feel reluctant to be saved."

"Yet how long before you reach it?"

That was vile. It was unspeakable. "All right," he said. And for the first time, his voice betrayed signs of what he must be going through: a terror which even my own terror could only dimly comprehend. "D'you think I don't know? I'm sure the situation can be different in the open sea, when you've swum out so far that you're exhausted."

But then he stopped. Regained control.

"And if it's true you see your whole life pass before you..." He smiled, albeit twistedly. "Then at least it gives you something else to think about, doesn't it?"

I was forced to have a second go. "Is there no one? Are you sure?"

"Except my parents? No. No one who could give a damn."

I wanted to attest that I could. But, of course, it would have sounded glib. And anyway? Could I truly have given sufficient of a damn to stay with him through every stage of his disintegration – scarcely a case of being required simply to hold onto his hand? At that moment I might have believed my answer to be *yes*. But that moment was charged with an emotion which would have made any sacrifice seem easy.

Except the one he really wanted.

"Drowning," he said.

I nodded.

"Well, that should do it." For a second I misunderstood. But he was referring, I soon saw, only to the state of the room.

I followed him upstairs. "I'm going to get undressed," he said. "You run the bath."

I draped my jacket and tie over a chair, rolled up both shirtsleeves, unfastened the top button, did everything but use my elbow to test the temperature of the water – it might have been Philip I was going to see to, sail his boat with or his yellow plastic ducks. Then we'd play this-little-piggy-went-to-market while I dried him, repeatedly parting my knees to let him fall through, loving to hear his unremitting squeals of excitement. I could still hear them, very clearly. I did my utmost not to let them go.

Douglas came in wearing a bathrobe, yet did so long before the water was deep enough. "It's always slow. I should've thought of doing this earlier." He sounded matter-of-fact. He had

169

been down to the kitchen and collected me an apron, the kind that butchers wore. I took it from him but didn't put it on.

He sat on the edge of the bath. After a moment I did the same, at the opposite end, facing him. A picture of domestic harmony. Companionship.

I noticed he had knobbly knees.

"Another drink?" he asked.

"Yes."

He went downstairs again, brought up two filled glasses, resumed his seat. "Don't worry. They're clean. No risk of contagion."

"Oh, for God's sake!"

I had to turn my head and look the other way. And then I thought, oh what the hell? If I ever knew *I* was within minutes of my own death, I should like to see that somebody cried for me.

But at least on one level this wasn't of assistance. I noticed his bottom lip tremble. I said abruptly: "Zachary Cornelius. Do you know him?"

"Who's Zachary Cornelius?"

It wasn't a question to which I could provide much of an answer. The bath still wasn't ready. I babbled on about my meeting with Zack but panic was again threatening to paralyse me. Philip, I thought. *Philip.*

"Tell me of that dream you mentioned."

"What?"

"You said you had a dream." This made me think of Martin Luther King.

"Oh, that. Nothing to tell. Frankly, it's risible. I dreamt I had a son."

I hadn't realized he had meant that sort of dream. I'd supposed he was referring to some unachievable ambition.

"But I've dreamt it repeatedly and that's what makes it odd. Each time it's exactly the same. You'd think it was prophetic."

I seized on this last word. Almost with gratitude.

"Well," I cried, "supposing it was?" The bath appeared to be filling faster. "Supposing you *were* going to have a son? Supposing that dream was somehow *meant*?"

170

He shrugged. His shoulders looked less bony beneath the woollen robe. "Then it would be a miracle," he said. "I have never – not once - never in my life made love to any woman."

"And yet you keep on getting this message. If it's that persistent how can you ignore it?"

"You're not suggesting that a man with AIDS should now go out and propagate?"

"No. But…" I wanted to say that on the very rare occasion – one could hardly rule it out, surely? – miracles *might* occur.

He uttered a harsh laugh. "Of course, you could always place bets on whether I or the woman or the child died first. That would be interesting."

"Fostering?" I murmured. "Adoption?" I must have been drunker than I realized. These options sounded feasible.

"Mind you," he said, "*that* would have been the rational part."

"How do you mean?"

"Guess who my son turned out to be."

"Prime Minister? President?"

He shook his head.

"King?"

"No. But you're getting warm."

The phrase was unfortunate. Sweat was running down my neck and torso. I had to turn off the tap. I tried to make the movement look casual.

"You'll have to tell me."

"My son," he said, "turned out to be Arthur."

"Arthur?" I repeated, stupidly.

"*King* Arthur."

"*King* Arthur? Goodness!" I really couldn't think of anything more to add.

"But you know the story, don't you? That when Britain finds itself on the brink of destruction King Arthur will return to save it?"

"Oh," I said, "yes, of course! Isn't he sleeping in a cave somewhere? Glastonbury?"

"What, with his trusty steed alongside? When we need him he'll wake up and leap into the saddle? Ride hell-for-leather down the motorway?"

171

"Well, it's only a legend," I replied. I sounded practically defensive.

"Then tell me, why should I have dreamt – dreamt a dozen times over – that he was born again, and went to school, and led a normal childhood, here in Nottingham? And that, in addition to all of this, he was born on my twenty-seventh birthday?"

His voice had actually risen in excitement. It was indescribably dreadful how he suddenly remembered. How we both suddenly remembered. I believe that for fully fifteen seconds each of us had forgotten our surroundings; certainly the reason why we sat in them. For fully fifteen seconds he had seemed inspired. More than inspired. Elated.

But now, abruptly, he stood up. Took off his bathrobe.

He looked at me and shook my hand again.

"Oughtn't we to pray?" I suggested.

But the few sentences I managed to come up with sounded unnatural, false. He nodded his Amen. We hugged and then he stepped into the bath. "Thank you," were his last words. He raised his knees and let his head slip underneath the water. My sweat and my tears and my concentration on the future (scenes from a life I hadn't yet lived passed unconvincingly before me)…my sweat and my tears and the peeing of my pants – nearly, but not quite, the shitting of them too – all played their desperate part in the drowning of a man I used to say good morning to upon the stairs, and had never greatly liked.

6

So it was done.

So it was done and I was still here.

Zack was a fake.

He wasn't only a fake. He must be evil. He was inwardly as black as he was outwardly beguiling.

I had just spent the most horrific minutes of my life. Killed someone. Held a man's head under water and watched his frenzied splashings for survival, watched the bubbles streaming to the surface with tenacious, terrifying vigour. Been forced to watch because if I'd looked away I should undoubtedly have lost my grip – my God, how he had threshed and seemed to possess a strength belied by his frail body. My God, how it had lasted. And why? Why had I done it? I couldn't even feel any longer he had really wanted to die, not after all that flailing, those wild, reverberating thumps. More than once I had nearly stopped. But how could I have stopped, when the worst, or half the worst, or a quarter of the worst, had had to be over by then, when he was perhaps a split second away from that hoped-for review of his brief time on earth? How could I have raised his head only – it was possible – to have to re-submerge it?

Yet I was scared, scared now that it was over and his eyes gazed up at me quietly through the water, now that the bathroom lino was awash and my shirt and shoes and trousers were all drenched, my socks and underwear as well. Scared that he might have changed his mind. Scared that what had started out as suicide would now, in the eyes of the Law, have taken on all the aspects of a murder.

With motive the disputed ownership of whatever the downstairs room had been ransacked for?

But why had Zack wanted him to die?

And how had he achieved it?

This was the twentieth century, close to the end of it. Not the Dark Ages. How could I have believed even for one fleeting minute…?

Since my meeting with Zack on Saturday morning (Zack? *Zack*?), no, since my meeting with Zachary Cornelius on Saturday morning I had been in a state of trance – of hypnosis – of enchantment. I could see that now. I hadn't been like a real person living in the real world. I had been a marionette. Bewitched.

Bedevilled.

Spellbound.

I had thought he represented the Enlightenment. Of course he represented nothing of the sort. Despite his denial of it, he had most surely come from hell.

173

I sat hunched inside my car, forearms flung across the steering wheel, face pressing into damp flesh. Had the meeting with my mother, then – her half-forgotten dimples, flirtatiousness, Utility costume, black-feathered hat – had all that been hallucination? Were his powers so strong he could sweep me back to boyhood without preparation, transport my present body to address an earlier one, escort me there as keeper or control? If so, he could almost certainly have mesmerized a person into suicide. Drowning wasn't necessary. What would Cornelius care about the feelings of a dead man's parents?

But apparently his plan had needed to include somebody like myself.

Why?

I was a nonentity. I had nothing to offer. No special talent. Why should he wish to have me – or, for that matter, anyone else – convicted of this killing?

For beyond a doubt they would convict me. They'd find my jacket in the bathroom. Driving licence, credit cards, the lot. Fingerprints all over. I'd slammed the door as I came running from the house, but even if I hadn't, could I really have been bothered to go round trying to wipe away the evidence? Did I really care that much about my future?

I raised my head, dully. The women who had witnessed my arrival were gone, and so was the boy who'd been working on his bike. But there were others who could talk of my departure. I'd almost collided with the postman as I charged into the street. A neighbour, to whom in all likelihood he'd just delivered something, had still been on her doorstep.

So here was one murder hunt that wasn't going to cost the public tens of thousands of pounds. Only the motive would prove to be a puzzle.

I started the windscreen wipers.

I gazed at them, like Bob Hope gazing at a swinging brooch in *Road to Rio*.

Then I thought of something. I'd always heard that you were safe when orders proved abhorrent to your nature.

So? In that case had part of me actually enjoyed what I'd been doing? Found it fascinating, seductive? The lure of the

174

forbidden, the unique power of the strong? My God! Had it been *excitement* which had let my hands maintain their pressure on his skull – bone against enamel – while his hair straggled on either side of them like black seaweed?

No.

It wasn't true. It was not true. Just couldn't be.

No pleasure. No fascination. No excitement. Simply the thought of Philip. Of Philip and my life ahead. Those were the only things that could have made it possible, apart from the victim's own resolve to have it happen. I would swear to it.

I engaged the engine.

I had to see Cornelius.

I had to pray that I could find him.

I was scarcely aware of how I got back into town. But that was no different to the outward journey. Presumably I stopped at traffic lights and pedestrian crossings, presumably I got into the proper lanes. At any rate no police car gave me chase.

It was too early for that.

The road where he lived ran alongside the cemetery in which we'd met. I remembered my lightness of spirit as I'd approached this house on Saturday. But the memory now evoked only loathing and self-pity, literally a howl of self-pity. I hadn't known when I was well off.

I rang and the buzzer sounded without my needing to identify myself. Oh, yes, naturally! One of his party tricks! I felt relief along with, as I climbed the stairs, an onset of breathlessness. I even felt a modicum of hope. Now, at the very least, I'd get an explanation. Possibly a solution. I would know what I must do.

But it was a stranger who awaited me. Short and puny, sharp-faced, cross. Accusatory.

"You aren't the Gas Board!"

People had always hoped for something that I wasn't.

I said, "I'm looking for Zachary Cornelius."

"Who?"

I repeated it.

"You've got the wrong house," he said.

"I spent the evening here, the night before last."

"This flat's been empty for three weeks."

175

"No." A note of cunning, even of triumph, had seeped into my voice. "If I hadn't been here, how would I know about the sunset and the beach? The starry sky?"

He tried to close the door but wasn't fast enough. I shoved him back. The flat had two rooms and kitchen and bath. All walls and ceilings were covered in white. The paint could hardly be new. It looked dingy and didn't have a smell.

Dear God! Could I have imagined it? Could I have imagined *all* of it? From start to finish?

Think!

What other evidence? What other *absence* of evidence?

The Post-it note on which he'd written his address – on which I *thought* he'd written his address – was in my wallet. Allegedly.

My wallet was in my jacket. My jacket was on the chair. The chair was in the bathroom.

Allegedly.

The bathroom was in the house.

The house that Zack built? The house of cards that Zack built?

On the other hand, if I was really losing my mind, at least I was aware of it; and they said you couldn't truly be mad if you were still able to acknowledge it.

Or was this as fallacious as their claim about hypnotism?

In any case I apologized to the landlord. ("My God," he said, appearing to recoup some of his courage, "you're all *wet*!" We could see my tracks on the hall carpet.) I returned to the car. Sat back and covered my face with my hands.

Should I go to the police? Should I send them to discover Brian Douglas – on the supposition, naturally, of his being dead? Should I give them a description of Cornelius, say he worked for a syndicate promoting euthanasia? Say that I, as a sympathizer, had offered to help?

Would it matter if they didn't find him? Cornelius?

Was he even there to find?

I took my hands down from my face.

Yes, if I could have imagined that whole striking use of colour...? The events of these past few hours had been amongst the most vivid of my life, yet people sometimes clung to their delusions even in the face of reason. I knew that. Could it be the same with me? Was it possible that if I presently returned to the office I might encounter my colleague looking no less yuppyish than he'd done last week – or last year? Was it possible that I'd be able to say good morning to him on the stairs tomorrow just as naturally as if I hadn't drowned him in his bath today? *Was* it?

I sat in the car and experienced the beginnings of a sense of well-being. I was working the whole thing out so rationally. Step by lucid step. In the end I wouldn't even need to see the police. (Already the notion of what I might have said caused me to cringe. For example, how would Brian have felt to discover he had AIDS?) Because, when it came down to it, there was only one point unexplained. Why was I so damp? Obviously I saw that it was raining, that it was raining *hard*, yet even so…

But eventually the answer would come. In the meantime perhaps I ought to drive across town to the Queen's Medical Centre and place myself in the hands of some psychiatrist?

(Suppose it was a Dr Zachary Cornelius? That was another thought which actually produced a smile. No matter how strained.)

I switched on the ignition.

It was the last conscious thing I did.

Apparently I had a heart attack. Though I don't remember any pain. It was the kind of thing I'd always dreaded, and this attack was certainly no small one: long before the ambulance arrived I was viewing the situation from somewhere above the heads of the people who had gathered, and of the policeman who kept asking everyone to stand back please (by then somebody had wedged something underneath my chest to release the pressure on the horn). I was viewing it, moreover, with a remarkable degree of composure, which interestingly suggested I might be passing through a state of near-death detachment. I watched the jostling and regrouping of umbrellas and listened to the hushed exchange of anecdote. Then the ambulance was there and I saw two medics lift me into it, an experience not unlike that of supposedly standing in the Chesham Road in Amersham. I saw them check for vital signs, put a blanket over me and give me oxygen. I heard their observations on the state of my clothing and the fact I must have urinated – and felt glad I hadn't also defecated. Glad for their sakes, I mean, rather than my own; dignity didn't seem an overriding issue any more. At the hospital, they wheeled me inside, still with the oxygen mask held firmly in position, and muzzy scraps of conversation floated in and out of my awareness, though none of them connected with myself: one with the forthcoming election and John Major, one incredibly – but I thought I might have blacked out, had possibly dreamt this – with King George and the forthcoming coronation. Also, we picked up snippets of cheerful comment in the corridors whilst making for our destination. Our destination came as a surprise. I had expected the emergency department, not a delivery room. My arrival even coincided with a baby's startled bellow as it emerged from cosy shelter into cold electric light, and with the midwife's nearly simultaneous cry of reassurance, before she deftly cut the cord and wiped the baby clean and wrapped him up and put him into the waiting arms of my mother.

7

As she would tell me more than once in future years, and had told me more than once in past years too, I arrived early on the morning of Easter Sunday…"and thereby did me out of my lovely chocolate egg, you devil."

"Why?"

"Because you made me feel so ill. I got a thrombosis on account of you!"

("How to pave the way for chronic guilt," was what I felt like saying. But at the age of three – or, equally, thirteen – I had to express my sentiments with care, even when merely teasing.)

Expressing my sentiments with care wasn't easy. There were endless pitfalls. "What a precocious little fellow you are!" my father once observed, fondly. "Don't tell me we've a genius on our hands, I don't think I could stand it!" Pitfalls and temptation, especially when I started school…I had a strong propensity to show off.

Yet it was easier to handle in the playpen. For instance when I heard my mother tell a friend about Errol Flynn's sex appeal in *Mutiny on the Bounty* I may have practically ached to correct her, but I knew it wasn't possible.

And when on that same afternoon I listened to their optimistic reference to the Munich Pact I wouldn't even have wanted to reveal the truth.

I remembered peace for our time, naturally. I remembered such dates as September 3rd 1939 and May 8th 1945. I remembered Hiroshima and Nagasaki. In fact I remembered all the major events of the next half century about as clearly as most people would, except in the rare cases when a warning could have been instrumental in averting catastrophe. Hence although I knew that Mahatma Gandhi and Dag Hammarskjöld and John Kennedy and Martin Luther King and President Sadat were all going to be assassinated, and even in what order, I had no idea of the dates or the places. On my fortieth birthday, fifteen years before, I had read that on the previous day two Boeings had collided on the ground at Santa Cruz airport in Tenerife, killing over five hundred passengers, which was one of the few disasters I could normally have dated with exactitude; but now I should have to wait another forty years to read of it again. I knew about the enforced mass suicide of an American religious cult in which nearly a thousand people poisoned themselves or were shot, yet I'd forgotten it happened in Guyana in '78 and that the leader of the sect was called Jim Jones. I'd forgotten such unnecessary happenings as the Aberfan slagheap tragedy and the My Lai massacre and the destruction of a Korean Airlines plane in Russian air space; such things as Chernobyl and the Exxon Valdez spill, the Alpha Piper oil rig and the Zeebrugge ferry disaster.

I'd forgotten, even roughly, such recent dates as that of the explosion above Lockerbie or those on which the two Sicilian magistrates, Falconi and Borsellino, were blown up by the Mafia. I'd forgotten the name of the Yorkshire Ripper. And so on. And so on. I should never be allowed to change the course of history.

I didn't even know any longer that Timothy Evans had been hanged for a murder he didn't commit, or the year in which Marilyn Monroe ended her own life, or the names of the people taken hostage in Beirut. Although I spent countless hours in trying to pinpoint such pieces of information it was always wholly useless.

"But it's inevitable I shall be changing history," I'd said to Zack, in the flat he had apparently never inhabited. "In small ways. Others will work in those offices I won't return to; on the other hand, the jobs I do take will now be closed to their original holders. And even more than that...I'll be changing it because I won't be marrying the same woman, and this time will father a son who doesn't die. Besides, it's always possible I may have other children."

"Oh, well," Zack had conceded, "changing it in small ways, yes." In fact, to me they didn't seem so small. (I had thought, a little tipsily, I should like to have a large family.) "In time, of course, a descendant of yours could hugely influence the history of the world, but this wouldn't be allowed to happen until...what's the date on Monday? Right, the 30th...that's the one unbreakable restraint. After that, it's up to you."

"Not merely a restraint," I'd said. "An impossibility." For I could hardly imagine becoming a scientist, say, and as a brilliantly creative thirty- or forty-year-old discovering a cure for heart trouble or cancer; or a preventative for AIDS before the disease was even heard of.

(And I didn't yet know, on that warm Saturday evening in Nottingham, in a house overlooking the cemetery, that some forty hours later I myself should be coming into such close contact with AIDS or that I myself should then be stricken down with heart trouble.)

My views on Zack – as must be evident from all of this – had once more undergone a change. Not only had he existed and kept his promise, I had delightful proof he still existed. (Was *still* the proper word?) One afternoon as my mother was pushing my pram through the town – I think she'd paused to look into the window of the Bucks Library, on the corner of Woodside Close – there was suddenly a handsome and familiar face gazing down

180

at me and a finger playfully prodding at my tummy. "Who's such a pretty baby, then?" He was wearing a tweed jacket, shirt and tie, and even a trilby, despite the fact it was a pleasant day in June; and after I'd got over my surprise, though emphatically not my pleasure, I reflected a little dryly – remembering only jeans and T-shirt in March – that possibly there were *some* fashions he liked a good deal less than others.

Though on the whole, I supposed, he was more accustomed to wearing jackets than T-shirts.

"Who's such a pretty baby, then?"

To my mother no amount of admiration could appear way-out, especially if it came from a singularly attractive young man who remembered to ask all the right questions as though he were genuinely interested in hearing the answers. "You obviously like babies," she said. "Have you any of your own?"

"I'm not married," Zack replied.

"Do you live in Amersham?"

"No. Just a flying visit."

"I thought it strange I'd never noticed you." She then inquired if he were here on business.

"In a manner of speaking."

"A man of mystery," she laughed. "But what a shame!"

How forward she was, what an unobservant child I must previously have been.

"And here were you thinking," he said, "you might have found yourself a babysitter?"

I wanted to ask him how many such come-ons he normally received in the course of any one day; he heard me, naturally, and gave a surreptitious wink.

"You must be very proud of Ethan."

"There's never been a baby like him! And that's not just a foolish mother speaking, everybody says the same. He's so *happy*. He smiles and gurgles and looks at you all the time as though he really understands what you're telling him. And would you believe it, he never cries! Honestly! He never cries! Well, only *very* occasionally, when his nappy needs changing and he's got no other way of letting you know, poor little scrap. And he

181

slept through right from the day we left the hospital. My friends say he's a miracle."

"Are you a miracle, poor little scrap?"

"Piss off!" I gave a winning smile and gurgled irresistibly. It should have felt so odd –this reversal of our generations.

"I wonder if babies ever have problems," Zack asked.

"Not Ethan," said my mother.

"My greatest problem," I told him, "is sheer boredom. Obviously I sleep a lot but when I'm awake I don't find sucking my toes incredibly stimulating – even though I still can't get over my ability to do so, and intend to keep it going for as long as I possibly can."

My mother might be talking but there was something about the tilt of his head which assured me I had his full attention.

"My biggest frustration is that I don't have the strength to climb out of my cot and lay my hands on a good book. My biggest regret is that, apart from the toe-sucking, I don't feel much of a sense of wonder. And also…"

He glanced round at me in encouragement.

"Also, I'm a bundle of neuroses. Fifty-five years' worth of phobias and foibles – which is something, Zack, I truly didn't bargain for!"

I'm not sure how he managed it but it was as if he'd asked me to go into detail.

"Oh, all sorts of little irritations which make my stomach tighten and give me nervous indigestion. And I know this is devoid of sense but being so young doesn't mean I can't be hypochondriacal. My mother never seems to air the washing properly, my woollies often feel quite damp. Apart from that, there's the whole question of noise. Soundtracks from the cinema downstairs, people hacking in the street, dogs barking, the revving up of cars and motorbikes – there may be fewer of them but they take longer to warm up. All that kind of thing. Do you think you can help?"

He nodded, although ostensibly in reply to something my mother had just been telling him. A feeling of great calm possessed me.

182

"Won't you choose an occasion next time when we could have a proper conversation?"

But he shook his head, with pursed lips. He said, "You know, this is such a quiet and charming sort of place, I wish I could get to Amersham more often. But sadly all the things one has to see to in this life…! Ah, well. No rest for the wicked."

My mother laughed. "But just in case you should ever grow less wicked, we live in the flat above the cinema. There, you can see it from here. The Regent."

"Thank you," he said. He took out a notebook and wrote down the address. "My name's Zachary Cornelius, by the way."

"Mine, Sally Hart."

I admired the thoroughness with which he played his role. I told him so. "But what I'd really love to know is who you are when you *aren't* playing a role."

He put away his pen. I realized I couldn't receive any answer now. I wondered if I ever would.

Yet even as I wondered it (I wouldn't have thought this possible) I fell asleep. Next thing I knew, my mother and I were back at home. I speculated on whether Zack had departed by train or whether he had some other means of transport. I speculated both on where he might have gone and, still more engagingly, into what period. I felt privileged he'd paid me a visit but, despite his pursed-lip claim, didn't imagine lack of time could really be a problem. I hoped he'd very soon return.

I also felt gratified that my mother had spoken of me as she had. I aimed to be just about the most considerate baby ever known to man. (Obviously, apart from Jesus.) An equally exceptional boy and youth. But at the same time I didn't want to get labelled as a goody-goody or a bore. *Fine athlete with a kind heart, cheerful disposition, inquiring mind…* That would do. There wasn't a single good experience I meant to miss out on – although of course I would; you'd need a hundred lives, not simply two, to do all the things that were worth doing, see all the places, meet all the people. Even a hundred would be nowhere near enough. And that was what made my present incapacity all the more frustrating.

So there were certain drawbacks even in those early days. I hoped *especially* in those early days.

On the other hand, in spite of these, I had begun almost from the start trying to live for the moment: something I'd often attempted before but quickly grown discouraged over – always because after a week, or a day, when all the elation had worn off, I had simply found it too demanding. Now, though, I believed I should be able to develop a mindset which, with time, might become automatic. Live for the present. *In* the present.

At any rate, to kick off with, I was determined fully to appreciate my room: the one in which I'd slept till I was twenty-two, when the Regent had been demolished, to make way for a frozen food store. The room was certainly small, but small could equal snug. Also, it gave me back a view of the sky that would remind me now of the walls and ceilings in Cromwell Street, however much repudiated by the landlord, a view which even in my prior existence had constantly exerted a beneficial influence – providing interest, providing aids to contemplation. (And this time, I vowed, I *would* save up to buy myself a telescope.) The room likewise restored to me something I might have been at risk of losing, something which had always given me such pleasure, be it derived from gunshot blast or lion's roar or the clash of steel on armour – or just the sympathetic laughter of a streetwise blonde. I mean the soundtracks which floated up to me six nights a week and which were gaudily woven into the fabric of my youth.

Originally I'd liked the westerns best, and maybe that was still true, although I was regularly disappointed to find I'd gone to sleep before the final shootout. If the picture were a murder mystery Dad would tell me who the villain was and fill me in on the story as best he could; at most I was allowed actually to see one programme a week, although frequently I did a trade and saw two second-features – sometimes on a Wednesday and Saturday, so that I could flesh out the work of my imagination (yet this could often prove an anticlimax) – sometimes on a Monday and Thursday, so that for the next three nights I was able to have the enjoyment of a mental re-run. I seldom bothered with the musicals, but nevertheless it was agreeable to have Bing

Crosby or Dan Dailey or Betty Grable sing me softly to sleep on occasion.

The room, judged solely as a room, wasn't extraordinary; but it had been *mine*, a place of warmth and withdrawal during the day – and at night, because of my view of the sky, a launch pad for starships and manned rockets, which had eventually succeeded a well-worn magic carpet and the albatross upon whose back I used to fly…especially on Sundays, when the cinema was closed, and especially in winter when the comfort of my bedclothes emphasized the magnitude of my blessings. My reacquisition of this room – along with the books, pictures, records, ornaments that would gradually reappear as part of it – this alone could have compensated for any drawbacks arising out of my frustration.

(Okay, so I didn't get the freedom I'd been used to. I wasn't entirely my own boss. I could wait.)

Compensated for all save one of them.

The biggest.

But how on earth had I not thought to speak of it to Zack when I had spoken of everything else from barking dogs – and damp woollies – to nervous indigestion?

My memory of Brian Douglas.

That memory gave me nightmares. My mother had forgotten to mention there were times when I woke up screaming – although, it's true, she knew about only two of them; I could immediately contain my horror. If *only* he had died more gently! Zack had asked me to do it and because I trusted Zack I knew it had been necessary. And merciful. And right. But all the same…

If only he had died more gently.

I couldn't regret what I had done; how could I possibly regret it? I felt completely confident there was a heaven, and that Brian Douglas would have gone to it.

How *could* I regret it?

And yet. Every single time my mother put me in the bath – some thirty years, for Pete's sake, before Brian Douglas had even been born – I needed to school myself not to resist, not to grow tense, not to cry out in panic, and this, whether or not she laid my head back to rinse the shampoo from my hair, whether or not I got water up my nose or in my eyes or in my mouth. My God, I had to pray then – yes, how I had to pray – for Brian, for Zack, for Ginette, for every living thing upon the face of this earth, either now or in the future; my frantic prayers were not selective. In fact, I also prayed when I wasn't in my bath, every time for instance that I'd been laid down in my cot and after my mother had gone from the room. But that was something different.

Though always in the end it came back to the same thing.

Always the same thing.

If only he had died more gently.

8

For our first English homework at the Grammar, Mr Hawk-Genn told us to write a composition.

"On any subject. I want to gauge the kind of work you're capable of. The range of your interests, the depths of your imaginations."

"Oh, sir! Do we have to?"

"Mine isn't very deep, sir. I can tell you that right now."

"I don't have any interests, sir."

"Couldn't we learn a sonnet, sir? Hickory, dickory, dock…"

Poor Mr Hawk-Genn. I now understood he was a poet with a growing reputation – although this was something I'd discovered only many years later, after he'd committed suicide and I happened to see his obituary in the Telegraph. He was about thirty when I first knew him, quite nice-looking in a mildly effeminate way, a slight man of only medium height, with slicked-down flaxen hair, and a yellow cord jacket which stank of cigarettes. He left the Grammar before I did, having banged down a desk lid on top of a boy's head and given him concussion. The boy, a new boy, had been winding him up by opening his desk every few minutes to conduct a lengthy rummage and treating the class to a running commentary on everything he found.

186

We ourselves, as new boys, also thought we had the measure of him, even before he was five minutes into our first lesson. Whereas with Mr Horwood and Dr Derry and Mr Tank you realized you had to behave – to some degree it was a matter of reputation but to a greater one it was a matter of presence – with Mr Hawk-Genn it was believed that you could get away with anything.

And the pity of it was, he would have made an excellent teacher. He longed to enthuse us with his own love of language and of literature.

"He said on any subject," Gordon Leonard told the class at the end of the period, when the master had departed. "Let's write on rubbing up. Let's all write on rubbing up."

The first time I'd heard this, fifty-five years earlier, I must have been uncommonly naïve. I hadn't understood what the expression meant; hadn't been aware of the activity it specified.

"I know! We'll claim we've done it so much we've all gone blind but haven't yet learnt brail!" Gordon put out his hands and stumbled down the central aisle, zigzagging drunkenly and being helped along his way by sturdy pushes. "Alms for the blind! Alms for the blind! Hendrix, you've let off, you filthy beast. Don't try to deny it. You're *disgusting*!"

And I had used to think he was so wonderful: this nonchalantly dashing Gordon Leonard.

"Tell you what, though. Being serious now. We can time ourselves, see who can write the thing in under ten minutes. Say twelve at the most."

Then small, grey-haired, dynamic Dr Derry swept in, wearing his black gown, and the uproar was immediately quelled. He didn't say anything but merely turned his back on us, selected an unbroken stick of chalk, and stood thoughtful for a moment in front of the board. At length he began to write. The chalk squeaked unmercifully for over a minute – for over a minute and a half – for over two minutes. Some of us looked at one another and wondered if it was ever likely to stop. Even I wondered that, because when it came to the minutiae of my existence I had naturally forgotten more than I remembered. But finally the small man stepped aside and we saw what he had written.

187

"'Manners maketh man' is the motto of Winchester College and I should like to say how thoroughly I agree with that, and how I shall now do everything within my power to adopt such a laudable maxim, and to endeavour to live up to it!" We were then informed we should have to write this out a hundred times before tomorrow, obviously rendering every word in every line so legible that there could be no fear of our needing to rewrite it *two* hundred times for the day following. After that, there ensued a further silence which lasted, except for authorized interruption, throughout the whole of that miserable Latin period, our first, and possibly least enjoyable, of all that Dr Derry ever took us for.

I didn't know what to do about Mr Hawk-Genn. During those chaotic few minutes between classes I could perhaps have remonstrated, said, "Hey, he's all right, let's give him a chance!" But probably a better way was to try to win over Gordon in private, since Gordon was patently a born leader – or else hope to influence some of the others at a more conducive moment.

Meanwhile, there remained the question of the essay.

"Any ideas?" asked Johnny Aarons, as we sauntered home that evening.

"*A visit to the seaside*," I offered. "*The life of a threepenny bit.*"

"Gosh, yes. Thanks, Ethan. Original thinker – ahead of your time."

I smiled. "Talking of which, you know what I reckon I might do? *The shape of things to come*! But not according to H.G. Wells. According to E.B. Hart." It was a subject I'd often been drawn towards at prep school but which I now felt glad I'd saved. "I'd like – if I can – to produce something quite impressive."

"For Hawk-Genn? You'll be in a minority."

"Sounds like it."

"Minority of one."

"What about minority of two?"

"Hah! You know what old Dallas used to say about my English."

"But if I try to help with it?" In any case we'd frequently done our homework together – and Johnny's mathematics had always been far in advance of mine. "And why should we just sit back and let Flash Gordon run this show?"

It hadn't been a ploy but it was providential. A spot of rivalry existed. In times past they'd seldom vied for the greater share of my affection, yet to be better-looking and taller and stronger had certainly made something of a difference. For one thing, of course, it must have provided me with more confidence.

It was strange I'd again picked Gordon for a friend but perhaps in some ways we were closer than before – in part, I think, simply because I didn't fawn on him as I had used to. And, invariably more thoughtful when away from the crowd, he was by far the best person to go bird-watching with, or bicycling or camping with, a trait in him I had never before recognized, let alone appreciated. Also, as it happened, we were currently talking about buying a set of weights together, from the proceeds both of our paper rounds and of a visit from one of Gordon's great-aunts (he was a generous friend), then exercising in his father's garage. And since Johnny was less interested in physical and outdoor pursuits and more into music and the sciences – together, twice now, we had made an effective crystal set which passed between us on alternating weeks – they complemented each other these days much better than when I myself had not been so attracted to such things as hiking and football and fishing. (Though I always threw the fish back and still objected unreservedly to shooting.) Gordon's father was a keen huntsman who enjoyed baiting me on the subject of blood sports but nowadays I could answer in kind, whereas previously I'd avoided him or, if unable to do so, had addressed him assiduously as 'sir'. Previously, however, I had missed out on the tree house he had helped us build in their cherry orchard, the really splendid tree house which Gordon had also missed out on, since the idea for it and even the first rough sketch had emanated from me.

So despite the changes that had taken place in myself (I often remembered telling Zack I was afraid a higher IQ might alter my personality but I'd made no allowances for other, gentler things),

Johnny and Gordon were still my best friends, and it had felt weird on my eleventh birthday to have my mother snap the three of us in front of our prep school and remember the second occasion on which it had happened, with Zack and me standing on the opposite pavement and watching her flirt with Mr Dallas. When the camera had been put away I wouldn't even have been flabbergasted to hear a familiar stranger asking for directions to the station: a sly joke, maybe – a wink across the calendar – engineered by Zack. Gordon had asked, "Ethan, what do you keep looking for over there?" "What? Oh, nothing, really. Ghosts!" And he had laughed.

"Or perhaps I'll write about the building of the tree house," I remarked now. Johnny had been invited up to it a lot and though so far he had refused to come the subject was no longer awkward. "And how I told Mr Leonard I'd decided to become a vegetarian and that it was him who'd mainly been responsible!"

He laughed. "Interesting. But, no, I'd still rather hear about *The Future According to Hart.*"

"Okay," I said. "I'm happy."

"What aspects will you choose?"

"Thought I might have the Festival of Britain as my framework. Not really sure yet." Instead of getting it done in ten minutes – or even twelve – I could envisage it taking something more like ten *hours*. Or even twelve.

But I was wrong. It took me fifty minutes. It flowed. It flowed as fast as the ink from my Platignum – faster, in fact, since the nib kept scratching up the paper. It could have been a lesson in dictation, without all the pauses or the needless repetitions.

Yet it wasn't about the future. Mr Hawk-Genn had asked us to plan what we wrote so that it might build towards a satisfying climax or at least to a logical conclusion. Naturally I could see the sense in this but I had started writing with a mind that was practically a blank – save for the projected Skylon, save for the exciting Dome of Discovery.

And I found the result to be horrifying.

190

9

So okay. I hit him. Big deal. He was a weakling. *Messiah*? The man who was going to carry us to victory? You should've seen him. He couldn't even carry his own cross. Stumbling this way and that! Pitiful. They had to pull some foreigner out of the crowd. To get that bit of wood up the hillside for our self-appointed hero the Romans had to commandeer a wog! That's when I hit him.

And I promise you, that *really* threw him off his balance.

He looked at me. It was supposed to be one of those I-know-you-didn't-mean-it-I-forgive-you looks. Blood, sweat and condescension. Turn the other cheek. So I walloped him again.

Then everybody cheered.

All right, I'm not a liar, not everybody. A lot of 'em. But anyway I didn't hang around to milk my sixty seconds' worth of glory. I wanted to get up the hill before he did – *three* crucifixions there were going to be – I didn't want to miss a minute.

And at first it was fun, all but some of the women loved it. (Women of both sexes.) It came to *him* and they rammed that crown of thorns down even tighter. They bowed and spat and laughed and bowed again. They ripped off his clothes and pushed him to the ground. They stretched his arms along the crossbar – and still they joked and chuckled as they did it. They showed him the first nail. Good and thick and long and rusty; perhaps it had been used before. "This'll knock a bit of sense into you, Yer Majesty! Let in the daylight, as it were!" I saw his mother's face.

The stupid bitch.

Oh, God! Was it because the word rhymed? Bitch? Witch? I saw a woman tied to a stake and standing in the midst of fire. Even as I glanced, the flesh was turning to charred meat. I had to close my eyes. Me! Press my hands against my ears. It didn't help. I threw up on the grass.

Then people stared at me and backed away and I realized I'd been dreaming. I felt asinine – ashamed. Went hot, cold.

Unsteady at the knees. But, Christ Almighty! It was like the heat of those flames had been licking at my own body. I hardly dared look down. Half thought my garment would be scorched.

I made an effort, though. Huge effort. Controlled myself. Wiped my mouth clean. Cast out my own demons. *I* wasn't a weakling. I wasn't the kind of man demons should ever think to mix with. My God, I'd show 'em!

The stupid bitch, I said, looking back at his mother. Stupid bugger, I said, looking back at him. And for fully a minute I managed to enjoy his sweaty contortions almost as much as I had hoped. I remembered the insolence he'd shown towards my master when asked outright, "*Are* you the King of the Jews?" I bet he was wishing now he'd been a bit more diplomatic.

But then it happened again!

This time I saw a man on another kind of gibbet, only this time he was white-skinned like the burning woman (I *think* she was white-skinned!), pale-complexioned like all the strangely garbed spectators struggling now to get a closer view. Yes, white-skinned and writhing, with a rope around his neck (but not pulled tight, not yet; or do I mean, not any longer) and there was this…hangman? executioner?…playfully pricking out upon his stomach the journey which he meant his knife to take… Dear Lord! I felt the blade slice into my own gut, turn amidst my own entrails, cause the blood to run between my own outstretched fingers.

Yet there I was – still standing on the grass on Golgotha – thank God, oh thank God: me savagely scraping across the back of one hand with the fingernails of the other. I looked towards Jesus of Nazareth. But again! It wasn't him I saw. It was two street children in Guatemala City (which wasn't any place I'd ever heard of, I'm not an educated man, how could I be, just a slave in the governor's palace) – urchins whose eyes were burnt out by police cigars, their tongues torn from their heads with pliers.

And I cried out.

No more. No more. Please stop.

I wailed.

192

I don't know what cigars are, or pliers, or police, I don't know any country but this, or any customs but ours, or any times but the times I live in.

I'm not sure who I cried out to – though one thing's certain: I didn't expect an answer. When I got one I fainted.

"No, as yet you don't know them! But wait. Other customs and other countries – yes, and other times, as well. Oh, yes, Cartophilus! You'll most certainly *get* to know them!"

<u>10</u>

It was several days before he commented. He had our exercise books piled in two heaps in front of him.

"Shall I give them back, sir?"

"No, Nesbitt. Not yet. Later."

"Oh, go on, sir, let me do it now."

"I said – later."

"Please…" Nesbitt, already on his feet, clasped his hands in piteous supplication. He looked like Al Jolson about to sink onto one knee before a picture of his mammy.

"Sit down!"

Nesbitt sat down – on the floor between two desks. The titters turned to laughter. There came, too, a smattering of applause.

I myself stood up.

"Oh, Andrew, stow it! It isn't funny. We want to hear about our work."

The ensuing hush was one of amazement. At that moment nobody looked on me with favour, not even the master. But I suddenly drew my shoulders back and thought, Oh what the hell, I know I'm doing right, surely I'm doing right! And the reflection steadied me and helped me stand my ground – do so, moreover, with an air of assurance even Gordon might have envied. I felt I was making my bid for top dog in the Mafia.

"Thank you, Hart," said Mr Hawk-Genn. "That's more than good of you, I'm sure."

His irony appeared ungracious but at least if I wanted to be noble the laughter of the class was now with him rather than against him.

"It's interesting it should be you," he said.

"Sir?"

"My saviour."

It occurred to me this really had to be an error, his admission that he'd needed saving, hadn't been in control. But the silence remained absolute: everyone caught unawares by such an unexpected development – on top of which it seemed blessedly certain that, whether or not I was now in the running to replace Legs Diamond, I was no longer any candidate for Teacher's Pet.

"I just wanted us to get on, sir."

"And that's what I find interesting."

"Why, sir?"

I was still standing and, even if puzzled by the sarcasm, still feeling competent to handle things.

But I suddenly wondered why I'd stood up in the first place. Had it been courtesy? Or had it been arrogance?

"Well, Hart, let me put it this way. There are those who didn't do the work – and I shall have a thing or two to say to them. Osborne, for instance, Whittaker, I trust you're both listening. I trust you both have convincing explanations. Also Simmons, Brown, and…" (he ran his finger down the register) "…ah yes, *you*, Wilkins! Why have none of you done the work I asked for?"

The silence lasted while each of these in turn made his poor pathetic excuse. And though each in turn played to the gallery, each in turn found his material less rib-tickling than he'd envisaged.

"Well, enough of this. Unless your work is handed in without fail by lunchtime tomorrow – and unless it's of a considerably higher standard than most of what I have in front of me at present – then you can make your excuses to the headmaster and that's it. You may all sit down again. No, Hart, not you. Where's Yardley?"

The boy who was more often known as Lavender stood up.

"Yardley, well done. If we have time, I may ask you to read it out. But pay attention to my comments at the bottom."

Lavender smirked a bit and sat down.

"Nesbitt, give him back his book. No – give it, don't throw it!"

Nesbitt walked to the back of the class, pulling faces as he went, and returned Lavender his book.

"Fletcher?"

Simon stood up.

"Fletcher, your spelling is appalling and your grammar at times odd. But the story was good fun. I enjoyed reading it. Thank you."

Simon was a shy boy and didn't look round for appreciation. I took to him nowadays much more than I had used to.

"Aarons? One or two interesting ideas quite pleasantly expressed. Try to keep that up. Leonard? May I ask how long you took to do this work?"

"I don't know, sir." Now we did get a low ripple of laughter and Gordon glanced behind him. He had been bragging about how he'd scraped in under seven minutes, according to his father's stopwatch.

"Half an hour? More than that? Less?"

"Maybe slightly less."

"Twenty minutes?"

"Not sure, sir."

"I see. Well, Leonard, how about rewriting it for me this weekend? The idea of your tree house – I found that appealing – perhaps because I grew up in the middle of a big city. Will you try to take a lot more care this time and do yourself some justice?"

Gordon shrugged. Again he glanced round at the rest of us. Whatever – quite – had happened, he encountered a pretty thin response.

He said in a mumble: "I suppose so, sir, if you like." He was permitted to sit down. I was the only one left standing, except for Nesbitt, who had returned Johnny's and Simon's books and now returned Gordon's.

"All right, Nesbitt, you may hand back the rest. But while you're doing so I want to say *this* to the majority. Don't let it happen again! Do you understand?"

I didn't understand. I had tried over mine and surely he must have been able to see that. No, perhaps I hadn't actually *tried*. But at least there'd been a prior determination to do so.

My book wasn't amongst the others.

"Which leaves us merely with our friend here."

If my book was lost I'd have been singled out with those who hadn't handed anything in. So was it a case, I wondered, simply of his having been shocked by what I'd written? I myself had been shocked by what I'd written. But not so much on account of its sensationalism or its crude blasphemy. Nor, come to that, on account of its less crude blasphemy: the idea that God could have so disregarded his son's anguished entreaty from the cross, *Father forgive them*; could, besides, have had so little understanding of what had turned Cartophilus into the brute he was; could in fact have *overreacted* as he had, by dishing out a punishment so wildly disproportionate – no, I was shocked not so much by the *content* of what I'd written, as because I couldn't think where any of it had come from.

"Tell me something, Hart. Precisely what sort of a fool do you take me for?"

"I don't take you for any sort of fool, sir."

"I think you must." He had now conjured up my book from between the pages of his register. "I don't know yet what source you've copied from but rest assured that if you don't tell me I shall find out. You really had the gall to believe you could pass this off as your own work? Well, let me advise you, I do *not* take kindly to plagiarism! Who can tell me what plagiarism means?"

But he was too worked up to allow enough of a pause for anyone to tell him anything.

"I'll tell you what it means. It means copying, often word for word, what somebody else has written. In effect, it means lying. Cheating. Taking low advantage." (Robin Baines – in the middle of the front row – shook his head and tut-tutted.) "Doesn't it, Hart? Isn't that the proper definition? Or have you a slightly different one?" He stared at me and defied me to contradict him.

I was not enjoying this. I said: "I try not to tell lies, sir. I don't believe I ever have." I realized that 'ever' was relative but reckoned they'd all assume that I meant only the past eleven and a half years. "And I don't cheat." (Or was it cheating to have Johnny help me with my maths and try to help him with his English?) I wasn't sure about taking low advantage. "In any case I'm not a plagiarist."

But that was showing off again and it was showing off which had brought me to this present pass. I was assailed by self-distrust.

The silence continued. I faced the master with what I hoped was a total lack of priggishness but merely having that thought go through my mind had possibly reduced my chances of success. Luckily the bell went. It startled me; maybe most of us. Perhaps Mr Hawk-Genn had never known his pupils so reluctant to take their leave. It was the final period of the afternoon.

He had told me, crisply, to remain behind.

"Come over here," he said, when finally the room was empty. "Sit down."

On the teacher's dais he'd placed another chair.

"Please look me in the eye."

I did.

"Ethan, I shall ask you only once." My full name, of course, was written on my book, as well as in his register. "Tell me the truth and we won't say another word about it but if you persist in – "

"Sir, I didn't copy so much as one syllable. I'll swear it on the Bible if you like. But I really do promise."

He sighed.

There followed a long silence.

I hated anyone to imagine I told lies.

"I suppose in that case," he said, "I shall simply have to believe you."

I don't know if it had been the passion in my voice or something that he might have seen in my expression.

"Although – I've got to add – contrary to every conceivable expectation!"

He wiped a hand across his brow.

"But if all this is pure invention...then I don't know what to say." His eye travelled down the first couple of pages. "Clearly

197

it's powerful stuff. Practically uncanny coming from a lad of eleven. Do you mind if I smoke?"

He used his matchbox as an ashtray.

"You *are* only eleven?"

It was ridiculous, I didn't even like to nod. But in any case the question was rhetorical.

"Ethan, where do you get your vocabulary? The adult way you phrase things?"

"Couldn't it be, sir, that I read a lot?" I indicated the essay, added uncomfortably, "I'm sorry about calling the Virgin Mary a bitch and Jesus a – "

"Yes, well, that wasn't you, was it? It was the character you wrote about." He drew lengthily on his Senior Service and gazed for a moment at its burning tip. "What gave you the idea of writing about the Wandering Jew? I gather from Mr Marne that in Scripture at present you're dealing with King David."

I hesitated.

"The Wandering Jew?" I asked.

"Didn't you even know who Cartophilus was?"

"No. The whole thing, you see…the whole thing sort of wrote itself. In a way all I did was hold the pen."

"But obviously you've read about him?"

"I suppose I must have."

"Don't you remember?"

"No, sir, but I think it might have been the radio." Indeed, it almost had to have been; either the radio or some article in a newspaper or magazine, interesting at the time but quickly forgotten. That's what I'd been telling myself over the past few days and on the whole it satisfied me. If I'd ever read a book on the subject, whether five years ago or even twenty-five, surely I'd have realized.

"Your parents talk to you about such things?"

"No, sir."

"And hanging, drawing and quartering…?"

"I know I've read of that. I almost wish I hadn't."

He lifted a shred of tobacco off his tongue.

"And why on earth Guatemala City?"

I shrugged.

"Ethan, has it ever happened to you before, anything of this sort?"

"No, sir."

"Did you tell your parents?"

"No, sir."

"And yet you brought the work to school? Presented it for assessment?"

By now, of course, I was wishing I hadn't. And I didn't even understand what had made me – again, this unconquerable urge to flaunt my cleverness? Or a feeling that, because I'd had no control over what I had written, it might have been intended to be made public.

For if I hadn't brought it to school I could so easily have replaced it. After all, it was only fifty minutes I had lost, except perhaps in one sense – that the exercise had depleted me. I couldn't have written anything else that same evening.

He gave another sigh.

"What worries me, Ethan, is where all these awful images proceed from. Are you in any kind of trouble, or torment? Do you often think about such things as burnings and torture and crucifixions?"

"No, sir. No more than most."

"I'm not sure that at your age you should think of them at all. Ever have bad dreams; anything like that?"

He must have seen me falter.

(Yet at the same time I found it consoling I could still hear a whisper in my mind: *appreciate the present*! You're sitting here in bright September sunlight, in a haze of ever-swirling chalk dust, facing a man who's deeply well-intentioned but ridiculed and unhappy and who'll have killed himself in less than twenty years' time. Don't let this moment pass you by.)

"Well, do you?" he persisted.

"Only one," I said. "Occasionally."

"What do you dream?"

"I dream I'm drowning someone."

"My God. Why? Do you know why?"

I bit my lip but then said carefully: "I once saw a man drown."

199

"And is this the person who figures in your dream?"

"Yes."

"And did you believe *you* were responsible?"

"Partly. But, sir. I'm coping with it. If you told my parents it would only upset them and there'd be nothing they could do."

He stubbed out the cigarette. We watched its thin, expiring gasp of smoke. He almost took another, then looked at me, decided not to.

"I will say this. You certainly have the air of somebody who's coping. Except for…" He tapped the book on his knee.

"And please don't mention it to Mr Saunders."

"No. If I do speak to the headmaster it will only be because I think you have exceptional gifts."

"Because of that one essay? No, sir, you'll soon find out it wasn't typical. Some kind of aberration."

I wasn't being modest. I didn't have exceptional gifts, other than the one I'd received nearly twelve years earlier. Neither in this life nor in my last had I shown any particular aptitude for writing, nor ever possessed the sort of imagination which could reach out beyond the limits of my own experience. (Except to have me flying on a magic carpet and suchlike.) The only card I still had up my sleeve was the shape of things to come – and even then I wasn't sure I could describe it well enough to interest readers unaware it was a bona fide revelation.

"Well, anyway," he said, "we'll see. Whatever happens you mustn't feel pressured."

He stood up and put his smoking materials back in his pocket.

"I suppose you wouldn't like to talk to a doctor about this other thing – this drowning? You don't think it might help?"

"No, sir."

"Fair enough. But if ever for any reason you want to change your mind…" Then, oddly, he held out his hand. As I shook it he said: "Sorry about all the unpleasantness in class. I hope you'll be able to forgive that."

I told him with conviction that it hadn't been his fault. "And you know, sir…in a way I'm even glad this happened."

"Yes, I am, too."

I held the door open and we said goodnight.

11

If only he had died more gently…

A terrifying notion came into my head. In March of 1992 would I be called upon to drown him for a second time?

I couldn't.

I wouldn't.

So I made a decision.

I should have to make sure I was a long way from Nottingham during the days surrounding my birthday.

12

It was the forty-first wedding anniversary of my mother's parents. (My father's were dead.) The year before, we'd had a slap-up celebration at the Golden Hind but today would be a somewhat quieter affair: Nana and Gramps and my mother's widowed sister and unmarried brother and our three selves. Also, it would be a daytime, not an evening, do. The anniversary this year fell on a Sunday.

In fact, it was to be no more than a glorified Sunday lunch, made special by having chicken in place of a joint and white wine instead of water. The chickens, two of them, were to be eaten cold, with salad and new potatoes, because it was July and for the past week the weather had been sultry. In a bucket in the bathroom – on a bed of melting ice beneath a deepening, gentle sea – the four bottles of wine clinked pleasantly.

That morning, while putting out the breakfast things, my mother was laughing but prepared to panic.

"Do you realize they'll be here in three hours and I've hardly done a thing? Such an idiot! What *could* I have been thinking of, yesterday?"

"But yesterday you made the cakes and the trifle and you and Ethan enjoyed your picnic in the woods. You weren't just standing idle."

"Thank you. So I've now got half the pudding prepared and maybe half the tea. Oh, wonderful! What about all those potatoes which need to be scrubbed, the salad which needs to be washed, the chickens which need to be cooked, the nut roast which needs to be seen to? What about the table which needs to be laid, the eggs which need to be beaten, the chickens which need to be carved? Bethel, remind me, please, what have you done with that magic wand?"

"You know," said my father solemnly, "I think they could have done with you ten years ago as Mr Churchill's speech-writer. Have we ever heard such rhetoric?"

"There's also the present to be wrapped, the card to be written. I'd also like to have a bath and wash my hair and spend a bit of time on getting *myself* ready. There are probably dozens of other little also's that I've overlooked."

"I don't suppose his trifle would compare with yours, either."

"I wish you'd be serious for a moment."

"You know you'll get through it all just fine." He lightly smacked her bottom as she leant across the table to position the Post-Toasties. "You know you have a highly domesticated husband and at times a semi-domesticated son – "

"Yes, I do have a domesticated son, thank God."

"I shall ignore that. And after all it's only your mum and dad and brother and sister. It isn't the King and Queen. *Then* you might have had reason to worry."

"It isn't funny," said my mother. "I happen to believe I should try to treat my family as if it *were* the King and Queen. And if you hadn't…" (she glanced in my direction) "kept us awake last night…reading…I'd have been up a couple of hours ago, possibly three, getting on as busily as I had meant to. It's all very well for you to make jokes." She herself was half joking. But only half.

Even at fourteen, even with the accumulated experience of – give or take – seventy years, I found it oddly disturbing to know my parents had a sex life. I ought to have been pleased, and in a way I was, and yet it was by no means as simple as seventy years should have made it. And I wondered if Dad saw a suggestion of this in my expression.

202

"You're very quiet, my son."

"Just thinking."

"That's my boy, and don't I know what you're thinking about! Why, about how you're going to take over and solve all your mother's little problems." He pinched my cheek in imitation of Alec Guinness's Fagin. "*Jewel!*" he said. "*Treasure!*" he said. "*Angel!*" he said. Three pinches in total, although I tried to duck away. "Now all you've got to do, young prince, is keep your reputation alive for just one more morning, earn yourself three bob into the bargain and let your mum retire to beautify herself, put on her regalia, practise her curtseys…and for a further two bob let me have my own bath in peace and read the News of the World in time to get that scandalized look off my face before our royal visitors arrive!"

Today, though, his humour was falling flat. Inwardly – and uncharacteristically – I railed at the awkwardness of life. I'd had literally years in which to remember the importance of this date and I had actually only remembered it while listening to the crystal set less than thirty minutes earlier. Listening to, of all things, the weather forecast!

"Dad, this is rotten. I was going to tell you both. I've got to go out."

"Oh, Ethan!" cried my mother, and now the last sign of her being able to laugh had totally vanished. "Oh, no, but you can't! I've been relying on you! Where have you got to go?"

"Aylesbury."

"*Aylesbury!*"

This wasn't just down the road; it was about fifteen miles from Amersham. And although the train service wasn't bad, even on Sundays, there'd also be a lengthy bike ride at the other end. There was no way I could hope to get home before the arrival of our guests.

"Son, you can't," said my father. "That's all there is to it. Who were you going with? Well, whoever it is, give them a ring and explain that your mother needs you."

"I can't."

"Of course you can."

203

"I mean, I'm not going with anybody and there's no way I can put it off."

"You aren't making much sense."

"Dad, I have to see someone."

"Who?"

"I'm afraid I don't know her name."

My father looked at my mother.

"No, it isn't like that," I said. "It's – "

"Ethan, frankly I don't care what it's like. Not now. The thing is – you're not going."

"I've got to."

"Sorry."

"But I shall have to, whether or not *you* allow me." This was miserable. At fourteen I was already much taller than my father.

"Ethan, be careful. I feel tired. I'm not in any mood to mess about. Walk out of here this morning and you need never bother to return."

"Bethel!" screamed my mother. "No, obviously he doesn't mean that, Ethan. But all the same – "

"I'm sorry, Mum. Dad. I really am. But look, I'll make a start on the potatoes. And I'll be fast. They may not take much more than fifteen minutes."

My mother looked as if she were about to cry. "No, you haven't eaten any breakfast. Whatever happens, I want you to sit down again and eat your breakfast."

"Yes, sit down again and eat your breakfast," said my father. "And while you're doing so, you can tell us what this is all about!"

But I didn't sit down. Now that he was struggling to recover his temper I became aware of losing mine. I, too, was feeling tired; I, too, had been having orgasms. (I didn't much like the thought of Zack knowing, nor indeed my Granny and Granddad, but the drive at times was just too strong.) I had lost my temper before, of course, by no means the saintly individual I had hoped and prayed to be, yet at least it hadn't occurred often and at least I'd always done my best to make amends. Each time it happened, though, I hated it – hated it.

"No, I can't tell you. You've simply got to accept my word that it's important. I'd have thought by now you might have learnt to trust me."

I could have said worse. I was relieved I didn't actually say, "Sometimes I think you're apt to take advantage," because I knew my parents depended on me for dozens of things that fourteen-year-olds didn't normally get asked to do (from mending fuses, replacing washers, cleaning windows, to wallpapering and painting, and digging the allotment) and I was really glad this was the case – in theory I wanted to be made use of, always, and as fully as possible – but nevertheless I wished I could sometimes get round things by resorting to a meaningless white lie, the sort that hurt nobody and simply eased away the complications.

"All right! Go off on your little jaunt," said my father.

"It isn't a little jaunt and I can't see why there has to be this huge to-do about it, why you're overreacting as you are. As you said, it's only *family* for heaven's sake, and all of them would be only too happy to pitch in if necessary. I know they would. Honestly, Dad! I *know* it!"

But by this time my mother was actually crying. On the one hand I was tempted to put my arms about her but on the other I felt it was all so unnecessary; and in any case my father was there to put his arms about her.

He called after me. "Next time someone says how wonderful you are, I think we may have to reconsider!"

"Yes, I'm sure," I shouted back. "Why don't you tell them how you always like to take advantage?" I had to have the last word.

Already, though, as I was cycling down to the station, teeth uncleaned, hair unbrushed (and this was a day we'd all been looking forward to), the tears were welling up in my own eyes; and would have been easier to hold back if only they'd been due to frustration. But they weren't. Inevitably they'd been brought on by remorse and shame. I should have handled it far better – that whole silly scene which had sprung out of nowhere! If only I had been less tired! If only I had been more prepared! I would have liked to ride back right then and there and throw my arms

205

around the two of them and confess I'd spoken wholly out of turn and without having meant a word of it. But I hadn't got the time and, besides, what could I have offered that would have made the situation any more acceptable? I wished I could have spoken to Zack.

I often wished I could have spoken to Zack. Zack, whom I had seen only once since infancy. And even that had been four years ago.

I'd been wandering on my own round Woolworths, or, more precisely, standing at one of the long counters looking a little aimlessly at cigarette cards.

"I hope this isn't how you normally spend your time," he'd said. It was as though we saw each other every day; there was absolutely no need for formalities or catching up.

"Why? What should I be doing?" Then I put my arms around his legs for a moment and held my head against his stomach.

"Reading something improving, not gazing at pictures of Susan Hayward and Jean Kent."

"I'm always reading something improving." But my grumble was as counterfeit as the reproach it was in answer to.

"Like what, at the moment?"

"*Confessions of St Augustine.*"

"And before that?"

"Bertrand Russell."

"Where do you find such things as *Confessions of St Augustine* and Bertrand Russell?"

"There's a secondhand bookshop in – " But then I saw his face and realized he knew perfectly well.

"And I think if you were genuinely enterprising," he said, "you might have learnt to hide those gentlemen behind dust jackets borrowed from *The Famous Five* or *Just William.*"

"Oh, you do, do you? *William the Showman*, actually, and *Swallows and Amazons*. But Mr Marshall in the bookshop believes I've got the best-read family in the whole of Bucks and that there's always one of them celebrating a birthday. He feels sorry for me and lets me have things for practically nothing. Oh! I've suddenly got an idea you may know Mr Marshall! If you do, please tell him how his kindness unfailingly touches me. Tell him I shall never stop feeling enormously grateful to him."

"Point taken. How are you enjoying your childhood in general?"

We were walking slowly round the various counters.

"Oh, it's brilliant!"

"Tell me."

"I don't know how. Do you want a list of things?"

"Why not?"

"Well…" Where did I begin? A sense of wonder had gradually been restored to me, a boy's-eye view of the world that noticed as if for the first time the patterning on a snail's shell or the inside of a foxglove. It had been fun being pushed along in one's buggy, having rides on shoulders, owning a tricycle, scooter, roller skates – electric train set – wind-up gramophone. It had been fun to stay again with grandparents, riding in an open car, eating honey from the comb, scattering grain for their Rhode Island Reds, going mushroom picking in the dawn. It had been fun being taken to children's plays and circuses and pantomimes, and knowing that this time one had to hang onto everything one could, since it was all so transient and precious and unrepeatable. (Essentially unrepeatable.) But it wasn't easy in a few minutes, and without warning, to pick out the thousand contributing ingredients. "I honestly can't do it justice."

"But if you're not even going to try I shall think it very feeble. And feel truly disappointed."

I needed no greater incentive. As well he knew.

"Okay, then. Completely at random. One's first glimpse of the sea out of a train window. Birthday parties. The smell of a grocer's shop. Tobogganing on a tin tray. Treasure hunts. Riding on a pram base. Running after car tyres. Playing rounders. Storming the enemy's camp, or castle, on summer evenings in the dark. I think this all sounds very naff."

Zack was riffling through some sheet music. "It's 1947," he said. "I don't know the meaning of that word."

"But naff or not…it's been phenomenal!"

"And what about your looks?"

"My looks? Oh, fine. Yes." But somehow they didn't seem so important any longer. Maybe they would come to do so as I grew older and got interested in girls, or maybe it was the usual story of someone wanting what he hadn't got and not reflecting too much on what he already had. But at least I liked to think of meat and fish and peanut butter slowly transforming themselves into muscle. (I hadn't yet become a vegetarian. Why *not*, I was to wonder later.)

"I note you've made no mention of the poor, the maimed, the halt and the blind."

"What about them?"

"Renewed opportunities for the helping thereof."

"Don't mock," I said. "It may not amount to much but I do try."

"I wasn't really mocking."

"I'm only a little boy of ten. Unfortunately there are limits to what people will accept from little boys of ten."

"You could run errands. Read newspapers. Make lovely cups of tea." He smiled, spread his hands, then added, "But never mind. You'll get older. I give you my word on that."

"Big-Hearted Arthur," I said.

He turned from his desultory inspection of assorted loose biscuits and looked at me closely. "Why do you say that?"

I was cock-a-hoop.

"Oh, Zack, you surprise me. I thought you knew everything. And you haven't even heard of Arthur Askey!"

"Ah, right. 'Hello, playmates'... 'Bzz, bzz, bzz, bzz, honey bee, honey bee...'"

"Too late," I said complacently. "You can't bear to think I caught you out, that's your trouble."

"You jumped-up specimen! Don't break a lance with me!" He smiled as he ruffled my hair.

I'd never met that expression. "Is it derived from jousting?"

"Which in turn derives from *jouster*, Old French. To fight on horseback."

"That's something I'd like to take up as soon as I can."

"Jousting?"

"Ha-ha! Yes, and fencing – why not? But what I really meant, as I *think* you must have known, was horse-riding."

"I agree. It's an imperative. It's also great fun."

"Along with polo and squash and boxing and…" I laughed. "Zack? Do you ever get the feeling I've a lot to make up for?"

When I'd said that, I had been talking only in terms of wasted time, but ever since then the phrase had intermittently reverberated, and taken on a different connotation.

"I've got a lot to make up for," I thought now, as I cycled down the hill towards the station.

Once more, when he had gone, it struck me that I had spoken largely of inanities (no doubt carried away by the sheer exhilaration of seeing him again – *very* schoolboyish) and still hadn't alluded to the thing which really cut to the heart of my being: my unshakable guilt over Brian Douglas. It seemed there might be a basic malfunction in that part of my memory, self-regulating as soon as Zack had gone. But it also seemed, whether I alluded to it or not, that he must surely know. Yet why in that case didn't he help? God surely knew, as well – why didn't *he* help? The prayer for Brian Douglas – and for myself – was constantly in my thoughts and yet my burden remained intact (the cross I had to bear, as Miss Evers at the library would have phrased it, an expression I abominated with a force that simply wasn't rational and could sometimes make me shudder). The nightmare continued as before, though not so frequently – only seven times during this past year. It was enough. I didn't have to be asleep to remember its content.

I got to Aylesbury at half-past-ten and then cycled to the village where Major Shipman lived. The Major was one of my father's bosses. He and Mr King owned not only the Regent but, in Chesham, the Embassy and the Astoria, as well as other cinemas in nearby towns. I had met him and his wife on several occasions, received good presents from them over each of the past six Christmases, as well as from Mr and Mrs King – Dad had come back from the war in September 1945 and had almost at once been taken on as the Regent's manager – but I'd never visited the Shipmans at their home, and indeed it wasn't them I'd come to see today. (As a matter of fact, I knew that on the

209

following morning the Major would be calling on us and bringing a tinful of his wife's meringues.) Luckily, though, the way to the village had been decently signposted.

I hoped to heaven that the Shipmans had only one set of neighbours nearby, for if there were houses all about, then my job would be a lot more difficult, as well as considerably more embarrassing. I began to sweat as I cycled and this wasn't entirely due to the humidity.

It was fortunate, however, that the land wasn't hilly. If it had been, my Aertex shirt would have felt still damper than it already did.

It was also fortunate that, yes, Apple Tree House was the only dwelling in any direction that could have been called close to Shipman's Farm. But my heart was showing no signs of slowing down in gratitude as I pushed open the front gate and walked along the narrow path between rows of neatly planted vegetables, rows prettily interspersed with pinks and marigolds and lavender. Perhaps the apple trees – or at least apple *tree* – were in the back garden. The house itself was unpretentious: redbrick, small and functional: and looked more in keeping with its vegetables than with the high-sounding name picked out for it.

A man of about fifty answered my knock. He was in his shirt and braces and had a crumpled sheet of the Sunday paper dangling from one hand.

I wished him good morning and asked if his wife were home. I knew I sounded polite and middle-class and stupid.

"No, what do you want her for?" His eyes appeared to narrow. "If you're trying to sell her something, lad…?"

I shook my head. But instinct had told me not to deal with anyone other than the woman of the house, not to blunt my message by talking either to the husband or the son. In her absence, though, I wondered if maybe I *should* talk to the son.

"Not here, either. If you must know, they've gone to church, the pair of them. Another hour, round about." Happily he didn't again ask what I wanted, nor offer to take a message. I settled myself on the ground outside their gate and leant back against the low wall of the garden.

He'd been right about the timing but wrong about their coming back together, and because she was alone I wasn't sure until the last moment that this was the woman whom I had to speak to.

Yet what was encouraging, she gave me a smile as she drew near. "Tired? You haven't got a puncture?"

I scrambled to my feet.

"Could I ask you something?" I didn't like not knowing what to call her. And *ask* sounded better than *tell*.

"A glass of water? Certainly, my love. Might even find a bit of squash to go in it. My goodness, it is hot, though." With the screwed-up handkerchief already in her hand she wiped at her forehead. "Real close and muggy. Full of all these horrid gnats and midges." She inspected her handkerchief and maybe saw that she'd put paid to one or two of them.

"There's going to be a storm," I said.

"Good thing. That's what we need all right, something to clear the air." She had now turned in at the gate. "Mind you, we expected one yesterday, and the day before that, too. Will you come in with me or would you prefer to wait out here?"

"No, I know there is. Going to be one. A storm. In an hour or so. That's the reason why I've come." I was conscious of not having started very well.

She looked at me uncertainly.

I didn't hesitate.

"There's going to be a storm and your cottage will be hit by lightning. And your son will be killed if he's lying down."

She didn't say anything.

"I'm sorry if I put it bluntly. But I didn't know how else to tell you."

In a moment she recovered her composure. Or her power of speech.

"Listen, love, you can't go about frightening folks like that – making up wild stories – I think you'd better be off without that glass of lemonade…as a bit of a punishment, you see. You didn't look the type of boy who'd go in for silly pranks like that."

She turned her back on me then and started up the path. I ran after her, caught her by the arm. The warmth and moisture of her flesh was disconcerting.

"You've got to believe what I'm telling you!"

"No, I think I've got to do nothing of the sort!" Angrily, she shook my hand away. "Now I don't know if this is *your* idea or whether you've been put up to it but I'm not having it, do you hear, and so you'd better be off before I call my old man out here. Or before I telephone the police, which is more what you deserve. And if you ever dare to return…well…" She clearly couldn't think what might make a sufficiently awful threat.

"Please listen. Please! I know what I'm talking about."

"Oh, I haven't got time for this. Already late and if lunch isn't on the table by one I'll have a sulky husband for the rest of the afternoon. I can't be doing with that."

"And if it is on the table by one," I said, "you'll have a dead son for the rest of your life. Would that please you better?"

"Colin!" she called.

"Listen. How do you think I know that your son always goes to lie on his bed immediately after Sunday lunch?"

"Colin!" And then for the first time since I'd revealed the purpose of my visit, she looked at me with more curiosity than annoyance. "How *do* you know?"

"But it's right, isn't it? He does always go upstairs to lie down after lunch?"

"Are you a friend of Billy's? No, you couldn't be, I've never seen you. Who have you been talking to?"

"Nobody. I promise. But your house is going to be struck by lightning shortly after two and Billy's room is right beneath the point where it will strike. His bed – moments later – will be nothing but a mound of ashes. Whether or not he's on it will be largely up to you."

The front door opened.

"Oh, there you are," the man said. "I thought I heard you call. I was on the lav." I remembered – as I didn't always – to offer up a thank-you. "That boy still here? What does he want, for God's sake?"

"Nothing. Nothing. I'll be in in half a jiffy."

212

"Well, it's getting late," the man observed, with noticeable truculence. "Don't give him any money, if that's what he's after."

He returned inside but left the door open.

"How do you *know*?" she whispered, urgently.

"Just do."

"That's not an answer."

"I mean, I have this… I sometimes know that things are going to happen."

"Like what?"

"But that's got nothing to – " Yet then I thought I would never see her again; could it really matter if I broke the rules for once? "Oh, like the King is going to die next February. Like on the same day Princess Elizabeth is crowned we'll get the news they've conquered Everest. Like, in the year after the coronation, Roger Bannister is going to run the four-minute mile…" It was surely important I should try to impress her.

"And like someone who'll never make the headlines is going to be struck by lightning in an unknown village at the back of nowhere. Why?" She added in the same near monotone: "You don't even know our name, do you?"

I said: "It isn't much I'm asking. Only that you delay your lunch a bit. What have you got to lose by it?"

"Oh, you haven't met my husband!" Yet at least she was now smiling faintly. "The name," she said, "is Cooper."

"Thank you, Mrs Cooper."

"And you? What's yours?"

There came the initial clap of thunder. We instantly looked up.

"So will you make lunch late?"

She nodded. "I may be as touched as you. But whether you're touched or not I can see you believe in what you're saying."

"Yes, absolutely. So if it's the only way, you'll have to turn the clocks back, won't you? I can assure you, even if he twigs, the sulks won't last for very long." I smiled, then picked up my bike from the grass verge. It occurred to me I should have been a recognized authority on that – on turning the clocks back.

"You haven't told me your name," she said.

213

"But remember. You've promised. And you'll soon thank God you did."

I waved as I cycled off. Turned my head just once and she was still standing there. I felt the first big drop of rain.

By the time I got home I was soaked. Nana and Gramps, Aunt Gwen and Uncle Max were all sipping sherry in the front room.

"Ah, there you are, you bad lad," said Nana – invariably more stern than Granny used to be. "You must go immediately and make your peace with your mother. She's highly displeased with you."

"And so's your father," said Gramps, cheerfully.

"And so's your venerated uncle," said Max, "who's absolutely starving. And so's your sadly disreputable aunt – who always kowtows to the winning team. All-round disgrace. I wouldn't be in your shoes, not for anything."

Gwen hugged me like he had, however. ("My goodness, how *wet* you are!" It could have been a bad moment.) "But I'll come with you into the kitchen and see if I can't cushion the blows to some extent. Max, why don't you come, too, and lend us a bit of moral support?"

"And bear in mind," said Gramps, "that none of this will matter a hundred years hence! In the meantime, we'll try to save you a glass of sherry."

The only deeply distressing thing about it all – I could so vividly recall the last occasion. My mother had certainly got up late, just as she had this morning, but she'd been singing as the two of us scraped the potatoes and set the dining-room table, as we polished the glasses and shone up the silverware and made the napkins into little hats (although I couldn't remember that I'd done much more than that – nor, I think, had Dad). And when everybody had turned up early in Uncle Max's car, we'd all stood merrily about the kitchen, sherry glasses in hand, my mum laughing as much as anyone at the signs of chaos in the sink. Nana and Max, anyway, had briskly disposed of most of it, with dishcloth and tea towel respectively. Gramps had endeavoured to whisk the cream; but been told he hadn't got the wrist for it. And Gwen had been separating the eggs for the mayonnaise instead of pushing protectively in front of me as we went into the

214

kitchen and declaring as she did so, "The return of the Prodigal Son! We've *all* been telling him off! You should just have heard Mother, even the grownups paled! She made him promise – "

But her sister – Gwen's – hardly appeared to be listening. "Look at you, Ethan! Oh, for heaven's sake! Go and get out of those wet things! Dry your hair! And I'd like to know what time you happen to call *this*."

I glanced at my watch. It was shortly after two.

Yet although the action had been almost automatic she thought I was being facetious. "Oh, I've a good mind to send you straight to bed, or get your father to. You've thoroughly ruined my day. I hope you realize that. You've thoroughly ruined my whole day – and I was so much looking forward to it!"

*

"Yes, the goodness of the Lord!" said Major Shipman the next morning, stroking meringue crumbs from his white moustache and gazing reflectively into his teacup. "Yes, indeed!… Don't know why he'd concern himself with Billy Cooper, mind, who's always been a bit of a ne'er-do-well, besides at times not seeming altogether there. Still, might mend. Might mend. The ways of Providence are often somewhat strange. (And, poor lad, one's only too happy, of course, for his deliverance.) But makes you think, doesn't it? Miracles and all that."

"Who was the boy on the bike?"

"No idea. Vanished into thin air. Could have been a ghost – all sorts of stories going around. Mavis Cooper said she asked him twice but never got an answer."

He paused.

"Apparently the poor old King's going to die next year. And Everest is going to be climbed on the same day as the coronation. And somebody called something is going to run a mile in…well, she wasn't quite certain. Still, have to see, won't we? You been thinking of running the mile, young-fellow-me-lad?"

215

Before, it had been all long faces, and condolences by proxy. Today it was mystified speculation, and shaken heads, and gaiety and laughter.

13

"I suppose you feel proud of yourself?"

I thought he meant smug. I had smugness on the brain. I knew I showed a tendency towards it, even though I also knew I had no reason to. It made a perennial and insidious enemy. "Rid me of it, then." Not that I thought he would – or even at heart wanted him to. I wasn't a puppet. I had autonomy. I realized it was a battle I should have to fight alone. I didn't even say it.

He'd just got on. There was always a long wait at Rickmansworth while they replaced the engine – the electric engine which had brought us out from Baker Street. For the rest of the way we should be steam-driven.

I was aware there was little point in asking him why he'd been at Rickmansworth.

Apart from myself, the carriage had been empty. It was supposedly a non-smoker and yet it still smelled of tobacco – the smell of tobacco and the dust of ages would live on forever in its patterned green upholstery. My initial exclamation of delight had instantly subsided, along with my grin of welcome. He was angry and I hadn't yet seen him angry. His mood was symbolized, and nearly given shape to, by the darkness of his overcoat. Although it was the same period of spring as the one in which I'd met him nineteen years previously – even a day or two later – the weather continued wintry, with reports of snow still falling in the Highlands. It was true I'd seen him all in black before but it hadn't been a reflection of the way he felt. His uncovered blond hair again made me think of a flame, yet this time he put me in mind not of a beacon but of a black candle at a witches' sabbath.

"Don't be cute," he snarled. 'Snarled' is clearly an exaggeration, even if in spirit it didn't seem like one. There'd

216

been no smile, no form of greeting, just the staccato delivery of that first question. Or statement. *I suppose you feel proud of yourself?*

He sat huddled in a corner – as far from me, it felt, as he could possibly get – for I had been sitting in the one diagonally opposite when he got on, and he had probably assumed that I would stay there.

So in the end I did, suddenly too proud to move in closer when I knew I wasn't wanted.

"Why have I made you so angry? What is it I've done?"

"I'd prefer it, please, if *you* would tell *me*!"

I held onto the broad leather window strap – gripped it tightly – without even realizing I did so.

"I've been getting a bit above myself. I know I can hide it from others but that isn't quite the point, is it?"

"Don't be dense. I'm well aware that you've been doing your utmost to get on top of that."

His acknowledgement of this – under such circumstances – was worth more than he realized. (Except, of course, it wasn't.)

I faltered.

"Is it sex?"

"No, damn it, it is not sex."

I searched my memory for a sin I hadn't recognized as big enough to provoke this present outburst.

"Zack, I don't know. I'm sorry. Is it lack of charity? Lack of tolerance? Lack of understanding? Is it laziness? Self-absorption? I'd hoped I was improving."

"What about basic dishonesty?"

I stared at him.

"And you don't even know!" he sneered. "To be dishonest and know it is one thing. But when a person's principles are so non-existent that he doesn't even realize…! Oh, yes, go on, cry," he said. "That's bound to answer everything!"

Yet for once they were indeed tears of anger, in no way of remorse or shame. And I thought that his referring to them like this (they hadn't even overflowed) seemed not merely unnecessary, but shabby and contemptible.

"All right, Zack. I don't know what I've done. I suppose I've been kidding myself but everybody kids himself about something. That isn't such a crime."

His look became sardonic.

"And if you want to talk about basic dishonesty," I continued, "in fact you could say my whole life is basically dishonest."

"Interesting," he said.

"But that's your fault as much as mine. I even think *you* could be more dishonest than me. It was never part of our agreement that I shouldn't just go my own way, lie, cheat, steal, waste my time – exploit my situation – do whatever I felt like. It was never a condition I'd behave."

"You wouldn't consider that great gifts carry their own conditions? Their own responsibilities?"

"If they do, it was a bit deceitful not to point that out at the beginning."

"Nonsense. You should have been aware of it."

"No. Any honest businessman shows his customer the small print."

"Unless he prefers him to write his own."

"What! Write his own small print? My goodness! Optimism!"

"Yes," he said.

"What does *yes* mean?"

"That then he'll always choose his customer with extra special care, won't he? Or at least – will do his best to!" He emphasized those last few words in such a way as to denote, presumably, his own abysmal failure.

"My God," I murmured, "you're such a bastard!" I could only think about how hard I'd tried – how very, very hard – over the whole of the past nineteen years.

I received an icy stare.

"It seems another birthday," he said, "hasn't brought any very marked advance in wisdom."

"That's rich. I don't know how old *you* are – or should I perhaps say ancient? – but you're obviously feeling it wasn't all that wise to have picked on me in the first place. I'm sorry I've proved such a disappointment. I'm sorry I've buggered up all your lovely, fine, do-it-yourself small print."

218

I turned my head towards the window, let go of the leather strap almost before I'd become aware of holding it; saw the harsh red marks it had made upon my palm and fingers. I stared across the track at a poster for Ovaltine – the healthy country life it represented, the rewards of a good day's honest toil, the peaceful rosy future. The tears spilled from my eyes and now I let them run.

Idiot! And you had thought your worst problem had been complacency: complacency freshly engendered by two days spent in London distributing largesse – almost the very shirt off your back, why don't you say, although in fact it had only been your new padded mackintosh. But at the bottom of Villiers Street there was an all-night coffee stand where I had met a tramp whose teeth had actually been chattering. I hadn't meant to give away my clothes but the relevant shops had all been shut and if I'd simply handed him the money...

I'd been able to buy him some food, however, plus a bottle of beer and a packet of cigarettes. Afterwards I'd done this for several others I'd found stretched out along the Embankment and sheltering under doorways in the Strand, although it was mainly money I'd been planning to distribute. At the start of the evening I'd had nearly five hundred pounds tucked into various pockets.

And with that much money on me, plus a burning desire to be in one of those places where it might accomplish the most good, yes I had certainly been like a young Lord Bountiful bestowing charity and getting a buzz out of doing so. But I was deriving this buzz more because I genuinely wanted to help than because I thought it turned me into such a great fellow. And wasn't it better to do it even for mixed reasons than not to do it at all? My last life had been so completely wasted I didn't regard it as astonishing that, given the opportunity, I should go all out trying to justify this one. Who wouldn't? Okay, I was plainly having setbacks when I'd thought that I was making progress. But nevertheless...

Though at the moment, it seemed, smugness wasn't my only problem. Self-pity was pushing its way in.

Then there came a jolt which signified that the new engine had finally been connected. I was damned if I'd feel self-pity. I blew my nose and wiped my eyes and turned my head back. He appeared hardly to have moved.

"All right, Zack. I'm sorry. I don't know where I've gone wrong – I mean, not in any vast and catastrophic way – and I can see why that on its own should make you angry. All I can say is, if you'll tell me where the trouble lies and if it isn't too late, I'd like to begin again. Please."

"No, isn't too late." But the steeliness of his expression hadn't changed.

"Then tell me how I've been dishonest."

"I said no. I want you to tell *me*."

"You can't be talking of the thousand pounds I won?" Over half of it had gone to charities that dealt with famine in the Third World.

"Can't I?"

"Well, you never suggested that I shouldn't gamble."

"And am I suggesting it now?"

"But then what…?"

Yet, looking at him, suddenly I saw.

"You're saying that of course it wasn't a gamble?"

"But more importantly, what are *you* saying?"

"No. It wasn't. You're right. Yet it didn't occur to me that I was doing wrong. In fact it seemed…almost a heaven-sent opportunity." I smiled. Wanly.

He didn't. He didn't smile at all.

"And should it have occurred to you?"

"Yes. I suppose it should."

"Suppose?"

"I still can't help thinking you're overreacting."

"You've always thought that *everyone* was overreacting."

"But was it so wrong? All's fair in love and war. And with bookmakers – "

"Don't give me that crap."

"I was merely going to say that with bookmakers – "

"All's fair in love and war."

"Zack. It's only an expression. I wouldn't stand by it."

"You just did."

I tugged at one of my earlobes and decided I shouldn't try to defend myself. I looked over at the picture of a mother and toddler bouncing a beach ball at Rhyl: *Fine sands – bracing air – beautiful scenery*. On the other side of a small central mirror there was a father as well: paddling and splashing with his wife and two children at Scarborough. I couldn't let him get away with it.

"And anyway, Zack, you'd had almost a year in which to prevent me. Surely you knew why I was saving up so hard?"

He must have done. Twelve months before, hearing of someone who had done well on the Grand National, I was suddenly reminded that the following year – when I was working at the Times Bookshop in Wigmore Street, instead of, as now, being on vacation from King's College Cambridge – that in 1956 I had won a few pounds on a horse called E.S.B. He was practically the only horse whose name I remembered, for he was the only horse on which I'd ever won. Definitely not as a result of studying form but because a friend and I had spent a coffee-break that March inventing middle names for our colleagues: one of these being Ernie Blick, a lad in the stockroom so po-faced he inevitably became Ernie *Sunshine* Blick. It was an adolescent game but for some reason those initials stayed with me long after all the others had faded. I had greatly liked this friend, Kenneth, and as a matter of fact only that same afternoon, my mission having been completed, I'd called in at the bookshop and chatted with him for fifteen very pleasant minutes, initially of course about books, but then about other seemingly unrelated topics including the Grand National. It had been extremely pleasant, yes, but rather melancholy too. I should have liked to speak to Mrs Morton, who had once said when she'd heard me singing from the *Noel Coward Song Book* (there was a copy of it visible this afternoon – I saw it on the central table; could it be the selfsame copy I had leafed through and sung from previously?), had once said that my tenor voice was charming – she herself, between the wars, had sung in operetta and she had chosen the word with kindness and with care – and who, even as I watched her single out *Gone With the Wind* for her present customer, had already, in a sense, been dead for countless years; should have

221

liked to speak to Mrs Morton and Jenny Nyman and to Anthea, Annette, Rosemary and many others. So in the end I felt a little wistful as I walked towards the station, for it had been a good time in my life, full of hope, appreciated not simply in retrospect but even as I'd lived it. While talking to Kenneth I had as usual tried to take in every detail, would have loved to see the small canteen again, hear the echo of our laughter and our silly conversations (I particularly remembered a discussion concerning men's body hair – sparked off by my own arms and William Holden's chest), would have loved once more to visit the quaint Victorian lavatory with its wooden seat, flowered porcelain and air of cocooned and comfortable solidity. Also, while speaking to him, I'd grown conscious suddenly of straining to glimpse some spark of bewildered recognition in his eyes, as I thought there might once have been in my mother's outside Warwick House, this probable absurdity being heightened, of course, by my catching sight of a salesman whom I didn't know and who had presumably been taken on in place of me. Kenneth had sometimes come my way in the evening, travelling on the Met as far as Harrow, but it was too much to hope that tonight would be one of those times for visiting his grandmother. I thought about returning to the shop before the end of my vacation and after some further congenial talk casually suggesting we should meet. But why? We had lost touch, anyway, after the shop had finally closed – someone thought he might have emigrated – and when at a later date I'd tried to track him down again I was no more successful. Perhaps I shouldn't have returned at all. It was one of the few moments I had felt something close to regret for my Nottingham decision, and it hardly helped that I knew it was illogical.

Now, scarcely an hour later, I was experiencing a similar uncertainty, a similar illusory pang. It occurred to me I must be tired. "Surely you knew why I was saving up so hard?"

"Of course I did. It was a test. I kept hoping that you might come to your senses."

"It was only – "

"Ethan, don't you dare!"

I'd been going to say robbing the rich to feed the poor. Until a moment earlier I hadn't even thought of it, not remotely, as being *any* form of robbing.

"If you'd got to me sooner I could at least have given the money back."

He made no answer. Quite possibly he couldn't think of one but this didn't dispose me to feel that I had scored.

"Anyhow. Just bear in mind," he said, "that there are tests and tests. This isn't the end of everything. Catastrophic, remember, was *your* word, not mine. "

"What do I have to do to be forgiven?"

His tone appeared to be lightening. "Well, for one thing, not catch your death of cold. You'd better take *this* overcoat. I think in all likelihood you're going to need it more than me."

The idea of possessing something of Zack's gave me pleasure in itself, but the idea of his presenting it immediately after such a very low point in our relationship made it even more valuable. I wondered if that was why he'd worn it.

"What do I tell them, then, at home?"

"That you were given it. That it was warmer than yours. That you then gave your own away."

"Is this another test?" I asked.

14

Again…no mention of Brian Douglas.

But a way of dealing with my guilt was beginning to suggest itself. It was outlandish, the sort of inspired lunacy that only came at night and guaranteed you got no sleep. It certainly brought no other guarantee; not even a clear picture of what I would be aiming for. If I spoke of it to anyone but Zack I should either be avoided or sent to a psychiatrist. Yet I knew it to be right – it was as if something had gone click inside my soul – and years before I could even start to put it into practice it was already obsessing me. I believed I had been shown the outline of my life's work: as nebulous as a figure glimpsed through fog but just as certain to take solid shape.

And it was all due to Brian Douglas.

15

And when Abram was ninety years old and nine, the Lord appeared to Abram, and said unto him, walk before me, and be thou perfect, I will make thee exceeding fruitful, and kings shall come out of thee.

At ninety-nine? Not bad. Do you think the Lord might have similar objectives for me? (But all I really want is this: that he'll just get off my bleeding back!) Ninety-nine is currently my own age. Recently, someone asked when I had last got it up. Salacious old bugger. Naturally I wasn't going to tell him I couldn't remember, must be thirty years ago at least. That's an added grievance, of course. Having all this time and still being deprived of a good fuck.

Not that longevity would be all it's cracked up to be even with a rampant cock. Well, not for me. Can't speak for Abram!

You get so tired. That's the thing. You've had enough. You want to put an end to it. Rest. It isn't just the aches and pains – and, yes, I really do mean pains – the heart attacks, the strokes, the rheumatism, arthritis. The cataracts, the deafness. Non-stop wheezing. And it isn't just seeing your mates drop dead all round you, in truth I never had many. It's everything. It's the damned monotony, it's the damned exertion. It's the damned business of having to get up in the morning and then having to go to bed at night – though knowing you won't get any sleep. It's the damned business of having to fill up all the time in between, find food, rely on people who aren't reliable, people you'd rather spit in the eye of, not have to feel obliged to. We Jews are supposed to venerate old age but I know there's always someone ready to snicker behind my back, make fun of me, point me out as a freak and an outcast. A leper. I'd rather be a leper – much. You *die*, of leprosy. Your days are numbered. Me, I don't even know if my *centuries* are numbered! My God, before long I'll be reduced to crawling about on my hands and knees – with creaks in every joint, agony in every movement – seeing nothing, hearing nothing and stinking to the high heavens. *That*'s not the way I was brought up. Hygiene was always important, who wants to stink? So when you get right down to it it's not only the tedium and the pain and the exhaustion, it's all those never-ending *small* humiliations. When you're doomed to eternity how are you meant to trim your toenails?

Too often now I think about my childhood. When I was young I had no time for either of my parents, any of my family. But I was wrong. I see that more and more. I wish I didn't. It's sentimental, it's disgusting. Last night I even had to wipe away rivers of rheum and snot when I allowed myself to reminisce.

I still see my mother as a young woman, tend to forget that she became a fishwife. Screaming old harridan. Even my father can sometimes seem all right. I hate it that my early years – before that bloody man was crucified – should now be turning into something sacred. Precious. It wasn't much of a life, even then.

I'll tell you what's precious about life. I've thought about this. It's the fact it's short, it's fleeting, you don't know when it's going to end. You want to hang onto it, hang onto it at any price. *Death* is the thing that's precious about life.

So when you realize you're not going to die…

But don't think I haven't tried. I've tried by jumping off a cliff. I've tried with knife, and rope, and poison.

Yet nothing works, absolutely nothing, even though I can break every bone in my body – back, neck, arms, legs – which accounts for the shape I'm in now, all the twists and the deformities. I'm not just a freak, I'm a monster, beside me Cerberus would sweep the board at any beauty contest. It also accounts for the fact that, as I said, I can't even sleep at night, there's no position I can lie in for longer than three minutes. So no escape, you see. Not even on those rare occasions when I can scrounge a bit of wine. A *bit* of wine, a whole amphora wouldn't help! I say scrounge because I haven't any money, how should I have? Quite often I starve and thereby add to my manifold physical attractions an air of charming emaciation, and to my manifold physical discomforts the ache of gnawing hunger. I'm deprived not merely of food but – far worse – deprived of the consolation of knowing that at least I'll starve to death.

So wouldn't you think I'd have learnt sooner? After that dive off the cliff-top? But the thing was, although the chance of survival was only about one in a million, I'd believed that *I*, wouldn't you know, had been that poor, dumb, millionth sap. So I drove a knife through my chest. And, oh God, the *agony* of it! You need courage to do these things. You need courage to do them and courage to recover from them; or would do if you had the least bit of choice in the matter. And yet, even then, I thought I lived because I'd missed my heart, the physician said I had, anyhow. But in truth it could have been plain desperation that permitted me to think it. After I'd hung myself, and swung three feet above the ground for six whole hours, scrabbling and clawing for my breath, I finally had to acknowledge it: that there was never going to be, *ever*, any hope of a way out!

This, though, didn't stop me from rushing at the henbane, packing it into my mouth, gulping it down unchewed, in the second I fooled myself they might be looking the other way. They, my persecutors. And I got the convulsions all right, the sensation of having swallowed shards of heated glass that burned and tore relentlessly at my gut. But when I was next able to think, in the intervals between the torment, I knew I hadn't caught them by surprise. Whatever surprises might be going I was the one who'd always be on the receiving end. The bastards.

Sodding bastards.

Yet…why the plural? I see I keep on doing it. Persecutors, bastards. Why?

Of course there's a lot of nonsense talked these days about a father-and-son act, and I've even heard mention of some crazy ghost wanting to turn it into a trio! But when I'm not getting too distracted, I still always think of *him*, not them – I mean, if I have to think about it at all, which thankfully doesn't happen often. *Him* being that same goddamn bullyboy who buttered up Abram and could obviously be pretty free with the goodies if he thought it was going to pay. I mean! Imagine a fellow of my years still being able to get his leg over and squirt his juices in the right orifice. Lucky git. I bet *he'd* done more than his fair share of sucking up.

But even luckier git. Better far than fucking. *Then Abram gave up the ghost, and died in a good old age, an old man, and full of years.*

That's happiness, true happiness! Beats bonking. Every time.

Because if I knew that, like him, I should die at a hundred-and-seventy-five – in other words, ninety-nine years down, seventy-six to go, well past the halfway point – then maybe I could bear it. Even looking as I do now, even functioning as I do now, *not* functioning as I do now, then maybe I could bear it. Just to know that one day all of this would come to an end. Another seventy-six years. *Finito*.

But wait.

Other countries? Other customs? Other times?

Well, I'll tell you. In my heart I dared to hope that all that nonsense had been forgotten. Or never seriously intended. Meant only to frighten and confuse.

For – think about it – sixty years! *Over* sixty years! Wouldn't you imagine they'd have felt impatient to get on with it, witness its results, an experiment as exciting as that? Because that's what it would have been, of course. An experiment. (And presumably, in *their* eyes, an exciting one.) Which perhaps they'd now discovered – glory be – that they weren't capable of carrying out. Faces all covered in egg! How are the mighty fallen!

An enterprise dreamt up on the spur of the moment – and possibly fairly soon regretted.

Though be that as it may, they must have realized they'd let too much time slip by, far too much. "Oh, yes, Cartophilus! You'll most certainly *get* to know…" Yet in the first place I was no longer mobile and in the second place I had cataracts. How could I possibly get to know?

Yet, even so, I was worried. One night I thought about the Witch of Endor – I don't know what put *her* into my mind. No way was I thinking of journeying to Endor or of travelling back through past centuries; it was enough that I must travel forward through future ones. (You see, I still hadn't *quite* convinced myself.) Besides, I now had a fear of witches, since I'd seen that woman perish in the fire. But the notion remained with me: might witchcraft cure my ills? After all, I couldn't go on like this, not unless they simply put me in a cage and left me there as some interesting exhibit – a decrepit, aging, floorbound, defecating beast, barely recognizable as human.

And it defied belief to suppose that *that* could have been the projected manner of it. Some sort of travelling peep show? "Step right up and see the world's oldest and ugliest inhabitant!" No, surely not. To get to experience different lands through only the smells that drifted between the bars of some endlessly swaying cage? Or through the barely heard ribaldries of those who came to gawp at me? That couldn't be what they'd had in mind.

So the question then remained. *If* it was going to take place, *how* was it going to take place? Was it conceivable there could be anyone out there – other than a witch or a warlock or an outcast of some other variety – who might have the potential to help me? And even if they had the potential, would they possess the generosity? Remember, I was penniless. Would it be within their nature to take pity?

*

However. Finally it happened. Somebody *did* take pity.

She set down her buckets and her yoke and procured me bread and gave me water and didn't seem to mind that she almost had to shout at me on account of my poor hearing. I felt so starved of talk, of normal human intercourse. I would have liked to touch her face but didn't dare request it – my warty fingers, no doubt filthy nails. And anyway. Again it was only sentimental: who cared what she looked like, so long as she delivered?

She wasn't a witch. She couldn't deliver. Not directly. But it was she who told me of the wizard who had recently arrived in Jerusalem. "I could take you to visit him," she offered, "or…"

I pictured her looking first at me and then at the state of my hovel.

"Or perhaps he could visit you here, if you'd be willing to receive him."

Willing? I'd have been willing to receive King Herod if King Herod could have offered me the least degree of hope.

*

So he came. Not Herod. The wise man she had spoken of.

"I hear you need assistance."

What glorious words! To show my gratitude I would have sunk down on my knees if I'd been able.

"You can help me die?" I whispered.

"But haven't you been doomed to live; to wander over land and sea for all eternity?"

"*Wander*? Is that what they call it? No, doomed to *drag* myself along! Inch by painful inch."

"Nobody can help you die."

I moaned. My gratitude was short-lived. "How can you 'assist' me, then?"

"Through making sure you *don't* have to drag yourself along. Inch by painful inch."

"And how, exactly, do you mean to accomplish that? Foot by painful foot wouldn't be so much of an improvement."

He stared at me, severely. "By offering you the chance of a new life. A new life every century."

Oh, a new life every century? Why, yes, of course! Why hadn't *I* thought of that?

This fellow must be mad.

"You are very much straining my patience, Cartophilus – but no, in fact, I am not mad."

Well, he patently had powers. Possibly it would be foolish to underestimate them; and I shouldn't have been so quick to let him know I did. Hot-tempered, that's me. But even if by some outlandish chance he *was* capable of doing what he claimed…no, I just couldn't believe it.

"So what can I say," he murmured, "to make you believe it?"

229

And then, ironically, I did. It was as simple as that. But it wasn't the actual question which convinced me – no, of course not – nor the fact he could so clearly intercept what I was thinking…although that, too, was certainly impressive. No, what convinced me was the way he'd *put* the question. The softness of the voice he'd used. For I had suddenly realized something. I could actually hear him! I could actually see him! The process had been a gradual one, but if he was talking miracles I now had proof that he could do it – well, ears and eyes, at any rate. Which was a persuasive testimonial…especially to somebody as keen to be persuaded as I was.

And from that instant I trusted him. Well – as fully as it was in my nature to trust anyone.

"I'm sorry I was sceptical," I said. "Born again?"

He nodded. I really saw him nod. It was amazing.

But this might have been simply in acknowledgment of my apology. I had to get it straight. No ambiguity.

"Reborn every century? Is that what you're saying?"

"Yes."

In other words it almost seemed… Well, it almost seemed as if my punishment was about to be suspended. Or lifted. Or evaded. Eternal life – the thing all mortals hungered for. (Especially if, like me, they had their doubts regarding heaven.) No more a punishment at all. A positive reward.

But why? Clearly, there had to be some catch to it. There was always a price tag. Nothing was for nothing.

This time he didn't respond, though – and I remembered that only ten seconds ago I had apologized for my scepticism. So be it! I let my mind dwell on the sheer restfulness of lying in a crib.

"Good health?" I persisted.

"What? Oh, good health. Yes, certainly. You'll be a normal child. A normal youth and adult. With everything normality implies except that – "

I laughed. "Except that I'll still live to be a hundred?"

"That wasn't what I had in mind."

"Money?" I asked. "Will I have money?"

"That all depends. If you want to be well-off it's obviously something you can see to on your own account."

230

Slowly, I digested all this information. "Every hundred years…made young again! That's staggering. Really staggering."

"Yes. I'm glad you look on it like that."

"Though on the other hand… Do you mind if I make one small suggestion? A hundred years is a long time. Couldn't we make it fifty?"

"No," he said.

"Seventy-five?"

Although he shook his head he didn't look reproachful. I sensed that with a bit of coaxing I might be able to swing it. "So much sympathy," I said, "so much compassion! I'm sure the two of us could come to an agreement."

"Are you?"

"Hugely beneficial to both parties." I rubbed my hands.

"How so, to me?"

"Oh, I can see you're a real gentleman. A philanthropist! I can see you'd like to make this world a better place."

"Aren't I doing that already? Your own small part of it, anyway?"

"Oh, you are, you are! You're the kindest person I have ever known!" I could tell he was amused by my flattery – even if I could also tell he didn't mean to be swayed by it. (Yet the funny thing is, it wasn't altogether flattery. He *was* the kindest person I had ever known.) "All right. Not seventy-five. I accept that. But does it have to be a hundred?"

I really felt he might be weakening. "That all depends," he said.

"Depends on what, O wise one?"

"On how things go."

What an irritating answer!

But no matter how I wheedled I couldn't get him to expand on it. I heard my tone grow plaintive.

"I don't want to live so long," I grumbled. "Not to a hundred! Please! No, never again!"

(Okay, so I was stretching a point. Though only by a few weeks – a few short wretched weeks. No. A few *long* wretched

231

weeks! He said: "By eight months and four days, if we want to be accurate." Why did he think that funny?)

But would you believe it? Already I was grumbling. I should have been dancing.

Tomorrow I'd be dancing.

"A newborn baby finds it difficult to dance," he remarked.

"Besides," I pointed out. I wished to demonstrate he wasn't dealing with an idiot. "When I'm newborn I shan't even know I've any reason to dance, shall I?"

"Yes."

"Exactly," I agreed.

But then – the very next second –

"I shall?"

"As I was about to tell you a short while ago. You'll be a normal child and youth and man in every respect save two."

I felt apprehensive.

"First," he said, "the matter of age. But you're aware of that."

"And second?"

"Memory."

My apprehension dwindled. "You mean I'll be forgetful? Hardly to be wondered at over the course of centuries!"

"No. I mean the opposite. Your memory will be excellent."

So what was the disadvantage *there*? (Though perhaps I'd only inferred one. Ever the pessimist! Yet – following a life like mine – certainly not without cause!)

"From your own point of view," he said, "the disadvantage will be this. You'll remember more than you would want to."

"Oh, I think I can live with that."

But suddenly again, on a far less casual note, "More than I would want to? What kind of thing?"

"Every kind of thing."

"*Every* kind of thing?"

"You'll remember, for instance, how you struck the Saviour. How you repeatedly tried to kill yourself. How you became an animal. How you – "

I was appalled.

"No, *stop*! All the things I'd most be wanting to forget!"

He ignored my interruption.

232

"Though undoubtedly you always *were* an animal! I should have said – how you became an out-and-out grotesque!"

His tone remained pleasant, despite his statement having been as damning, virtually, as any statement *could* be. But, for the moment, that wasn't what mattered. What did matter – overwhelmingly – was that even as a newborn I'd be remembering all the horrors I'd assumed I should now be leaving behind. I'd be carrying the full weight of my past even into my cradle. From my cradle I'd be hauling it every interminable step of the way into my grave – and out of my grave – and back into my cradle. It would be *unbearable*.

Iniquitous. Indescribable. Wouldn't it almost be better not to – ?

"No," he said, "think straight, man! What – remain as you are? You can't have forgotten that at the very least now you'll be able to sleep at night?"

Yet even this was qualified.

"Or if you *don't*, it won't be due any longer to crippling physical discomfort, which – although you didn't realize it – must often have neutralized the pain of thought."

He added, "Naturally you won't be attempting suicide again, now that you're familiar with the consequences?"

No. At least I had learned *that* much.

"And you'll have bread, you'll have wine, you'll have all the things you might have thought would give you pleasure. Even sex, Cartophilus, you'll be able to squirt your juices once again. It's just that you'll also have a new ingredient – an ingredient invariably withheld from others. Your memory of past lives."

I muttered: "*Mercifully* withheld from others."

"That all depends – doesn't it? – on the quality of the past lives."

I considered this a phrase I could very easily grow to hate. Already had. How many times had he used it? *That all depends…*

"I'm sorry, Cartophilus. Those have to be my terms."

"And you let me think there wasn't any catch. You really let me think there wouldn't be a catch."

He hesitated.

233

"You're right to point that out. It wasn't my intention to mislead."

"Hmm," I answered, doubtfully.

"Whether you believe me or not is immaterial. But at least I'd like you to forgive me."

I, too, hesitated.

"I don't know."

"That's a shame," he said, "because forgiveness of course – "

I cut him off. "What I *meant* to say…"

"Yes?"

"What I meant to say was…" I gave a shrug. "That all depends."

There followed a moment of silence. I wondered if I'd have to explain. But then he laughed.

Properly laughed. Laughed with genuine enjoyment.

Which – I have to admit – did a lot to sweeten things.

Yet even so. Didn't he understand that there was weariness of spirit – oh, my God, was there not weariness of spirit – at times every bit as burdensome as the greatest weariness of body?

"Remembering things," I said, "will be to go on experiencing them! To go on reliving them! For ever!"

He offered no reply.

There ensued a further short silence.

"And bearing in mind that you did mislead me," I observed, "are the terms you've mentioned utterly non-negotiable?"

"Utterly."

Contained in that question had been a degree of humour which he clearly hadn't recognized. My tears began to well. I fought furiously to stem them.

"Yet if it's any consolation," he remarked, "I can add that every thousand years or so you'll have the slate wiped clean."

"Oh, thank you!" I said. "Every thousand years? What a remarkable selling point; you should have introduced it earlier!" (My natural aggressiveness…perhaps accentuated, because of those ruddy tears. I knew it wasn't appropriate. Basically, he was my benefactor. Basically, he was my friend. But all the same… Well, I ask you!) "Every *hundred* years… Every *thousand* years… Can't you think in anything but round figures?"

234

"Maybe I can," he conceded – frankly, more gentle than I would ever have expected. "So let's amend it a little. Every thousand years, *more or less*. How's that? One lifetime in ten. But the key factor is…on those occasions you won't have any memories left at all. It'll feel as if you're starting out totally afresh."

"Just one in ten! I shall go crazy!"

"That's up to you," he said. "You might go sane."

I steadied myself.

Took a deep breath.

"Couldn't we make it one in seven?"

"No."

But then he laughed again.

"I can respect the haggling," he said. "It's the whining I don't take to."

He placed his hand upon my shoulder, gave it a squeeze. Nobody in over half a century had done anything that simple or so suggestive of friendship.

"You're right," I said. "You're right. I wouldn't take to any of the whining, either. 'What an ingrate!' I would say. 'Doesn't he know when he's well off?'"

I added quickly:

"So couldn't we make it one in *three*?"

It was a universal wheeze. He was meant to say: *One in three; a moment ago it was one in seven*! *Oh, very well, I suppose we'll have to split the difference*! *One in five*!

That, anyhow, would have been something.

Because one lifetime in ten! Ridiculous! And every lifetime lasting a hundred years! Ridiculous! Hadn't he discovered yet that *all* of human existence was inescapably messy? What about seventy-three-and-a-half, or thirty-nine, or fifty-five, or even eighty-six-and-three-quarters? Eh?

"Well, that all depends," he said.

16

I remember the night the Regent closed. At least I was more understanding the second time around. About the way my father felt. The end of an era. An era only fourteen years old – for *him* – but the cinema business was changing: all bingo now, soon to be bowling (soon to be Iceland). For the final week he would have liked to show a selection of classic movies, a fresh double programme for each of the six days, but for some reason it wasn't possible. He ended up with *Carry On Nurse* – I think the second in the series – and an Audie Murphy western. Good popular stuff, of course, but even then the last performance wasn't well attended. As the main feature was approaching its end Dad took up his position in the foyer, just as he'd done for practically every final performance of the day since 1945; only, his demob suit of the first years had been replaced, as soon as coupons allowed, first by one dinner jacket and then by another. My father wasn't a handsome man but he looked distinguished in his dinner suit, it gave him an air, and he always seemed a little like the squire – no, there was nothing of condescension in it – more like mine host seeing his guests off at the end of what he trusted had been a good evening. He felt personally responsible. If someone occasionally told him he thought the programme had been rotten, a total waste of time, it genuinely distressed my dad, even if it didn't altogether surprise him; he always hoped, even with the poorest pictures, that some sort of alchemy might be occurring in the darkness and all his patrons would emerge in a glow, feeling that the world was truly a better place. Poor Dad. In some ways it was his whole life, the enjoyment of those groups of people underneath his roof for three or four hours at a time. He hated it whenever the projector broke down or the heating system packed up. He really worried about what records should be played before the house lights faded.

The final night was different in one way from all the others: a table was brought into the lobby, a table then set with glasses and bottles of wine and bottles of cream soda. There were cocktail sausages and squares of cheddar cheese, bowls of crisps and

236

nuts, plates of biscuits. He'd hired two hundred wineglasses but realized by the time the main film started that despite all his posters and a message to his patrons in the local press he was going to need hardly a quarter of that number. In the event he didn't need a tenth. People seemed unexpectedly awkward and in a hurry to get away, like worshippers slipping out of church by a side entrance in order to avoid the vicar. The modest party he'd envisaged (I knew he had prepared a speech) had turned into a mere sprinkling of embarrassed customers and stilted conversation and unhappy silences. Even Doris the usherette and Mrs Wilson at the box office had both made excuses, one to do with her own health, one to do with her mother's, and the projectionist was a kind man but very shy and he too asked if he could possibly cry off. Both the Shipmans and the Kings had declared that, regretfully, they couldn't come.

So it fell to my mother and me to help Dad through as best we could. Mum got the giggles.

In fact she was almost drunk. Knowing the quantities of wine which wouldn't be required she had slipped downstairs much earlier than was necessary.

She looked very pretty in her red dress and black heels. Always much fairer than my father or me, she had recently lightened her hair still more and it suited her. She called it her Grace Kelly look.

Fifty-five years ago I had been as merry as her and giggled every bit as much. I had ended the evening by suddenly being sick and not even getting to the lavatory. (And my father, bless him, had never uttered one single word of reproach.) This time I went easy on the wine and tried to make her do the same. But I proved as unsuccessful here as I'd been in discouraging Dad from holding such a function in the first place. My endeavours to keep her upstairs, entertained by games of gin rummy and silly impersonations and by putting on her favourite records, had only managed to make the matter worse.

"Oh, Ethan, don't be such a spoilsport! You can see how much your father's over-ordered."

"But it's all on sale or return. We don't have to polish it off."

237

"My darling, you should let yourself go a little. I sometimes worry about you, my sweet."

"Why?"

"I don't know that you always get the fun out of life that you should."

She hadn't said this the first time.

"Mum, it's been a wonderful life. I'm the happiest man in the world."

"Sez you!"

She touched the tip of my nose with a forefinger. She was already on her second glass.

"You know what really worries me? I'd hate any son of mine to turn into…"

Now she dipped her finger into the wine and flicked at me two drops.

"Turn into what, Mum?"

"Oh, but you mustn't be offended! A prig – just a teensy-weensy bit of a prig! A very little one." She measured it: about an inch high.

It speaks volumes for my advanced development that I was, in fact, considerably offended.

"The way you seem to hold yourself aloof; to stand on the outside and quietly observe the rest of us. As if in judgment. Only sometimes. It isn't serious. But, Ethan – promise. We don't want a prig in the family, do we?"

"I promise we don't want a prig in the family do we." But I couldn't make my voice as light as I had aimed for.

"Oh, and now I have offended him! Come on, drink my health. Then dance a little dance with me. Tell me I'm forgiven."

"Mum!"

For she had now begun to hum it: *Tell me I'm forgiven, for making you cry…* And she had taken my hands and was pulling me back and forth in a grotesque parody of some form of light fantastic – could it be a quickstep?

"There you are! You see! So stiff. You should unbend. There's nobody watching, nobody passing on the pavement. You could even do a striptease."

None of this had taken place before.

238

"Come on. Do a striptease! I feel so absolutely convinced you would strip to advantage! What a long time since I've seen my little boy all bare."

She retrieved her glass and raised it to me as she swayed in a far more graceful imitation of a dance than when she'd had to propel her lumpish son in front of her.

She winked at me.

"Mum, I'll be right back. Just a minute or two."

I found my father standing at the rear of the stalls and looking as if he were positively willing his patrons into finding the film funny; assessing the frequency and depth of their laughter in relation to last opportunities. Lost opportunities.

"Dad. Mum's in the foyer getting tight. I think you ought to be there."

"Your mother? Tight? No!"

"Well, no. Not tight. But well on the way."

"Oh, let her be. She enjoys her little glass of wine; doesn't often get the chance. And I ordered far more than we need."

"She won't thank us, though…not if we let her make a fool of herself."

"Baloney," he said. "It's the last night. It's a celebration. I may well come and get tight, too. To keep her company. You mustn't be a wet blanket."

Spoilsport. Prig. Judgmental. Wet blanket. All within the space of five or ten minutes. Was that really the image I projected? Perhaps the image I projected wasn't particularly important yet the happiest man in the world now felt remarkably deflated.

I went upstairs to the flat, bypassed the lobby. Sat on my bed and tried to pray but felt too rebellious. Hard done by. Hurt.

Prigs and judges and wet blankets: weren't they far more the types who'd be able to pray?

It was a Saturday. I'd come home this weekend especially for my father's big event, to see whether, having failed to persuade him not to hold it, I could help him improve things in any way. I had bought *A Pictorial History of the Talkies* to present to him at the end of the evening – or, rather, to leave casually lying on the table by his chair – in appreciation, partly, of that particular act of forbearance he didn't even know about but which had been one of the many kind things I would chiefly remember him for. Tomorrow I'd be returning to Cambridge.

I had stayed on at Cambridge to do an MA. Now, sitting on my bed – and very much in the light of what my parents had just said – I briefly reviewed my university career. Reviewed my sixth-form days. Reviewed my whole social history. Perhaps I *wasn't* the life and soul of the party but I had never set out to be. Perhaps I *didn't* too often throw back my head to enjoy a really good laugh yet I wasn't that type. I would smile at things and softly chuckle. I hoped that I was fun to be with – always tried to be a good companion. But in spite of my increased self-confidence, I still had moments of shyness, was still at times a scaredy-cat, although I thought this wasn't obvious. I tended to be serious about life, more so perhaps than I had been in the past, more into politics and world affairs and all that sort of thing, but I wasn't a wet blanket.

Or was I?

People sometimes said, "A degree in *Divinity*? What in heaven's name made you choose *Divinity*?" And I would have to answer lamely that I found it interesting. "But what are you going to do with it? You're surely not planning to enter the Church?" (Few remembered to say 'Synagogue'.) "No, no," I'd reply, "nothing like that. Future still very vague!" But Divinity didn't turn you into a wet blanket.

Did it?

And could I really be judgmental? For twenty years I'd tried to echo John Bradford who in 1550 saw a group of criminals being led away to execution and exclaimed, "There but for the grace of God goes John Bradford!" Besides, I had far too much to remember from my previous existence (as well as having plenty to remember from this one) to be in any position to throw stones. I truly didn't believe I was judgmental.

But prig? I looked it up in the dictionary. A person who is smugly self-righteous and narrow minded. C18: of unknown origin.

Certainly my life was not developing in quite the way I had imagined. I had pictured myself sowing my wild oats, having a swinging sex life well before the Swinging Sixties, going all out for a stage career. I had always envied actors...those who were constantly in work. I thought I knew my goal.

But I found that what in fact had appealed to me was really the camaraderie of the theatre, the laughter, the sense of belonging, the thought of cutting a figure. I possessed no burning ambition to act. And since there were thousands of others who did, was it then fair to take up room which somebody else would occupy more worthily?

And as for the sex: was it shyness, or the spirit of the nineteen-fifties, or an unwillingness to engage in merely casual encounters? Don Juan no longer seemed a character to emulate.

Yet did this turn me into a prig?

In any case, I told myself. You were what you were. You did your damnedest to avoid the pitfalls. And when you couldn't manage it, it was best that you should know. Clearly.

Then you went on trying.

Full stop.

End of conversation.

I returned downstairs.

As I did so, I heard the National Anthem. My father was already in the foyer – as he would have been on any other evening – gently rubbing his hands while he waited. My mother was tapping her foot quite happily to a tune that now remained inside her head. But she looked all right; only my father's worried glances might have suggested otherwise. The vanguard of the audience came dribbling out, mainly comprised of the younger element, the ones who'd been sitting in the back row and who would now have to find new venues for their petting. My father said, "Good evening, would you like some wine?" and held out a filled glass in either hand. These first arrivals looked at one another and giggled and murmured, "What's this for? – yeah – don't mind – ta!" A card had been screened during the interval announcing that there would be wine served after the performance, and why, but not everyone, plainly, would have had their eyes fixed on the screen. I went and helped my father pass round the drinks and the savouries. By now the main body of the audience was either slipping out – with heads studiously

241

lowered – or else lingering, irresolute. But there were perhaps three or four couples who showed the right amount of appreciation and regret. "We're so much going to miss our cinema," they'd say, "what a shame this all is!" "Yes," I'd reply, "rotten old television, let's hope at least it has the grace to feel guilty!… And did you happen to see any of *these* at the Regent?" For Dad and I had spent a cheerfully nostalgic morning going through his stock of old posters, picking out those which were either the most colourful or else advertised our favourite movies, then pinning them up wherever we could find the space. *Bandit of Sherwood Forest*, *The Ghost and Mrs Muir*, *Born Yesterday*, *Magnificent Obsession*, *Guys and Dolls*… There must have been about fifty of them. "Do you think the day will ever come when we can buy old films and play them on the box?"

But such questions didn't accomplish much. I had wanted to get Johnny and one or two others to come – Gordon had by then gone off to be a pop star – yet Dad had asked me not to, on the grounds that somehow it wouldn't seem quite honest, nor quite dignified, and certainly the first of these objections had got through to me. Johnny and Simon, however, and some of Mum's and Dad's own friends, along with Gwen and Max and Gramps and Nana, would definitely have put a bit of a sparkle into things – even if privately they *had* considered the whole proceeding a mite pathetic.

"My father's really choked," I said, "to hear the Regent's going to be demolished." But only two people asked me if he had another job or where we were now going to live. In fact we weren't sure. There were several months before we'd have to move, and I was still trying to deter my parents from finally picking on London. They hadn't been happy there before. My father had missed his allotment – there'd been a waiting list in the area where they'd settled – and the only sympathetic job to come his way had been at the Classic in Baker Street, which had turned out to be another cinema soon having to douse its lights. They hadn't made any real friends in London, either. It had all been rather gloomy.

But it proved impossible to find the proper arguments.

Tonight, though, my mother did her utmost to enliven the proceedings. She hadn't yet become depressed, as was going to happen in the years ahead.

"Would anybody like to dance with me? Poor man's Grace Kelly. Looking for the poor woman's *Gene* Kelly. Any takers? Roll up!"

She weaved amongst the rest of us and undeniably added some much-required pizzazz. "'Ten cents a dance, that's all they pay me, oh how they weigh me down…'"

Also variety.

"Anyone here do conjuring tricks? Juggling? Has anybody any balls?"

She sang again.

"'Knees up, Mother Brown. Knees up, Mother Brown. Under the table you must go, ee-ay-ee-ay-ee-ay-oh!'"

My father did his best, as well…to carry on doggedly with his own one-sided conversations and pretend he saw nothing wrong. By now, though, people were either standing there and frankly watching Mum, or else edging towards the doors like a dribble of tactful sheep. It must have been evident to him for sometime that his little speech of gratitude and regret and good wishes wasn't going to be called upon. I felt sad for him, and slightly angry. It was what I think he'd regarded as the climax of his career, albeit with supposedly another fifteen years to run.

Mum finished her song and performed a curtsey. Unfortunately she wobbled – and then fell. The floor wasn't carpeted, she fell with quite a bump. Dad and I rushed over. She seemed disorientated, blankly shook her head when asked if she was hurt. She stood between us. Looked around in sorrowful surprise.

And then, without a word, she soundlessly – but copiously – threw up. Eight people, not counting Dad and me, had their coats and trousers and shoes and stockings pretty well splashed. One woman even asked to have her handbag sent to the cleaners.

17

The following August, my parents having bought a place in East Finchley, Johnny and I took a furnished flat in Camden Town. "That's nice," said my mother. "Two good Jewish boys setting up house together. Don't forget on Friday nights to light the Sabbath candle! Have a mezuzah at your front door!" In Amersham, neither before the war, during it or afterwards, had we ever lit a Sabbath candle, set foot inside a synagogue, or had a mezuzah at our front door. Therefore, she was being humorous. But her humour had been ironic, as well as heavy-handed. In truth, she had been a little miffed by my decision to leave home.

And after we'd been there only a few days – in fact it was our first Sunday and we were sitting, pyjama-clad, over a celebratory brunch of fruit juice, scrambled egg, hot rolls and coffee, with the newspapers spread out beside our plates and overflowing onto our laps – Johnny suddenly said, "Let's go to Paris for the New Year!" He was looking at an article about Versailles.

By the New Year he would have completed his first six months at Air France – he worked in their reservations department in New Bond Street – and would then qualify for fantastically reduced travel (if only on a stand-by basis) which someone flying with him could also enjoy.

"Great! I'd love it! But how can you be certain you won't be working at the New Year? Doesn't everybody fight tooth and nail to get it off?"

But this was just small talk, what I sometimes thought of as keeping up appearances. I knew damned well he would be free – even if I hadn't expected mention of it for a further week or so. Memory plays tricks. I could have sworn it had happened in the Old Bull and Bush, up in Hampstead.

Johnny was fair-haired and of medium height and had the air of a serious-minded student – especially when he wore his glasses – not of someone who had frittered away the past six years in a series of dead-end jobs in Amersham. Indeed, I'd done my best to nag him into staying at school and going to university, reading for a degree in science or in music. But he'd been keen to be out in the world and his parents had backed him. Yet when I remembered such things as the crystal set, far more *his* accomplishment than it had ever been mine, I kept being cross at his shortsightedness and the thought of all that he was missing.

However, it mightn't be too late. I'd spoken, *ad nauseam*, about the fun of my own undergraduate days – the balls and the picnics and the punting, the all-night discussions fuelled by wine and chocolate biscuits, the playing of the drums and saxophone at dawn in misty meadows near the river bank – until at last he'd asked me, please, for the love of Mike, just to put a sock in it. I wasn't sure this was altogether a bad sign.

"Well, if we're really off to France," I said, "tomorrow I'll inquire about evening classes in French."

"But we're only going for a couple of days! And in Paris, you'll find, you don't even *need* French."

"Oh, it's all right for you. You get practice at work. But for me, when I actually scraped through my 'O' level, old Horwood nearly fainted from the shock of it."

No, that had been the last time – again I'd got muddled – this time my pass was more respectable. But Johnny probably thought I was simply being modest. And he knew that modern languages had never been my forte. Even having a French wife hadn't helped me much, for both Ginette and her parents spoke excellent English and by the time Ginette had lived in Britain for twenty years most people were surprised to learn she wasn't British.

Previously I'd been content not to have to make the effort. Now things would be different.

"I think you're a nut," said Johnny. "Just two days!" he repeated.

"This won't be the only time I'll go to France."

"Maybe not, but on that principle you might as well take evening classes in Italian too – throw in Spanish, Greek, German and Serbo-Croat – people are getting better-travelled all the time."

It was through Johnny I had met Ginette. She had become a colleague of his at Air France, some five years hence. Ginette had stayed a year; Johnny had stayed for nearly two decades. But he hadn't risen very high – too many people chasing after too few openings – and finally he'd handed in his notice in a fit of pique, before finding any other employment. From then on his life had further deteriorated. In fact, our destinies had been disturbingly alike: two reasonably bright boys who'd messed around and never fulfilled one tenth of their potential. Yet we hadn't even remained close. I didn't much like his wife but it wasn't until he'd walked out on her in the late seventies – as well as on his job – that I lost touch with him completely and had a letter returned to me, 'Moved away, address unknown'. This had been a year or so before Philip died, when Ginette and I had still had…I am tempted to say a good marriage but it couldn't have been that, a good marriage would have better absorbed the stress, would have survived as something other than a travesty. Ironically, I think my own domestic happiness had been hard for Johnny to accept; and perhaps, as well, his seeing me so often could only remind him of his youth and the dreams he'd had of fame as a composer – although, damn it, I don't know how he'd thought he was ever going to achieve that, without the proper grounding. *Despite* his frequent references to songwriters who couldn't read a note!

In any case it was essential to get him away from Air France before he'd been there very long. His marriage had been childless – Sandra hadn't wanted children – and she'd been terrified of flying too, so after the first half-dozen years he hadn't even travelled much. She had joined the company a month or two before Ginette.

Furthermore, it wasn't enough to get him away from Air France. He also needed to be pushed towards university and/or a fulfilling career.

Does this sound manipulative? High-handed? It certainly sounds like, "Please do as I say, *not* as I do," for my own future was still far from finalized. At present I had a job as a porter at the Royal Free, although for some time I'd been making inquiries about careers as diverse as those in the charity field and the London fire brigade and bomb disposal work; inquiries, even, about a career in the Church of England, regardless of those clear denials, perfectly sincere when made, to anyone who had previously questioned my choice of Divinity. Nor did I feel the need to mention to my parents (yet) that earlier in the year, at Cambridge, I had been both baptized and confirmed. I regarded Christianity not as a new faith but as a logical extension to my old, an extension which I had long been heading towards; during my past life almost as much as during this present one. I meant to be as certain as I could – this time – that I got things right.

Yet in the meanwhile, because I intended to be thorough, there was the question of my learning French; and also, because I intended to be thorough, there was the question of my marrying Ginette.

The order, obviously, is wrong.

But to put it bluntly – even coldly – I needed Ginette if I wanted Philip.

Philip wasn't due to be conceived until 1966 but it would be wonderful for him to have siblings – as well as wonderful for us, of course; and some of those siblings could be older just as easily as younger.

To put it less coldly: I remembered Ginette as she was at the time of our meeting and during the first fifteen years of our marriage; and I knew she would never have grown bitter if, firstly, Philip hadn't died (and Philip wasn't going to die) and – secondly – if I had been a better husband (and I was going to be a better husband). And just as when my mother had succumbed in her middle seventies, lined and strained and petulant, it hadn't taken me long to cast off the image of her old age and envisage her again as she had been in her heyday…so my renewed youth caused me to think of Ginette in the same fashion: laughing and vivacious and full of devilment. In the end I felt there was nothing cold at all about my decision to woo back my wife.

Previously, as I say, I'd met her in London, but of course I had often visited her parents' home in the Boulevard Beaumarchais, near la Place de la Bastille.

Now, however, I met her on the eve not simply of a new year but of a new decade. It seemed appropriate.

I'd taken Johnny to a nightclub in the Latin Quarter called Les Enfants du Paradis. I had been there with Ginette on another New Year's Eve and knew it was by no means the first on which

247

she'd celebrated beneath its imitation theatre boxes, gilt cherubs and maroon rococo plushness – its seasonal balloons and streamers. The chances of her coming here tonight seemed roughly even. But I reckoned that if I didn't see her I could just hang about her apartment block the following day, even though this would present the problem of what to do with Johnny, and also of what to tell him.

That might be something I should need to sleep on.

We had both brought evening clothes. Me, I'd done remarkably well at a secondhand store just around the corner from where we lived, while Johnny, being about the same build as my father, had borrowed one of Dad's suits and shirts. As with most men, dinner jackets became us. We turned up at the nightclub feeling debonair and elegant and British. We had each drunk a couple of Pernods back at the hotel.

I'd reserved us a table by telephone from London. In return for the airfare, I had determined to give Johnny a really memorable New Year's Eve. My having planned it so far in advance, moreover, had provided a further incentive to work hard at my French. I'd set myself a four-month goal and as well as the evening classes had attended conversation circles, bought records and spent an average of three hours a night on study. It had paid off. When it came to our break I could speak the language with competence, which boosted my morale hugely. Whether Ginette was there or not we were going to have a good time.

But she was there – although, incredibly, for the first moment I didn't even recognize her. I saw this young woman in a strawberry-coloured dress and for the fraction of a second was prepared to be deflected by a stranger. The impact tonight was as strong, every bit as stunning, as it had been fifty years ago.

"My God!" I said.

Johnny followed the direction of my gaze.

I told him, recklessly: "That's the girl I'm going to marry."

"Oh, right. Not bad. For myself, I've lined up Audrey Hepburn."

"Just look at her! Isn't she everything you ever dreamt of?"

248

"I suppose you haven't noticed that big blond fellow next to her? From her present expression I'd say he might be everything *she* ever dreamt of."

"Only because he's just made her laugh at something. In any case," I smiled, "irrelevant. How do I get to talk to her?"

"Don't they have a Gentleman's Excuse-Me, then, in France? Or what about a nice Paul Jones?"

"No, you don't understand. I'm being serious."

"Then why not simply go across and ask her to dance? You're looking sufficiently fetching. Once on the floor you can tell her of your marriage plans."

"Good idea," I said. I stood up.

"Great Scott! Can it really be the lad's not bluffing?" He pushed my wineglass towards me. "Dutch courage."

"I don't need it." But halfway across the floor I decided that I did. I returned to Johnny.

"Her parents are also at the table. I didn't see that."

"But why does that affect things? Besides, they could be his. And at least it will provide him with people to chat with, while you're proposing to his girlfriend. Or maybe his fiancée."

Yet my knowledge of the outcome was no longer enough, suddenly, to furnish the requisite bravado. The eventual outcome, I reminded myself. Perhaps, after all, I *would* have to wait until she joined Air France at the start of her projected year in London.

I sat down again.

"Funk!" he said.

I took a sip of wine, several sips of wine. "Hold on. I've got to work this out."

I crossed my arms and stared down at my pumps. If in the long run I was going to marry her, I had nothing to lose in the short run by possibly making a fool of myself. Five years from now, in London, either she wouldn't recognize me or if she did we would laugh about the incident – by then it might even have acquired an aura of romance. By the same token, although I had nothing to lose, I clearly had much to gain: at the very least, several years' worth of consummated love – and companionship – and support – and freedom from impatience; but more than that, the possibility of other lives, the lives of our children, who, if I failed to act, then lost their chance for ever. So. It was my unknown children I heard crying out to me; and saw reflected in the glossy surface of my new pumps.

And, in that case, when would there ever be a better moment than this one? For if I waited in the Boulevard Beaumarchais tomorrow – and she came out of the block of flats alone – and if I caught her up and said, "Excuse me but didn't I see you at the Enfants du Paradis last night…on the strength of which may I invite you to a cup of coffee?" – in short, if everything went as swimmingly as I could possibly have hoped for, there would still be the problem of what to say to Johnny. I could hardly acquaint him with the truth. And I wasn't prepared to lie, not even in a fairly trivial way: "Such a coincidence, you're never going to believe this!" – while a refusal to tell him anything at all might have set a severe strain upon our friendship and certainly blighted a thoroughly happy New Year.

So it had to be tonight.

"Well, this is it!" I said. Up on my feet again.

"Really? You're fantastic! If you do carry it through I'll never cease to speak of you with solemn, awestruck reverence."

"Will you apply to university?"

"What?"

The words had come to me unbidden. They seemed like a message of confirmation. This was the path which I was meant to follow.

I repeated my question.

"Hey! You've got a hope! What? In exchange for your making sheep's eyes at some dolly bird you fancy?"

"Yet supposing I get her to dance with me? How about that?"

"You really think I can be bought so cheap?"

"No, but I'll let you off needing to speak of me with solemn, awestruck reverence. Don't forget it's a lifelong commitment that you've taken on."

"Nah! I'll just never mention you again."

"Oh, come on, Johnny. Be a sport. I could be losing my nerve; bribe me in some way! Say at least you'll think about your 'A' levels if I do get her to dance."

I was so much in earnest that almost unknowingly I'd resumed my seat. Maybe he did perceive this as a second wavering of my courage.

"Tell you what," he compromised. "If you get her not just to dance with you but also to marry you I'll go for my 'A' levels, apply to university *and* speak of you with solemn, awestruck reverence."

"Promise?"

"Promise."

"Even if she turns me down tonight I can redeem that pledge on the day she eventually marries me?"

He contemplated my outstretched hand for a moment. "Oh, why not? I've decided to be big about this."

We shook on it.

It immediately occurred to me that Zack would speak of the Grand National syndrome, tell me good intentions didn't alter things. On the other hand, his advice on how to explain away his overcoat had also been dishonest. (In fact, I'd told my parents the exact truth: that I'd given my mack away but that somebody I'd met on the train had considered I looked cold and so replaced it.) Whilst bearing this in mind I silently passed on to Zack what Mr Dallas had always told us in relation to English grammar. When *at last* we knew the rules, he'd said – supposing that far-off day should ever arrive, he'd said – we might then, very occasionally and if we absolutely had to, he'd said – be permitted to break them.

And suddenly I wondered. Could that have been the reason, or at least a part of the reason, why Zack had given me his overcoat? Along with such an evidently unnecessary lie? As mute endorsement of Teddy's grudging dispensation?

Or was I rationalizing?

In any case, I grinned. "All's fair in love and war!" I said. And naturally Johnny thought my defiance was directed either towards him or towards the French contingent sitting across the room. All four of them.

It was now half-past-ten. One of the cabaret spots began. From my own point of view this at first seemed like bad timing, since it gave my nerves more of a chance to exasperate my

251

bladder. And although it was performed with talent – a lengthy (far *too* lengthy!) apache dance – I couldn't find it enthralling. But at least it supplied an opportunity to pray. I felt there was a lot riding on what might happen in the very near future.

The performers were applauded and bowed their way out of the spotlight. Ginette came onto the dance floor with her blond boyfriend; there was no denying his attractiveness and – stupidly – I felt jealous. Johnny didn't help.

"You know, it isn't going to be that easy. She looks quite cosy in his arms." After the quick violence of the apache dance the band had started up again with something smoochy.

"Stop it!" I said.

He looked at me in some surprise.

"I mean…," I amended, sheepishly.

"You mean…*stop* it?"

I managed to smile. "That just about conveys it."

The waltz came to an end. Ginette's parents had also been on the floor, and now there was a change of partners between the two couples. The music continued slow.

"Wish me luck."

Then I walked over and tapped Monsieur Tavernier on the shoulder. "Would you permit me, sir, to dance with your daughter? I do have a special reason." Obviously I spoke in French. The couple came to a standstill.

"And what is your special reason?" asked my former (future) father-in-law: so familiar in his discreet smell of expensive cigars and cologne, his compact dynamism, his five-o'clock shadow and his small humorous eyes. I had always got on well with him.

"Next April," I said, impressively, "it will be the fifty-sixth anniversary of the Entente Cordiale – the fifty-sixth, monsieur!"

"My word! I really didn't know! Next April, you say?"

I looked at Ginette and gave a grin. My nerves had settled, I felt immediately at home. "She's also the prettiest woman in the room but what has that to do with anything?"

Ginette lowered her eyes, demurely. And deceptively. "You have an unfair advantage, monsieur: your being alone in a

252

strange country on New Year's Eve. I should be very hardhearted to refuse. Don't you say so, Papa?"

"I suppose I do, my child. And another thing I would point out. There will be practically nothing left of this dance if we continue to deliberate."

Saying which, he gave me a nod and turned away. The orchestra was playing 'Volare'. Ginette had always made of me a fairly graceful dancer. (My mother might now have been surprised.) For a moment I simply enjoyed the sensation of having her once again in my arms and of rediscovering her favourite perfume, Shalimar. But it was potent stuff – the feel of her, I mean, rather than merely the scent. I began to get a hard-on.

I said, a bit abruptly: "My name is Ethan Hart."

She laughed. There seemed no reason for this unless she'd guessed at the cause of my abruptness and of my swiftly loosened hold.

"And mine is Geneviève Tavernier."

Ginette was her second name. I had always called her that because it was less of a mouthful than Geneviève and she didn't like abbreviations. Besides, its anglicized pronunciation inevitably reminded people of that veteran car out of the British film comedy. "Ethan, I am not an old crock," she had pouted, "and I will not be named after one!" I decided on the instant that this time I would call her Geneviève, with the French pronunciation and with no attempt at shortening. It would mark a little difference, another pleasingly unsuspected departure from the past. A further symbol that could have meant nothing to anybody except me.

"You speak French very well, monsieur."

"Thank you, mademoiselle. But something tells me you speak English every bit as well. And probably better."

She looked surprised. "No – no – I keep meaning to make a proper study of it. But I don't suppose I've spoken more than a dozen words since the *bac*. My mother is quite fluent, though. Maybe I should fix you up with her?"

"You're very kind. Yet I ought to say that although I let you think I was alone tonight it isn't quite true. I'm with a friend. But

253

my friend is a man and it might attract attention if I were to dance with him. So to that extent you were certainly right to take pity on me."

"I think I took pity on you because you were English and away from home." She laughed. "Or possibly because you were English, period. Oh, no, I'm sorry, that was a mean and silly joke – but I suddenly thought of you boiling all your meat and then eating jam on it! I am so sorry to make fun of you."

"But that is not true!" I said. "It is a lie! It is a – it is a – " I couldn't find the word for myth. "Like King Arthur and the Knights of the Round Table," I explained. "What do you call that sort of story in French?"

"*Légende.*"

"Yes, like a legend, a kind of legend, but... Oh, very well. What you've accused us of is a lie and a legend."

She laughed again. "The Legend of the Boiled Meat and Black Cherry Jam! It has not quite the same ring of romance to it. I mean, not to a French person. No doubt the English could get to feel properly romantic over it."

Then, unhappily, the dance ended.

"Please. Another one. I haven't asked you yet to marry me."

But all the dancers were now beginning to leave the floor. I turned towards the bandleader and asked him pleadingly for just one more – *tout de suite*! – clasping my hands to him rather like Nesbitt had once done to Hawk-Genn; but though he smiled he shook his head and shrugged as if his musicians were to blame. "Typically French!" I said to Ginette – to Geneviève. "So practical. So unpoetic. Thinking of nothing but the next Gauloise."

"But even if you're right," she answered, reasonably, "my boyfriend might not like it: your asking me to marry you."

"Dog in the...something," I said.

We had another spot of bother over that, a little more understandably. (*Il fait l'empêcheur de tourner en rond* as opposed to the word for myth – which happened to be *mythe*.) "You see," I explained, "your boyfriend is never going to ask you to marry him. Take my word for it."

"But he already has," she said. "Several times."

254

And then I did the unforgivable. It was shocked out of me. I'd suddenly remembered; or suddenly made the connection. I wasn't on my guard.

"My God! That's not Jean-Paul?"

She had often told me that Jean-Paul was the most persistent of her suitors, would never take no for a final answer. Sometimes she had said she ought to have accepted him; and less and less had there been any air of jokiness about the manner of her saying it. Jean-Paul had not only been handsome but he had become rich and had acquired the reputation of being an excellent father to his six children.

Now she had taken a couple of paces backward and was gazing practically openmouthed.

"How do you know about Jean-Paul?"

"I…"

"How do you know?"

"You see, we've met before – you and I – in a previous incarnation."

"No," she said, "seriously."

"And we got married and you were always throwing Jean-Paul in my face. You told me how he was forever asking you to marry him and how you should have done so because he was very handsome and became rich and, besides all that, was a wonderful father to his six children. It was a sort of family joke – well, not really such a joke, to be honest. You used to taunt me with it, rather. You see, we weren't very happy."

I spoke quickly but she was still staring – although now, to my inexpressible relief, she was starting to laugh again. "Oh, what a fool you are! Do many of the English behave like this? I always understood the English to be stuffy. No sense of humour."

"It's all that jam they have to spread on their boiled meat. Could you do that and retain your sense of humour?"

"No, probably not. But, monsieur, I am intrigued. If we've been married before – and yet weren't very happy – and I was beastly to you – then why do you want to marry me again?"

"Oh, because this time it will be different. Enormously different. I shall cherish you. You'll never experience a single moment of regret."

"Ah, my! *That*'s very comforting! I may have to accept."

"And you were only beastly to me because I was beastly to you. In fact, I'm sure I was the beastlier."

"You have an unusual way of putting yourself across."

"I can afford to tell the truth. You see, I'm a reformed character. And in future I shall make you a fine husband."

"I don't believe you can ever have been that beastly." Fleetingly she touched my sleeve. "How many children did we have?"

"Only one. That was a sadness. I don't know why we didn't have a dozen. This time, however, we'll make up for it."

The dance floor was deserted; had been, maybe, for some minutes. Abruptly becoming aware of this and abruptly becoming aware that I should take her back to her table and so risk losing her for the present I said something that must have seemed a little out of tune.

"My Geneviève – but we shall be so very happy!"

I immediately tried to give it a lighter touch, yet it had come out sounding like what it was: a *cri de coeur*: and for the moment she was disconcerted.

I said: "Don't worry. That wasn't me. That was David Garrick, impersonating me. An instant of deathless drama but I'm afraid I forgot to warn you."

"Ah, then, were we married in the time of David Garrick, too?"

I shrugged. "Oh, as to that…well, who can say with any certainty?" It seemed all right again.

But the next second it wasn't so all right. We had been joined by Jean-Paul and Jean-Paul wasn't happy. His fair skin was suffused by a flush of – at best – impatience. "Ah, *chéri*," said Geneviève. "Meet the gentleman from England. Monsieur Gérald, Monsieur Hart. Monsieur Hart claims to be my long-lost husband."

He shook my hand and muttered a conventional greeting, yet he didn't respond to this statement with the slightest air of interest, let alone amusement.

"There is some evidence in support of it," Geneviève persisted, wide-eyed and meaning to impress. "He knew your name, Jean-Paul! So how do you account for that?"

"No doubt he overheard someone using it as we were making our way to the table."

This was an explanation which happened to suit me, even if it did carry certain undertones. To wit, I was a spy. A grubby opportunist.

"Oh, Jean-Paul," she said, "how prosaic you are! Even on New Year's Eve. How unpoetic! How practical! How typically French!"

"Geneviève, you are wanted back at the table. Besides, it seems odd, your continuing to stand here in this way. You are drawing attention to yourself."

Geneviève gave me her hand. "But we can't help that, can we, Monsieur Hart? Not if while standing here we make such a very handsome couple?" She was obviously annoyed with Jean-Paul, a little unfairly, on account of his failure to enter into the spirit of her game. "Ah, well, monsieur. It has been nice. I shall remember this encounter."

I kept hold of her hand for several seconds longer than was needed – or even proper – and looked her in the eye as I did so. "*Au revoir*, Geneviève. *Bonne année*! *A la prochaine*."

Jean-Paul gave a little *tst* of irritation. He took Geneviève's arm and firmly led her away. I myself returned to Johnny.

"Well done," he said. "I watched you both. It looked as though you were really...I don't know...getting through to her. Smarmy devil."

He had risen, expressly to shake my hand and clap me on the back.

"So what happens now?" he asked.

"I know her address. Tomorrow I go and sing 'On the street where you live' on the street where she lives."

"You do, do you? So I have to play the abandoned tourist?"

"Johnny, it's for your own good. Remember that. But let's not think about tomorrow. Right now I'm going to order some champagne. This is an occasion which I feel demands it."

"In a place like this, champagne is going to knock you back a bob or two."

"So much the better," I said. And actually I meant it. One of my constant small battles was against meanness. When for fifty years or more you've been a little tight with your money, the defect isn't one you can easily eradicate, just because you want to.

"Hope you won't regret it when you see your bill! Hope you won't regret it in the morning!"

He obviously didn't intend it but his tone was faintly taunting. This implicit reminder that the crest of the wave descends into the trough was no doubt timely yet I could have done without it. For some reason it made me think of the last New Year's Eve on which I'd seen Ginette; and suddenly a chill passed through me. It was impossible to imagine Geneviève as the same woman. Impossible – and yet only too possible as well – to imagine me as the same man. We hadn't even stayed up until midnight. We'd had a glass or two of sherry, yes, watched some television, spoken as little as we usually did, gone upstairs about eleven – upstairs and to our separate rooms. But it wasn't as if we hadn't started out, then too, as lively, decent, well-intentioned people, both of us. It wasn't even as if, fundamentally, we hadn't each *remained* decent and well-intentioned, although certainly not lively.

No wonder that I shuddered.

18

We got married in Paris, in June 1960; and in the following September Johnny enrolled at the City of Westminster College in Victoria to study four 'A' levels. Less than a year later he passed them all and – having applied to Durham to read for a degree in music – he never met Sandra and was never lucky enough to have Geneviève for a colleague. In fact, Geneviève never went to Air France. Apart from all else, she was too busy bringing up babies. Anne came in 1961, Jacqueline in '62. After a two-month honeymoon in France we had returned to live in Lincoln: a rented house in Steep Hill, quite close to the cathedral. There I studied for three years at the Theological College, which I could scarcely have managed if my parents-in-law, bless them, hadn't been helping out financially. Life was good. Life was terrific. My wife and my daughters were as lovely as any man's wife and daughters possibly could be. And I had very much chosen a career which suited me. My studies weren't purely academic, either. Far from it. I spent a lot of my time getting out into the villages around Lincoln, being inducted into preaching and pastoral work, hospital-visiting, school-teaching, learning about mental health and psychiatric care – I mean, learning about them as much on the job as in the classroom. And then towards the end of my course the college found me a position in the one city which I'd been holding out for. At Petertide I was ordained as deacon in Southwell Minster and having been licensed to St Andrew's in Nottingham I then began life as a curate. My curacy and Geneviève's new pregnancy roughly coincided. The following year I would be twenty-seven. I wanted the baby to be born on my birthday and I prayed that it would be a boy.

Obviously I knew I must be grateful for whatever God sent, but to have a son born in Nottingham on my twenty-seventh birthday had been an overriding ambition since my late teens. More than an ambition. A necessity.

And he had to be called Arthur.

"*Zut*! What kind of crazy British name is that? In France they would just laugh at it. This isn't Camelot, it's not the Middle Ages." Geneviève ran her finger round my ear enticingly – along the nape and round my other ear. "Darling, why can't we have Philipe? Even Philip? I know you like Philip, you've already told me so." I promised her that Philip would be the name of our next son and remained adamant on the choice of Arthur. Since, for the girls, I had wanted Sally and Rebecca, but had prudently given in to her on each occasion, she knew she wasn't justified in denying me the name I wanted now. "*Merde!*" she said. "I hope that it will be a girl!" But her pout turned – as I had known it would – to giggles when I told her that even the crazy British might consider this a touch eccentric: a little girl named Arthur. It also helped that I had deliberately brought the topic up in bed and that I knew her ticklish spots and had most shamelessly exploited my knowledge.

However, I still realized there was something virtually unbalanced about the way I felt. I was objective enough to know that if I'd met anyone who had advocated a similar scenario, or even smilingly encouraged mine, I should have given them a pretty wide berth. And yet the thing was in my blood. I lived it, breathed it, thought about it as I went to sleep, thought about it when I woke.

For Arthur – of course – was to be my means of recompense to Brian Douglas: the son he'd never had, never could have had, but who was going to make his dream come true – as literally, that is, as lay within my grasp and within Arthur's own predisposition and abilities. A senseless vow maybe, made to myself, not even to the man whom I had so finally, if ambivalently, sinned against...or in any case not made to him directly. Senseless and perhaps inordinately presumptuous.

Yet wholly inescapable.

Or so it had seemed.

But also... Wasn't it significant that from the time I'd made my vow I hadn't once been troubled by that nightmare? A nightmare hitherto relentless?

Okay, this could well have been psychological. Yet, even so, I saw it as a sign.

Though again I agree: I was always fairly good at spotting signs.

On the 20th of March 1964 I wrote a letter to my former English master and sent it via his publishers. It was a short letter in which I simply told him I had read his poems and how very much some of them had meant to me – and in which I asked if we might meet, possibly in London. I don't know which was dominant, my sadness or my guilt, when two days later I received an answer not from him but from his editor, to the effect that Humphrey Hawk-Genn had "very tragically passed away on

March 9th," barely a fortnight earlier, "just when he seemed to be getting fully into his stride, potentially a most tremendous loss to the world of English letters." I was shaken, and castigated myself for days because I hadn't written sooner. There wouldn't have been a thing to stop me. But I'd thought I still had plenty of opportunity and hadn't made allowance for the fact that time so often caught me out: either by the sheer rapidity of its passing or, indeed, by the exact opposite. Still. Since my feelings of shame and inadequacy, which even prayer apparently could do little to exorcise, were obviously of no value to anyone, it was as well that by then my birthday was approaching and that things about the house were hectic: Geneviève was expecting to go into labour at literally any moment.

And she did so – most wonderfully – at 9pm on March 27th; and our child was born a little under six hours later. And he was our first boy and when he was merely minutes old Geneviève held him to her with tears in her eyes and whispered, "*Oh, mon petit mignon, que tu es beau! Tu es tellement beau, mon chéri, que je te pardonne immédiatement que tu t'appelle Arthur.*"

19

Nottingham in the middle sixties was a lot pleasanter than in the early nineties – even though the mystifying vandalism that could tear down acres of fine Georgian housing in order to replace them with unmitigated ugliness was by then well under way. We lived in Forest Road, which was peaceful and tree-lined, in a late-Victorian house that belonged to the Church and was not only about the same age as our old one in Park Avenue, but likewise had three floors and knew all about rattling window frames and irrepressible, frequently icy, draughts. (And *here* we had no central heating.) St Andrew's was roughly equidistant between the two. Sometimes I used to cycle up the hill expressly to have a look at No 17 – which was now let out to students – and to remind myself of how extraordinarily blest I was; and that I should never, ever, start to take for granted a life so cram-full of miracles. Park Avenue represented deadness; or, at best, limbo. Forest Road, on the other hand, seemed practically in paradise.

<u>20</u>

Arthur grew up against a background of classical music. I'd put a record-player in his nursery and from the very start kept it softly on the go, or as much as was feasible – at least it had an auto-changer. But oh, I thought, for a tape deck complete with auto-reverse or an eight-track cartridge player! Or what about, just possibly, an endless loop? Anyhow, I was doing my best to be inventive in that region, and, more practically, to inspire Johnny to be inventive in it, too. At all events Arthur, when awake, was seldom without good music for any appreciable length of time; and even when he was asleep wouldn't some part of his brain, or soul, still be receptive to it? Both the girls had been breastfed and at first I felt disappointed that on this occasion Geneviève had dried up, but in one respect I came to look upon it as a blessing: that I myself could spend time with him during the night, either for one feed or for two, and thus provide not only more music but poetry as well – including passages from Shakespeare and Chaucer – while my son sucked, pausingly, upon his gently sloshing Cow & Gate. Under this general heading of poetry there also figured occasional readings from the King James Bible. Both Testaments.

All right, you may laugh. I admit that on one level it was ludicrous, the idea of a month-old baby being subjected to Middle English. But on the other hand…what harm? There weren't going to be any end-of-term tests, I would fight against unacceptable pressures being imposed by a too-demanding father. At the worst, perhaps, he would get a bit muddled. But if he started speaking in Tennysonian verse or soaring biblical cadences while clamouring for his potty, or for Marmite on his bread, all this could be sorted out when it happened. Surely it was worth an element of risk?

262

Geneviève didn't know at first about our son's early exposure to literature, for although she wasn't disapproving of the music – well, not exactly – there was one aspect of it that worried her.

"Why now? It may be good or it may be…*inutile*, but why didn't you do any of this for Anne or Jacqueline?" Hairbrush poised, she watched me in the mirror.

"I should have done. I didn't think."

I should have done. I hadn't thought.

"Then why didn't you think? Experiments are fine but – do the girls mean less to you than Arthur?"

"No, of course not." Nor did they – considered purely as persons and personalities. "Surely you know how much I love them. Have I ever left you in any doubt of that?"

"Not until now."

"Sweetheart, I can only say I had my studies to contend with when the girls were Arthur's age – so much was going on – everything, everything, was new to us…" I spread my hands and hoped for understanding. We both watched our reflections.

"Then it isn't just because they were girls but now you have the boy you always wanted? Oh, I remember how everything had to be so completely right from the very first minute you knew I was pregnant. Even the name…"

"And didn't everything have to be so completely right from the minute I knew you were pregnant with Anne, and then with Jacqueline? Didn't it?"

"Yes, but not quite in the same way. And you were never so concerned before with – oh, I don't know – with whether they were warm enough…or too quiet…or lying in the right position… You never once mentioned *ce cauchemar effroyable*, this thing you call the cot death."

I should plainly have foreseen all this.

"So I ask again. It isn't because, deep down, you think that girls are somehow less important than boys?"

"Darling, I swear it."

"You're sure?"

"I promise you I couldn't be more sure." It was at times like this that I got glimpses of the woman I had left at an earlier dressing table, a mere mile from the dressing table at which she

263

now sat. Such glimpses were a little frightening but in some way reassuring. Ginette was integral to Geneviève; Geneviève was integral to Ginette. There was no fear that, over the years, the two would grow apart.

She allowed herself to be convinced. And in the circumstances I decided not to pick her up on that statement she had made: 'the boy you always wanted'. It was a complete misreading of the case. If we had to speak in those terms at all, then Philip was the boy I'd always wanted. It was partly for Philip – very much for Philip – that I had gone through all of this in the first place. Although I was now indescribably happy to have gone through all of this in the first place, there was a strong chance that if it hadn't been for Philip, Arthur wouldn't even be here. Nor would Anne. Nor Jacqueline.

The situation developed one night when Geneviève, happening to wake and go out to the loo whilst I was feeding Arthur, heard me reciting to him.

> "'Where the bee sucks, there suck I
> In a cowslip's bell I lie…'"

"Oh, darling!" she remonstrated. "What are you doing to him? My poor little pet! *The Tempest*? He's barely five months old!"

Irrelevantly, I was impressed she knew it was *The Tempest*. But then I remembered we'd seen a production of it at the Theatre Royal only the previous year. I made a stupid joke.

"You're lucky it wasn't *Titus Andronicus*."

She looked at me angrily. "*Assez de faux-fuyants!*" She came and gathered up our bright little son in his Babygro suit and took the bottle from me and the wooden chair. Arthur looked surprised but interested. Geneviève kissed him under his chin and made him chuckle. "*Ah, ton coquin papa! Que fait-il? Mon petit chou, mon pauvre petit! Where the bee sucks, there suck I. Ma foi!*"

Arthur renewed his chuckle.

I'd felt tempted to say I'd been entertaining myself rather than him. But the pause had given me time to realize I mustn't.

"You go back to bed," she ordered, in a harsh tone. I was clearly in disgrace; Arthur hadn't saved me. "If you must feed him poetry, what's wrong with Jack and Jill or Baa-Baa Black Sheep?" What indeed? In my zeal I had wholly overlooked the nursery rhymes, perhaps on the assumption that he'd soon enough get to know those anyway. And as Geneviève now pointed out: I had told them often enough to his sisters. "And why must it always be Mozart or Vivaldi or Purcell? Why not Piaf or Trenet or Aznavour? And turn off that machine please, *whoever* it is. *I* am going to sing my son a lullaby…in French. I am going to have a whole long conversation with him, about silly, unimportant things…in French. So there!"

I laughed and put my arms about her shoulders and kissed the crown of her head. "Oh, I'm all in favour of his learning French! You know I am."

Then I went back to bed grinning, having given Arthur, too, a kiss on the crown of his head. But since I was no longer sleepy I read a short story and waited for Geneviève's return. I didn't want the day, or at least the dawn, to go down on her resentment.

Yet, following this confrontation, there was something which now nagged at me. It wasn't that I thought Geneviève capable of sabotage – she wasn't at all, not on a conscious level – but she was a person who very much went to extremes, and I could imagine her thinking that if Arthur had to be force-fed on music, he also needed to know about Gershwin and Kern and *Oklahoma*! Again, I had no real quarrel with this, only believed he didn't require a *grounding* in it. So I took to popping home a little more often than I had, and began to worry that my parish duties might suffer on account of it. For the first time it struck me that if I wanted to take a more active part in my son's upbringing – in my children's upbringing – I might have to think about giving up church work and looking for some sort of evening job instead. Or night position. On a temporary basis anyhow.

About five months later there arose a further contretemps.

I had offered to take the girls to the local swimming pool – Geneviève herself didn't care for swimming – and I'd automatically assumed I should also be taking Arthur.

265

"What! Are you crazy? What would you do with him?"

"How do you mean?"

"Clearly you can't have him in the water with you."

"Why not?"

"Why not? Because he's still a baby. Because he can't even walk. Or perhaps you hadn't noticed?"

"It's catching on in America that it's easier for babies to learn to swim before they can walk."

"Ethan, I don't care what is catching on in America. You are not taking Arthur to the swimming pool."

"I only wanted him to get used to the feel of the water. To realize how much *fun* it is."

"He can do that in his bath, thank you."

"I wasn't going to say, 'Go on, swim three lengths.'"

"I wouldn't put it past you. With that poor little baby I wouldn't put anything past you."

"Oh, darling!"

"Sometimes I think you're not safe to leave him with."

"This is ridiculous."

"And what about your daughters? You have daughters, you know. Little girls of three and four years old! And a lot of fun *they*'re going to have with their daddy if he's spending every minute looking after the baby he's carrying! A fat lot of help with *their* swimming they're going to get!"

"Dammit, they've got water-wings. I could easily give them a hand under the chin. *Just* as easily as if I wasn't holding Arthur."

"Oh, treats! What little girl ever wants to splash and race and ride upon the shoulders? But you can still do all that, of course, holding Arthur? Or have you perhaps left him by this time – how do you put it – to sink or swim? Sent him off on his fifty or sixty lengths?"

"All right, let's forget it. It obviously wasn't a good idea. I'm sorry."

"And suppose that one of the girls got into difficulties? What then? You make me sound unreasonable but I wouldn't have a moment's peace. I didn't raise my children to let them all be drowned." She was beginning to cry. "Not by you nor anyone."

266

I slammed out of the room. It was the first time I'd really lost my temper with her. I was angrier than I'd been in years.

It was the angriest I'd been since before I met Zack...originally met Zack.

But, of course, we were fairly soon reconciled and I took Anne and Jacqueline to the pool and it was fine – Geneviève was right – Arthur *would* have been in the way.

Yet our quarrel left me miserable. For many days I kept returning to it in my thoughts, wasting time and energy by wishing I'd avoided it, wishing I hadn't lost control, wishing I'd stayed to comfort her when she had cried. Such behaviour seriously dented my image of the perfect husband I was trying to be...an event possibly overdue and very necessary. The only clearly positive things which resulted from it, apart from the relief and pleasure of our making up, was that it reminded me of how careful I should always have to be, and that when a month or so later I asked to take Arthur to the pool on his own, Geneviève agreed without any fuss, even though he still couldn't walk, the lazy little brat.

At eleven months my unconcerned son may have been a lazy little brat; at almost twenty-eight his deeply concerned father was getting ever more industrious. Once Arthur was finally sleeping through, I began to get up two hours earlier every morning and go down to the kitchen, the warmest place in the house, to make myself a pot of strong black coffee and spread my books all over the table and start to study. I studied world history – the word 'world' now figured a lot in my endeavours – world politics, world religion, world mythology, world geography. I rotated and integrated and imposed on myself no deadlines, as I had while learning French, because on all such subjects it was clearly absurd to set limits. Gradually I would try to add at least the rudiments of all the major ideas and beliefs which people had at various times held, as well as the rudiments of philosophy and psychology and astronomy, physics, chemistry, biology...well, in short I wanted to become as well-informed as it was possible for any layman to be, not for the sake of my own education but for the sake of my son's. *Yet please – please! – don't ever let me pontificate.* This was a prayer I now added to my many others. *I want to teach, but don't let it appear like teaching.* Let me be lively and stimulating and funny and relaxed. Endlessly patient. Tolerant and understanding.

Save me from solemnity.

I began my course of studies, appropriately enough, by reading about King Arthur; both the Celtic warrior *and* the creator of the Knights of the Round Table. It was strange I hadn't thought of doing this before. Right at the beginning I didn't even know which of them was spoken of as being the one who would return.

The Once and Future King.

21

"Death to the infidels!"... "Enemies of Christ!"... "Child killers!"

Oh, how they hated us. A lot of them regularly came to borrow money and I don't know how they'd ever have got on without us, but oh how they hated us, these solid citizens of York. Often they didn't pay the money back – so then we'd have to take them into court; and often too, for no reason at all, they'd spit on us in passing, or even assault us...sometimes, for a great joke, corner one of us and force him to eat pork, at other times beat us up so cruelly our blood would run between the cobblestones. Somehow those robes of ours seemed always an affront. We tried to make them look less costly and occasionally risked taking off our yellow badges. But our swarthy skins and Semitic features invariably betrayed us and so invited trouble; and there'd have been fines to pay, perhaps imprisonment, if the papal authorities had ever heard we were defying regulations. Besides, it appeared to most of us dishonourable: we aimed to wear our badges with distinction. With pride.

A lot of it had to do with the crusades. A priest from the Christian Pope had come to the marketplace on a recruiting drive, to get men to join the armies in the Holy Land and take up arms against the infidels.

"But what about the infidels in York?" That had been the immediate reaction of the crowd. "All Jews are infidels!"

So it seemed there was just as much anti-Jewish as anti-Moslem hysteria sweeping through the city. And even the Pope himself had warned the English to beware of us: we exerted a 'corrupting influence on Christian souls,' he had written. That priest in the marketplace was a demagogue who hardly cared in what direction the passions of the mob would flow.

It hadn't always been like this. Intermittently we'd been allowed to get along in peace – especially when King Henry ruled. He'd treated us well. It was largely due to him we'd usually won our cases at the assizes. (Even if we *did* have to send him a tenth of all our damages!) Throughout King Henry's reign, York really hadn't been – well, by and large – such a bad place to live.

I'd started off in Lincoln, I'd spent the whole of my last life there...although until I was old I never used to think in terms of this life, next life, last life, why should I? It was a passing stranger in our tiny synagogue on Steep Hill who drew me to one side and acquainted me with how things stood. He told me that a thousand years ago I'd struck the Messiah while he was on his way to crucifixion. I couldn't believe I had done that. I still can't believe it, not deep in the heart of me. Done something so contemptible? Something so utterly vile?

I mean, I'm not a saint. My God, you should have asked my wife, Rebekah, about that. I'm not even a passably good man, I've never pretended to be. No patience, that's my trouble. I *do* sometimes lash out, not so much physically any more, but with a vicious and irrepressible tongue. *Intolerant* is what I am, although at least these days I usually feel ashamed and seek forgiveness. But what I'm saying is – I may not be a good man but I can't believe I would actually have *hit* somebody when he was down, not even somebody in whom I'd felt so disappointed, some self-proclaimed deliverer. You see, I know only too well what it's like to be spat on and reviled, what it's like to be the underdog.

But if I didn't know it *then* and if I really did strike him – as I suppose I must have done – well, at least I've got to be

269

improving. This travelling wise man, I'm not sure what to call him, in fact he reluctantly admitted I might be making progress – well, half reluctantly, half teasingly, it seemed like an odd mix. (*Certainly taking your time about it* was the phrase he used.) And though, as I say, I didn't quite believe him at the start – how could he even be a Jew, with a countenance as fair as that? – I was obliged to stop and listen on account of some magnetic power he had, magical maybe (since, later, no one could remember seeing him), and I was also obliged to believe him afterwards, *long* afterwards, just by the very fact of my staying alive so incorrigibly…and then by the very fact of my coming back, so incorrectly.

Therefore, I'm making progress. I believe that, too, and if there's hope for *me* there must be hope for anyone.

Improving…and the knowledge that you're improving makes you want to improve still further, like when you've first got a bit of money saved and you're keen to see it grow.

Improving.

But at what a cost.

Because I've got to tell you.

I've spilt blood! I've spilt a lot of human blood.

Spring, 1190 – and I myself am older than the century. There's this man called Malebisse, Richard Malebisse, who's the arch-conspirator against us Jews. And some months back he borrowed heavily from one of my neighbours, Benjamin of York. But, only a short time later, categorically denied having done so. Declared his signature was forged.

The case was about to come to court. Malebisse would definitely have had to cough up. But one stormy night in mid-March he and a band of his henchmen broke into Benjamin's house, killed him, killed everybody, then set the place on fire and carried off what treasure they could find.

I heard the screams and smelt the smoke but thought at first these were only a part of some appalling dream. I believed that Benjamin had fortified his windows, doors and courtyard gates just as we all had, and kept servants always on the watch just as we all did. So by the time I'd struggled up and managed to get downstairs and out into the street, the murdering cowards had made their getaway. But I knew that it was Malebisse, because my own two servants saw him and soon afterwards, anyway, before he fled to Scotland, he even bragged about it. Drunkenly. Claimed recognition as – get this! – 'the man who gave the signal for the massacre'.

That's right. Massacre.

For by the middle of the next day the narrow streets were all but jammed with looters on the rampage, with murderers crying out for vengeance. Vengeance for what, you ask? Vengeance for the fact our forefathers had come to England with nothing? Had by sheer hard work turned that nothing into something? Vengeance for the fact that a year ago hundreds of Christians had died in York from a localized plague which hadn't killed a single Jew? For the fact that three 'boy martyrs' had recently been canonized in England because *we* allegedly had killed them – ritually and horribly – by crucifixion?

Or was it vengeance for that most terrible crime of not sharing in their beliefs? Of being more thorough in our ablutions, more particular about our diets, more anxious to teach our sons whatever we could teach them?

More intent on securing for ourselves a close-knit family life? Was it because they felt jealous of this – or threatened by it – or what?

Anyhow.

By now it was nearly dark and the whole of the Jewish population had been smoked out and was running for its life – or I, for my unmutilated limbs. There were fewer than two hundred of *us*; of *them* there were many thousands. We thought about hiding in one or other of the city's forty churches, or in the crypt of the Minster, but that rabble would no more have respected the holy laws of their own places of worship than the sanctuary of ours. So we decided to make for the castle.

We made for it along the back alleys and even – the more nimble amongst us – over the rooftops, and prayed we wouldn't be anticipated. Behind the thickness of castle walls we might be safe; or certainly as safe as anywhere. The Royal Constable would have to let us in, since we went in fear of our lives and were as much the subjects of the King as were those who'd do us

271

harm. In a day or two, we thought, the situation must surely be defused…either by the authorities or by the elements: it was excessively wet and windy. Disappointed of their sport, please God, and lacking the stamina for any lengthy siege, the crowds would eventually drift home in search of food and sleep and dry clothing. Besides – didn't they have their livelihoods to think about?

We assumed that getting to the castle would be the hardest part. We did so in little groups of two or three, and in the main, though terrified, were able to slip through successfully; only nine of us were seen and chased – and caught and killed. Plainly, I would have made a captured tenth, if it hadn't been for the two young men who gave me their support, half lifting me between them as they ran. We huddled against walls, pressed into doorways – once disturbed a pair of sheltering cats which, stepped on in the gloom, sprang into screeching life. Often we heard the clamour of the crowd come agonizingly close, and saw the blaze of torches lighting up the brickwork only yards from where we cowered. But, yes, in the end, fighting for every breath and with the sweat of fear making our robes feel even damper and more weighty, we got there, to the castle. We got there and the Constable had been prevailed upon to admit us and safety seemed – almost – within our grasp.

Yet there were those who didn't trust the Constable and infused the rest of us with their suspicions.

Until, eventually, we locked the man out of his own castle.

Which proved a wretched move. The Constable appealed to the Sheriff of Yorkshire. And the Sheriff decided to use his soldiers to eject us.

The soldiers joined the mob now waiting jubilant beneath the battlements. The people cheered at their arrival. They believed the presence of the troops bespoke the new King's sanction for the way they were behaving. It was a kind of royal warrant.

A white-robed monk, parading back and forth along the walls, whipped them up into an even greater frenzy. The soldiers had a battering ram with which they stormed the gate.

By then, in spite of our more confident predictions, the siege had lasted several days. Several days of prayer and fasting and of trying to keep our spirits up, days of darkness and of hunger. Of shivering and of fear.

Of the screaming of babies, the sobbing of children.

Of acts of kindness and of sacrifice.

Confessions in the dark.

In conditions such as these…you learn about your fellow beings.

But this was the end. There remained only one course available to us if we wished to avoid a lingering death.

If *they* wished to avoid a lingering death.

Yet only exceptionally do we Jews commit the sin of suicide. So it was agreed that the men should first cut the throats of their children and their wives, then kill each other. Which was how it started. But the rising consternation as the children realized what was happening, the stifled sobs and hysteria of the mothers, the final terror in the eyes of women who had always been so giving and were now so dearly loved: all this led inevitably to a weakening of resolve. Strong men, hardened men, world-weary men – they found they couldn't do it.

And so it was that with the regular and horrifying thud of that battering ram shaking the very floor beneath us, the very walls around us, I felt obliged to volunteer my services.

Oh, God! Dear God! I dispatched maybe sixty lives in the space of just ten or fifteen minutes.

And it didn't get any easier, not even after practice. "Peace, and may the Lord receive you," fifty or sixty times over. All of these people were known to me, some of them were my friends, had shown me many kindnesses. This was a kindness I was showing in return but the thought did nothing to increase my courage – possibly the two most difficult throats to cut were those of the strong young men who had recently supported me, saying as they did so, "Are you all right, old Solomon, rest a moment, have no fear that we'll desert you."

Only fifteen minutes, yes, but undoubtedly the most debilitating of my life…or lives. When I was the only living thing left in that foul-smelling room, I sank down on my knees through sheer exhaustion and slumped red-handed and wet-robed across the nearest pile of corpses.

273

Not a minute too soon. Already they were battering at the dungeon door. The hinges were about to give.

And, oh, you should have heard them shouting at us. Telling us to come out to be slaughtered. Asking if we had crucified any little boys recently. Describing the terrible things they were going to do to us as soon as they had broken through.

I lay there stiff and cramped and aching, my nostrils filled with the stench of dead humanity. But I knew I couldn't fool them into thinking I was dead. Uncontrollable breathing – shudders – tear ducts. I prayed. God, in your infinite mercy, take me forward to my next life. Don't let me fall into the hands of these barbarians. Pardon my sins. Show me pity.

Take me.

But in truth I had no faith that his mercy *was* infinite. Or that he hadn't simply left me to the devil.

22

We were having problems we hadn't had before.

Down-and-outs. Charitable appeals. Flag days.

But mainly down-and-outs.

Although in Birmingham, where we lived now, there weren't as many destitute and homeless as there would be later, not nearly, there was still a distressingly large number. I felt a need to give, and to give substantially. I knew I would sometimes be duped but this seemed unimportant. "For I was an hungred, and ye gave me meat… Inasmuch as ye have done it unto one of the least of these my brethren, ye have done it unto me." I wanted – no, felt driven – to act out the teachings of Jesus as fully as I could. I didn't wait to have hands held out to me in want, I searched for those who looked as though they needed help. No special virtue here, I simply couldn't stop myself. In fact, in some ways I felt it was very far from being a virtue. Witness the dissension it provoked at home.

"But this is madness. We are getting into debt."

She was always accusing me of madness, though this took many forms. Prison-visiting, "when you can't even find the time to visit your own parents!" Helping out in missions, "until you're practically sleepwalking and no doubt thoroughly in the way of those whose job it is!" Giving shelter to derelicts, "who might steal everything we have, or be sick on our Persian rug, or even murder us while we sleep – though on these occasions, as you very well know, I never do sleep! Not that you ever care about *that*, naturally!"

"And not only are we getting into debt," she added now, "we are getting *steeply* into debt! Frighteningly so! What a fine example to our children!"

She had been talking, of course, only about financial management, but inadvertently had gone straight to the nub of it. When I was out with my children – and I was out with them as often as I could be, despite her taunts about not visiting my parents (which I didn't believe justified) – when I was out with my children I neither repressed this urge towards giving, nor exaggerated it. Actually, all four of them put it down to 'Daddy being in one of his crazy moods', a phrase they had possibly picked up from Geneviève herself. But whereas Anne and Philip would speak about it with me, and sometimes shyly hold out a coin on their own account, to the 'poor people who just aren't as lucky as we are', Jacqueline and Arthur often appeared uncomfortable, Arthur even more so than his sister. "Don't, Daddy – don't! It makes us look so silly. And Mummy says they only drink it." Later I heard Philip say to him, "If they have to drink money they really are very poor people!" and out of the corner of my eye I saw the six-year-old Arthur – having first decided, erroneously, that my attention was engaged elsewhere – give him a pinch.

Philip was three. He was our youngest and our last. Geneviève had put her foot down about having any more – and indeed I had even had a fight to secure Philip. I wasn't sure what I'd have done if she had continued adamant; his life had been more crucial to me than Arthur's – although in a vastly different way. He was precisely the same Philip as before, good-humoured, generous, funny, endlessly endearing. We enjoyed a rapport, he and I, which I knew to be very special but which I didn't feel in the least guilty about. Clearly, I tried to keep it secret.

We had other problems, Geneviève and I, again related to money, or partly so. Partly related to prestige. Not all that much related to education.

"Darling. How would you feel about our keeping the children at home and educating them ourselves?"

I'd realized this would be contentious but I hadn't known how to lead up to it in easy stages. It wasn't as though the three who were already at school were unhappy there – bullied or repressed or friendless. It wasn't as though they weren't doing well and getting good reports. They just weren't doing *as* well, obviously, as if they'd been getting a lot more individual attention. "Wouldn't you like the thought," I said, "of being able to control our children's progress? Academically?"

"No. I should hate it. I should find it terrifying."

"One person on his own maybe. But the two of us together. Think how enriching it could be: widening our horizons, drawing us closer, all the time teaching us something new."

"Why, don't you feel we're close now?"

"What I meant was – it could form yet a further bond between us."

"No, you don't feel we're as close as we should be, do you?"

"Geneviève, I love you. Very much. You know I do."

"Pooh! You love everybody."

"That's nonsense. But don't let's get sidetracked. We were talking about the children."

"No. I think you were talking about Arthur."

"Darling, *all* our children. I haven't got a particular preference for Arthur…except in some ways. I have a particular preference for each of our children…in some ways."

"What about Anne, for instance?"

I hesitated.

"The way she buys us presents for no special reason. The way she's always wanting to give us small surprises. A dozen things."

"And Jacqueline?"

"Oh – Jacqueline. The way she looks like you; the way she walks about in your shoes, little coquette, and looks so very pleased with herself...so *mignonne* and adorable. The way she's so determined and will stand up to anything, large dogs, angry parents, but then will suddenly get very shy as well..." My grin broadened. "Why do I have this strange idea you might be testing me?"

"Perhaps because you always think that, in the end, everything comes back to you."

"Ouch!"

"You always rely on your charm to get you your own way. Your own way in everything."

I wasn't sure that I could see any connection. "But, darling, won't you *please* try to stick to the subject? Which is about teaching our kids at home."

"Ethan, you're not being serious about that? No, you can't be!" She stirred her coffee for the second time. "In any case. A partnership, you said. But you meant *you*. Right? Basically, you meant *you*. Yet how could you ever stay at home long enough to give a proper education?"

"Well, that brings us to my next point." I announced this, wishing I had a little more of my second daughter's fearlessness.

My next point involved leaving the Church. Leaving the Church involved moving to rented property probably inferior – greatly inferior – to that which we'd grown used to. I had already been asking questions about possible night work in hospices and hostels – hostels, say, catering for ex-offenders – or in refuges or old people's homes. Geneviève would also need to take a job. None of this would be easy. But I hadn't envisaged it as impossible.

"No, I refuse to talk about it. I refuse! Now you really have taken leave of your senses."

"Geneviève, this means a lot to me. Right or wrong, you can't dismiss it out of hand."

"We're nearly at the end of your second curacy. Nearly there. Your being a vicar means a lot to *me*. All those years of study. (Which, perhaps you need to be reminded, my father mainly paid for!) All those platitudes. All those expressions of...?"

277

"Piety?"

I offered the word grimly.

"Pretensions of caring."

"No, I do care. I care very much. But there are other curates, other vicars. Our children have only one father and I genuinely believe I've a duty to them which transcends – "

"And what about your duty to me?"

I looked down into my own coffee cup.

"Because," she said, "please glance around you! We're surrounded by people with young families. But the fathers are normal loving fathers who want the best for their children – like we all do – yet don't expect their wives to give up everything, go out to work, have no fun, never see their husbands..." Since we now lived very close to a large housing estate where there was much poverty and drunkenness and wife-beating – in stark contrast to the parish where we'd started out in Nottingham – I felt her picture was not a fully impartial one, any more than was her subsequent comment. "They'd be amazed to hear a smart middle-class person like you thinking for one *second* of taking on anything so far beneath him. Working as a porter – or a cleaner – or a janitor! So immature, so irresponsible! And what would you suggest for me? To superintend a public toilet?"

This was quite a diatribe and there were occasional disadvantages to Geneviève's having so quickly acquired such very good English.

So I let the subject drop, and continued to pray about it and try to be thankful. But Geneviève remained immutable. I couldn't believe that God wanted my marriage ruined for the sake of a unilateral decision which was in any case debatable. And why had he encouraged me to enter the ministry in the first place if I was only going to let down so many who'd been relying on me? Certainly my children hadn't been relying on me, not for their education.

So that same September, September 1970, I became a fully-fledged vicar, with my new incumbency in Dorset. Geneviève was happy and busy and full of common-sense supportiveness; there was no question but that I'd done the right thing. Friends from Amersham, Nottingham and Birmingham came for the

278

induction, and Geneviève's parents flew in from Paris, and from London Johnny brought not only Mary, his wife of six months, but Gordon Leonard as well, whom he had bumped into one day in Selfridges. Gordon, on hearing of the event, had thought it would be fun to join in and had phoned me that very night. In fact, to be completely accurate, it was Gordon who'd brought Johnny and Mary, in his latest Porsche. And it *would* have been fun...well, to an extent it *was* fun...all of us making do together in our grand new vicarage, rustling up a totally impromptu supper. But my father had just died from lung cancer (his funeral had been eleven days earlier) and though Mum came to Bridport – driven there by Max, with Gwen in the back seat – still, the fact that my dad couldn't be with us inevitably cast something of a blight, at least as far as she and I were concerned, and probably Gwen and Max as well. "He was so proud of you at Southwell and later at your priesting," said my mother. "And he was so looking forward to being here with us this afternoon!" I told her I was sure he *had* been here with us this afternoon but I suppose she saw this only as some typically churchy remark. Anne, too, said that it wasn't the same without Granddad, Jacqueline agreed, and Philip climbed onto my mother's lap and put his arms about her neck and looked into her eyes and said, "I *loved* my granddad!" I said, "Yes, I know, Pip, we all did. Didn't we, Art?" and Arthur said, "'My daddy said his daddy's dead, the moment I got out of bed!' Granny, I want to be a poet when I'm older, and that's a poem I've made up." I found I had to restrain myself, the vicar so recently returned from his induction and from the small party thrown afterwards in his honour – the small party at which he'd spoken a few honeyed words to every member of his parish then present in the church hall. Had to restrain himself from giving his older son a fair old clip round the ear.

I plodded on, regardless. As Arthur grew older it seemed to me he became less and less the sort of person I had hoped for. But I didn't want to judge and I *did* want to stay true to my prayer – what had it been? – for patience, tolerance, calm and understanding! And in many ways, too, he was undeniably kindhearted, there were moments when he really surprised me with his thoughtfulness. But he was naturally rightwing and chauvinistic. Narrow-minded. Or so it appeared. And whereas the others would all, more or less willingly, help out with chores about the house, Arthur often took a lot of persuasion and might then only perform his share with resentment. He insisted on rosters, which was fine, but if the rosters got snarled up, as for one reason or another they invariably did, he wasn't adaptable, he just got angry and refused to step in, unless, that is, Geneviève bribed him…which she knew I didn't approve of and which generally, therefore, I didn't get to hear about till later, if at all. Arthur didn't profit from example, either. In fact I think he probably reacted against it; the rightwing business might well have been a pose – although his mother could also on occasion display similar proclivities. But he glowered more often than he smiled. He was far more inclined to indulge in tantrums than any of his siblings and to hit out with apparently minimal provocation. Perhaps his namesake had been that sort of fellow too; perhaps it was appropriate for a king, certainly a fifth-century king, to be obstinate and aggressive, arrogant and something of a Philistine. Yet Arthur – *my* Arthur – didn't appear to exhibit the qualities of leadership which might have excused, or explained, those other facets of his character. One sensed an underlying weakness, rather than a latent strength.

Philip was much more, was exactly, the kind of material I had hoped for and expected. But Philip wasn't Arthur. He hadn't been born in Nottingham on my twenty-seventh birthday. He hadn't been the focus of a dying man's recurring dream. It contravened the rules to attempt to give to Philip the role that had been designed for Arthur. For surely it *had* been designed for Arthur?

But I plodded on, regardless. What else was there to do? I'd got into the habit of preparing my son for kingship and – as I say – who was I to know what changes the years might bring, or what groundwork should have been laid by the time those changes had occurred? And if Arthur didn't seem responsive, certainly Philip did – and, to a lesser extent, the girls. So, to put it at its lowest, at least those three were likely to benefit from the kind of education and example with which I sought to supplement their schooling.

There was a date engraved upon my memory: November 23rd 1980. On that day I felt tempted not to let Philip out of the house, not for a moment, but clearly this was paranoid. Before, we had been living in London; Philip had been attending a grammar school in Hampstead. The car which he hadn't seen until too late, hidden from his view by a parked delivery van, would still presumably be speeding along that same stretch of the Finchley Road at 4.25pm, and the van would still be stationed in the same position, but nobody would step out from behind it at 4.25; assuredly not Philip, who'd be three hundred miles away. Poor Mrs Bancroft's life – along of course with Geneviève's and mine – wasn't again about to be destroyed; supposing that it ever had been. I hadn't felt inclined then to call her *poor* Mrs Bancroft, although undoubtedly she must have suffered.

But even so, despite all the differences between that time and this, I felt scared. The closer drew the day, the more apprehensive I became. It was absurd.

Prayer didn't help. I decided the only way to cope would be through direct action – through my personally ensuring that no one else's child was going to fill the vacuum left by our own son.

"Geneviève, I've decided to go to London tomorrow." After Bridport I'd been sent to Newcastle.

"Oh, yes. Why?"

"Something I've got to see to." There was a funeral arranged for the afternoon, which my curate would now have to handle. Otherwise, providentially, there was nothing that couldn't be rescheduled – not even, for once, a meeting of any kind.

281

"I thought that tomorrow we were supposed to be having a quiet evening at home." On such occasions, by way of minor celebration, she often planned a special dinner.

I said: "I could probably make it back by eight, or eight-thirty."

"What can you possibly need to go to London for, at such short notice?"

"Ah…secrets!" I tried to make it sound as if, for instance, I were going to look for her Christmas gift there; although what I could get in London that I couldn't get in Newcastle, or what would be worth all those hours spent in travelling, might present me with a real quandary. "But, look, why don't you come too? Make it a day out? I'd only have to desert you for about an hour."

"Oh, it may be all right for vicars to swan off at just a moment's notice. It's obviously much harder for the vicars' wives."

Nowadays, Geneviève had mixed feelings about the role of vicar's wife. She still thought it carried a certain cachet and even enjoyed the element of exposure – was happy to think it would be noticed when she put on a new dress or styled her hair a bit differently. Always vivacious and popular, she liked to believe she was fairly much at the centre of things, had her finger on the pulse. But on the other hand it annoyed her that a vicar's wife was so often regarded as being a mere adjunct of her husband, an unpaid worker who was available at any time to come to coffee mornings, sort out grievances, open fêtes, answer the door to hard-up strangers. "I am spied on, I am spied on!" she had once cried. "I can't do anything without the whole world knowing! I am not a person in my own right!"

I'd suggested she should take a job. "To escape the claustrophobia, I mean."

"A job! What am I trained for? Selling in a sweet shop?" (At least she didn't allude to public toilets.)

"Then why not train for something?"

"Well, perhaps I shall. One of these days. When Philip has left home."

Arthur was now at sixth-form college, the two girls had already started at university. Geneviève had often spoken about studying for a degree herself but I didn't think she ever would.

In the meantime, perversely, she didn't really mind serving on committees and being always in demand. She probably felt as pleased as she felt disgruntled that she *couldn't* swan off at just a moment's notice, although if truth be told she often had.

I emerged from Finchley Road Underground in good time. When I reached the spot where the accident had taken place there wasn't as yet any van parked there. However, I knew that one must come. There was a space waiting for it and no reason why that space should not be filled. And come it did: at twenty-one minutes past the hour. The driver climbed down and took out of the back two large boxes containing packets of matzos for a nearby convenience store.

Although I thought I'd forgotten what he looked like I recognized him immediately, believed I should have recognized him even in Oxford Street or Newcastle. He gave me a cheery smile, just as if he recognized me too, and fifty-five years ago I would never have imagined myself capable of responding. I wondered if Philip had once been the recipient of that same cheery smile.

I stationed myself in the gap between the van and the vehicle to its left, blocking the way to any schoolchild who might be in a hurry to get home, and stayed there, not only until I'd seen Mrs Bancroft drive past, searching for something in her handbag – "Why, that bloody bitch!" I thought – but until the delivery man had returned and with a further pleasant nod driven out into the traffic. For this I had rescheduled my whole timetable and paid to travel these three hundred miles. But at least it had enabled me to deal effectively with my conscience, had provided precious time to read, had put me in the path of an old vagrant I should never otherwise have met – well, more than one, of course, but one I thought of in particular. Had placed in my hand a hatbox which came from New Bond Street and which had something inside it that – I felt confident – could rival even Parisian chic.

When I got home there was a note from Geneviève.

"Philip hurt in accident. Serious. We're with him at the hospital. Come as fast as you can."

Also on the table was a duck, only half unwrapped.

I couldn't understand it. Why had they allowed Billy Cooper to live? Why had they allowed Anne and Jacqueline, and Arthur, to be born? (Whom did I mean by 'they'? The Fates – God – Zack – whom?) Had there been something in Philip's future life which overstepped the bounds of acceptability? Some accident or atrocity that one of his children or descendants might have caused, bringing destruction to those who simply weren't expendable? All questions such as these I only asked myself a long time afterwards. For the moment I went off the rails – at least inside my head I did – even if, on the outside, I might have appeared to be getting by. People were kind, sympathetic, supportive. The girls came home and didn't go back to Durham until the following January. Arthur, normally undemonstrative, kept giving me hugs for no apparent reason. I suspected that he cried even more than his sisters. I often noticed his red rims and twice found him washing his face at unusual times. I began to feel that during all these years I might gravely have misjudged him. Had never really known him.

I was equally surprised by the lorry driver. I mean by my own attitude towards him. Especially in view of how I'd recently reacted to Mrs Bancroft. Geneviève beat at him with both her fists and had to be, quite literally, pulled off. But I felt no animosity at all. If it hadn't been him it would have been somebody else. In fact, I felt sorry for the man: why should this quiet-spoken, pleasant-faced individual, devoted father of two, need to go through life knowing he had killed a boy of roughly *their* age? Would he think of Philip every time he looked at Diane or Harry, particularly when one of them was celebrating a birthday? If Philip had *had* to go, why couldn't he just have died instantly, painlessly, from some rare, congenital, wholly undetected heart complaint? I didn't understand the ways of God. But I told myself that this was his loss, not mine. I couldn't give a fuck about the ways of God.

Yes, it was God for whom I saved my animosity. God and Zack. I hadn't seen Zack in over twenty years. He had clearly

284

washed his hands of me. A little thing like the loss of a favourite son was obviously too unimportant to merit the time-consuming inconvenience of a visit.

Fuck Zack.

People said that I was wonderful. How did I manage to remain so calm, so active, so forgiving? Mixed in with their admiration – if indeed any of that was genuine – was undoubtedly a deep vein of criticism. The subtext read: how can you be so cold, so distanced, so inhuman?

I didn't give a fig for the subtext.

Geneviève certainly felt no admiration. "Who are you? What are you? Why don't you rail and cry and beat your breast? You always told him that you loved him. What hypocrisy! The only one you ever loved was you. You're the only one you ever will love. You see – I understand you now!"

She pushed me away when I tried to comfort her, when I tried to hold her in my arms and let her howl. "Oh, yes, I know," she said, "you like to feel superior." I saw history repeating itself, would never have believed that it could happen like this...so flagrantly! When her parents arrived to take her home to France – they'd been travelling in Australia at the time of the accident, impossible to get hold of – I had no idea what she might have told them during the car ride from the airport, or might have written in her letter, but they were atypically cool towards me for the few days they remained. After Christmas, when Geneviève and the children came back from Paris (all three of them had just paid lip service to the idea of staying behind with me; Philip would never have done that), I guessed our marriage would be over in everything but name. I hadn't even felt convinced that Geneviève *would* come back. Or not for any length of time.

But she did. And our marriage was over. In everything but name. Never once did we make love again.

My friendship with her parents surprisingly revived.

My friendship with my wife just couldn't make it.

Perhaps it never had a chance.

Because when, the following February, Gordon Leonard returned from wheeling-and-dealing in Las Vegas and Los Angeles, he learned from Johnny what had befallen us; and came posthaste up to Newcastle – by air. Ironically, that week of his arrival, I happened to have been on a retreat, in a monastery in Norfolk, trying to find some pattern to my life, some plan, some meaning; trying to gather strength, to make my peace with God, to learn from him the way I must proceed. With Geneviève. With Arthur. With everyone.

With everything.

I came back on the Friday evening to find the vicarage empty. There was a light on in the hall and my supper in the cooker and, once more, a note left on the kitchen table. But this time in an envelope – and sealed. Normally the only envelopes Geneviève employed in her communications with myself were used ones which she wrote on the back of: see you at about ten, make sure you heat the pie through properly.

The first time she had met Gordon had been at my induction in Dorset. They had hit it off immediately, anyone could see that. Part of the chemistry had obviously been sexual. But for ten years – or so I was informed under the harsh fluorescent light and with a tap dripping in the background – they had held out against temptation. Yet now, she asked, why fight it any more? Clearly she and I no longer had a future. She felt that with Gordon she could make a fresh start.

The clothes she hadn't packed, she said, could be given to Oxfam. Evidently we should need to be in touch over details of the divorce – or would it be better to wait to hear through our solicitors? Arthur liked the idea of living in London and of completing his 'A' level studies at some technical college. Naturally I could see him whenever I wanted.

End of twenty-year marriage, or nearly twenty-one. I'd walked back from the station planning to take her in my arms, override her protestations, romance her, ply her with pretty things: with bottles of champagne and candlelit dinners and weekends well away from the parish; yes, actually to begin again, a *third* beginning, renew all those resolves I'd made at the start of the second. And I'd felt confident. When once determined on a particular course of action, I was usually able to carry it through.

286

But why in God's name had Gordon come back from the States during that specific week?

What made it worse: there'd been a retreat a fortnight earlier I could have gone on. I remembered praying about it. So shouldn't I have been given some glimmer of a premonition? The faintest stirring of a merciful sixth sense?

I didn't even believe they had always held out against temptation. There'd been frequent shopping and theatre expeditions which she'd made to London at times I couldn't get away. In retrospect, I supposed her bubbliness on such occasions should have alerted me to something, even when I'd supposed that basically we were still happy. But it hadn't alerted me to a thing. I'd never had the least suspicion.

Yet had this been only because I would have deemed such qualms unworthy? Or more because my stupid male vanity couldn't accept the fact she wasn't sufficiently fulfilled at home?

Oh hell!

Oh hell, oh hell, oh hell!

I took the train to London early the following morning: resolute to win her back and sure that in the long term I represented at least as good a bet as Gordon, whose tastes up till now had always seemed to run to women in their twenties. I was prepared to do battle; and I trusted in my ability to be persuasive. But the porter at Gordon's Knightsbridge block informed me that Mr Leonard had left about two hours earlier for the South of France, accompanied by a ladyfriend and a young gentleman – they would be gone for several days.

At first I felt tempted to follow them. They would probably be easy to find, I thought, staying at one of the best hotels in Nice or Cannes or Monte Carlo. And it would have been a fairly dashing line to pursue, one that would have been likely to appeal to Geneviève. But I had my responsibilities: a sermon to be preached the next morning, a heavy week ahead – with my curate and his wife departing late this afternoon to attend a family wedding in the Algarve and then remaining there for several days. The timing of it all continued to amaze me.

Besides. Think how embarrassed Arthur would have been.

But forget that untimely return from America. Why in God's name had Johnny and Mary had to bump into Gordon, ten years ago, in one of those art-deco lifts at Selfridges? To avoid such a meeting they might only have had to arrive a dozen seconds earlier. Or a dozen seconds later. It all seemed somehow...so perverse.

Was this my punishment for having persuaded Johnny not to remain at Air France?

For having – once again – bet on a certainty?

No. I refused to believe that.

I rang my mother, met her for lunch and told her what had happened. Her sympathies lay mainly with Geneviève – I wasn't surprised. She had once warned me she thought I was neglecting my wife in favour of my children. While she was talking, it occurred to me that Geneviève had never spoken of Jean-Paul as being an excellent father, not this time around. Indeed, she had hardly spoken of him at all. But in our last life there hadn't been any Gordon Leonard, had there, resplendent on his dashing white charger? Or in his dashing white Porsche – his Jaguar – his Lamborghini?

My own days of excellent fatherhood were over; would-be excellent fatherhood. I felt I'd now discharged my duties to Arthur, my duties to Brian Douglas. The fact I'd failed both of them in what I'd set out to do was unfortunate but irrelevant. Let Arthur make of himself what he would. Now my duties lay primarily with my wife, my mother and my parish. Anne and Jacqueline were both so attractive they would soon almost certainly find themselves husbands. (And I had dared to think that *Arthur* was a chauvinist!)

But over the next few days I changed my mind about the nature of my duties towards my wife. Who knew? Maybe Gordon would indeed prove to be the person who could make her happiest. If this were so, then I should clearly serve her best by standing down. If, on the other hand, things didn't work out for them, she would at least have flushed him from her system, and *that* perhaps would be the best time for a new start. I still believed a new start could reanimate our love and restore to it the strength it had possessed in the beginning. But then, of course, I had believed this before and mundanity had obtruded. There was no guarantee, I supposed, that mundanity wouldn't always obtrude. I still hoped, not very nobly, that one day I'd be able to find out.

Slowly, too – very slowly, it took more than a year – I changed my mind about the nature of my duties towards my parish, or in fact towards the cloth. It wasn't that I saw myself as being played out. It was merely that I thought I could perhaps be more useful elsewhere. I now had no family commitments. A man without family commitments was a relatively free agent. And as I had pointed out to Geneviève over a decade before…there was no shortage of good vicars.

I had to try to be of maximum service.

That was now my one reason for continuing.

To leave the Church wasn't all that simple – there were many attempts at dissuasion – but at last I was working out my notice. While I did so I took a crash course in nursing and first-aid. It was my idea to do some voluntary work abroad, most probably in Africa, and see what opportunities suggested themselves during my time there. But then, in 1983, practically upon the eve of my departure – to Tanzania – there was that earthquake in Turkey in which the death toll eventually rose to two thousand. On the day the news reached Britain I booked my flight; and three days after that was slowly making my way by train towards the devastated areas. And there I didn't any longer need to wonder how I could best make myself useful. Any able-bodied man who was anxious to help would have been welcome but one with nursing skills was additionally so. I thought I'd found my niche; had soon learnt enough of the language to be able to communicate reasonably well, if ungrammatically; had been prepared to stay on indefinitely to assist rebuild broken communities – even literally rebuild, for I was ready to turn my hand to anything.

But then, a year later, there was the famine in Ethiopia, and the year after that the cyclone and tidal wave which hit the Bay of Bengal and as a result took the number of dead and missing as high as fifteen thousand – and where, again, to bring succour and comfort to those suffering people felt like the most important work anywhere on earth.

In any of these places I could cheerfully have stayed put, but somehow, when news reached me of the next famine or natural disaster – or even, once, of the next war – the urge to move on was always so strong as to prove irresistible. Lee Marvin's *wand'ring star* seemed nothing as compared to mine.

I'd meant to return to England in 1990, not simply to recharge my batteries but to learn about Geneviève and Gordon and to see my children, but was stopped by a further earthquake, this time in Iran, where apart from the thirty-six thousand dead there were a hundred thousand injured; and then in '91 there was the famine in the Sudan. I had flown back very briefly in 1987 when Gwen had written to say that my mother was in hospital, and thank God she did, for Mum died just two days after I'd got there. She had been lucid, for the most part – and loving – and cantankerous – and had seen Geneviève fairly often, it appeared, though Geneviève had just then been in Italy, spending practically a year in Rome and Florence as part of her degree course in European Studies. ("Happy? I suppose so. But I never liked *him* that much – not even when he was a boy. Too glib, too plausible, too jolly pleased with himself. Not a patch on Johnny." But she hadn't spoken like that on the day I'd gone to her from Knightsbridge, so I wondered what, if anything, this change of view might indicate. Paradoxically, though, it made me remember chiefly how generous he had been: when finally we had sold our weights, for instance, he'd insisted I take half the proceeds. It had been good to have him as a friend.) I had returned to Guatemala City immediately after the funeral. In early 1992 I knew Somalia was going to be the place I should go to next, either there or Bosnia and Herzegovina, where the situation seemed so grave some said it could be hatching an apocalypse, but I wanted – no, not wanted, somehow felt compelled – to be in England for my birthday. Not just in England, either; Nottingham. I believed this part of my life had to be sloughed off *officially*, and that my birthday – or, more properly, the second day that followed it – would be the time when this would happen. After that I would be…well, mortal again. No longer the bearer of a charmed existence. Did such a thought please me, or perturb me, or neither? During the past nine years I had been totally absorbed in what I did and knew that I had been of use. Which, of course, was happiness…of a kind. But I wasn't sure when I'd last been happy, I mean *happy*-happy. Possibly not since my arrival back in Newcastle on the day of Philip's death; certainly not since my arrival back in Newcastle on the day of Geneviève's departure.

Not *happy*-happy.

My return, then, to Nottingham was one I felt I had no option over – I was being led there hypnotically – despite the freedom of choice which I'd experienced in every other way. I thought it was intended I should meet Brian Douglas. This second encounter, second because I didn't count our occasional nods to one another on the stairs, this second encounter would undoubtedly mark my final break with the past, the bit of ceremony which I believed to be required.

I no longer feared I might be asked to drown him again.

Or, rather, I no longer feared that anything could have the power to make me agree to it.

Somehow I would save him.

24

So…Monday 30th March 1992…and naturally it was raining. Steadily. I got to the office at about ten. Even now, even towards the end of the phenomenon, I was still surprised at how things remained just as I remembered them. Yet perversely I was more surprised when they didn't: small details present I'd forgotten, small details absent I must either have imagined or transposed.

I'd have liked to see the name on my own door. But here – from the reception area – it wasn't quite possible.

Iris finished putting through a call to Mr Walters.

She looked up at me with her usual friendly smile. "May I help?"

Although I'd stood and watched for a few minutes in the sixties while this office block was being erected, it was ridiculous to think I hadn't actually set foot inside it or exchanged pleasantries with any of these four young women for well over half a century. It felt more as if I'd been on just my annual break.

"I'm here to see Brian Douglas."

"Mr Douglas? Oh – do you have an appointment, sir?"

"No. But I believe he'll want to see me; may even be expecting me. My name is Hart. Ethan Hart."

"I don't think he's come in yet."

"You mean, he's sick?"

"Well, it's not like him to be late, so – yes – he may be. I'll check with his secretary."

"No, I was wondering in general. Does he have…does he have problems with his health?"

She laughed. "Not unless you count the odd hangover!" That laugh, so well remembered. "Oh, Debbie, there's a Mr Ethan Hart in reception asking for Brian… What? Yes, I thought I hadn't seen him. No, he hasn't called in… Just a tick." She looked back at me. "Is it something that his secretary can deal with?"

"No, thanks. That's all right. I know where he lives."

I'd have liked to stop and chat. But after I had passed comment on the weather I couldn't think what else to chat about. It suddenly struck me it was a long time since I'd tried to savour my surroundings. I felt regretful as I said goodbye. A bit melancholy.

I travelled to Sneinton by bus. The bus was crowded. I sat beside a young woman with a baby on her lap and a wet umbrella she couldn't decide what to do with. I took charge of the umbrella and was sorry when she finally got up. Hearing about her life with Jason, and even about the continuing disapproval of her parents, was preferable to merely sitting and becoming nervous; although otherwise I would have tried to pray. After she and Jason had gone, my prayer in fact began with them but then widened to include everybody on the bus. I nearly overshot my stop.

292

In the street where Brian lived there weren't any women talking on the corner, nor was there any young lad pumping up his tyres. I guessed I was a little earlier than before. The rain hadn't yet turned to a drizzle.

But the door was opened just as quickly. I hadn't been looking forward to this moment: to seeing a face I had last seen when it was under water, to meeting eyes I had last met when they were either insentient and blank, or filled with such emotions as I might variously ascribe to them. For fifty-five years Brian Douglas had lived with me both day and night – become in a sense my most intimate companion. I'd wondered if out of all the people I had ever encountered in this life, always excepting Zack, Brian might be the one person who was going to recognize me. Despite the change in my appearance.

There was a change in his own appearance. It wasn't simply that he wore a suit this time, a suit which I might – or might not – have seen at the office. His body underneath it looked more solid.

And, above all, I felt relief. It reminded me of what had happened once (or indeed twice) when I was young. I'd been standing by the graveside at my grandmother's funeral – Granny's not Nana's – and then I'd been awoken by a tap on the door, and she had brought me in my breakfast.

The sheer joy I had experienced was something I'd never forgotten. Even though she had actually died less than a year later, I'd felt those nine-and-a-half months had come to me, on both occasions, as a treasured gift.

"Ethan Hart?"

"Yes."

"Come in, sir, I was expecting you."

He didn't sound the same, either. This wasn't a man who was dying or who was wanting to die. This wasn't a man who was going to require any saving. My relief and my gratitude – if possible – intensified.

After he'd taken my umbrella and hung up my overcoat he led me into his living room. That certainly remained as I had first seen it. No emptied drawers or overset furniture.

I turned and faced him. "I don't know why I'm here. Will you fill me in?"

"No, I'm sorry, sir. I'm not the person who can best do that." He glanced at his watch. "But you won't have long to wait. And in the meantime, Mr Hart, may I offer my congratulations?"

"I'd rather you didn't call me sir. Nor Mr Hart. My name is Ethan. Congratulations on what?"

"On coming through."

"You may do so with pleasure. But it seems to me I had no choice. Being invulnerable."

"On coming through, I mean, with such distinction."

I pulled a face and shook my head. "But, anyway, thank you." I gave him my hand and thought about the last time we had shaken hands: barely a minute before he had stepped into the bath.

I said: "I'm sorry I was forced to – no, I'm sorry that I chose to – "

He waited. I finished very lamely.

"I'm sorry for what I did."

"And what was that?" He smiled. "But first things first. May I get you some coffee?"

"Good God!" I said. "You don't remember?"

"Then obviously we *have* met before? I wondered."

"Most certainly we have." Though, unsurprisingly, I balked at revealing under precisely what circumstances. "You spoke about a certain dream you'd had."

"Well, that doesn't surprise me, not in the slightest! I know the dream you're referring to. Old Chaos?"

"You didn't use that phrase, but it was clearly what you had in mind."

Old Chaos. The bottomless pit towards which – in theory – all of civilization was now being irresistibly drawn. Well, *almost* irresistibly drawn.

"Yes, I was obsessed by it!" And then he gave an exclamation. "In fact – hang on a tick – I think I *am* remembering! I said that if ever I had a son...? But now that sounds so incredibly presumptuous! Why should any son of *mine*...?"

He broke off; looked uncomfortable.

"And talking of presumption," he added, "when I spoke of the Once and Future King I believe you mentioned Glastonbury. Is that right? And I have an idea I may have asked…"

"Go on."

"Whether you thought that Arthur would simply leap onto his trusty steed and tear off down the motorway? No! Please tell me that I didn't!"

"Well, if you did, I certainly don't recall it."

It must have been the first time in my life – in this second portion of my life – that I had ever, consciously, told a lie.

"Thank God for small mercies," he sighed.

"But, in any case, why would it have been presumptuous?"

"Perhaps I used the wrong word. Discourteous? Disrespectful? Appallingly so. I know this can't be seen as an excuse but plainly at the time I didn't appreciate…" He stopped again.

"Yes?"

"About the dream."

"What didn't you appreciate?"

"That you were the one whom it involved."

"You mean, because I tried so woefully to take it over? I only feel ashamed I couldn't make it work."

He stared at me.

"But didn't you realize, sir?"

I waited.

"There was no question of your taking it over."

"I'm afraid I'm not following you," I said.

"At no stage did its focus even slightly shift."

"I think I'm still being slow."

"From first to last that dream was about *you*!"

He wasn't to blame, of course. It could hardly have been his own fault if they hadn't clued him in.

And only a second later I would have realized this.

But in the meantime I had snapped at him.

"Oh, for God's sake, man! Talk sense! Do talk sense!"

He looked surprised. As clearly he had every right to. I struggled to retrieve my calm – and pretty soon apologized. "But you had just come out with something so *monstrous*! Worse than monstrous! Blasphemous if you but knew."

"Blasphemous?" His expression had lost its air of startled hurt, yet he still appeared bewildered. "But why?"

"Oh, God! Have I really got to tell you?"

Despite the oath, however, I was speaking more calmly. More deliberately. Partly, this could have been because at the same time I was having to fight back an urge to vomit.

The shock had come too fast. How long had I known? Thirty seconds? Forty? Hardly more. It was the sheer immensity of his mistake – or, at least, what I had seen as his mistake – which had broken through the barrier. Had briefly unleashed my innate, if generally controlled, fierceness of temper.

"That dream," he'd said, "was about you!"

But then, suddenly, it was as if I'd always known. Not always, no, but virtually from the moment I had opened my book to begin that troublesome essay for Mr Hawk-Genn; from the moment I had poured out that hugely awful first paragraph.

Now I swallowed, and cleared my throat, yet still couldn't get my voice to sound quite natural.

"You talk of crisis and disruption," I said. "You talk of the return of Arthur. And you talk about these things – "

At first I couldn't even say it. I forced myself to say it.

"And you talk about these things to the benighted oaf who struck the Saviour on his way to execution."

Brian Douglas didn't flinch. He only said: "And who five centuries later found his way to Britain."

"Oh, yes." My laugh was bitter, brutal, full of self-loathing. "Didn't you always know that Arthur was a Jew? Not just a Jew. A disgrace to every decent Jew who ever lived?"

He shrugged. "Well, to be honest," he smiled, "I never heard it mentioned, one way or the other."

25

Other memories came: flashes from a past life of the kind Brian Douglas had once hoped he'd get in his bath – although now, presumably, he didn't remember whether he'd had them or not. I saw a hermit living in his shack in the woods at St Albans and looked after in his dotage by the monks; that was during the thirteenth century. A beggar travelling throughout Germany, ragged and hirsute, during the sixteenth. A gambler in Italy the century after. I had a glimpse of him in 1772 sitting for his portrait in Belgium. God knows how I knew it was 1772. There wasn't any calendar.

And – yes – I saw him, too, in Powys, in fifth-century Britain. Chieftain of a warring tribe.

Although these were simply glimpses, I felt an affinity towards the man, maybe not a liking but an interest in his welfare and an immediate acceptance. The empathy I felt for such as Isaac Laquedem in Brussels, Solomon in York, Arthur at Tintagel and even Cartophilus in Jerusalem was so strong, so instinctive, it could only have been inspired, I realized, by direct experience. I sat there feeling no longer nauseous, but dazed – utterly dazed. I had a mug of strong black coffee in my hand, yet I was hardly aware of it, and lifted it to my lips only absent-mindedly.

It seemed that every time I did so, however, I saw reflected in the depths of that dark liquid a further facet of my own personality.

26

Brian went out – ostensibly to brew more coffee. Zack came in. It was thirty-six years since we had last met but the moment I saw him I lost all trace of my resentment.

He told me his apparent withdrawal had constituted the final test. In truth, he'd never withdrawn, not for an instant. "But I needed to know that you could make it on your own. Even in the hardest of circumstances."

"Why?"

"No, don't be difficult," he said.

I laughed. "I mean – do you have plans for me?"

"Certainly I have. So long as you'll be happy to fall in with them."

I felt honoured and numbed and undeserving. Perhaps the fact of feeling numbed prevented me from feeling frightened. But, although I sensed that fear might come, I also sensed that I'd be able to handle it. Anything. Whatever there was in the future could never be worse than much of what there had been in the past. And, whatever now befell me, I knew I shouldn't be alone.

"But, Zack? Whatever induced you to take a chance on *me* – on me, of all people? Such an obviously lost cause?"

"The harshness of your punishment," he answered, simply. "I had a fellow feeling."

"Why?"

"We were *both* such lost causes."

"Have I asked you this before? During other lives?"

"No, you were never ready to do so."

"Good. I'd hate to think I was becoming a bore."

"And that sense of fellow feeling," he added, "was probably the very thing which they'd been banking on. They're enormously devious." He said this with a smile.

"I'm not with you."

"Look. *You* wanted to make amends. *I* wanted to make amends. Forgiveness was out of the question for myself but at least I wanted to be the means of *your* being able to achieve it. Perhaps I just wanted to show I hadn't forgotten, not completely, how to be one of the good guys."

"Well, if you want my own take on it – and whether you want it or not, you're going to get it – you're not merely one of the good guys, you must be one of the all-time, all-round best." I grinned. "*And* I seem to remember having told you so before. 'You're the kindest person I have ever known!'"

"Yes, flattery, flattery," he murmured.

298

"Not at all." But then I returned to his earlier comment. "Devious?" I said.

"Yes, William Cowper had it absolutely right. 'God moves in a mysterious way, his wonders to perform.'"

"But what was he banking on? God?"

"On *you*, Ethan! On you! On your becoming such a downright, positive force for good in this world."

"Huh!" I said.

"Huh!" he mimicked.

"Well, in any case, that was obviously no credit to *me*. It was all of it down to you: your showing me the way, your setting the example – your obliging me, even, to compose my own small print! Always it was down to you! So answer me this, Zack. Why is it out of the question for *you* to be forgiven?"

He gave me what he thought were reasons. But they didn't amount to much. Not in my eyes.

"Yet surely, if God represents forgiveness and mercy, and *you* are repentant…?"

For I couldn't bear the idea that, thanks to Zack, I myself had been slowly hauled towards salvation, whereas there had clearly been no one around to do the same for him. ("Perhaps I scare people off?" he smiled. "Perhaps they reckon I'm overqualified!") I couldn't bear the idea of me going forward into light, while he himself had to remain in the darkness.

"Just because you were once ambitious," I protested. "Just because you were once tempted and gave in to your temptations… Just because you once led a rebellion…"

He tried to make light of it. "An awful lot of 'onces' there, for an educated man! And, anyway, who knows? Maybe my time will come."

"Well, it better had! Because when I die, Zack, if they refuse to have you back in heaven, then I shan't want to be there either. I'd rather be with you."

"I don't think they could ever have counted on such loyalty!"

He still made light of it but I could see that he was moved.

"Or love," I added.

"Ethan, let me get this straight. What scared you most at the beginning was that I'd try to claim your soul. Now you're

299

actually offering it. But have you considered? You know how I react to temptation!"

"Which makes me think you need me all the more. And need me somewhere I'll be well posted to keep an eye on you."

"You aim to infiltrate the underworld?"

"Something like that. Why not? But did the G-men *usually* discuss their plans with the gangland bosses?"

He looked thoughtfully across the chasm which, metaphorically speaking, separated our two positions. "The idea has a certain irresistible charm," he said. "The Wandering Jew keeping an eye on Lucifer. Am I my brother's keeper?"

"No, Arthur keeping his eye on the Bearer of Light. And being in the right place to do so, to know the very instant that temptation waves hello. Plus, attempting to repay an unpayable debt. And, yes, I *am* my brother's keeper; and I'm certainly not one of those who regard you as being overqualified! So? We can argue this, if you like, all the way through to the Second Coming, but what I reckon is, it means you're stuck with me. That you always *were* stuck with me. From the moment I hit Christ, Zack, I think your days were numbered."